ALL IN GOOD TIME

THE LONG ROAD HOME, BOOK THREE

AN AMISH ROMANCE

LINDA BYLER

Good Books

New York, New York

The characters and events in this book are the creation of the author, and any resemblance to actual persons or events is coincidental.

ALL IN GOOD TIME

Copyright © 2022 by Linda Byler

Good Books is an imprint of Skyhorse Publishing, Inc.®,
a Delaware corporation.

Visit our website at www.goodbooks.com.

10 9 8 7 6 5 4 3 2 1

Library of Congress Cataloging-in-Publication Data is available on file.

Print ISBN: 978-1-68099-783-5
eBook ISBN: 978-1-68099-832-0

Cover design by Create Design Publish LLC

Printed in the United States of America

PART ONE
May and Oba

CHAPTER 1

Eliezer Weaver was known as "Eli" in his family and at school. He was a dark-skinned, husky little boy who had entered first grade in the fall, a happy, robust individual with a mop of curly black hair and dark brown eyes that danced with good humor and mischief. His wide smile was quick, often revealing the gaps where he'd lost his baby teeth.

Dressed in the conventional denim broadfall trousers, brightly colored shirt, and black leather shoes, with a bowl-shaped straw hat crimping his head full of curls to his skull, he hopped and skipped his way to school, swinging his metal lunchbox until the apple rolled against his peanut butter and honey sandwich, smashing it flat.

He walked with the children from a neighboring farm; the oldest girl, Elmina, in seventh grade, was asked to look out for little Eli. He was as quick as a young colt, and as unruly, Elmina complained to her mother, who took the situation in hand and went to see Eliezer's mother. The slight, blond May, with the huge brown eyes, invited her in, nodded her head with growing concern, and thanked the woman for bringing the matter to her attention.

Eli was properly chastised, then cuddled on his mother's lap as she softly told him the dangers of cavorting across a country road, occasional traffic or not. He watched her earnest brown eyes with a sincere heart, a wish to do better. Until the next time.

His father was Andy Weaver, a big teddy bear of a man, with a shock of wavy brown hair and squinty, crinkling bright blue eyes. He was a large man and so in love with his slight little wife that he radiated goodness. After five years of marriage, their love had grown to include Elizabeth and Veronica, known as S'Lizzie uns S'Fronie. The S sound pronounced before the actual name was a western way of identifying the female version of the name. In the German dialect, their mother was known as S'May.

Elizabeth was tall, with a head of unruly hair like her father's. May thought it was the most beautiful hair, a heavy, rippling mass of brown beauty, which made her smile, though she kept the joy all to herself. Vanity and praise were not what a child needed.

After five years together, Andy had been instrumental in helping May over the rough patches, the dark times that would return from time to time, leaving her haunted by her past, in doubt of her own salvation in Jesus Christ. The birth of her two daughters were her greatest joy, but coupled with the worst of the darkness afterward. She was told she had the "baby blues" and needed to take better care of herself.

And how did one go about taking care of oneself if there was a busy two-year-old in the same house with a squalling newborn, her body racked by a near constant onslaught of colic? The mother-in-law put the baby's left elbow to her right knee, drew her up like a pretzel as her cries increased. Then she would cuddle her, pat her back, and the elusive burps would come to the surface, but only after May had broken out in a sheen of perspiration, weak and so very tired.

It was all a part of life, although Andy said there would be no more after Veronica's cries of pain proved to nearly undo him. Eli, however, seemed to think it was his personal duty to see the household run well, in spite of the chaos after Veronica's birth. May would find him in the kitchen, plying the broom across the floor, carrying dishes to the sink, wiping down the oilcloth table covering.

And he sang the songs he heard from his mother's lips, the old hymns from the brown *lieda buch* (songbook), his head nodding, his toes tapping as he made up a lively beat in his own musician's heart. Singing was his way of expressing the bubbling joy of his life. *He got that from his father,* May would always say to herself as she watched him absorb the words from any song he heard, then hear him sing them to himself as he played on the floor.

Andy was not his biological father, but he was certainly a wonderful replacement. He genuinely loved little Eli, viewed him as the one reason he was fortunate enough to have won May's hand. He had accepted him, along with May's checkered past, and felt himself blessed beyond reason.

LIFE IN THE small brick ranch house near the farm had been close to idyllic, until the day May had helped her sister-in-law pack their belongings for a move to neighboring Geauga County. A stack of yellowed newspaper had been handed to her from the old man along the same road, where he resided in all his eccentricities in a house not much bigger than a chicken coop, nor more attractive.

May had spread open a page, found the article about the small plane going down somewhere in the Northwest Territory, the lone survivor listed as Oba Miller. The name Obadiah Miller, his age, and place of birth were all screaming at her from the page. Almost, she had fainted, the shock of finally, at a time she least expected it, having found a clue to the whereabouts of her lost brother.

With shaking hands and a mouth gone dry, she had managed to convey the strange phenomenon of finding the article, stumbled home to spread the page on the table for Andy to see, and then spent months trying to get in contact with her brother, the last remaining member of her family.

He had been in a hospital in the city of Toronto, Canada, but seemingly vanished after months in a doctor's care. Finally, on the advice of the kindly bishop, they traveled over a thousand miles, found the hospital, gathered all the information possible, and after a fruitless week of spending all their savings for food and lodging, finally found Oba in a rehabilitation center on the city's outskirts.

She would never forget the moment they were shown to his room. She found a small cubicle, with one window, where he sat in his wheelchair, gazing out over the city, his shoulders hunched like an old, old man, his elbows resting on the arms, his hands dangling toward his knees.

She felt Andy's hand on her shoulder and looked up at him gratefully before saying hoarsely, "Oba?"

He stiffened.

They waited as one hand dropped to the wheel, turned the chair around. She would never forget the old, pale, ravaged face of her brother, the eyes so dark with pain and despair, the bitterness having taken away every spark of life or hope.

"Oba?" she said again, holding out both hands, entreating him to accept her, to recognize the fact they were here, had come so far, gone through so much in order to find him.

"It's you," he said softly. "May."

Andy released her, and she flew to him, threw her arms around his too thin frame and held him as if she would never part with the poor thin person he had become. Her face was disfigured with the years of sorrow rising to the surface, tears of relief and suffering, of remembering and wondering and hoping against the crushing obstacles in her way. She cried, sobbed on his shoulder, then knelt in front of him and put both hands to his face, gazed deeply into the dark eyes so much like her own.

"Oba. Oba. Oh, Oba," she whispered brokenly.

"Yeah, it's me." The voice was dry, grating, but there was not a shadow of emotion. Nothing.

May stayed on her knees, her hands going to the top of his thigh, then gasped. "Oh Oba . . ."

There was only one whole leg. One shoe. The opposite leg was simply gone, about mid-thigh, where the leg of his trousers was folded back, empty. She searched his dark eyes, shivered at the dead cold stare emanating from the depth of his gaze. His perfect features were twisted with disdain, his mouth a cold, hard sneer. It was the expression she remembered after the worst of Melvin Amstutz's whippings.

"How'd you find me?"

He looked down at her, but it was as if his eyes saw nothing—they only served the purpose of being in his face. *That beloved face,* May thought. *No matter how hard or cold, he's here. In this room with me.* May was crying softly, so he looked to Andy. One sharp look, knifelike in its unfair appraisal.

Andy stepped forward, extended a hand, his blue eyes wet with the tears that mirrored his wife's intense emotion. "I'm Andy. May's husband."

A mere nod, the hand ignored. Andy let it swing to his side, then stuck both hands in his pockets. Oba's cold gaze swung to May.

"So you got married? Surprised you're Amish." He wiped the back of his hand across his mouth and sneered, one corner of his mouth lifted.

May got to her feet, her eyes never leaving the beloved face. "I did get married." She reached for Andy's hand, leaned against the strength of his arm. "This is my husband, Andrew Weaver. We have three children." She didn't say anything about Eli's biological father. That would have to come later. "Tell me about your leg."

"What is there to say? They cut it off. Thought I would lose the other one, but it seems to be usable. Plane wreck."

May nodded, took a deep breath. "Yes, Oba, that's how I found out about you."

LOOKING BACK, THERE had been false starts and stops along the way, but in the end, they persuaded him to come live with them in the small ranch house. At first he had been belligerent and refused to go, not wanting to come within miles of the Amish community. But what was the alternative? Andy was skilled at persuasion, and he made the decision as easy as possibly for Oba. No, he did not have to join the church. How he lived was his own choice. No, he did not have to be seen or acknowledged by anyone in Ohio, least of all the relatives who had spurned him, packed him off to Arkansas to be mistreated by the hands of a cruel uncle.

"Just come stay with us," Andy had pleaded. "We want you."

Oba refused, and Andy and May eventually went home without him, but they didn't give up. May continued to write him letters telling him of the children, describing what his room in their home would be like if he came, telling him how glad she was to have found him.

Oba considered returning to the wilderness, but had no stomach for it. The Zusacks had come to visit him a couple of times. Sam was a silent ghost of her old self, and Brad and Rain spouted off about the love of Christ and the redemption of his soul, but he remained firmly entrenched in his deep, dark pit of hopelessness and anger. More than ever, now that the leg was gone. He was sure Sam didn't want half a man, and neither did anyone else, so he shook his head and told them all to get lost. He wanted to die, like a horse or a dog, be wiped off the face of the Earth and know nothing afterward.

He sat alone, sullen, mocking those around him. He got into arguments, refused any suggestion of a prosthesis, and swung around the grounds and down lengthy hallways on wooden crutches, the solid thump a warning to everyone in his path. Anyone brave enough to make overtures was almost always turned away either by a lack of interest or an angry rebuttal sending the hapless newcomer scurrying.

In less than four years, he had aged beyond reason, fully entrenched in a dark world of unhappiness, a bitterness so thick it surrounded him like an electrical charge. His rehabilitation long completed, he barely escaped admittance to the psychiatric ward of the tall cement block building next door, also known as the mental institution, the nut house. He had nowhere to go, no relatives, no friends, and no purpose in life other than clinging to his hateful attitude toward God and every human being on the face of the Earth.

Until May arrived.

It was eight and one-half months later when May and Andy returned to Toronto, and this time Oba gave in, partially. He was going with them for a visit. An indefinite stay. He'd go back to California maybe. But he would not stay with them.

The long ride home to Ohio was a nightmare of obscenities, refusal to cooperate, a stream of snide remarks or black silence. Almost, May felt the beginning of fear. Had they bitten off more than they could handle? Was Oba so far gone there could be no redemption?

May placed her trust in God alone, knowing that since He had graciously led her to Oba, He would provide for the remainder of the journey. God would not promise an easy ride, but He would be worthy of her trust.

And so Oba was put up in the spare bedroom with a comfortable double bed, a chenille bedspread in a shade of blue, two dressers, a small desk, cozy rugs, and sheer white curtains that blew in the early summer breeze, the scent of new-mown hay that made his throat tighten with remembering of his past. He remembered every road, the brick house, Simon Weaver's farm. Everything. For two months he stayed mostly holed up in his room as he kept a firm grip on his bitter feelings. Andy and May stayed true to their promise and had no visitors, did not impose restrictions, allowed him to eat and sleep without interference. He never asked questions, answered when he was spoken to, but only when he felt like it. He watched the children with dark, brooding eyes, asked no questions, and never offered a sign of friendliness.

Eli, in his winsome way, tried his best. He hovered, asked childish questions, brought books to be read, a box of crayons and a tablet, but was always turned away. May explained Oba's behavior as best she could, so after a few weeks, Eli continued to watch Oba but left him to himself, like an extra piece of furniture no one thought about anymore.

May tried. She explained Eli, told Oba the story of her relationship with Clinton Brown and her eventual leaving of the Amstutz farm. Yes, he remembered Clinton. Arpachshad's brother. What did they call him? Drink? Yeah, Drink. He fished all the time. Fell in. Oba almost smiled when May laughed gleefully.

Sometimes, he would have a mostly one-sided conversation with Andy, on his good days, usually in the evening out in the backyard with the family when the heat of the day dissipated to the time when dew fell, the sun slid below the horizon, and a comfortable breeze cleansed the air. But that was as far as anyone attempted to draw him out.

On one summer evening, May had made a pudding with heavy cream, Knox gelatin, eggs, sugar, and a buttery graham cracker crust, which she kept in the Servel ice box until it was very cold and refreshing. She cut it in squares and proudly dropped slices of luscious Red Haven peaches on top, with another dollop of whipped cream. She placed six small plates on a tray, carried it out to the backyard, and announced the dessert in merry tones.

"Graham cracker fluff, guys!"

Andy leaped to his feet, took the tray, set it on the picnic table, then bent to kiss May's cheek.

"You are the best wife in the world," he whispered in her ear.

She looked up at him, and they exchanged a sweet longing.

Oba did not miss the magnitude of the moment. He lowered his eyes but felt the stirring of his own longing, his own desire to experience the same happiness, and just as suddenly, squelched the uncomfortable feeling with the safety of his customary bitterness.

He knew no one would want him, and he didn't want anyone, either. The closest thing to love he had ever experienced was the beautiful girl of the North woods, Sam. The one and only girl he had ever truly wanted. But as all things in his life, it was not to be.

"This is so good," Andy said, beaming at his wife.

"Thank you, kind sir."

May's eyes twinkled as she looked up from feeding little Fronie, a miniature version of herself, the blond hair braided into submission like a crown around her delicate head. Eli was pushing the peach slices to the side of his plate, spooning the whipped cream into his mouth. Oba watched as Eli looked first to his father, then his mother, before flicking his peach slices into the grass beneath the picnic table.

He looked straight at Oba, a long honest look, before arching one eyebrow expertly, as if daring him to tattle.

Almost, Oba smiled. He allowed his eyes to crinkle the tiniest bit for only a short moment.

"Eli, hurry up. Finish your pudding," Lizzie called from the end of the bench, leaning forward to see his face.

"Why?"

"We need to play horse. I'll be Clara, okay? You be the horse."

"Yeah! Sure!"

Eli gobbled the pudding, leaned back, and swung his legs off the bench, then ran off with Lizzie on his heels. Andy watched them go, then pushed back his plate, sighing contentedly before commenting on the children's constant energy.

"Remember playing horse, Oba?" May asked anxiously. He had been in one of his darkest moods all day, which served to bring May a sense of failure, of foreboding.

"Yeah."

But he clearly did not want to be questioned or included in a conversation, so May's eyes swept over him before she sighed and put Fronie on the grass with a spoon to play with, smoothed the pleats of her white apron, and turned to Andy, giving him a bright smile.

IT WAS ON a hot Sunday afternoon, the time of day when most folks are resting in a breezy spot outdoors, or finding the coolest spot in the house to stretch out on the couch, when the rattle of steel wheels on gravel awoke Andy from his semi-sleeping beneath the maple tree in the backyard. May was putting Fronie to bed, and Oba sat in his wheelchair on the lawn, reading a book he had no interest in but had picked up out of boredom.

The open, roofless courting buggy was occupied by a lone woman. Oba watched the horse. He didn't know much about horses, but that looked like a good one. He thought May had promised him there would be no visitors.

Andy got to his feet, strode across the lawn, extended a hand, and shook the woman's hand. Hard, from what Oba could tell. She turned to tie her horse, then dusted her hands by clapping them together, drawing up the corner of her brilliant lime green apron, and wiping them well.

The screen door was thrown open, and May appeared, both arms extended, rushing to greet an obviously dear friend. He could only hear snatches of their conversation and shrank back in his wheelchair wishing himself invisible.

"Oba!" May called out.

He looked up.

"Do you mind if Clara joins us for a while? I know we promised no visitors, but she's practically family."

Oba shrugged, leaving the air empty of an answer.

They walked toward him. The woman had the reddest hair he'd ever seen and a dress the color of pond slime. She had a figure like a stick and was ugly as all get-out.

She reached him, stood directly in front of him, and placed her hands on her barely existent hips.

"Can't you talk?"

Oba waved a hand, as if to get rid of an annoying insect. He would not meet her eye.

"You know, you need to straighten up, fella. After all Andy and May have done for you, you're still acting like a spoiled brat."

Oba looked up, shocked. No one talked to him that way. No one. He would have slugged anyone who dared approach him in that fearless manner if he could have reached them. Andy cleared his throat uncomfortably. May looked devastated.

"My name is Clara Yoder. I'm the one your sister lived with before and after Eli was born. She talked about you."

"Is that right?" Oba's voice was hoarse.

"That's right. What happened to your leg?"

"I'm sure you've heard."

"Yeah. May told me. I was trying to start a conversation is all."

"You can stop now."

"What if I don't want to? What if I'm curious about a lot of things? I remember you. What were you, ten, twelve when you were taken to Arkansas?"

"None of your business." His words were raw with contempt, the ever prevalent animosity with which he viewed the world.

"Why, sure it's my business. I have no intention of staying away from May here just because you're scared of people or whatever. So get used to me. Besides, looks like you need all the help you can get, and in case you haven't noticed, May's got her hands full with three kids."

Oba's mouth literally hung open in disbelief. He caught himself and closed it.

When there was no reply forthcoming, Clara lifted her chin in the direction of the amputated leg. "Can you walk?"

He turned his back and twisted his shoulders in his chair, purposely.

"Is that an acquired skill, ignoring people?" she asked.

In one lightning move, he turned, glared at her with eyes sparking dark scorn, and let loose a string of horrible language, punctuated by a fist pounded on the arm of the flimsy lawn chair.

May flinched and Andy shifted his weight uncomfortably, but both of them held their peace.

Clara laughed.

Oba kept his eyes on her, waited for the flinching, the shriveling embarrassment sure to follow, the signal that he would be left alone.

"Whew!" she said and laughed again. "That, my dear boy, is some salty language."

Oba's best weapon of defense was to withhold answers. People who tried to be friendly normally floundered pretty quickly if you left the air empty of normal conversation deemed necessary by folks who talked way too much. So he said nothing.

Ignoring the stiff silence, she sat down on the grass in front of him, arranging herself in the most unladylike manner he could possibly think of. No Amish woman wearing skirts sat cross-legged.

"So, if you can't talk or walk, life must be pretty dull, huh?"

"Why don't you get lost?" Oba growled.

He reached down to release the brake on his wheelchair, put both hands on the wheels, and pushed himself backward.

Andy sprang forward to help him, May bustling along by his side.

"Where you going?" Clara called.

"Away from you."

"Really? Looks like that's pretty rough going there. You know what you need? A motor, a gas engine, mounted on that thing. Either that, or an artificial leg. What are they called?"

She hadn't planned on an answer, so when none was forthcoming, she took it in stride, turning to watch the anxious Andy and May flutter and hover like mother hens. She shook her head.

Eli walked up to her and sat down, cross-legged, imitating her perfectly.

"Now you made Uncle Oba mad," he said soberly.

"Uncle Oba needs to grow up, Eli," she said, ruffling the dark curls on his head.

"You like my hair, don't you?"

"I love your hair. It looks so stiff, but it's so soft."

"My hair is different from all the other children's."

"Right. Same here. No one I know has hair this color, or a thousand freckles like me."

Eli nodded solemnly. "My skin is darker."

"I love your skin color. It's like maple syrup. Or honey."

"That's what Mam says." He gazed up at Clara wistfully. "Did anyone make fun of your freckles in school?"

"Of course they did. Children can be mean, sometimes. Although, I don't believe they are cruel on purpose. They often say what they think without realizing they're being hurtful. Why? Do the children make fun of you?"

"No. Hardly ever. Just sometimes they'll say I look toasted. I don't look like burnt toast, right?"

"Certainly not. They used to call me Sour Milk. Or Speckles."

Eli lifted his face and howled with genuine laughter, his white teeth lined up perfectly, like corn kernels.

Clara looked down at him and winked. "So we're buddies, right? We don't let anyone push us around."

"Uncle Oba will."

"I'm not afraid of Uncle Oba. Your parents need to stop babying him. He could easily walk and live a normal life, and I'm not going to stop until he does."

Eli shook his head. "Boy, oh boy."

"Yep, that's right. Boy, oh boy."

She got to her feet to help May with the tray of mint tea she was carrying, smiled into her friend's eyes, surprised to see the spark of disapproval. *Boy, oh boy.*

CHAPTER 2

It was so hot the following week, no one felt comfortable from the early morning hours to late at night, tossing and turning on sweat-soaked sheets till exhaustion finally sent them into a restless slumber. Every morning the sun rose, a fierce, orange orb of pulsing heat, the atmosphere brassy with shimmering heat waves, the limp leaves barely stirred by a merciful breeze. Andy searched the sky for signs of rain. His blue eyes squinted as he searched the horizon, licked a forefinger, and held it aloft to find the direction of a breeze, searching hopefully for an eastern air. He watched the chest-high cornstalks turn into parched, curled leaves, the deep green color turning olive-hued in the heat of the day. The wide steel-wheeled wagons created a thick cloud of dust, the horses' wide hooves stirring up little puffs of it as well. The grass by the fencerows turned brown with a thick coating of it; the window screens in the windows turned gray as the dirt clung to every available surface.

May carried the galvanized watering can from the rinse tubs to the garden, patiently saving the cucumber stalks, the heavy growth of lima bean bushes that would not produce beans without moisture.

Eli walked beside her, carrying a small bucket, the water spilling against his patched denim trousers, one arm extended to balance the weight. He watched his mother carefully, then imitated her exactly, bending his back so the water would soak around the plants without being wasted.

May glanced wearily at the thermometer tacked to the clothesline pole and sighed audibly to find the mercury creeping toward ninety degrees, so early in the forenoon. The heat and lack of rain was wearing on everyone's good humor, especially Oba, who refused any form of work or entertainment. He sat and brooded without sufficient activity to keep his mind or body occupied, pushing May to her wit's end.

Elizabeth, the brave little soul, was doing her best to talk to him in the shade of the front porch, prattling nervously as she pushed the porch swing with one foot, barely able to cling to the seat as she did so.

"Did you have breakfast?" she asked in her lisping voice.

"No."

"Do you want some? Mam let us have corn flakes because it's so hot. Do you want corn flakes?"

"No."

"Are you sure? Corn flakes are better than oatmeal."

"Are they?"

"Yes, they are." She considered Oba's face, the way his blond hair hung into his eyes, hiding the deep brown or any expression that might have formed there. "You need a haircut," she observed.

Oba said nothing but shook the bangs out of his eyes as he watched Andy walking across the field from the farm. His shirt seemed to be dark with perspiration already, his step measured and slower than his normal energetic stride. He let himself through the gate, then walked up to the porch, lifted his straw hat, and threw it down before running a hand through his hair.

"Good morning, Oba," he said, flopping on the porch swing as he lifted Lizzie on his lap. He looked down at her upturned face, kissed the top of her head, and smiled at her, the smile lingering till it included Oba. There was no response, but Andy was used to that.

"You want to ride along to town? I broke the shaft on the mower engine."

"You know I won't ride in a buggy."

"I'll get a driver."

"Nah."

"Why not? You can't sit on this porch all day."

"Why can't I?"

"Well, I guess you can. As long as you're contented that way."

"Do I have a choice?"

"According to Clara, you do."

"Who's Clara? Oh, her. I can't stand that woman. If she ever comes around here again, I am out of here. I mean it."

"She's alright, Oba. Really." Andy squinted his eyes, laughed his good-natured laugh, and went to find May, seeing if she needed anything in town.

Oba watched the bluebirds in the pear tree, twittering and hopping around each other. He knew they'd already raised a pair of babies, knew when they'd flown and where they came to look for mealworms. He also knew which barn cat had robbed the robin's nest, devoured the poor pink baby robins, leaving the anxious parents fluttering over the empty nest, their children murdered by the evil prowling cat. It didn't seem fair, the way the mother robin had spared nothing, sitting in the cold spring rain and wind, hatching her babies, just so the cat could climb the small pine tree and devour them.

He felt no pity for the robins, just a burning desire to get revenge on the cat. He didn't know if he was capable of pity but knew the anger that welled up in him quite easily. If he had a shotgun, he'd lie in wait for that cat. He didn't care that it was Andy's best mouser.

It was so hot. So humid. His leg ached. What they called phantom pain. As if the rest of the leg were still there, and the air around it still held the pain of being crushed. Why was he still here? Why hadn't he died with Alpheus and Jonas?

His previous life in the wilderness seemed like an alien world now. It was so distant. And yet that world still contained the girl he could not have. Sam. Well, it was for the best. She could never have accepted his moods; Lord knew May could barely put up with him.

He hated Ohio, resented the horse hitched to those stupid surreys. Why would anyone drive a horse and buggy? He had no plans of attempting any such tomfoolery. Although he'd never be able to drive a car with only one foot. That red-haired thing could keep on talking about a prosthesis all she wanted; he was having no part of it. It was bad enough, being cross-hatched with vicious scars across his back, and now being only half a man with one leg. And so his thoughts rambled on, mostly based on himself, the cruelty of life, of fate, the unending blackness of a life without hope.

He was so immersed in his thoughts, he did not hear the crunch of metal wheels on gravel until he looked up and saw the dreaded courting buggy flashing in the sun, some half-crazed horse lunging into the collar at an alarming speed.

It was her alright, hauling back on the reins like an idiot, trying to stop the headlong dash with very little room to spare. Besides having that abominable red hair, she was as crazy as a bat. He turned his chair, ready to push into the house and out of sight. The last thing he needed was another conversation with her.

He pounded on the screen door, which brought Eli, his own personal doorkeeper, his deep brown eyes alight, a smile on his face as he opened the door and held it. Oba could have done this himself, but Eli seemed to thrive on helping him whenever he needed it.

He settled his chair at the kitchen table, his back turned to the door.

"Hey, are you here? May!"

"I'm here." May turned from her sewing machine, a smile on her face as she greeted her friend.

Elizabeth and Veronica looked up from their play, and Clara bent to hug them both.

"S'Lizzie uns S'Fronie!" she chortled. "My two best girls. And how are you, Eli?"

"I'm making a sparrow trap, Clara. Dat said if I catch sparrows, he'll give me one penny every time I get one."

"Hey! That's good." She turned to Oba. "And how are you?"

He glared at her.

"You still don't like me, huh? Well, get used to me, Mister Obadiah Miller, because I'm not done with you yet. I have a number for you to call. This is a doctor in Cleveland. He specializes in artificial limbs. Prosthesis. I want you to go there."

"Those things cost a fortune," he growled. "Who's going to pay for it?"

"We'll figure that out later."

"I told you I won't strap some clumsy thing to my leg."

"Yes. I believe you told me." She paused. "I am hoping we can come to an agreement. Before you think of making the trip to Cleveland, I want to see you on crutches. Leave this house. Come on down to my horse farm. You need to take an interest in something other than yourself."

May poured glasses of cold mint tea, the set of her shoulders giving away the tension she felt. Oba was like a gun with the safety off; it simply was unsafe to meddle in his own world of loss and self pity. She knew Clara was fearless, but with Oba, she was afraid she would overstep her boundaries.

"Tea, anyone?" she chirped, trying to lighten the sizzling static emanating from Oba.

"Thanks, May. This weather is like a desert. I'm always thirsty." She sat down, too close to Oba for his comfort, lifted the glass of tea, and drank thirstily, then set the glass down with a forthright *Ahh.* "You make the best tea, May."

"It's a mixture. Spearmint, peppermint, and apple."

Oba narrowed his eyes, scrutinizing Clara. Didn't the woman have a self-conscious bone in her body? Her arms were tanned, but riddled with freckles in spite of it. He'd never seen skin like hers. You'd think she might want to cover up more than she did. Even the neckline of her dress was open, the straight pins placed down too far for all those freckles, plus the color of her dress was a screaming magenta, a pinkish red that did nothing to tone down her red hair.

He had never seen anyone like Clara. He wondered vaguely if she was normal, or if a little something was missing.

"So, what do you think, Oba?" She turned to face him and gave him the full benefit of her yellow-green eyes, alight with interest. Not a trace of shyness or self-consciousness, only a frank, forthright appraisal.

That nose, he thought. Caught off guard, he shrugged, before lowering his eyebrows and shaking his head.

"Oh, come on now," she said.

She had no intention of backing down or giving up, and he had no intention of accompanying her anywhere, to any hospital or horse farm. He had no desire to let her blab on and on about how much she knew about horses, when he himself knew so little. He'd driven the hateful mules with mouths as tough as shoe leather from the bits being yanked around by the irate Uncle Melvin but had never been allowed to work with the driving horse who flattened his ears and turned his rump to release a well-aimed kick to protect himself from delivered blows.

He put his hands on the wheels, pushed away from the table. He felt suffocated, tamped down. He caught May's anxious eye and wheeled sharply to the left before rolling himself to the screen door. He couldn't believe it when Clara put her hands firmly on the handles of his wheelchair and yanked him backward without speaking, surprising him so much he couldn't think fast enough to put the brakes into use.

"Don't you know how rude it is to leave a question unanswered? To roll away from a person who's trying to help you? You should be terribly ashamed of yourself, for what you are putting your sister and her husband through. You thrive on pity and isolation. Well, let me tell you, that is a one-way street to losing your mind, so if you find yourself in some room painted a sickly shade of green, between the brick walls of a mental hospital, you have no one to blame but yourself."

Oba flinched, visibly.

He was incredulous. No one spoke to him in this manner. No one. For once, he had nothing to say. He felt the anger rise but also felt it sputter before it raged into a full-blown tantrum. He floundered, tried to regain firm footing, opened his mouth for a well-placed retort that would redeem him from this onslaught of unkindness.

"Think about it, Oba. You're young, your whole life is ahead of you. You sit here, your muscles weakening, your mind cluttered with bitterness. I know your life was hard—May told me everything. But right now, you have choices to make. Serious life-altering choices. Just trust me a little bit and I'll do everything to get you on the road to better health."

"I can do it by myself when I'm ready. You don't have to be involved."

May held her breath.

Clara gathered more steam. "If left to yourself, things will only worsen."

She was cut off by an angry outburst from Oba, who told her in clear terms that he had no plans of allowing anyone to become involved in his life, so she might as well go back to her horse farm.

Much to his surprise, Clara sighed, then turned to May and the children, thanked her for the tea, and said it was time to go back to work. Ignoring Oba entirely, she walked away with quick, long strides.

He didn't want to watch but could barely keep from turning, curious to see how she managed to loosen that crazy horse and get in the buggy before he took off. He turned sideways, turned his eyes to see her loosen the neck rope, rub her hands up and down the horse's face, then slide one hand down the sides of his neck before clipping the rein to the hook, the signal to all horses telling them the driver was ready to go. The horse pawed the ground as Clara held the reins, ready to climb into the buggy. The horse shook his head from side to side, took one flying leap before she was ready, leaving her dragging back on the reins, calling out the necessary *whoa* before leaping onto the seat as fast as lightning.

But the horse was angry now, confused, undecided whether he should go or stay. So he stood, shaking his head from side to side, snorting, pawing. Oba could see his flanks trembling. He became aware of May's quiet presence, her hand on the handle of his chair.

Clara leaned forward, called out, "Yup. Come on, Star. Time to go." All the coaxing did no good. So Clara leaned back in the seat and waited. He'd go when it was time.

May called out. "You want me to lead him?"

"No. He's being cranky. He's not used to being tied."

Oba watched. The woman was incredible. How could she sit back against the seat, the reins held loosely, without being afraid?

The horse was a genuine balker. They could rear up on their hind legs, throw themselves, and bring down a thousand pounds of solid horseflesh, breaking a good pair of shafts and overturning the light buggy in the process. He didn't appear to be older than two or three. Yet Clara sat there in the hot morning sun as if she were taking a rest on a chair beneath a tree. From time to time, she made a funny noise with her mouth, which only brought another shake of the horse's head.

Eli started to laugh, said Clara would have to sit there all day. He wanted to go sit with her.

"No, Eli, you cannot sit on that buggy. The horse is not safe." May gasped as the horse reared up on his hind legs.

Up and up, his front hooves pawing empty air, before coming down in one running leap, the light buggy lurching haphazardly behind him. Clara waved one hand above her head, her white covering and a slice of brilliant red color from her shoulders visible through the cloud of dust raised by the pounding hooves.

May exhaled sharply without realizing she had been holding her breath. She gave a low laugh and shook her head before scooping up Fronie.

Oba continued to watch. He wanted to ask her to stay, wanted to know more about this horse farm, but his pride would not allow it.

Really now. He couldn't stand having her around, so why this curiosity about her farm?

He remembered his father being gentle with the Belgian work horses. He would let them rest in the shade of the huge oak trees that grew along the fencerows, their sides heaving as sweat ran in rivulets down their great flanks. He could smell the salty odor of the sweat mingling with the scent of freshly mown grass as he sat with his father in the hot June breeze.

Then there were the battered mules in Arkansas. The homely creatures with gigantic ears and heads much too big for their skinny necks, their slatted ribs and sharp hip bones a testimony to his uncle's stingy feedings. He'd laugh his mocking snort, say the mules could survive on brush and weeds, like a goat. If Oba had ever felt raw pity, a feeling so sharp he had felt a physical lurch in his stomach, it was the first few years in Arkansas.

The mules plodded along endlessly, took the crack of heavy leather reins and the hissing sting of the whip, trotted whenever they were asked, stopped when Melvin hauled back on the reins, opening their mouths and raising their enormous heads to ease the harsh yank of the steel bit on the soft flesh of their mouth. All day, they went without a drink, standing sleepily at the hitching post in the brutal southern sun while Melvin sat at the kitchen table with his family, drinking glass after glass of cold water, slurping up his bean soup, and stuffing half slices of bread and butter into his gaping mouth.

Oba swallowed. His eyes turned into narrow slits of remembered scorn. He wondered vaguely what had become of him. Him and those three boys. Not that it mattered. For the rest of his life, he would carry the years in Arkansas on his back, a visible history of rampant abuse by a violent man who lived with a dangerous nature and who covered it well in everyday life.

Melvin was the reason he had no respect for the Amish church, although May had warned him repeatedly about judging the whole community by the misdeeds of one man. Forgiveness and acceptance was a long way off, of this one thing he was sure.

ANDY HEARD ABOUT Clara's balker from a gleeful Eli as they sat around the supper table enjoying bowls of cold fruit soup, an Amish staple in hot weather. Fresh peaches were sliced in a bowl, covered liberally with sugar, then slices of bread torn in strips, and cold, creamy milk poured over everything. There was a side of cured beef bologna and a chunk of cheese, the good waxy Swiss kind with the slightly rancid odor, the perfectly rounded holes created by the aging process. There were cold glasses of mint tea, the ice box with the large square of ice on top keeping the food from going bad. In winter, when the lakes froze to a good twelve inches or more, the men were kept busy cutting wagonloads of chunked ice and storing it away in icehouses, packed and insulated with sawdust. Without electricity, it was a solution to spoiled food in summertime.

Eli lifted his arms to show how high the horse had gone, his large dark eyes sparkling.

Andy laughed, and May shook her head.

"She knows what she's doing. I haven't heard of one dissatisfied customer after buying a horse from her."

Caught off guard, Oba blurted out, "You mean, she sells horses? She actually raises them? Surely she doesn't . . ." He stopped, looked at Eli, who was all eyes and ears. His mind was quick and sharp, absorbing most conversations and remembering every word.

"She sure does," Andy said hurriedly. "She has one of the best bloodlines in Ohio, if not the surrounding states. If the Amish believed in registering horses, keeping up the paperwork and fancy names the way the English do, she'd be a famous horse breeder."

May clucked and rolled her eyes in Eli's direction, who was engrossed in fishing out the last of his peach slices, leaving the soaked bread till last.

"Sorry, May," Andy said, regretting his slip of the tongue. Children were kept strictly from any language pertaining to reproduction, so it was never spoken of in their presence.

Oba absorbed Andy's information in silence, but his interest was definitely aroused. No wonder the woman was so brash, so outspoken. She was more like a man. Especially the way she tried bossing him around about going to Cleveland.

He wasn't going. Bad enough to be here among the Amish without sponging off their charity while they all sat around with hopeful eyes and clucking tongues, waiting for his prodigal return. Sorry, folks, but a straw hat and a bowl haircut, a horse and buggy, and a fat wife were not for him. Besides, how could he hope to enter any society on a wheelchair? He looked at his crutches, knew he should use them more, but felt more like an invalid using them than he did in his wheelchair. For the thousandth time, he hated his stump, that half leg as worthless as six fingers on one hand. He was an oddity, someone young children watched with frightened eyes, someone to pity.

THE MONTH OF August waned and the stifling heat of the long wearisome nights abated, leaving Oba in a better frame of mind. He'd eyed the crutches for weeks before finally deciding to give them another try. He stuck them beneath his arms and swung around the yard. At first, his weakened arms ached within the first minute, and he collapsed into a lawn chair, his chest heaving as drops of perspiration dripped from his brow.

Eli ran alongside, shouting encouragement, his black curls bobbing in the hot wind. Later, Oba found him by the sandbox, trying to fit a small piece of wood onto a broomstick to make himself a pair of crutches. After that, Andy did design and build Eli a simple pair, which proved to be invaluable for Oba. Eli kept up a barrage of questions, pleading with him to go here, go there, come on, Uncle Oba, we can go to the farm, to the shop, to the henhouse.

Sometimes he did. His shoulders strengthened, his back no longer ached. May caught them racing across the yard, taking unbelievable strides with the crutches, Eli fully capable of keeping up. May often marveled at the child's athletic abilities, the way he seemed to be a natural runner and could throw a ball with surprising skill for one so young. And her heart would feel the old familiar pang, the remembered lost love of his father, Clinton Brown, also a young man of athletic prowess.

Oh, bless his heart, she would think, as he moved so well, swinging the crutches with his well-formed arms, the thin, white short-sleeved shirt already becoming snug across his chest. Her eyes stung with tears, but only for a moment. Then she remembered the gentle kindness of the big, burly husband that God had given her, a gift so precious she would never forget to appreciate him. She lived in undeserved love and safekeeping, a haven of trust and kindness. But she never regretted her years with Clinton or the gift of Eli. So amazing, the community's support and acceptance. Her love for Lizzie and Fronie was no less, only an expansion of her heart. And she wanted more children, of course. She dreamed of giving Andy a son, their world complete.

All in God's time, she thought. *We'll appreciate one day at a time.* She had never imagined this a month ago. Oba racing—yes, racing—across the yard on his crutches, his face tanned, his blond hair bleached by the sun. And he was actually laughing, if only for a short time.

Every two weeks they all piled in the buggy and made their way to church, leaving Oba alone at home. They had promised him they would accept any decision he made, so they stayed true to this, allowing him to sleep late before getting his own breakfast. Once, he had seen them leave and thought how unusual it was that the child was being accepted by the community, his dark face and springy black hair so obviously different from Lizzie and Fronie's porcelain faces.

Andy and May had something special, he thought. Andy was a real nice guy, one who never irritated him, never rippled the waters of his underlying bitterness. In spite of himself, he found he looked forward to suppertime, the time when Andy would walk across the fields, carrying his sweat-soaked straw hat, relishing the breeze through his wet hair. Even with his shirt soaked with the escalating temperatures, he was smiling, calling out to the children who would drop everything and run to him.

And Andy's first sight of May upon coming home was almost a sacrilege, the light in his eyes reflected in hers. They were the only couple he had ever known who always hugged each other upon either one's arrival or departure. His own parents had never fought, yet he couldn't remember seeing his father put his arm along the back of the couch where his mother was seated.

And he still yearned to find a love like May's, though he hated to admit it even to himself. He could not imagine meeting anyone or allowing himself to become attracted to a girl, so he did not venture out, it being far easier to let all of that go, with his battered and broken body.

He found he was never jealous of May. He knew she deserved so much goodness in her life, unlike him, who questioned the existence of God and ran away from any mention of Jesus Christ dying for him.

Maybe for good people He did, but not for him.

And yet he had seen angels. He had. He had felt the presence of his parents. He rolled over and turned his face to the wall.

CHAPTER 3

WHEN THE COOLING WINDS OF AUTUMN BEGAN TO WHISPER through the pine trees and the leaves on the sugar maples turned a dull shade of green before the edges showed signs of red, Clara finally arrived on a Saturday afternoon, after chores were finished. May had looked for a visit for a month but heard nothing from her at all, and she had sensed a cold shoulder from her at church. Knowing Clara, she figured it was very likely due to Oba's refusal to see a doctor.

Eli was overjoyed and ran out before she climbed down from the buggy, with Lizzie and Fronie on his heels. Oba looked up from the puzzle he was working on, frowned, looked at May, and said he was going to his room.

She laid aside the garment she was mending, smiled at him, and said he might not want to. Clara had probably brought her ice-cream freezer and the mix she was known for. She'd talked about it all summer and hadn't done it yet.

Sure enough, when he looked out the window, the children were bouncing up and down, clapping their hands as Clara hoisted a wooden ice cream freezer from the buggy. Andy strolled toward her, a broad smile on his pleasant face, untied the horse while he talked, then led him off to the barn. Looked as if she was staying awhile.

He couldn't help noticing the brilliance of her dress. A shocking shade of green. How many outlandish dresses did she have? She banged through the door, the children hovering at her heels.

"Hi May!"

"Why hello, Clara! What a surprise!"

"Yeah. I had three yearlings to work with through the month of September. Horse sale in Oakley, and then council meeting and communion, you know. Hi, Oba. How are you?"

He lifted his face, glanced across her shoulder, and nodded, then went back to his puzzle.

"Does that mean you're doing well?" Clara asked, pulling up a chair to join him at his card table.

Really? Oba thought. He shrank away from her, feeling accosted by red hair and alarming colors.

"So, Oba, have you given any thought to the doctor in Cleveland?"

"No."

"Ah, come on. I don't believe that. Surely you've had time to think about it. I would love to see you enjoying life like a normal man. You know it's possible, don't you?"

She was separating pieces of the puzzle with long, slender fingers, fingers tanned by the sun but without any freckles. He noticed the freckles on the backs of her hands and found himself wondering if they appeared only on skin exposed to the sun or if they covered her entire body.

"Hey, here's a piece."

He looked at what she'd done without comment.

"They say these prostheses are heavy and sort of clunky, but you'd get used to it. You could work at my horse farm after you learned to walk."

He glared at her, his eyes boring into hers with what he hoped was enough anger to stop this foolish prattle. But she was undeterred and barged ahead with as much finesse as a bulldozer. She met his eyes with bold determination, never flinched, sat up even straighter and more formidable.

"Can't you talk? What is this rude manner? Where in the world did you learn to ignore people when they talk to you?"

May listened to this from her place at the stove, putting the kettle on for coffee. She held her breath.

"Sure I can talk. But not to you, coming in here and telling me what to do. If I choose to spend my days doing nothing, it's none of your business. I'm not your 'project.'"

Clara leaned forward, her eyes flashing yellow light. "I'm not going to leave you alone. You're a grown man. You need to work, make your own way. I don't care if you're handicapped or not. You can't live here sponging off Andy and May. You can't be gainfully employed without an artificial leg. It's time you get off your duff and get to work."

A hot wave of anger coursed through his veins. He lifted the card table with one hand and threw it across the living room, puzzle pieces flying like shrapnel. May covered her mouth with her hands. Eli's eyes opened wide as he looked from one to the other, and Lizzie ran to May and buried her face in her apron.

Clara remained seated, exposed to Oba without the card table. Oba remained where he was, breathing hard, staring at her, she staring at him. The room was as still as a tomb.

"You feel better?" Clara asked.

"Yes."

"Really? You're a spoiled baby. Now go pick up those puzzle pieces. Go on."

"I can't get down on my hands and knees."

"Why not?"

"Why don't you try getting down there with one leg?"

And Clara did. She slid off her chair on one knee, balanced herself, and began to pick up the pieces. He looked at her narrow waist and thought she was so skinny he could likely span it with both hands. She looked up and told him to get down here and help.

"Don't, Oba. Don't. You won't be able to get up," May said breathlessly, unseating Fronie and rushing over to help. She would much rather remove adversity, make his life easier, than put him through shame or discomfort. She gasped when Oba slid clumsily out of his chair and rocked unsteadily on his one knee before placing both hands firmly on the floor. He began to pick up pieces of the puzzle.

This scene is what Andy found when he walked into the house. He stopped.

"What?" he asked quietly.

Clara sat back on her heels, smiled up at him, and told him to get down and help. Being the kindhearted person he was, he obeyed, scrambling beneath the couch with his large hands to look for missing pieces. When the puzzle was all put back in the box, they got to their feet, except Oba, who had no idea how he'd get back on his chair without the benefit of one knee to support him as he pulled himself up with the other. May moved forward to help, but Clara pushed her back, made a face to warn her away. Before she could stop him, Andy moved forward, stood above, and asked if he needed help.

"I don't know how I can get up," Oba answered.

"Well, you can't. Here. I'll hook my arms beneath yours and lift."

Clara stepped up, pushed the wheelchair closer. "Here. Grab hold of the arms. Put your weight on your knee, then pull." She motioned Andy away.

To her surprise, Oba did what he was told. She put the brake on both wheels, then grasped the handles, putting all her weight against the pressure he applied as he struggled to pull himself up. He tried, much to his credit, but his arms were still weak, too weak to lift up his own weight.

Then Eli stepped up. He put one small, dark hand beneath Oba's arm and said, "Come on, Uncle Oba. You can do this. Your arms are strong from using the crutches."

Oba's face was red from exertion, his legs shaking from the unusual position. He felt dizzy, disoriented, forgot Andy, May, or Clara, but was gripped by an overwhelming need to do this, to prove to himself the fact that he could accomplish the impossible. He gripped the handles again and squeezed his eyes shut as he strained to lift the weight of his own body.

Clara braced herself each time he made another attempt. May looked as if she would burst into tears, but Andy seemed to get the message and stood back, crossing his arms.

Finally, when he pulled himself halfway, with Eli shouting encouragement, he teetered on the brink of losing his balance, before righting himself.

"Take your time," Clara said.

And he did. Perspiration beaded on his upper lip, he shook like a leaf, and he was on one foot, gripping the arm of the wheelchair in a viselike clench.

Andy stepped forward. Clara motioned him back.

And Oba turned, sat panting in the wheelchair, his head lowered as he regained his breathing.

"You did it, Uncle Oba! Yay!" Eli shouted, dancing on tiptoes.

And Oba smiled. He shook his head and smiled a rueful grin of embarrassment mixed with a sliver of pride. For the first time since the plane wreck, he felt a sense of purpose, even if it was a very small one.

He felt two hands on his shoulders, rubbing appreciatively.

"You did it, Oba. Imagine what you can accomplish from here on out."

He dismissed the rising irritation at Clara taking the liberty to rub his shoulders the way she'd praise a dog or a horse and resisted shrugging off the touch of her hands. When had he last felt the touch of another adult? It was odd to be praised and, yes, touched. When she took her hands away, he almost wanted her to rub his shoulders again.

Almost.

The evening was a great success. The ice cream mix was put in the hopper, ice chipped off a block with an ice pick, salt added in layers to melt it efficiently. The end result was a creamy concoction with chunks of fresh peaches on the side, a bowl of buttered popcorn, and steaming cups of coffee.

Oba was quiet, for the most part. He watched the children inter-
act with Clara, thought it a pity she would never be a mother. She
tried drawing him into the conversation repeatedly, but the only
reward for her effort was a mere shrug or a nod, sometimes a "yeah."

"So, Oba, when are we going to Cleveland?" she asked, as she
gathered dishes to take to the sink.

"Never."

"Why not?"

"Because."

"That is no answer. You need to see what a good, experienced
doctor will say. Please? For Andy and May?"

He shook his head.

Then Clara did something totally unlike her. She knelt in front of
him, took both his hands, and asked, "Promise me you'll think about
it?"

He looked down at the the long fingers without freckles, the
thumbnail chipped and broken, wondered how much work this
woman accomplished in a day. The touch of her fingers, her hands,
were not repulsive. He could not have imagined this a few months
ago—even a few hours ago—would have done anything to avoid her.

He nodded.

She pressed his fingers with gratefulness.

"Good. Just think about it."

COUNCIL MEETING MEANT lengthy church services, which only the
adults attended, which meant leaving the children with older children who were responsible at childcare, or someone from another
district would keep them at their house.

The services were made up of stories in the Old Testament, the
lessons of the *fawa eldra* (forefathers), the ones whose lives all led
up to the coming of Jesus. These stories were an important part of
Amish culture, kept in high esteem, as was the telling of the *ordnung*
(rules) afterward.

To most of the congregation.

There would always be the stragglers, the rebels who found it difficult to be put into the same box as those who loved obedience ... such as those who enjoyed bright colors and red scarves and kept a radio under their bed, who dealt in horses and scorned any smidgen of piousness or self-righteousness.

For council meeting, Clara dressed in a plain brown dress, combed the brilliant red hair into submission with a wet comb, put on an expression of hopeful acceptance, and went to church, driving the quiet, aged Standardbred she hoped would raise no eyebrows. Council meeting was serious stuff, although she didn't really get it, the way it was so important to wear plain shoes or tie your covering just so, or why she couldn't have a small tractor to haul manure. Plus, her conscience prickled uneasily, thinking of the radio under the bed. That, and the last horse she'd sold Enos Schlabach wasn't quite the trotter she'd told him he was, the way he shied about trucks and flapping objects beside the road. She soothed herself by thinking he deserved to be spooked a couple of times, the way his eyebrows wiggled at her, plus those few suggestive remarks.

She knew she was not truly attractive or desirable, so he must be flirting out of pity, to make her feel better about herself. Well, she didn't need some married hayseed to make her feel attractive. She was downright homely, an old maid without the blessing of any physical beauty, and this came from God, so why worry her head about it? When May and Andy married, of course she'd gone through her own shadowed valley of longing, who wouldn't? But that was past now, and she'd gone back to living alone, working with the horses and listening to her new radio in the evening.

And now there was Oba. Her personal mission. She was going to fix that guy, no matter what. Whoever heard of a perfectly good man going to waste like that? She had a pretty good idea of what he'd gone through down in Arkansas, though she guessed even May probably didn't know all of it. Well, no excuse. Water under the bridge, gone with the sands of time. Folks had to pick up the leftover pieces of their past and keep going, their faces to the sunny future.

And that May. Sorry, but she was part of the problem. She did way too much for him, like a jumping jack the minute he yelled for something. And he did yell. Sat there like a big lump and demanded a cup of tea, a glass of water, the paper, a spoon. Come on. And that habit of not talking. There was nothing about that whole deal she could stomach. She felt like reaching out and slapping him.

He was very handsome, so easy to look at. Just a gorgeous man, that was all there was to it, with that blond hair and brown eyes, just like May. Those perfect features, the chiseled chin with a dimple in the middle. She knew a handsome man when she saw one, and Oba was one of them. The reason she could freely talk to him, touch his shoulders, argue her point about the prosthesis was the fact she could never allow herself to be attracted to him. He was a good bit younger than she was—he was like a nephew, a cousin, perhaps a brother, in time.

Yes, the rehabilitation of Oba Miller was up to her, and her alone, so it was a good thing indeed, this not being blessed with physical attributes. She was older, homely, and free of any thoughts that would eventually lead to heartache or disappointment.

She didn't enjoy council meeting much and spent most of the time thinking about Andy, May, and Oba. She knew the neighbor girl, Emma, had been asked to watch the children. Joe Troyer's Emma, a young sober girl who had not yet become a member of the church. She was pretty enough, so Clara imagined Oba talking to her, perhaps striking up a friendship. Wouldn't that be something? She wondered what a young girl would think of a boy with one leg, then dismissed the thought. One thing at a time. First, get him the leg; second, get him back to work; and third would be finding him a companion. Which led to the big question. Would he ever return to his Amish roots? He certainly had no intentions the way he sneered about it all, but who knew?

She awoke from her intense thinking and planning when the minister repeated the phrase used before prayer, then fell on her knees with the rest of the congregation, covering her face with her hands so everyone would think she was deep in prayer even though she was actually thinking about that horse she sold Enos and hoping he wouldn't shy too much. Not enough to cause an accident. The radio under her bed weighed on her shoulders, but she shrugged it off and told God she'd get rid of it tomorrow.

She helped serve the meal after services, carrying trays of cheese and pickles, spoke to her friends, the married women, the elderly ones. Relieved to be free of another council meeting for six months, she felt quite buoyant and happily carried bowls of bean soup to the cloth-covered table. She was pleased to bump into May, giving her a huge smile.

"Come over this evening, Clara," May said. "Do."

"Oh, I don't know, May. It's late already. Who would do my chores?"

"You can do them late. I made meatloaf, your favorite."

Clara's eyes lit up. "You make the best."

THEY SAT AROUND the kitchen table enjoying heaping plates of the fragrant meat loaf, mounds of mashed potatoes with browned butter, fried zucchini, applesauce, and slices of homemade bread with raspberry jam.

Clara leaned back when May appeared with a German chocolate layer cake, frosted with brown sugar, coconut, and pecan frosting, and a bowl of late peaches with whipped cream.

"You are the best cook in Ohio," she observed.

"Oh, I wouldn't say that," May said, color rising in her delicate cheeks. She never took a compliment easily, always blushed or denied anything and everything, which Clara found endearing. She was one of the few genuinely humble people she had ever found. Lots of people trained themselves to appear humble, strove to be quiet and sweet and everything a good Christian should be, but were not truly poor in spirit, meek, the way May was. She hoped their friendship would last as long as they both walked the earth together. Or until the end of the world, the way Jess Detweiler had spoken of Christ's second coming being so soon, the way the world was headed for destruction by the evils of man.

She cut a slice of cake, leaned over to ask Eli if he wanted any, laughed outright when he wrinkled his nose and whispered, "I hate coconut. It gets in my teeth."

Andy grinned. "What did you say, Eli?"

"I don't want a piece of cake. Just peaches." He looked apologetically at his mother, who nodded knowingly.

"It's alright, Eli. I know you don't like coconut. I made the cake for Clara."

Oba looked up from his plate.

"Clara rates pretty high around here, I noticed," he said, sarcasm biting uncomfortably.

With the ease of her self-confidence, Clara seamlessly assembled her weapon. "Why wouldn't I? I saved your sister."

"Yeah." A rude mockery.

Clara put down her fork, gripped the edge of the table with both hands, and said slowly and quietly, "Well, unlike you, some people recognize kindness, then appreciate the fact they needed someone in their time of trouble. See how happy they are? This family? Yes, I was there for her. I was only a link in God's plan, but I was there."

Oba was silent.

An uncomfortable silence hovered over the table, the only sound the steady scraping of utensils on china, a glass lifted, the squirming of the children. Oba glanced at Clara, dressed in a decent color for once, saw the lack of embarrassment, saw how completely situated in her own sense of worth she really was. She spoke her mind, simply flung it out there, and calmly took the response without flinching. There was nothing hidden, no guile, nothing.

For the first time, he recognized a spark of something other than distaste. If she had really saved May, was that why Eli, and May for that matter, were accepted as a part of the Amish church? He could only imagine her headlong attempt at persuading those in charge.

His curiosity won over, and he opened his mouth, then closed it again when May said, "You were definitely a link, Clara."

"I was. And I've been blessed by it."

"Were you . . .?" He stopped

"Was I what?"

"Were you the one who persuaded the Amish it was okay to accept her?"

"Well, I talked to the ministers. The deacon and the bishop."

Oba looked at her, found the yellow-green eyes looking back, open and as frank as a child's. He couldn't help comparing her to the poor girl who had come to keep the children. What was her name? Emma? Such a pitiful mess, completely undone by his appearance, scurrying around like a frightened mouse, keeping her distance as if he would growl and leap after her in his wheelchair.

Clara was a mature woman, sure of who she was, completely unattracted to him. He was, or had been, accustomed to giggles and batted eyelashes, open flirtatious smiles containing vain and empty egos. Well, except for Sam. She had been different.

She had been his first and only love. The stirrings of desire he had felt as a youth did not compare with his feelings for Sam. A shadow passed over his features, a sadness softened his eyes. A love lost was better than not having loved at all. Wasn't that a true saying? He would forever cherish the image of Sam swinging the wonderful curtain of blue-black hair, gathering, twisting it into a ponytail. If they could have been together, the sight of her would have been sufficient, enough oxygen for his survival.

He could never go back. Even if he gave in to the thought of an artificial limb, the skills the Northwest required were far above anything he could hope to attain. To take Sam out of her natural environment would be nothing short of cruel. It was over, but he could cling to the images of her beauty for the rest of his life, which was something.

He looked up to find himself under scrutiny, Clara's eyes boring into him without actually seeing him at all.

"You know, Oba. You need to go with me. I know you won't make the phone call I want you to make, so I'm going to go ahead and do it. I'll get a driver. Andy and May can accompany us, and we'll make a day of it. Do some shopping. Andy's mom could keep the children. Right, Eli? You love to go to Mommy's house."

He nodded. "Where would you go?" His little brow was puckered with confusion. In the insulated world in which the children lived, Cleveland, a doctor, an artificial leg—all these things were completely foreign, so he had reasons to be alarmed.

Patiently, Andy explained the hospital, the city, everything.

"Well, then, I want to go." Eli was adamant; he wanted to see these building and all the cars and the people.

May looked at Andy and an agreement passed between them.

"We'll talk about it, sonny," Andy said kindly.

"Just a minute here," Oba growled. "I'm not going. That's it."

"Oh, come on. You are, too. It doesn't mean you have to get the limb immediately—it's just so you can talk to a doctor and consider your options."

Clara was buzzing with frustration. She rose from her chair to pour herself yet another cup of coffee, raised the pot, and asked if anyone else wanted more.

"I won't sleep well if I drink another cup," May said, laughing.

"Oba?"

He shook his head.

"Well, it's settled then. I'll do the calling on the telephone and be over sometime next week to let you know."

"Wait a minute. I told you 'no.' I'm not going."

"Yes, you are going. All expenses paid. It's your only chance at a half-decent life. I'm simply not accepting a refusal. After you've talked to a doctor, you can make your own decision, but the first shove in the right direction comes from me."

"But why?"

"Well, Andy and May will be moving to the farm soon, and Andy could use some help from a man. That farm has a lot of acres, well over a hundred. He can't do all the work by himself."

"I told Andy I'm not a farmer."

"You can become one. What else would you do? You'd have an awful time making it in the world, and you know it. What kind of job is available for . . . for someone like you?"

"Say it. Say 'handicapped,'" he sneered.

"You want me to use that word? Alright. You are handicapped, and will remain handicapped until you decide to do something about it."

"A . . . a fake leg is no promise."

"It's a beginning."

Andy agreed with Clara, voicing his opinion in his usual low-key manner, and when May saw Oba was not becoming pinned in, irate, lashing out the way he always did, she added her opinion of approval as well. Eli listened, absorbing the adult conversation the way he absorbed everything, with studied concentration and a mind seemingly older than his years.

"Do it, Uncle Oba. Do it for Dat and Mama and me and Lizzie and Fronie."

He thought awhile, then added. "And for Clara."

CHAPTER 4

IN THE FOLLOWING DAYS, OBA BECAME LOST IN INDECISION and feelings of frustration. He wished he'd never met Clara, although he no longer thought of her in the derisive terms he had previously. He kept to himself, putting up an invisible shield. May understood and didn't interfere; she explained to Andy the silence was his way of shutting the world out.

He wheeled himself out to the front porch, shivered as he contemplated the change in the weather. The heat of summer had dissipated, the humidity and scorching heat replaced by a tentative crispness in the morning. He imagined walking down the steps, his footsteps crunching on the gravel driveway, the strange sensation of being upright.

What were the things made of? Leather? Wood? In the modern day, anything could be possible, the way television was finding its way into homes, planes were new and improved, cars long and sleek with innovative fins, something about aerodynamics. Electricity was no longer the marvel it had once been, but an accepted normal flow of life in many homes.

Lights switched on, there were electric washers and dryers, electric ranges and refrigerators—everything was becoming better, easier, at least outside the Amish community. So why wouldn't there be new developments to help people like him? He hated thinking of himself as a handicapped person, but he guessed that was exactly what he was, a helpless lump who succumbed angrily to his fate. He wasn't sure whether he believed in God, but if God was real, Oba sure had it in for him. Why was he chosen to endure all he had? And so his thoughts tumbled over each other, always coming back to himself and life's unfairness.

Back here in his hometown, the presence of a faith in God was undeniable. These folks lived in a quiet dependence on the invisible Higher Presence, never spoke of it, or hardly ever, yet moved in quiet serenity as the days passed. In sunshine and rain, in cold and heat, the atmosphere of peace seeped between the cracks of his armor, softening a very small amount of his heart.

Except for the flamboyant Clara. She disturbed all his hard-won sense of calm, for sure.

He wasn't sure if he could survive the city. Panic clenched his chest at the thought of looming skyscrapers and cars rushing past. Of being on a four-lane highway hemmed in by fast-moving automobiles and lumbering trucks.

That night, after he fell into a restless slumber, he dreamed he was on stilts, those wooden ones his father made for him. Blocks of wood, triangular, nailed to sturdy, smoothly planed poles, leather straps to keep your foot in place. Once he'd had the skill, he could make huge strides, up high, charging along like a champion.

In the dream, he was capable of anything. High above the four-lane highway, he strode along with gigantic steps, leaping, flying, without effort, carried along by a sense of joy and self-confidence unlike anything he'd ever experienced. He opened his mouth and cried out with sheer jubilance, sang and shouted and cried.

He woke up crying, his cheeks wet with tears. He reached over on the nightstand for his handkerchief, blew his nose, and flopped back onto the pillow, clinging to the pure feeling of exuberance. He told himself it was only a dream, nothing more. But what if he really could walk again?

CLARA ARRIVED RIDING a fiery red horse with flaring nostrils and no sense of restraint. Oba actually didn't see her coming in the driveway, but heard May gasp and exclaim from her stance at the kitchen window.

"Oh my, Clara," she said.

She swung through the door, all loose flapping hair, wearing denim trousers beneath her skirts, bringing the smell of hay and raw earth. She was covered in horse hair, with the apology of one who says it only to be conventional. He felt the old irritation rise in his chest but watched with narrowed eyes as she wiped down the front of her rust-colored dress.

"Hey, good morning, all!" she shouted.

May put her hands on her hips, regarded her friend with consternation. "Now, Clara, that is about the limit. Aren't you afraid someone will see you riding around like a man?"

"Why would they?"

"There's usually a horse and buggy on the road on any given day."

"Oh, pooh! Who cares?"

Oba grinned, then hid his smile before she could see.

"It's not just that, but the horse looks unsafe. Wild!" May exclaimed.

"Barb? She's a real baby. Just full of energy. She's not real good in the buggy, so I'm training her to ride. I'll probably have to sell her as she's hard to have bred." Without missing a beat, she turned to Oba. "Hey, back there. Come on out to the kitchen. I got you an appointment. Dan Walsh is our driver. November second at 12:00 noon. The Cleveland Clinic. Doctor's name is something Brown. I can't pronounce his first name. Something starting with Ark."

At first, Oba did not make the connection, till May looked at him, the question in her eyes. He noticed the color seeping from her face.

"It couldn't have been Arpachshad, could it?"

"Yup. Exactly. How did you know? That is some name."

Clara bent to inspect the warm cookies laid neatly on a snowy tablecloth. "What kind?"

But May was staring at Oba, and he was staring at her, each one lost in memory. Of a time in Arkansas as children, when a boy named Arpachshad Brown wanted to be friends with Obadiah Miller, and Uncle Melvin never allowed it, said he had no business running around with the coloreds.

Arpachshad. As lighthearted and free as the wind, spending his days down by the river, dangling earthworms on a string suspended from a willow switch. They called him Drink, for having fallen into the river. And Melvin pronounced him worthless, a ne'er-do-well, the way he was allowed to do what he pleased. Oba saw the remembering in May's eyes and had to turn away, his face working to contain the emotion.

"What's wrong with you two? What kind of cookies, I asked?

"Oh. Yes. Peanut butter. They're peanut butter cookies."

"You look scared. Did you hear what I just said?"

"I did." May nodded.

"What is wrong with you?"

Oba shook his head. "We used to know someone name Arpachshad Brown. He was—*is*—a colored boy from Arkansas. Although I can't believe it's the same person. He would be too young to be a doctor. Perhaps a relative."

Clara gave Oba a sharp look. "An omen. A sign from God. That is exactly what it is."

BY THE TIME the second of November arrived, Oba was resigned to going. He couldn't deny his curiosity any longer—not just about the possibility of a prosthetic leg, but about the possibility that this Arpachshad was the same one they knew from childhood.

He was dressed in black Sunday trousers, a pair May had sewn and pressed for him, the belt snug around his hips, a light blue button-down shirt, and a light coat. He wasn't Amish, he told himself, only wearing the dress pants May had sewed out of necessity. His long blond hair was trimmed and combed, so he knew he was presentable, sitting in the wheelchair, waiting on the driver.

The station wagon was blue, with faux wood panels along the side, blankets and pillows in the back for the children, Andy in front with the driver. Clara, May, and Oba sat in the back seat. The arrangement suited him just fine, not having to make small talk with the driver or talk to May and Clara, who seemed to be doing fine on their own. He was glad to be going away in a car, but no one would have to know that. He needed to keep the upper hand, without allowing anyone to think of him as a charity case. He was merely allowing them to try out a newfangled thing, one Clara had thought up, just to see what he would make of it.

He'd never walk again, couldn't imagine lifting or moving anything with his stumpy leg. But he'd wait and see.

Clara was dressed in all her brilliant finery, the only sober saving grace her black jacket, which only set off the lime green of her pleated skirt. Her red hair was tamed into a semblance of humility, wetted and combed, no doubt. Her green eyes looked out on the landscape without missing a thing, commenting on the homes, cars, the corn fodder going to waste.

They reached the city an hour before the appointment, the driver gripping the steering wheel with both hands, keeping his eyes on the moving traffic ahead of him, the responsibility of his passengers weighing heavily on his mind. A graying, retired gentleman in his early seventies, he made extra cash hauling the Amish to places not accessible by horse and buggy.

The skyline was amazing, the horizon like the misshapen teeth of a broken comb, the river like a shard of broken glass. The sky seemed colorless, a haze of steam, smoke, or exhaust hovering above the many highways, streets, smokestacks, and chimneys. When they poured into the city with the rest of the traffic, they seemed to be swallowed up by the enormous mouth of the bustling metropolis, the tall buildings towering over them, shutting out the wind, the sun, and the clouds.

Oba felt swallowed by a vast stillness, the buzzing of cars an elevator into an abyss from which there was no return. He kept his face to the window, watched bridges with trucks and cars streaming across, before the scenery was shut away by the unforgiving walls of the city.

The Cleveland Clinic was an imposing glass, metal, and brick building, dwarfing the pedestrians and modes of transportation alike. Oba was wheeled through the doors into the lobby where they all conferred with one another. It was decided that Andy would stay with the children, allowing May and Clara to accompany Oba to the doctor's office at an adjacent building. May was his sister, and Clara was the one would who be responsible for the finances of it all.

Oba frowned. Why did she have to go? Why not only May? But knowing her, she'd have to be front and center. He shrugged to himself, found the sense to keep his mouth closed, in spite of wanting her to stay with Andy.

She would galvanize the conversation, he knew she would, while he'd sit there like a stump without any will of his own. He was prickling with irritation, felt restrained and locked away, as the women moved him along hallways, through glass doors.

He waited, kept his yes on the tile floor, tried not to meet anyone's eyes. It was a trick he'd learned early on. If you looked down without seeing anyone, it was the same as not being there at all. There was no accountability for sitting in a wheelchair with one pant leg tucked under, one foot on the footrest. He was comfortably invisible. He heard Clara say his name, to the receptionist no doubt. Another prickle of irritation. Full steam ahead, he thought.

Then he felt May's soft hand on his shoulder, felt the chair begin to move, the nurse stepping aside to let them pass. There was small talk, introductions, everything he so thoroughly disliked. But he got through it without any artificial smiles, bowing, or scraping, as he called it.

The door opened. A pair of brown leather shoes, trouser legs. A booming, "Mistah Obadiah Milluh."

He looked up to the round, gleaming face he vaguely remembered. A meaty dark hand was extended.

"Doctuh Brown."

"Yessir."

Oba shook hands, felt his own hand crushed between enormous fingers. Two bright curious eyes bore into his own.

"I saw the name on the charts. Didn't I used to know an Oba Milluh?"

"You're Drink?" Oba asked, quietly.

The light of recognition was kindled, followed by a roar of approval, a series of backslapping, fist bumping and shoulder grabbing.

"Yeah! Back in Arkansas. Wasn't that something?"

Guffaws of turbulent laughter, the nurse holding her clipboard to her chest, unsure of her next step.

They quickly caught up on each other's pasts, but with appointments pressing, they had to get down to business. May searched his face for signs of Clinton but knew her secret had never reached his brother, so why bring it up now?

She felt her pulse beating rapidly in her throat, was glad to have the chair to support her. They gave him the needed information, and Doctor Brown proceeded to roll up the trouser leg. He was stopped by Oba saying he didn't appreciate Clara in the room and would she please leave?

Clara fairly hissed her displeasure and refused. "If you're going to start all this again, I'm not paying for it, okay?"

"I don't want you to see it."

"I'm going to."

"No."

"Well, I am."

"Get out."

"No. If I'm going to be the one helping you with this, which I know I will be, I deserve to be right here and see what the doctor says. What's the stump end of a leg?"

"The lady has a point, Obadiah," Doctor Brown said kindly.

And Clara stayed.

The white, misshapen leg was thrust beneath the fluorescent lights, revealing every horrible dimple and slash, healed with a layer of red, pink, and deathly white skin. It was his worst nightmare, his shame revealed for three people, sickening them, thrusting him into his pool of dejection. To sit with a trouser leg tucked in was one thing, but to be exposed to prying eyes was cruel.

The doctor was professional, touching, measuring, asking him if there was more tenderness here, or here. He pronounced it a clean amputation, a good job in the professional sense. Of course, May stayed in the background, but Clara's beaky nose and freckled skin were right there in line with the doctor's, examining, curious to see what her own verdict would be.

She was the most annoying person he had ever met.

Then, she dared to reach out and place her hand around the part of his body that disgusted him. He didn't look at it himself, so why did she have to, then have the nerve to reach out and touch it? He looked down at the freckled arm, could not bring himself to see her hand with the long, slim fingers, wrapped around the shame of his amputated leg.

Then he felt the gentleness of her touch, felt the warmth along his veins. She drew back at the same moment he did. Their eyes held. She removed her hand. The air surrounding the amputated leg felt chilled, hostile. Something passed between them.

What?

He didn't know. He only knew there was no disgust, no loathing.

And Doctor Arpachshad Brown told him he could see no problem designing a prosthesis, but it would take quite a few visits to the clinic.

"I'll come with him," Clara said quickly.

He told him there would be hard days, frustration and pain. The prosthesis was built of leather and wood, the straps would chafe, the leg was cumbersome, but it was so much better than depending on a chair or crutches.

In time. Certainly not at first.

May stayed quiet, watched the doctor's dark hands, so much like Clinton's, and had an urge to tell him his nephew was here, but waved it away. It would bring confusion for Eli, at a tender age, which she felt was unwise.

Some day, the truth would have to be revealed, but not now.

They spoke of Arkansas, laughed a great deal about the waters of the great Mississippi River, the days Arpachshad wandered away from the cotton fields.

"I hated the cotton fields," the doctor mused, his fingers to his chin. "I started reading textbooks about medicine and never looked back. After my time as a medic in the war, I went to medical school, got my degree, then went for the study of orthopedics. And here I am. You wouldn'ta thought it back then, huh?"

Oba shook his head, smiled.

"You know, we all find our talents, what we love to do, what keeps us interested and happy. This is my calling. Medicine."

Oba nodded.

He found himself deep in thought on the return trip. The twists and turns of life. How far the doctor had come. It could not have been easy, in a white man's world, struggling up the social ladder. While his brother fell in love with May, took her away, only to find he could not support her because of their biracial union. Life was hard, too difficult to figure out.

Clara, for once in her life, was strangely silent. The children were exhausted, sleeping soundly in the back of the station wagon as the humming of the wheels lulled them into relaxation. Andy talked to the driver about crops and finances, the president, and the invention of the latest war plane. Oba had to admit he looked forward to his next visit.

ELI WENT TO school every day, as eager every morning as he had been on the first day. He loved his teacher, his classmates, his schoolroom, the work he did, everything. It seemed as if his life began the minute he walked into a classroom.

Sometime around the middle of November, he stumbled down the stairs in the morning complaining about pains in his stomach, his face contorted as his hands gripped the belt of his trousers. May was concerned and gave him a cup of peppermint tea, which seemed to lessen the pangs, and he ate his oatmeal and ran off to meet the neighbor children for the daily walk to school.

When May asked how his day was, he answered in his usual confident, cheery manner, but his mother watched the hint of a shadow on his face and wondered. As the week went on, the stomach pains continued, until May told him he had better stay at home that day, lie on the couch for a while, and see if it would help.

He stood up straight and shook his head.

"No, Mam. I can't do that. I have never missed a day of school."

"But you will someday, Eli."

"No, I can't do that."

But May insisted that he stay home. That afternoon, his stomach pains easing up, he ran beside Oba when he swung back and forth on the lawn with his crutches, the doctor having told him to do everything possible to strengthen his body as he waited for the prosthesis. Back and forth, he ran in the cold wind that carried falling twigs, bits of corn fodder, and a few brown oak leaves. Oba was breathing hard, his face red with the cold and the exertion. Finally, he flopped on the porch and threw his crutches to the floor, with Eli beside him. They sat, breathing hard, saying nothing.

After Eli caught his breath, he looked at Oba very seriously. "Uncle Oba, what is a Negro?"

"A black person."

"Am I a Negro?"

"No."

"The children . . ." He stopped, blinked his huge brown eyes, and took a deep breath. "A boy—his name is Robert—told me I am a Negro. He put his arm against mine, to show me I am not white. He said Negroes come from monkeys."

Oba looked down into the upturned face, the hurt and bewilderment obscuring the bright lights dancing there on any given day. His heart twisted with an actual physical pain, remembering his own adjustment in Arkansas when Lemuel Yoder told him he was an orphan, and orphans had to be sent to the children's home eventually. Without hesitation, he'd growled, lowered his head, and swung his fist blindly. He remembered the satisfying impact of his hand on the side of Lemuel's face, followed by another sound crack on his left cheek. Lemuel cried out and came for him, blindly, furiously, but Oba jumped aside and Lemuel lost his balance, sprawled in the dust. Oba jumped on his back, pounding his head, shoulders, anything, the primal need to injure, to maim, his first priority.

The teacher pulled him off, took him to the woodshed and administered a sound spanking, then wrote a note to Melvin and Gertie. It had been his first encounter with Melvin. Oba still being a young boy, Melvin hadn't used the horse whip, but a thick willow switch that stung like fire. It hadn't drawn blood or created white scars, only added insult upon insult, one beating on top of another. He never had a chance to state his case, had no one to tell why he sat on top of Lemuel Yoder and pounded him good. His hatred blossomed against authority then, and that emotion prevailed his whole life, especially after repeated whippings without justice.

His back was a mess of white welts, like puffy train tracks or the lines on a map. The scars on his back were a road map to resistance of anyone who tried to exercise their will over him, to control his behavior or make his decisions. That was the number one reason he could never be Amish.

He looked into the hurt in Eli's eyes and saw his own boyhood. A fierce sense of protection welled up in him. He looked long and hard at Eli, and told him he'd go to school with him on Monday morning, and that he had nothing to worry about, none of that was true.

He told Andy and May.

May broke down, weeping silent, bitter tears, her delicate blonde head bent in the gaslight of evening, after the children were in bed.

"I was always afraid of this. I know I will have to suffer for my past sins. The Bible plainly tells us, we reap what we sow. But must poor Eli suffer because of me?"

Andy was by her side in an instant. "May, May. Please don't. It breaks my heart to see you cry. We'll take care of this, together. I'll talk to the teacher. And I think perhaps this is the time to speak to Eli about his father."

"No, no. I can't do that. I can't. I can't," May moaned, her sodden handkerchief held to her mouth.

Andy's face was tormented with his wife's sorrow. He held her against his chest as he knelt beside her chair until the storm of weeping had passed. When she sighed and looked up, he gazed into her swollen eyes with so much kindness, Oba felt like an intruder to be able to witness such love.

Then Oba spoke.

He told them of his own childhood, the lack of understanding, a fair trial and punishment on his antagonizer. May was shocked. Oba nodded at her.

"You don't want Eli to find a base for the hatred I kept in my body. If he isn't allowed to be heard, he will not turn out well, especially if you don't tell him the truth about why his skin is different."

May nodded, her face a mass of anxiety. "But how will we tell him?"

"We will. He's so smart. He'll grasp it."

"At seven years of age?" May wailed, unable to fathom what the news would lay on her precious, carefree son.

"Brace up, May. Be grateful for the chance to tell him. Think about it. If I wasn't here to tell you all of this, you might never understand the importance of setting a good foundation."

"Yes, yes, of course," May whispered brokenly.

So May broke the news to her small son, alone in the bright sunny kitchen on a Saturday morning when Andy took the girls to the farm.

She told him Oba had told her what someone at school had said, and the part about monkeys was untrue. She took both of his hands in hers, looked into his innocent brown eyes, and with gentle words, told him of her past, being rescued by a kind young man who was born with brown skin and beautiful black curls like his own.

"He is your father, Eli. He was. He died one dark night, when he was out looking for work, in a city that was not welcoming to us. He died before you were born, and he went to Heaven to be with Jesus. He loved me, and he loved Jesus. Now Andy is your father, and he loves you the same as the girls. Sometimes he loves you more."

For a long time, Eli was silent as he absorbed his mother's words. Then the questions were pelted at her, quick and fast, a small line of confusion appearing in the smooth skin between his eyes. And May answered them as gently and as honestly as possible. She held him close, murmured words of assurance, allowed him time to think of more serious questions that would eventually need to be asked.

Finally, Eli breathed a long, trembling sigh, sat up straight, and looked hard at his mother.

"I guess, then, someone will have to go to school and tell Robert Mast. He shouldn't be allowed to say such things and make me feel bad. If I am not white like all the others, he should know that Jesus loves me as much as He loves them. Right?"

And that was carried out in a Christian manner, with Andy and May visiting the school, having a talk with the teacher, who was told about Eli's birth, which she had heard through the active grapevine anyway.

Eli was given the chance Oba never had, a chance to be treated fairly in love, with two parents whose first interest was the well-being of their son.

CHAPTER 5

IT WOULD HAVE BEEN BETTER IF ONLY DR. ARPACHSHAD Brown had been in the room, without Clara hovering, watching every move he made. The prosthesis was a clumsy affair. He felt ashamed of it, as if it had the power to mock him. The leather straps gouged his tender flesh, the top of the artificial limb all wrong. With patience and plenty of grumbling, he managed a few painful steps, his unused hip crying out in agony.

The bill was paid. The doctor wished him well, told him to make that call if he needed assistance in any way. Oba was polite, shook hands, thanked him properly, but knew the hateful thing would be propped in a corner, or even better, stashed in his bedroom closet as far out of sight as possible.

The entirety of the trip home, he sat in the back seat and sulked. He felt defeated. What was the use of going through all that when there was no way on earth he would ever become used to maneuvering through his days dragging that cumbersome thing around?

He knew he would have to seek employment, do something with his life, but the more the thought nagged him, the darker his days became. How did one go about navigating the world of employment if you were seated in a wheelchair? Who would hire you? And if they did, it was strictly out of charity, nothing else. His future stretched before him, a long dark void, an uncontrolled free fall into nothing.

HE STAYED IN his room, appearing only when hunger or thirst propelled him. May's face took on a pale hue, her large eyes dark with worry. She baked his favorite black walnut cake, made the ground beef noodle casserole he loved, grabbed his arm in desperation, pleaded with him to come spend time with the family or get some fresh air.

Andy knocked on his door, was told to get lost, and like May, he spoke through the door, pleading. They knew he was in a bad way.

And then Clara arrived. She blew in with the cold north wind on an overcast day, the red scarf tied securely around her face, her hands chapped with the cold. She put her horse in the barn and fed him a forkful of hay, knowing he was too skittish to stand at the hitching rack in the cold.

She spoke with May in hushed tones and pursed her lips as angry sparks ignited her yellow green eyes. She was furious, but did her best to hide her true feelings from the gentle May.

She turned without hesitation and strode purposefully down the hallway to the guest bedroom and began to pound on the door.

"Open up!" she shouted.

When there was no answer, she continued. "If you don't open this door, I'll get a screwdriver and remove the latch. If you don't believe me, watch."

No reply.

So she did. She removed the knob, inserted the screwdriver, and sprung the latch. It opened with a satisfying click.

"If you don't have any pants on, you better get them on, because I'm coming in."

She found him reclining on two pillows, covered with a warm quilt, fully dressed, his hair lank, unwashed, a week's growth of blond hairs like bristles all over his face. When he refused to look at her, she sat down on the bed, put her face close to his, and asked just what he thought he was doing.

He kept his eyes averted, refused her a reply. Clara looked up to find May hovering anxiously, the two girls peeping around her skirts.

"You must really enjoy making other people suffer, Oba. You sit in here, wielding power over your loved ones, feeling powerless and weak yourself. You are a coward, Oba. No guts. You have never been told this, I'm sure, but it's time you hear it. Stop thinking of yourself. Start caring what you're doing to Andy and May. I don't care about the money, and you don't have to do it for me, but I want you to know you have a whole life ahead of you. You're wasting everything God has ever given you."

"I have no interest in doing anything to please anyone," Oba growled, his voice like sandpaper grating on rough wood.

"But yourself," Clara cut in.

"Leave me alone. I want to die."

"No, you don't. You are afraid to die. You're doing this to make everyone else as miserable as you are, and the only reason you're so miserable is because you choose to be. Where's the leg?"

"In the closet."

It was a start. She yanked the door open, drew out the artificial limb, straps flopping about, then set it against the bed, where it slid to the side and crashed to the floor. Oba mocked her with his eyes.

"Get out of bed and pick it up," she ordered.

"I'd sooner pick up a rattlesnake."

"Pooh. I'd love to see you pick up a snake. You'd be scared out of your wits, and you know it."

He let her have the full benefit of his anger.

"Go ahead. Hate me all you want. I'm not going to let you lie in bed slowly losing your mind. Pick up the leg."

She waited. She crossed her arms and waited. She pulled up a chair and sat in it and waited. She turned to May and said she might as well make coffee, and did she have any of those sugar cookies left?

When May left, Clara got up, went over to the bed and picked up his leg, swung it across the top, and flung the quilt away. He was so surprised he had no time to resist.

"Now bend over and pick it up."

He didn't. She crossed her arms again and waited.

"I'm not a coward," he said.

"Yes, you are."

"No, I'm not. I ran a dog sled for miles. I lived in the Northwest, in the wilderness. You don't know me at all."

Clara said, "I know all that. I'm not particularly impressed."

After that statement, he had nothing more to say.

She continued, "If you had any courage, you would not be sitting in this room, on this bed, in the middle of the forenoon. Pouting."

"My leg is cut off!" he shouted.

"So what?"

Again, he was speechless.

She came to sit on the side of the bed, pushed her face close to his.

"Your leg is gone, right. So what are you going to do about it? I was born skinny and ugly, flat chested, with flaming red hair, and crosshatched with freckles. No normal man has ever looked at me, let alone asked me to be his wife. No one has ever asked me for a date or wanted to spend time with me alone." She snorted with derision. "Except, of course, some depraved individual who thought he could overpower me in the horse stables. So I've lived my life with an aversion to men, confident I can do everything they can." She became quiet, her breath coming quick and fast. "My looks are nothing to be proud of. In a sense, I am handicapped as well. It shouldn't be this way, I know," she continued. "But it is."

When he said nothing, she said, "At least you're a handsome man, leg or no leg."

He glanced at her, embarrassed.

"Now get out of bed, roll up that pants leg, and try this thing on."

She lifted the leg, ran a hand across the smooth surface of spliced wood, felt the joint, flexed it, then examined the straps, while he watched.

She said, "It's made from very light wood. Likely a wood grown in a foreign country. What did Dr. Brown say?"

"He said a lot of things," Oba said wryly. "You were there."

"Well, let's get on with this," she said briskly. "Roll the pants leg up. You know what? You should actually cut the pants leg off."

"No."

"Why not?"

"I don't know. Too final, I guess."

Clara looked at him. "You think it'll grow back or what?"

In spite of himself, he began to chuckle, an unaccustomed rumbling in his chest he tried hard to suppress. Clara let out a startling whoop, then let the artificial limb slide to the floor as she laughed a deep sound that came from the depth of her stomach. At first, he smiled, then contorted his face muscles to keep from joining her, and finally, grinned broadly, wholeheartedly. She sniffed, slanted him a look, and smiled.

He shook his head, met her eyes, then looked away. He was terrified to feel the lump form in his throat, the burning in his nostrils. He gulped, waved her away, turned his face to the wall, but the sobs that tore from his throat were so powerful, his entire body convulsed. His shoulders heaved as the guttural sounds came from his clenched mouth.

Clara waited, then felt her own tears rise to the surface. She leaned over and put a hand on his shoulder and kept it there a moment before she began a gentle, rhythmic motion. She felt the flaccid muscle, the bone beneath, the wasting away of what had once been a powerful young man, and a great pity welled up in her.

"Oba, it's okay. You don't have to be ashamed for me to see you cry. That is a sign of a true man."

She spoke in a voice quite unlike her, soft, gentle, feminine. He shook his head, lifted one hip to search for a handkerchief, a gesture Clara found vulnerable, like a small boy who had been hurt at school and needed his *schnuppy*. When he lifted his reddened eyes, she could barely muster the strength to hold his gaze and shrank from the dark, troubled pool of sadness and torment she saw there.

"You okay?" she whispered.

He nodded.

There was a quiet reprieve, one filled with understanding, a soft-ening of the atmosphere surrounding them. Clara wanted to speak, wanted to know more about the cauldron of hurt and disappointment simmering below the surface, but knew she did not have the courage. She'd called him a coward and found, in a moment of compassion and intimacy, she was the worst kind. So she stood up, clapped her hands, and told him she'd get this thing on him if it took all day.

He said nothing.

It was not too difficult with May's help. The hardest part was the sensitive stump, unused to any chafing or pressure, so they formed a layer of sheep's wool before tightening the buckles. Oba's mouth was twitching, a small line of perspiration forming above his upper lip, but he waited, did what they asked of him.

He wanted crutches for support, so they were brought. He put them beneath each arm and stepped out with his foot before drag-ging on the prosthesis. He winced, keeping his weight distributed on the crutches. May held her breath without realizing it and exchanged a look with Clara, who stayed on the opposite side. Lizzie and Fronie watched from the doorway, wide-eyed and frightened.

"Through the door? You alright with that?" Clara asked.

He nodded, and they stepped away. It was heartrending to see the effort he put into it, after his adamant refusal, and neither one wanted to see him revert back to his old exile, hiding away in his bedroom. Clara knew it would all take time and probably more patience than she was capable of, so now that she'd gotten the ball rolling again, she'd leave it up to May—and likely Eli—to help Oba stay motivated.

SHE STAYED AWAY for a week, determined to give Oba a chance to progress on his own. Clara stayed busy—she cleaned her house, did laundry, wrote lengthy letters about Oba's progress to her relatives in Indiana, and worked with her yearlings.

But she thought of Oba, the way he had shifted from anger to bit-ter sobs, and wondered how many more wells of misery were capped and ready to burst open.

Why did she care? Was it the responsibility she felt to May? Was it only natural to have a spirit of nurturing, a motherly instinct to protect? Yes, she was childless, would always remain so, and perhaps this need to take care of someone was just something all women felt.

Well, she'd see. She'd try and get him walking with that leg of his, then she'd work on getting him into society, help him meet a nice girl who would love him in spite of the prosthesis. He had needs like any normal young man, although she realized it would take a special young woman to be his wife. Her thoughts traveled through the community, peered into homey kitchens and upstairs rooms, picturing the older girls who were not dating.

Rudy Troyer's Sally.

Dan Mast's Amanda.

Then there was Sollie Wengerd's Lydia. Now there was a nice girl, probably over twenty-one years of age. She was attractive enough, although not as good looking as Oba. He was, like May, blessed with every good feature God had ever invented.

She found herself peering closely at her own features, evaluating, comparing, something she hadn't done for quite some time. She came away with the same thought she always did. She was not an attractive person. Never was, never would be.

She shrugged her shoulders, put wood on the fire, got down the cast iron pan, and made herself some sausage gravy. She stirred a batch of biscuits, worked the dough on the dough board, cut perfect orbs with a biscuit cutter before lifting them with a spatula and plopping them on an aluminum cookie sheet.

Her thoughts went to Oba again. How would she feel if a man—not necessarily Oba—was seated by the table, waiting for dinner, keeping a conversation flowing? She berated herself for even having such thoughts. She had never needed a man to keep her company and she never would. But while she sat eating her favorite food, she couldn't help but imagine the hominess of it, the cozy feeling of sharing food, discussing ordinary happenings of ordinary days.

She scraped her plate, wiped the last of the gravy with a section of biscuit, sat back, and belched comfortably. She brought her gaze to roam around the house, the perfection of the sturdy rooms, the comfort and orderliness of her home. A quick appreciation for the inheritance from her parents arose, the realization she was well to do for a single girl, able to run the horse farm efficiently—although she did hire a boy from time to time.

She wondered how far Oba would go with that artificial leg. It was a cumbersome thing, would take days of patience and determination, and she was unsure whether he had enough of either one. He was just so weak. So uncaring about building his strength, not even caring enough to get out in the world to try to acquaint himself with anyone or anything. If he kept this up, he'd turn into a babbling recluse.

AND SO SHE found herself at May's door. She blew in with the cold air, the scent of horses clinging like a second skin, her red scarf untied, hanging around her neck, the red skirt billowing around her ankles.

She surprised the family, who had just finished the noon meal and were seated around the table drinking hot cups of peppermint tea. There was a half-eaten apple pie at Oba's elbow.

"Sorry. Forgot to knock," Clara called out.

"Don't worry about knocking, Clara," May laughed, her face glowing with appreciation at the sight of her.

"There's apple pie left," Andy said, gesturing toward the dessert.

Oba wondered why there were never formal greetings when she arrived. He'd never met anyone with worse manners, and yet she had told him he was rude. As usual, his skin prickled at the sight of her; he wished her gone. Instead, she slid on the bench beside Eli, put an arm around his shoulders, then asked how school was going, before reaching for the girls.

May hurried to the stove for tea, smiling at the obvious affection Clara displayed for the children. Andy handed over the pie, grinning broadly, then asked if she'd be able to help May with the packing.

"What for?"

"We're moving before the winter sets in. Dat is ready to let go of the farm."

Clara put two fingers to her mouth, said "Hmm."

"What does that mean?"

"Well, who's going to milk all those cows?"

"I am!" Eli shouted.

"And me!" Lizzie echoed.

Clara laughed. "It's a lot of work, for the amount of help you have." She looked directly at Oba. "You better get your act together with that prosthesis. Andy's going to need another man, you know."

Oba ignored her.

"Did you hear what I said?"

May looked steadily at her plate, cringing inwardly. She thought surely Clara would learn to back down. It was so apparent that Oba did not want to give her the information she wanted. He was hurting, had always been, and if he had no one to protect him, well . . .

Clara went on as if he had given her an answer.

"You know, I heard of a man who walks so well with his wooden leg, no one can tell he's wearing one. You should find someone who has been through what you have. You know, it's always a help to hear of another's experience."

Oba got to his foot, reached for his crutches.

"I see you're not always dependent on the wheelchair anymore, which is a good thing."

Oba swung himself out of the room without looking back.

May was upset, but it was not in her nature to be confrontational, so she looked at Clara, gave her a weak smile, and shrugged. "He's hurting, Clara. He's not like other people."

Clara gave her a long steady look, an unwavering accusation without disguise. "May, I told you before. You can't protect him from the blows of life."

"But . . ."

"No. I'm sorry, but you're part of the problem."

Andy did not appreciate Clara's harsh manner with his beloved wife, whom he knew shrank from all forms of adversity. "Clara . . ."

"I know. You don't want to hear what I have to say. Do you want help for your brother, or don't you? There is only one way to help him, and that is giving him the push he needs. If he doesn't want it, well, he's going to get it anyway."

"But Clara, I'm afraid your way is not right in this case."

"It is. Trust me."

SHE WAS THERE, washing dishes, packing cardboard boxes, singing, talking, a bright presence that filled the house with vitality. May worked alongside her friend, exclaimed with her about the amount of worldly goods they had accumulated over the short span of years.

Clara lifted a stack of linens from a drawer in the bathroom, counted the sheets and pillowcases, then yelled down the hallway, where May was packing things in the children's room.

"Seven sets of sheets!"

"Oh yes. We were given so many wedding gifts. I know."

"That is amazing. The kindness of our people."

May chose to remain silent, the distance between them an obstacle. But also, she intended to keep from Clara the resentment that was slowly growing in her heart. The truth was that not everyone in the community was kind. The situation at school had been tamped down, but the slow burn continued unchecked, with sunny Eli arriving home from school with a quiet face, chewing his nails till they were mere stumps.

No amount of inquiries made a difference, with Eli shaking his head, saying no, no, everything was fine. But she knew everything was not fine.

In church on Sunday, she had witnessed a sad spectacle, that of old Mommy Hettie, handing out the pink mint candy to a crowd of children but turning away from Eli, who eagerly waited his turn. When he saw there would be none for him, he turned away, the smile erased, his dark eyes shadowed with rejection. Hettie watched him go, her lips pursed, her old eyes glittering with righteous refusal. And an arrow of pain had become embedded in May's heart. To Hettie, this child was cursed, a spawn of the devil, conceived in sin and tainted with it for the duration of his life.

Oh, she knew. May knew, no matter how hard some tried to hide it, the disgust would crop up from time to time, raise its ugly head, reach out with long fingers and draw her into its horrible embrace.

Yes, she tried to understand, reasoned with her own take on Hettie's attitude. She had been born and raised into this way of thinking, so there was nothing May could do or say to change it, but why must she take out her lack of understanding or forgiveness on poor Eli?

It wasn't his fault.

So Eli often found himself on the outskirts of the group of children in church, waiting hesitantly as white-haired, kindly grandfathers, their eyes twinkling with delight, would tell a story to the children, then hand out a gum drop or the ever-present pink lozenges.

As children do, he would forget, his sunny disposition returning as regularly as the morning light, which May felt was an undeserved blessing, this precious child rising above his circumstances.

She never told Andy or Clara, but kept the incidents in her heart, for the Lord to take away. He had been faithful in her life, had redeemed her by His grace, so could she do any less to those who trespassed against her? She loved the Lord Jesus, the beginning and ending of her faith, and lived her days in the realm of His blessing, aware of the fact that Andy, Eli, Fronie, and Lizzie were her own form of God's forgiveness.

And life was precious. There would always be imperfections, times of trouble and sorrow, but with the assurance of His love, anything could be overcome with His strength. Oba was a form of sorrow, of unending worry and fear she took to the Lord daily in prayer. She longed for his freedom from self, his unhappiness and despair changed into courage and love, but knew well she was powerless to provide it.

God alone held the key to his redemption.

May smiled to herself as she set a box of dishes on a stack of more boxes.

"May!"

"What?"

"I'm hungry."

"Andy won't be here for another hour. I have chicken and dumplings here on the stove, but it won't be ready till lunchtime."

Clara appeared, a vision of color in a flaming green dress, her white covering sliding around on her thick red hair, the tendrils loosening around her face as she kept up the frenetic pace of throwing things into boxes, running after Fronie and Lizzie to grab them up in her arms and tickle them till they giggled uncontrollably. The two girls adored their "Aunt Clara."

When Andy drove up to the house with a pair of Belgian work horses, May was surprised to see Oba seated on the side, his crutches beside him. His face was reddened by the cold, his blond hair disheveled, his coat opened as if the cold was merely laughable. And he was talking to Andy, waving his hands, animated.

When had he left the house? Had Clara's presence angered him to the point he'd swung himself clear over to the farm on crutches?

She crooked a finger to Clara, who was lifting the lid of the chicken and dumplings, pointed wordlessly, and watched as Clara caught sight of Oba. It was only later that she wondered at the look on her face.

CHAPTER 6

B Y THE TIME THE COLD WINDS BLEW IN EARNEST, WITH THE underlying threat of a real snowstorm, Andy and May were settled into the large white farmhouse where he had been born and raised. His parents simply traded homes with them, settling into the brick ranch house with a happy sigh of rest and contentment. Their work of raising a large brood of children, working the soil and milking cows as the seasons turned into years, was behind them now, the future of resting on their laurels into the golden sunset years before them.

Ketty had never been happier, her rotund form moving with surprising speed from room to room, exclaiming at the perfect size for three people (Simon and herself, of course, plus their youngest son, still at home), and how she would enjoy her coffee and raisin cookies after doing laundry. Simon smiled indulgently at his wife, said she deserved every well-earned rest she could find.

May was a bit overwhelmed at the size of the house, the yard, and garden—everything. But she would love being closer to Andy as he worked, to be able to watch him come and go with a team of prancing Belgians, to help with the milking, working side by side with him, to be a true helpmeet in every sense of the word.

Oba felt completely unmoored, in a way he did not understand. His bedroom was on the second floor of the farmhouse, the stairs an unnavigated question mark, one he had never tried. He wanted to leave, to disappear from this well-ordered household. He knew he was a burden to those around him, but knew, too, he had no other options, the world outside an inhospitable place, one in which he would not survive.

It all narrowed down to one thing, which Eli recognized early on. He would have to get up those stairs and back down again.

"Uncle Oba, going down will be easy," he offered.

Oba looked at his upturned face, gave him a small grin. "Sit down and slide, huh?"

"Something like that."

"Sure, but how will I get up the stairs?"

Eli put a finger to his lips, evaluating the stairs with wise eyes, then looked at the ever-present crutches. "It could be done."

May smiled at Andy, and he gave her a broad wink. Eli seemed so much older so much of the time, showing an amazing ability to reason things out. He was a big help to Oba simply by his willingness to help; his charming, little-boy eagerness was an underlying mood booster to his spirits.

"Try the bottom step, the way you get up on the porch, then keep going."

Oba looked at Eli, then at the stairs. "Who will catch me if I fall?"

"I will." Then he opened his mouth as he howled with glee.

So it was on a light note that Oba placed his crutches on the bottom step, swung himself up, hesitated, and then took another laborious step. Nothing about it was easy, but he was determined, so with the audience at the bottom of the steps holding their breath, he kept on, one step at a time.

When he got to the top, everyone clapped their hands and shouted approval, Lizzie and Fronie dancing with delight.

Oba grinned, lowered himself, and said, "I'm coming down."

And he did, sliding on the seat of his pants, sending the crutches in a haphazard slide before him. He bounced and slid his way to the bottom, where he sprawled awkwardly before lifting himself with the crutches.

There was a celebratory air at the supper table that night, amid the boxes and half-unpacked crates of dishes. The meal was simply a leftover casserole, an apple pie, and slices of bread with pear butter, but it tasted wonderful, with Oba in better spirits.

May felt as if she could conquer anything with Oba showing so much improvement. She washed the dishes quickly before following Andy to the barn. This was her first attempt at milking a cow since her days in Arkansas, but she hadn't forgotten a thing and she was eager to show her husband the skill she had always possessed.

She opened the door to the cow stable, a wave of the accustomed odor of manure, hay, grain, and silage bringing an unexpected surge of anguish. Her breath came faster, her fists clenched as she braced herself for the rushing memories that washed over her.

She could almost feel Melvin lurking behind the post riddled by cobwebs, a dark sinister figure who tormented her with hissing promises. The quick stroke of his hands as she poured a bucket of warm frothy milk into galvanized cans, unable to turn and fight him off. And if she dared attempt it, there would be consequences known only to her. And to him.

She began to tremble. Quick tears sprang to her eyes. Telling herself she must be strong, she clenched and unclenched her fists and squared her shoulders as she moved to the milkhouse. The smell of milk cans, the cooled water containing the smell of mold and iron, the wet concrete floor, everything about the place reached out and threatened to choke her. She sagged against the cold stone wall, bent her head into her hands, and began a mixture of ragged breaths and hoarse sobs coupled with intermittent moaning.

Andy swung happily through the door to find his wife in such a state. He stopped in alarm before going to her, his strong denim-clad arms drawing her gently to him, holding her as if he couldn't bear to hear the sounds from her throat.

"May, May. Tell me what's wrong. Am I expecting too much of you to take on the farm? Shh. May."

Great sounds of anguish rose in waves, sounds that could not be stopped. So he held her and prayed, his lips moving as he closed his eyes and allowed his own tears to seep from between the lids. With the depth of his love for May, these sounds were like a knife to his chest.

He stroked her back, told her he loved her, reminded her they could get through anything together. Finally, she took a deep shuddering breath, and strained against his arms as she searched for a handkerchief in her dress pocket. She shook her head back and forth before falling against him, her arms going about his waist in a viselike grip.

"Hold me, please hold me," she whispered.

The story came in bits and pieces of mumbled remembering, the shame and self-blame a tangled skein of years of being treated in a manner so devastating to a young girl. Andy felt helpless as he was confronted by this puzzle of her past. There was nothing he could do to protect her from what had already happened.

"Did you ever hear how a sense of smell will bring back memories faster than any other sense?" he asked, tenderly.

"No."

"I've heard it said."

"It must be true."

"Listen, May. If you would rather not milk, you don't have to. I can always hire someone, and in a few years, Eli will be able to milk a cow."

"No, no. I want to milk. I looked forward to showing you how good at it I am. I used to milk six cows, sometimes as many as eight."

"I'm sure you're very good." His eyes searched her face, looking deep into her trusting gaze, before he lifted his hand to wipe away the traces of her tears. "You know you are safe now, right?"

She nodded, then raised her lips to his, clinging to him as he kissed her with all the gentle love he felt in his heart.

SHE POSITIONED THE milking stool into place, sat down by a cow, and bent her head against the soft, smooth flank, the stainless steel bucket held firmly beneath the udder. With swift, sure strokes, she pulled on the soft teats, with thick streams of rich milk hitting the bottom of the pail with a pinging sound. Her fingers were strong, the muscles in her arms supple, but the unaccustomed squeezing soon tired her out. But she kept milking with determination.

She jumped when Eli came flying into the cow stable, felt her irritation rise like bile in her throat. She stopped herself from jumping up and berating him thoroughly, the way she would have liked to.

She thought of Leviticus.

Where was he now? Romping through the cow stable in Arkansas, how much had he seen? Had the boys always been blind to their father's incomprehensible behavior? She hoped fervently, hoped they had been far too young and innocent to notice. She swallowed back the rising flavor of guilt, of self-hatred. Had she truly done all she possibly could to avoid any overtures from Melvin? Would she be found innocent on the day of God's judgment? A yawning hell of remembrance threatened to drag her into its fiery depth as she valiantly fought every wile of the devil. How could it possibly be fair, opening a door to be thrown off guard by the familiar odor of a lowly cow stable?

Her lips moved as she began to pray. She begged God to take away this thorn in her flesh, this shadow repeatedly covering the light of her happiness. She brought her thoughts into subjection by her prayers and finished milking the first cow before going on to the second. She realized this was her lot in life, God had allowed it. She could never undo what had been done, and would always have to remember to move away from the darkness of her years in Arkansas, into the circle of grace and forgiveness from the father of lights, the beginning and ending of her faith.

IN TIME, THE farmhouse became home. Oba thumped his awkward way up the steps each evening until he became quite adept at maneuvering his way up and down. Clara stayed away for a while, allowing them to settle in, before arriving in the middle of a fierce snowstorm about a week before Christmas, riding the sorrel mare with the long mane and wild-looking eyes, bundled up so only her eyes were visible between layers of scarves.

The mare was in over her knees, the fine powdery snow spraying like clouds of white smoke behind her, bits of froth from the bit in her mouth clinging to Clara's black coat.

Andy stood in the barn door, his wide form filling the entrance. "Are you OK?"

Clara laughed, the sound ringing out through the gray, muted atmosphere. "If you really want to know, Andy, I'm frozen the whole way through."

"I believe you. Give me the horse and get to the house. I'll be in."

Clara banged into the washhouse and yelled for May as she struggled to undo the layers of knotted scarves. Her eyebrows dripped water and melted snow ran from her wildly disarrayed hair. May looked dismayed to find her in such a state and fumbled with the scarves while telling her, one of these days, she would find herself in a situation she could not get out of.

"I am half-froze. Shoulda checked the thermometer."

She hugged Lizzie and Fronie as they came running to her, then handed them a bag of gumdrops in brilliant colors. May smiled as she put the kettle on, laughed outright when she saw Clara's bedraggled head covering. Clara whipped it off her head and reached back to yank out a dozen hairpins, allowing the cascade of rippling red hair to fall down her back.

"My hair bun loosened, I guess. The wind is so fierce."

Oba entered the room in time to see the glorious head of hair loosened, finding the length of brilliant, rippling locks a bit disconcerting. If the hair belonged to anyone else, it would be astoundingly attractive, but on Clara? He wasn't sure what to think or feel.

Clara saw him in the mirror, his face a blank slate, his eyes averted after the first glance. She turned her head to one side as she drew a comb through the long, luxuriant tresses. Unselfconscious, without a thought to her own appearance, she said hello and how are you, then finished the work of folding all that hair up over the palm of one hand while pulling it firmly into place with the other.

He was mesmerized without recognizing it. He had never seen anything so fascinating. She jabbed hairpins into the thick bun of folded hair and took one offhand look in the mirror before plopping the white covering into place and ramming two straight pins through it, one on each side. She threw herself into a kitchen chair, looked at the kettle on the stove, and told May she was starved.

"You sure do have it looking nice here, May."

"Thank you."

"You know Ketty was no housekeeper."

May laughed. "I know. She's my mother-in-law."

"I should have helped you more."

"Oh no. Andy helped. Oba too. We painted most of the walls. Scrubbed floors and windows. Oba hung curtain rods."

"You did?"

Clara turned to Oba, her green eyes bright with approval. He found himself smiling before he could quite catch it. She caught his eye and nodded.

"So you're doing what you can? That's a start. Do you wear your limb?"

"Of course not."

"Why not?"

"Because it's heavy and cumbersome, and I hate it, that's why."

Clara eyed him levelly, then told him he might as well give up and get used to it. The longer he pushed it off, the harder it would be.

He watched the snow outside the window, ignoring her yapping. When she paused, he asked what was wrong with her, riding a horse through this, gesturing with a thumb jerked in the direction of the snow.

"I ride horses every day, in every kind of weather. It's what I do to make a living. If you wouldn't be so stubborn, you could ride with me. I can always use an extra hand."

"I don't like horses. I told you that."

"You can learn to like them."

May sighed, thinking tired thoughts to herself. Why couldn't two of her favorite people simply get along, even for one day? The storm outside was worsening, and if Clara remained as overconfident as she was now, she might not make it home. When Andy clattered into the washhouse, stamping his feet, the snow scattered from his clothing like bits of flying paper. He called out, warning Clara about the thing May had been thinking.

"It's not that bad," Clara said, without a trace of concern.

"Try making your way to the barn," he answered.

"It can't be that bad."

Andy shrugged, as if to allow her to have her own way. Eli looked up from his schoolwork, smiled, and shook his head at his father, a grown-up gesture of sharing his thoughts without comment.

They enjoyed a lunch of sausage gravy on toast, a fresh pan of fried potatoes so crispy they crunched in their mouths, with stewed tomatoes and applesauce. Talk flowed freely, with bits of news from around the community.

"Did you hear about Rudy Troyer's daughter, Sally?" Andy asked.

"No. What?" May asked.

"She has a date with Pete!"

"Your brother? Seriously? Oh, I'm so very pleased!" May exclaimed. "They will be perfect for each other."

But Clara's face fell, her eyebrows lowered. "Hmph. I had her picked out for Oba."

May winced, knowing this would not go well.

"Oba, you get to wearing that leg, you can ask a girl. Sally would be the best one of the three I thought about."

"Oh, come on, Clara," Oba growled.

May watched. She had never heard Oba use her name. Perhaps it meant he was becoming used to her ways, content to let her prickly personality alone.

"I'm not joking. You need to decide what you're going to do with your life and proceed to pursue a future."

"I'm not Amish. I have no intention of being Amish."

"Pshaw! You were born Amish, right here in Ohio, so don't go around thinking otherwise. It's all a matter of getting your priorities straight. If you want to be English, then what are you doing here, holed up like a hermit?"

Clara's words thumped between them with all the finesse of thrown bricks. May wished her best friend would learn to acquire a few social graces, if only to make life easier for all of them.

Oba glared at her, but did not give her the benefit of an answer.

"If you'd get to work on that leg, it would be a beginning of a future."

May was shocked when Oba's eyes fell, and he mumbled, "I know."

"'Course you do. You're just not facing facts."

Andy laughed. "You're not facing facts either, Clara. This storm is not letting up, and I'm afraid to let you ride home. I'm very serious."

"I'm not staying here, so you may as well forget it."

May echoed her husband's concern, but Clara would have none of it, saying she had chores to do, horses who depended on her for their food and water, a fire to keep going in the house or the water pipes would freeze, perhaps burst and create an awful mess.

No, she was going home.

Through all of this, Oba stayed silent but felt mounting apprehension. The thought of this thin woman staying astride a horse in the ever-increasing wind brought thoughts of the Northwest Territory, the mind-numbing cold and dangerous temperatures. He knew first-hand the disorientation of low temperatures and blowing snow, the world a soundless, reckless spinning of moving particles and winds seemingly out to destroy a person.

He watched as she shrugged into layers of clothing, wrapped three scarves over her head, around her neck, then pulled on a pair of heavy gloves.

Andy got to his feet, begged her to allow him to ride with her.

"What? On those klutzy old Belgians? No, I'll be home before you're out the drive."

With that, she waved a hand and let herself out the door.

THAT NIGHT, OBA could not get to sleep. The anxiety of the snow still scouring the upstairs window, the whirring of a loosened piece of spouting, the eerie moaning of icy winds, was almost unbearable. She had taken a risk, made a foolish choice, gone against the common sense of both Andy and May. He didn't especially care for Clara, but still . . . it was plain stupid of her to strike out blindly in severe weather like that.

Again and again, he pictured the image of flowing red hair and imagined her frozen dead, the hair trailing across the white snow like some tragic princess. The remaining family would have to be notified. No parents, but he remembered that she had siblings in Indiana.

He found himself unusually distraught. That was why he agreed to accompany Andy and May and the children when they ventured out in the bobsled a few days later to visit Clara. The storm was long gone, leaving behind piles of fresh snow. Andy and May said they just wanted to get out for a ride and see their friend, but both had harbored concern for their friend since the moment she had set out. So they hitched up a team of Belgians to the sturdy wooden sleigh, bundled up in layers of outerwear, heated bricks in the oven, piled sheep's wool blankets on the two seats, and started off.

Oba squinted his eyes against the blinding light of the sun on the crystal white snow. He shivered inside his heavy coat, but he felt the exhilaration, the lifting of sour spirits and long winter days. The Belgians were eager, excited to be freed from the restraints in the barn. Their ears were in constant motion, turned beautifully forward, flicking backward as they listened for Andy's commands. Their noble necks were arched, the deep, thick hairs of their manes jiggling along the top, the black leather harness with silver rings and buckles showing off the deep golden color of their bodies.

A dull *thwock, thwock* of their hooves became coupled with the whisper of the sled's runners on heavy snow, packed down by passing snowplows, but only a few motorists. The straps and buckles jingled, the sound like tinkling bells, and steam from the horses' nostrils flowed back, leaving a distinctive scent in the crystal air.

Oba looked around, feeling the pull of nostalgia. The clump of pine trees here, the aging cement block garage on the corner, the blue house with black shutters and the deep porch. How young he had been! How carefree, a smooth unsullied back and two sturdy legs, a mind unfettered by the evil ways of men. He wanted to go back, start over. But he knew with a sharp clarity he could never bring back his father or mother. They were buried in the cemetery nearby, their bodies decayed, gone completely by now. He wondered if bones lasted forever inside that wooden box they'd lowered into the ground.

His thoughts marred the beauty of the pristine snow, the blue of the sky and the green of the fir trees covered in layers of snow as thick as frosting on cupcakes. He slanted a look at Andy, wondered at his good humor, as regular as the rising and setting of the sun. His face was ruddy with the cold, his eyes as blue as the sky, the crow's feet around his eyes turned up, put there by frequent laughter. How did one acquire that level of merriment, flowing through life with no bitterness to resist?

The farm was quite picturesque, the way it was nestled among the trees, the pastures spreading out on both sides, the fences as white and as neat as the fresh snow. The house was small, compact, welcoming with that deep porch and sturdy porch posts. He could see young horses tearing around in the snow. But there was no sign of Clara.

For a moment, he wondered if she'd survived that trip home, felt a lurch when he thought of his wild imagining. There was no light in the house, but she might be in the barn.

Andy's face was serious as he brought the sleigh to a standstill by the barn doors, looked around at the seemingly deserted place. He looked back at May and the children, raised his eyebrows in question.

"I'll check the house, see if she's home," May said quickly.

Oba noticed the lack of shoveled walks, the snow a smooth, undisturbed blanket over everything. Horses whinnied in the barn. His breath quickened.

May floundered through the snow, a small black figure. She reached the porch, stomped her boots, and lifted a hand to knock, then turned the knob to open the door. Oba found he was holding his breath until she reappeared, motioned for them to come in.

So she had made it.

Andy put up the horses, then reached for the children before telling Oba to stay, he'd find a shovel and clear a trail to the house so he could make his way.

Clara was seated on an overstuffed chair, her feet in a galvanized tub of steaming water giving off an herbal odor. She was dwarfed by the giant chair, her slight form looking a bit subdued, vulnerable, in a dusty shade of green, one that made her red hair look auburn.

"Come in, come in. Don't let all the cold in. Oba, I am completely shocked to see you venture away from your house. What brings you?"

He found himself speechless, floundering uncomfortably for words before shrugging, seating himself on the couch, and setting his crutches neatly in a corner.

"Well, good for you, for thinking about me." She snorted, then gave a rueful laugh. "I think I might have frozen a few toes."

Eli burst out laughing, his mouth wide open, showing all his white teeth. He laughed so hard, he leaned forward and slapped his knees, then wiped his eyes. It was the relief of finding her alive and well—even if her toes were a little damaged. Everyone had to laugh with him, even Clara.

"It's not funny, Eli. Do you have any idea how painful frostbite can be?"

He shook his head, then began to laugh all over again.

"You should have stayed," Oba said.

"I know that now," she said curtly, without smiling.

She lifted her feet out of the tub, set them on a towel, as Andy and May bent to examine the damage. Oba stayed quiet, strangely repelled by her brusque manner. He hadn't meant anything by it. He was the one who knew about frostbite, having spent years in the wilderness of the Northwest Territory. When she showed him both feet, he bent over and examined them before reaching down to touch them with the tips of his fingers. There was no color, but some warmth, which was reassuring.

Her legs and feet were freckled, but the skin of her foot was soft, almost velvety. He felt the tingle start at his fingers and spread warmth up his forearms. He looked up to find her green eyes, asking for the verdict, for once appearing unsure of herself, vulnerable. His dark eyes stayed on hers, but he quickly put his hands in his lap, her foot an embarrassment.

"Well?" she asked.

"Give it a couple of days. You'll be alright," he said, but his voice was choked.

"Really?"

"Yes. I had feet like yours more than once. It's painful, but you won't lose your toes."

"Thank God. You know, Oba, someday you'll have to tell us all about your life in the North. I have a feeling once you begin to talk about it, it will be terribly entertaining."

And he found himself wanting to do just that.

CHAPTER 7

CLARA HAD MADE PLANS TO SPEND CHRISTMAS IN INDIANA with her siblings, but between the frostbite in her feet and the storm delaying the train schedule, she decided to stay on her farm in Ohio.

Andy and May planned a huge get-together, a mammoth Christmas dinner, hosting Andy's extended family, which left Oba to decide if he wanted to stay upstairs in his room, face the hordes of unfamiliar faces, or find somewhere else to go. He disliked the idea of being scrutinized, pitied, touched by people who did not know what to say or were so full of their own ability to be a perfect Christian they fawned over him with so much pious talk it made him want to throw up. Avoiding strangers was much easier than getting through all that, the rebellion raising its head until he had only loathing left.

He moped around the house, with May in a flurry of preparation. She cleaned and scrubbed, washed windows and floors, clothes, and anything left in her way, after which she began to bake and cook, the house filled with the scent of chocolate, roasting walnuts, caramel pudding, and so many cookies that he lost track of the dozens and dozens taken from the oven.

Small gifts were wrapped and hidden, the house filled with a general air of festivity, while Oba became steadily more withdrawn.

May was too busy to notice, but Eli sat beside him and asked if he was going to be here at the Christmas dinner, his large, intelligent eyes filled with love and understanding far beyond his years.

"I don't want to, but I don't have anywhere to go."

"You could go to Clara's. She's all by herself."

May lifted two cookies from a sheet pan, set them down slowly. "Oba, why don't you?"

"Why would I?"

"Why wouldn't you?"

He shrugged.

"Take your artificial leg, and she'll help you with it."

"No she won't."

"But you know she will. I'll call a driver for you, Oba. She'll be glad to have you, you know that."

Of course she would, he thought. He was like a younger brother, someone to nurture, admonish, get started down the right road. He felt enraged by this, the audacity of her presumed guardianship. She was not a substitute parent, not even a mentor or a friend. She went so far as to think about a suitable girl for him, as if she could add matchmaker to her list of accomplishments.

He didn't want some young simpering girlfriend. He didn't want to be introduced as a possible suitor, one-legged, damaged, his pair of crutches or his wheelchair a waving flag for produced results, which was always pity. The fancy word was empathy, but it only served the purpose of glossing over the carved pedestal of a righteous, lofty status, being better, more blessed, being whole and good and without the curse of one amputated leg.

And now, there were other complications.

Complications he could not mention to anyone, not even himself. How did one go about sorting feelings? Anger, distrust, dismissal, all woven together now with the confusing truths he could no longer deny.

She was not someone he wanted to be with as a sister. She was not completely unattractive either. He'd told himself that his loneliness had taken over his senses, thus bringing a kind of infatuation, her bright colors and loud manner, the swagger of her self-confidence a ray of color, a light at the end of his self-imposed tunnel.

He did not see her beaked nose, but saw the vivacious eyes, the slim fingers on well-formed hands. He saw the beauty of her freckles, was glad to see them on her legs and feet. Yes, she was older, but was there a sin in that? He blushed, thinking of her slim waist, her strong arms and legs, then felt a sense of self-hatred, a burning shame for admitting he had any desire for anyone.

The truth was, he was not complete. Who would ever want him as a husband? Who would lie in bed with a husband with one leg missing? And still, part of him wanted to keep the maelstrom of his feelings, knew his previous existence had been nearly dead, and this gut-wrenching discomfort of doubt and fear and excitement intertwined with a certain new longing. Perhaps it was an unreachable goal, but it was a goal, something to hold on to.

So he allowed May to call a driver. He bathed, dressed in clean clothes, took up his crutches, and asked May to bring the artificial limb to the car. Clara had no way of knowing he would be arriving, so if she wasn't at home, he'd have to return to Andy's house with all the guests.

But Clara was in the barn, her red scarf and wool coat covered in bits of hay, her hair in loose straggles, but a welcome on her face. Yes, of course, he could stay. Yes, come on into the barn till she was done. She retrieved the artificial limb, set it in its corner encased in the blanket, then put her hands on her hips and said, "Well."

He said, "Yeah. Andy's having a horde of relatives for a Christmas dinner, and I don't do well in crowds."

"Of course not. Okay. Let me finish up. Here." She shoved an old stool in his direction. "Sit."

"Thanks."

She went to one of the many doors along a wide corridor, slid it back, and said, "Come on, Bud."

She turned without waiting, and a magnificent brown horse followed her obediently, straight to the cast-iron watering trough where he lowered his gleaming neck to drink the cold clear water. She ran a hand along the length of his body, checked the shoes on his hooves, then untangled the long black hairs on his mane. She seemed to be as familiar with the horse as she was with anyone around her.

Complete confidence. Was that the reason she was a good horse-woman? The horses trusted her, and she trusted them. She stood back, clapped her hands, and pointed back to the gate.

"Okay, Bud."

Another gate, another horse. Behind the third gate a scruffy-looking donkey appeared, all ears and long shaggy hair, a face to be remembered. When the donkey spied a stranger in his territory, he stopped, his eyes opened wide, and he opened his mouth to expose long yellow teeth like overripe corn, then emitted a jolting bellow unlike anything Oba had ever heard.

"Mercy days, Fred!" Clara shouted above the din.

And Oba laughed, an unexpected burst of sound that surprised Clara and shocked poor Fred, who shied away from the intruder and refused to drink.

After he was retuned to his stall, she brushed the hay off her coat, then told him to follow her. She retrieved the artificial limb and made her way to the house. He was so adept on crutches, he had no problem keeping up, thumping up the steps to the wide porch and into the house. The house felt smaller and cozier than he remembered from last time. A teakettle hummed on a miniature cook stove, pine flooring gleamed, bright rugs were scattered everywhere. The furniture was all good quality, the counters cleaned and shining.

"Here. Give me your coat."

She held out a hand, and he laid his crutches across a chair before shrugging out of it. She returned from the washhouse, swiping at her hair, then gave up and began removing hairpins, talking all the while. Confident, unflappable, she regaled him with local gossip. She flipped the long, wavy strands into a coil on the back of her head while he tried not to watch, tried to be as casual and unfeeling as she was.

"It's good to have you here, Oba," she called over her shoulder as she washed her hands at the sink. "You know we're going to work with that leg, don't you? That's why you brought it, right?"

"Yeah."

"Good. So since nothing's stopping us, we'll get started. Sit down."

There was no resistance to her prodding and pulling as she expertly applied the sheep's wool, buckled and strapped everything in place, then stood back.

"Okay. Now. Since we don't have May, you're going to have only me to hang on to. Put your hand on my shoulder to get started. Here. Give me your hands. Both of them."

He did as he was told. He gripped her thin hands, felt the hard-knotted strength, allowed her hands to guide him to an upright position. It was like a knife through the stump of his leg, the way it had been the first time.

He groaned, reeled drunkenly.

"Hurt?"

He nodded, his lower lip caught in his teeth. She watched his face steadily, kept her grip on his hands, neither pushing him nor allowing him to back down.

"You okay?

"No."

When she had no comment, he put more weight on his whole leg, relieving the intense pressure where the amputation was thrust cruelly into the prosthesis. There was no sound in the house except the frenzied ticking of an old clock on the bureau, the kettle's humming, and an occasional creak of wooden siding where the cold contracted it.

"Got your balance?"

He nodded, concentrated.

"Alright, then. Try to lift the artificial leg. One step. Just one."

She held his grip, matched its power, took a step back, tugging gently. He drew forward with his hip, but nothing happened. He tried harder. The heavy wooden leg stayed on the same spot. Clara did not speak, kept her grip on his hands. The third attempt he tried so hard his entire body twisted, and the wooden leg stayed still.

"Hmm."

Clara let go of his hands. She watched as he grabbed at the air, clawed for anything to hang on to, before toppling back on the couch, his breathing heavy, his eyes dark with fury.

"I was thinking. You're trying to move your foot with your hip. I think you will have to think differently. Think of your prosthesis as a real foot. Move it with your brain, not your hip."

"Don't let go of my hands."

"I won't."

Again, he tried, and this time, the foot moved a few inches. Over and over, until he was exhausted mentally and physically, he moved the foot, inch by inch. She released his hands, and he placed only one on her shoulder. They developed a sort of dance, and were definitely making progress.

When he took an actual step, his face lit up, and he grinned down at her. "I bent that hinged knee," he said in awe.

"You did!" she exulted.

"It's the hip. The strap I hate so much."

"It works!"

It was a small victory, but Clara knew it was gigantic in Oba's mind. Her green eyes glowed her congratulations, and he kept his hand on her shoulder as they moved by mere inches across the living room. The pain was blinding, excruciating, but a necessary part of the development.

When he collapsed into a kitchen chair, he felt the exultation rise in his chest. He raised a fist in the air silently. Clara caught his eye and laughed outright.

"You came, you conquered!" she shouted. "Now, Mister Oba, I will have you introduced to every young girl in Wayne County. You will be the community's most sought-after bachelor. You are on your own two feet, a whole man. You're young, handsome, with a whole life of happiness in front of you."

Oba hung his head, his expression visibly darkened. For a long time, he said nothing. She took the chair opposite him, looked at his downturned face, and asked if she'd said anything wrong.

"Sorry, Oba. I'm always a step ahead, galloping on without common sense."

He knew what his goal actually was, now more than ever. He felt as if he had come to a crossroad, blinded with a thick blindfold, unsure of anything except the fact of his life being in ruins, debris scattered about in the form of anger, bitterness, depression, and self-pity. This Clara, this unlikely woman he had hated, had literally removed the blindfold. He wanted to tell her, no, she was not galloping ahead, but was so far behind she couldn't see him at all.

But what he did say was easier for both of them.

"I just don't want to be pushed into meeting young girls."

"Oh. Sorry. You mean not so soon."

"Not ever."

The look she gave him was quizzical, clueless. She shrugged her thin shoulders, said, "Okay, whatever you want."

He gripped the tabletop, held out his hand. "Try again?"

"Of course."

On his own accord, he put both hands on her shoulders, and she moved backward. They did not speak, with Oba concentrating on his efforts. They shuffled together, slowly, but steadily making small steps.

"If I knew how to dance, I'd ask you to dance with me," he said suddenly.

Startled, she looked into his pain-filled eyes, the eyebrows lowered to contain the immensity of it, and realized the courage and determination he was using.

"It hurts, doesn't it?"

"It does. But you help."

There was nothing to say to this, so she remained silent, her eyes lowered. He began to hum, a tune she did not recognize. She looked up at him, and he looked down at her. He went right on humming, then took his hands off her shoulders, balanced himself for a short time as he held her gaze. Slowly, he placed his hands on her narrow waist, gently. He felt the thin fabric of her dress.

"Put your hands on my shoulders, and we'll dance."

Clara swallowed nervously, suddenly wordless. She lowered her eyes, unsure of what was expected of her.

A short moment of unexpected bliss for Oba, the beginning of turmoil for Clara. Her hands on his shoulders dispelled all doubt and cemented the idea of his goal, set his feet in the direction that was right and good and solid. He had the rest of his life to remove himself from the cocoon that held him in its grip, and if this was his purpose— this sweet, cozy house, the woman he would never have imagined ever being remotely interested in—well, then, so be it.

Some women would have caught on that day, but Clara was so completely unaware of any change in Oba, she played along as if to humor him, still not absorbing his comment about meeting a potential girlfriend. He just hadn't met the right one was all.

The day was untainted by either one being ill at ease. Oba was filled with newfound purpose, Clara was as clueless as a newborn. Oh, she thought he was awfully handsome, sitting there at her kitchen table in the gray winter light. Handsome enough for Abe Weaver's Marion, almost. Although, she might be a bit spoiled, the way her mother doted on her. And everyone knew her father owned more than one farm.

They talked easily, naturally. She whooped and hollered and laughed when he asked her if she remembered how much he used to dislike her, would leave the room when she arrived.

He watched her flip ponhaus and break eggs into sizzling butter with as much confidence as she did everything else, amazed by the fact of his discovery. She ate like a man, lowered her head and put food into her mouth for the sole purpose of filling her empty stomach. She asked him to pass the butter, please, or the sugar, then applied copious amounts of each one to toast and oatmeal.

He told her about Sam, the Northwest Territory, Eb the sled dog, Jonas Bell, the wreck from the sky, the feeling of advancing death.

And never once did she mention God.

Among the Amish, God is naturally there. Everyone assumes the other is a believer in Creation; the birth, life, and death of Jesus; and God is in His Heaven controlling the Earth with his Majesty. So of course Clara did not bring up the subject at all, knowing Oba was born and raised in an Amish home. He didn't bring up his lack of faith, or his unwillingness to be Amish, or his years in Arkansas. He had no idea Clara knew of the full extent of Melvin's beatings, so it seemed as if they covered a large area of his life, when in truth, they had barely cracked opened the door.

He swung along behind her on his crutches to do evening chores, envied the ease with which she moved along the corridor. He asked her to exercise one of the horses, but she declined, saying she wasn't wearing trousers. He wondered exactly how she made any money, having to feed all these horses, and when he asked, she demurred, shook her head, and said she found money in the elderberry bushes down by the pond, then laughed at her own joke. He watched sparrows twittering in the rafters, and thought they wished them well, looking down from their perch. He was sorry to see the driver's return, but gave no indication of this to Clara. He merely shrugged into this coat, turned, and thanked her for having him.

"I enjoyed the day, Oba. Oh, here, don't forget the leg."

He laughed, "That sounds different." He became quite serious then. "Do you mind keeping it? It's better to practice here. May hovers too much, and the children make me nervous, running around. Could I practice here?"

"Of course. If it works for you, I don't mind helping you. I'm just surprised to see you've changed your mind. You put that thing away, stomped off, and quit."

"Yeah, well, things change."

FOR DAYS, CLARA tried to figure out why Oba was acting strangely, then came to the conclusion that he really did want to meet a young woman, but was embarrassed. It was the only reason he wanted to walk normally, but of course, he would not say this to her. So she went about her days planning her strategy, saying she needed a hired girl, a *maud* (maid), then she could introduce the two and get something going. Oba needed a goal, a motivation to go out and get a job. There wasn't much he could do for her yet, but eventually he could muck stalls, mow hay, or whatever.

She'd try Sally Troyer first. She sat down at her writing desk, asking if she was interested in some deep cleaning after the New Year, spring being such a busy time at the barn. She folded the letter, put it in an envelope, attached the stamp, and carried it to the mail box, imagining Oba's surprise when the attractive Sally walked into the kitchen, where he would be seated having a cup of coffee.

Oh my, but he was certainly handsome. Older than some, but the years added an attraction, a maturity, which she was certain Sally would find appealing. This was not the first time she'd made a good match. She had been instrumental in getting Ivan Mast to ask the girl he had always wanted, and never had the nerve to ask. She had him help her with a rowdy two-year-old stallion, and afterward, had given him the pep talk of his life. She smiled to herself, a smirk of confidence. Yes, she was a good matchmaker.

THE BARN WAS a haven for Clara, a place she could bury herself in her work and her love of fine horses. The barn was a symbol of all she had accomplished, her dream come to life. As a skinny, red-haired child, she had ridden the chunky workhorses, their broad backs swaying, the harnesses jingling as she clutched a handful of thick, coarse hair from the mane. She felt a sense of loss every time her father lifted her off, wished she could stay on the horse's back forever. The smell of horses, the way they moved, their expressive eyes and eager whinnying—everything about them fascinated her. Unlike other young girls who lost interest in horses or barn work after they became teenagers and began their years of *rumschpringa*, Clara's interested increased. She was a regular sight at horse auctions, standing beside her father, a tall, thin man with a beaked visage and a keen eye for a good trotter.

She yearned to ride a horse in the ring with the young men. Slouching like that, they were an embarrassment to the crowd. She knew she would sit a horse much better, control the frightened animals with ease. Plus, she would have a talk with that guy standing in the ring, slapping that short whip against the side of his leg, snaking it out occasionally when he thought a horse could use a bit more snap.

Oh, she would become angry, her face reddening, her green eyes snapping. A horse was never at its best when it was frightened, the whites of its eyes showing, its ears rotating wildly as it shied away from the cracking of the little whip. She would watch appalled at how the horse's haunches lowered to propel itself away from the man, as if in flight, then come up short against the boards at the end of the ring.

Once, when a skittish young horse had spooked and run headlong and out of control into the boards, dragging the man along as he desperately held to the lead rope, she had taken one look at the cut on the horse's chest and got to her feet before her father could stop her. She slipped through the crowd, squeezed through the gate, and walked up to the man with the whip and grabbed the small black menace from his hand. Caught by surprise, he relinquished his hold on it, and Clara lifted her arm high before flinging it across the ring. Seething with outrage, she closed both hands into fists, stamped her left foot, and stuck her red face close to his.

"Keep that stupid whip away from these horses!" she shouted, loud enough for everyone to hear.

Oh, it was a scandal. A genuine source of gossip among the Amish for years, that Clara Yoder, you know, Dan Yoder's Clara, red-haired and a temper to match. She had no business in that sale barn, standing there with all those men, it just wasn't a good thing for a young girl.

Clara didn't care. She wouldn't give two hoots for a good reputation. It just wasn't right to handle animals like that. The treatment of the poor worn-out creatures headed for the killer was bad enough, let alone antagonizing the healthy ones in the ring. Sometimes, she would make her way over to the pens containing the "killer horses," the ones slated to be turned into pet food, their hooves into glue. Her heart ached for those old, broken-down horses, their eyes soft with goodwill, accepting their fate. They had worked all their lives to please one master or another, and the only reward they would have asked for was a trough of grain and a pile of hay, maybe a green pasture with room to roam. Clara would slip into the pen, stroke their noses, slide her hand along the smooth part of their necks, below the scraggly manes, tell them they had done their job well, and that she loved them. She did love them but knew their work was done. She just wished they knew how much she appreciated them. Sometimes, she would look back to find an old horse eyeing her with an expression she could only describe as peaceful. Then she would bite her lower lip and squeeze her eyes tightly to keep from crying. Those times her father would look at her red eyes and know she'd been to the killer pen.

When she wasn't asked to be any young man's girlfriend, she shrugged and threw herself into the farm work at home. She learned to ride, clinging to the horse's back with her long, lithe form, no saddle necessary, and often, no bridle. Her brothers envied their father's admiration of her, but admitted none of them came close to handling a horse the way Clara did.

So without a husband, she took cleaning jobs and saved every penny until she could buy horses of her own. Eventually, with the untimely death of both of her parents, she inherited the farm and turned it into her dream, raising fine horses, which was what she loved then, and still did.

The barn was efficient, with a wide cement walkway between a row of stalls, room to store hay and grain, and a small room for all the paraphernalia that went with raising good horses, including a desk with paperwork. She often sat at her desk and looked out the window at the view across the pasture dotted with grazing horses, and in those moments she felt like a queen.

The barn was warm, moist with the horses' breath, the scent of stored hay and mixed oats and corn one she never tired of. She greeted each horse by name, then worked with the fiery sorrel mare in the gray cold of the winter day. Her fingers were stiff with the cold, her hands numb from the steady pull on the reins as she flew across the snowy back roads, her hooves making a steady *thwock thwock* in the wet snow.

Exhilaration flowed in her veins as the horse tore along, the snowy landscape a blur of white, the sky leaden and cold. This was her life, this was what she was born to do, and she planned to continue as long as the good Lord provided a sound mind and body.

Back in the barn, she checked on a chestnut mare, her black mane and tail glistening with frequent brushing. She was heavy with foal, her sides distended grotesquely. Clara had been watching her, fearful of a foal with enormous size, a difficult birth.

"Well, Lucky, you poor thing. You look miserable."

She did, pacing relentlessly around and around her stall. She wasn't due to foal for another few weeks, but Clara decided to clean her pen and spread a thick layer of fresh straw, just in case.

Her hands grasped the fork handle with ease, threw large amounts of manure on the wheelbarrow before wheeling it out to the wide doors along the back, where she dumped it on the ever-growing pile. Then she stood back to eye the alarming amount of manure, and thought a hired hand would come in real handy about now.

CHAPTER 8

BACK AT THE WHITE FARMHOUSE, ANDY AND MAY WERE SET-
tling in, becoming accustomed to the extra workload, that of milking
cows twice a day. May was a proficient milker, impressing her admir-
ing husband so that he grabbed her in the milkhouse and kissed her
soundly, looked deep into her shining brown eyes, and told her he
would never deserve her, even if he lived to be a hundred years old.
And May would repeat the phrase to him, both of them profoundly
pleased to find the same emotion in the other. Their love continued
to grow month by month, although in the way of all human beings, it
was not altogether perfect.

There was the ever-increasing problem called Kettie, the mother-
in-law. Buxom, round as a biddy hen, and as excitable, she scurried
around on small feet topped by swollen ankles and varicose veins,
her pleated skirt much too short for a woman her size. She rarely wore
stockings, her wide girth and excess poundage creating too much
heat, so her feet would begin a slow burn inside her black shoes and
stockings, creating a misery all its own.

Since moving into the small brick house with only one son left
over, and he having plans to be married, she found herself often just
rocking in her chair, thinking of her son and his wife situated in her
house back on the farm. One such afternoon, she heaved herself out
of the chair, pulled on a pair of rubber boots with breathless effort,
poked her heavy arms into a coat, tied an itching wool scarf beneath

her many chins, and ventured down the lane to the farm. When she arrived, she hesitated on the front porch before deciding it was not right to have to knock on her own front door, turned the knob, and let herself in with a resounding "Hallo-o-o!"

May was startled, to say the least, carefully laying little Fronie into her crib without waking her. She tiptoed out, closed the door softly, and peered around the door of the living room to find Kettie in the kitchen, her face the color of a ripe plum from the cold and the exertion of her walk to the farm.

"Oh, why hello, Mam," May said pleasantly, pleased to use the proper phrase for her mother-in-law.

"There you are, May. Why, there's Lizzie! Don't you go to school?"

Lizzie shook her head. "Next year," she announced proudly.

"Here, give me your coat and scarf," May offered, trying to keep from watching the rivulets of dirty water from the rubber boots pool on the clean linoleum.

"Alright. Good! Oh my, I'm so ready for some company!"

All Kettie's sentences needed an exclamation point at the end, the way she delivered her words in stentorian blasts, followed by bursts of raucous laughter, chirps and pouts and wiggling eyebrows. She was extremely opinionated, smart, aware of things around her. She read newspapers, books, and only sometimes her Bible.

May loved her, in the beginning, but as time went on, the love seemed harder to grasp, sliding like oil through her fingers, and was replaced by tolerance, then a weary kind of endurance. She did her best, always greeting her with kindness, listening to her colorful tirades with patience, marveling how this woman had ever raised a son like Andy.

She put the kettle on, knowing Kettie loved her strong coffee laced heavily with cream and sugar. The top of the cream, not the cream close to the milk, and brown sugar, not that white stuff. And she loved her pie. Any pie. She made custard pie like silk, a bubbly brown top, a crust that was so flaky it barely held together. She made pecan pie, and Montgomery pie, all the fruit pies, and green tomato pie well into the winter from her store of green tomatoes in the root cellar.

She thanked May for her cup of coffee and carefully added the required cream and sugar before sipping appreciatively. The she raised her eyebrows and asked for pie.

May smiled. "I do indeed have pie. I made fresh apple pie with crumb topping. Andy's favorite."

"Oh, did you really? You're a good wife. You know, I feel sorry for young husbands whose wives do not bake pie. I hear more and more of my good friends saying how their boys do without pie since they're married, and that's a shame. Every man needs his pie. Why, look at Andy. He was raised on pie."

"Yes, he was. He loves his pie."

Pleasant, smiling, May tried to put the abrupt appearance and the lack of polite knocking out of her head. She fixed her own cup of coffee, gave Lizzie a small cup of spearmint tea, and brought out the pie.

Perfectly rounded, the crumbs a delectable mixture of flour, butter, brown sugar, and a small amount of chopped walnuts, it was a better pie than Kettie herself had ever accomplished. Expertly, she cut into the pie, took out a piece for herself, then raised her eyebrows as she tilted her head to the side, examining the bottom crust before shaking her head.

"The bottom isn't quite done," she said, chirping with her tongue as she held out a thumb and forefinger, only a hair apart. The sound with her tongue was an indication of how *shaut* (what a shame) it was the crust was underbaked.

May felt a flush of irritation but squelched it quickly as she watched Kettie use the side of her fork to cut a generous bite, chewing and nodding. May waited, eager to hear the praise she felt sure would come.

"Sugar. Needs sugar. What kind of apples did you use? These seem a bit firm, a bit tart. But otherwise, the pie is pretty good."

After which she polished off not one piece, but three, still elaborating on the lack of sugar.

Kettie looked around the kitchen, the clock on the shelf, the gleaming countertop and stovetop, the bright throw rugs scattered about, and smiled.

"You sweep your floors every day, huh?"

May laughed. "Yes, but we have three children, you know."

Kettie looked pointedly at May's slim waistline.

"Fronie isn't a baby anymore."

May blushed painfully, avoiding Kettie's direct gaze. How could she tell her mother-in-law about her conversations with Andy, the deeply intimate and personal conviction he had, not wanting her small body to be carrying babies every year, the way so many young women did, birthing up to a dozen children or more, all in the span of fifteen to twenty years? He cared so deeply, cherished his wife so sincerely.

Kettie went on. "Jonas's Hannah, you know what happened there. They quit having babies and after a few years she ran off with the bread man. That was years ago. She should have been making her own bread, had no business spending good money on store-bought bread. That was her first mistake. Then, a few years went by with no babies—everyone thought she might have health problems. She had this flashy look about her. Well, look what happened. She spent too much money at the grocery store, too. She bought bananas in winter. So what does that tell you?" More clucking and eyebrow-raising.

May was at a loss for the proper response, so she shook her head somberly and said she was sorry to hear that.

"Well, yes," Kettie said, breaking off a section of crust from the pie, casting a long gaze at the remaining half. "We women are to take the admonishing of the Lord, and the Bible clearly tells us we will be saved through childbearing. All the discomfort and pain is good for our souls."

And so is the grace of our Lord Jesus, May thought, but she just nodded her outward assent and kept the peace. Immediately, Kettie was off on another ramble, this time the subject in question being Oba.

"Oh, he's doing alright," May said, cautious in her response.

"He needs a wife. But who would date a man like him? It's a pity, the way he has only one leg."

"Yes."

"Did he ever learn to walk with the wooden one?"

"He's working on it."

Kettie nodded, then regaled May with the story of her cousin Ruth's half brother's condition, the years of pain and misery from a back injury before dying at the age of thirty-seven and a half. She thought Oba wouldn't live to be an old man, either, the way he sat around and glared at the world.

"He needs good thoughts. I don't think he's born of the Spirit. You need to bring him to church."

May nodded thoughtfully, glancing at the clock and thinking of her stack of ironing. Would these visits become a regular occurrence? Sitting in her small brick house, without sufficient duties to keep her occupied, would Kettie arrive on a daily basis?

That night she talked to Andy about it. It was the time of night when they shared their deepest concerns, after evening prayers, lying in bed, a small candle burning in its pewter holder giving off a soft, yellow glow. It was a time of sharing their hearts, two people given in holy matrimony, blessed by the God of Abraham and Isaac, a time May cherished with an almost fierce abandon.

She brought up the subject in painful, halting sentences and waited for his answer with a strangely heavy heart. When it came, she was plummeted into a long, dark tunnel of fear and betrayal. He spoke firmly, as if reprimanding her.

"May, my mother will never change. Her ways are a bit harsh, and as you well know, completely overdone, but you are married to her son and therefore she is your mother as well. So try to accept her. It's the only way we can get along living here together. You know how much I love you and want only what is best for you, but I think my mother is part of the package."

If he had reached out and slapped her, it might have been easier. What had she done wrong? She had not done anything against him or his mother but had merely questioned whether he thought she'd be visiting every day and whether that was really necessary.

His mother's feelings were placed above her own. No, he did not lover her above all else. He loved his mother first.

So she cut off all conversation, turned her back, and snuffed out the candle, a move uncharacteristic of her soft, kind self. An unusually strong anger coursed through her body, so when she felt his large, calloused hand on her shoulder, she shrugged it off, plumped her pillow, thumping it a bit harder than was necessary.

"May?"

When the only sound was the wood falling in the grate of the living room stove, he repeated her name, tentatively.

Suddenly, she flipped on her back and said harshly, "So you love your mother more than you love me."

"Of course not. I just want you two to get along with each other."

She felt very much like Clara when she gave him no answer, but for one moment, it was a kind of liberty, a bit exhilarating, like a headlong slide down an icy hill with a runner sled.

"May?"

No answer.

"May? I love you. Please don't be offended."

But she was offended, and she wanted him to know he had hurt her deeply. But she decided to let him figure it out for himself and walked around the next day with an air of haughty pride, like an insulted princess, until he was miserable with the mistake he knew he had made but wasn't sure how to go about fixing.

And May learned she did not always need to be a doormat, something everyone took for granted and no one appreciated fully. She learned the ways of a woman, the little wiles and bits of wisdom life requires when a well-meaning but very bumbling husband gets out of line.

It was a marriage, and a very good, solid one, but since a marriage is never perfect, neither was theirs. In the end, she told him how he had insulted her, and he apologized for his harsh tone and also reminded her of his patience and acceptance of Oba, the most impossible person he had ever encountered.

And May's happiness retuned. She had begun to learn the need for good communication, and life moved on, the bump in the road navigated successfully.

SALLY TROYER WAS tall, slim, dark-haired, and dark-eyed. She had run her course of boyfriends and breakups and was bored with men and relationships. She was unaware of anyone living with Clara till she bumped into Oba in the kitchen. She took in the sight of his handsome face and astonishing blond hair and stopped short. Never given to social graces, she blurted out, "Who're you?"

Oba gave a steady evaluation and said, "Santa Claus."

"Very funny."

"I'm Oba. Oba Miller."

"You live here?"

"Of course I don't. Would that be acceptable, an English man living with an Amish woman?"

"Oh, pooh."

Sally waved him off and went to the barn to find Clara, who brought her back to the kitchen and introduced them properly. Oba said hello in an offhand way and Sally said something garbled before turning her back and asking Clara where her rags and scrub bucket were kept. Clearly, Sally was here for the cleaning, getting the job done as quickly as possible, and had no time for strange men seated in her way.

"Sally, why don't you sit and have a cup of coffee with us?"

"I don't drink coffee."

"Tea then?"

She glanced uncomfortably at Oba before saying, "Alright."

"Sugar?"

"Do you have honey?"

"Sure."

And so the stilted conversation moved along by jerks and awkward stops. Sally was the kind of person who had no outside interests and pronounced her words with an irritating lilt, as if mocking the subject and the people she was talking to.

"Oba is here to learn how to use his wooden leg," Clara said finally, trying to interest her in something.

Sally looked at Oba. "You have only one leg?"

"Afraid so."

"That's awful. What happened?"

"A wreck."

"Clara, I need to get started immediately. I can't sit here drinking this tea. I have a full day ahead." She glanced toward Oba's leg and shivered visibly, disgust written all over her face.

There was nothing to do about Sally and her total disregard of Oba except do her bidding, so Clara got up and gave her instructions for the upstairs bedrooms.

Coming back down, Clara flopped into a chair, grabbed her coffee cup, and took a large gulp, before banging it down in frustration.

Oba smiled at her. She did not return it.

"I told you I don't want to meet someone."

"That's not why she's here."

"You know it is."

Caught off guard by his total honesty, she went into a sulk, refusing to look at him as she grabbed the coffee cups and slammed them into the sink. She told him she was busy and went out to the barn, leaving him to strap on the leg and work on it himself.

Oh, she was plenty mad. She hated being caught out like that. Her pride was battered, ruined, actually. The worst part was the fact that Oba knew it. She could have shaken Sally. Talk about social graces. Huh. She had been prepared for a rocky start with Oba and Sally, with his handicap and all, but couldn't Sally have at least acted interested? That was what was wrong with young girls in this day and age.

Completely self-absorbed. She didn't even ask what kind of wreck. And that look she gave Oba. What was she thinking?

So her mind roamed across the community, thinking of a plainer girl, someone with a bit of sweetness about her, but came up empty. She stood absentmindedly stroking the nose of the restless mare, ran her hands down the side of her face, and told her if she didn't have this baby soon, she was going to be worn to a frazzle. Too many nights of having to get up and check on her.

She was startled when she heard the creak of hinges and noticed a stab of light when the barn door was opened from the outside. Her mouth flew open in astonishment when Oba made his halting way through the door, gripping the sides for support.

A hand to her mouth, she was rooted to the spot. He was breathing hard. She stepped forward to help him, but he held both hands up. She hurried to grab a stool, an old wooden one she would often use when she polished harnesses or saddles.

"Here. Sit."

He did, gratefully. There was a light in his eyes, a flush on his face, and he looked at her with what could only be called a triumphant look.

"Weren't you afraid?" she asked, suddenly close to tears.

"Of course. There's snow on the ground. But I didn't want to stay in the house with her."

Sally. Well, her plans had gone awry, for sure. But perhaps she had served another purpose altogether, sending him into a long walk by himself, the beginning of his freedom. Clara looked at him, her feelings a confusing mix of concern, frustration, and victory. He looked back at her and shook his head ruefully.

"So how soon will you introduce me to someone else?"

"Stop it, Oba."

He laughed outright, but it was not a mean laugh, or a mocking one. He reached out a hand and asked her to help him to his feet.

"Can't you do it by yourself?"

"I think so. But I want you to help me."

She watched him warily. He was not making fun of her at all, but had a serious look in his eye, a soft look, almost sincere. Mistrust rose in her, a fear of . . . she didn't know what. It seemed such a short time ago, the times he would leave the room when she arrived, refusing to answer her questions, being rude, obstinate. Was he merely setting a trap, trying to drag her into his pit of unhappiness?

"You can do it yourself."

He did not answer but simply leaned forward, got his good leg beneath him, and slowly drew himself to a standing position. The light was not strong in the dim interior of the barn, so she couldn't tell if he was in pain or if days of practice had helped to toughen the part of his leg where the skin was pulled and fastened across the end.

His steps were halting, his posture poor, but he kept going until he reached her, then stopped. She looked up at him, a question in her eyes, a sudden fear of the unknown making her uncomfortable. She stepped back.

"Clara."

She swallowed nervously. "What?"

"Don't move away. I need you."

His eyes bore down into hers, his face far too close to her own.

"No. No, you don't."

She felt as if she was in a strange land, a weird, unexpected place she could not figure out. What was he thinking? The atmosphere in the barn had changed and she felt completely disoriented.

She took flight. With a strangled cry, she moved away to the door and up the snowy path to the washhouse, where she banged the door shut behind her. She became so agitated she whipped her red scarf off her head, shucked her coat in one swift move, and stabbed it against the coat hook, missed, and tried again, blindly. When it fell to the floor, she began to cry. She bent over to retrieve the stupid coat, sniffed and sobbed, and blew her nose, which was where Sally found her when she came to ask a question about the closets.

Clara waved a hand and told her to let the cleaning go, just go. Get your horse and go. She thrust some cash into her hand, trying to hide her own tears.

Sally decided Clara was mentally unstable, and then met Oba in the barn, which gave her the creeps even more. She hitched up her horse and drove out the lane, bringing the reins down hard. She swung to the right with the back wheels sliding on the packed snow, glad to be rid of that place.

CLARA COMBED HER hair, fixed her white covering, smoothed her skirts, and gathered her knotted emotions. Then she went upstairs, brought down the broom and bucket of soapy water, restored the kitchen to its former cleanliness, and watched the barn. She took two deep inhalations, exhaled slowly, and told herself she was Clara Yoder, an old maid, undesirable as always. She would never allow herself to be drawn into a risky situation, and Oba spelled out danger if she ever saw it. He was untrustworthy, unstable. All he wanted was her money, a place to stay.

When the barn door finally opened, she could not step away from the window, but found herself gripping the edge of the sink as he stopped and looked toward the house, as if measuring the distance before starting out. Her first instinct was to go to him, but she made herself stay.

Who could explain the emotion which seemed to grip her? She thought everything was under control, but a fresh wave overtook her, as if a storm driving the helpless waters of her existence broke over her, took away her resolve, her resistance, and threw her into strange and untested territory. The figure of Oba blurred as hot tears coursed down her cheeks, her chest heaving as childlike sobs and hiccoughs tore through her throat. She realized she was completely undone and there was no way of hiding her distress. Desperately, she swiped at her face, blew her nose, then broke into fresh sobs. She ran to the bathroom to wash her face, then looked in the mirror with despair.

Well, good. If Oba even thought for one second he was going to get all amorous with her, this face would change all that. And she cringed with an inner self-hatred.

But she watched him make his way slowly and carefully to the porch, then stop, eyeing the steps before he grasped the railing. For the longest time, he tried working the leg with hip maneuvers, before finally grasping the knee with his hands, struggling to set it on the first step.

Clara moved to the front door, then changed her mind halfway. She stood beside the door and peered out, carefully remaining out of sight. It was heartbreaking to watch, the exertion and disappointment playing across his face, but she had to admire his determination. When he finally reached the top step, she moved away. She heard the front door open before her heartbeat began to race.

He called out her name. Her first instinct was to cover her ears, run in the opposite direction, find the cool, calm waters of her former life.

"Yes?" she said, her voice strangled with the amount of turmoil she had experienced in the past few minutes.

"I made it back. Where are you?"

"I'm here." She made an appearance stepping around the door frame. "You did. You made it back!" Clara put an earnest effort into her words, but her face was ravaged by the onslaught of bewildering agitation.

"What is wrong with you?" he asked, his eyes never leaving her face.

"Nothing. Why?"

"You have been crying."

"No. No, absolutely not. Why would I cry?"

"Clara."

She turned away. She loved the way he said her name, with a short *a* sound instead of the usual long *a*, the name shot through with . . . whatever it was. She was a mess, an old ugly redhead who dared, yes, dared to think an atrocious thought that had no business entering her head. What business did she have even imagining that he suddenly had romantic intentions? And yet how else was she to interpret that look in his eyes in the barn? Oh, her thoughts were a tangled mess.

"Look at me."

She made the mistake of doing just that and was swept away again into the choppy waters of strange new territories.

"Can I ask you a question?"

She nodded, her lower lip caught in her teeth as she tried to keep from losing her composure yet again.

"What does it take for someone like me to come back to the church? Would there be a problem with my age and having been in the world for so long?"

A great surge of relief caught her up in its soft velvety arms, followed immediately by a sense of crippling loss. "Uh ... well, I suppose you would speak to a minister, perhaps a deacon, but they will most certainly give you a chance to return."

"You think so?"

"Yes, I do."

"Well, then, I suppose I'll see what I can do about that."

CHAPTER 9

CLARA FOUND HERSELF SUSPENDED ABOVE A DEEP, DANGER-ous chasm, dangling like a moth caught in a spider's web. She stayed home and tried to return to normal as the days went by and Oba did not return. She got nothing accomplished and moved through her days without focus, without the needed calm and large amount of self-confidence that were her trademark. She wanted May, then did not want anything to do with her. She wandered from room to room, casting a baleful eye at the snow and pine trees bent over by the force of the strong winter wind. She thought of spring, the earth loosening and warming graciously, giving forth sprouted seeds, and felt a wave of beautiful sadness at the thought of all the dormant growth beneath the hard cold snow.

She considered seeing a doctor, wondering if there was a malfunction in her brain, a lack of oxygen perhaps. She couldn't eat—the breakfast she made for herself was suddenly repulsive. Finally, she couldn't take one more day of this strange malady. She went to the barn to harness the black Standardbred named Ralph and found Lucky, the gentle mare, with a brand new, long-legged foal, a skinny, spindly little thing with the exact same coloring as her mother.

Clara was delighted to find Lucky to be a good mother, birthing the foal all by herself, evidently proud and happy with her offspring. She did the necessary bookwork, praised and petted Lucky, pet the foal and allowed her to become used to human touch before spreading fresh straw. This was why she loved raising horses—the rewards far outweighed the sleepless nights and hard work.

MAY WAS EFFUSIVE with genuine gladness, reaching out to hold her tightly, then grasped her shoulders to look into her face.

"How are you, Clara?"

"I'm well. Doing great."

"Good. I'm so glad. You know I worry about you if you stay away too long. Winter months are hard on sunny dispositions, and you're so very alone."

"Oh, I'm fine. You don't have to worry about me, ever."

"But I do. You know I do."

"Where is Oba?"

"Oh Clara, I can hardly wait to tell you. He's out with Andy almost all day now. And guess what? He went to see Danny Weaver about becoming a member of the church. Can you begin to imagine my happiness? It's almost as if a light went on inside him and he is shucking that hard, bitter layer that kept him closed off from the rest of us. I don't know what to think. Half of me is afraid it's too good to be true. You should see him walk, Clara. He's come a long way."

Through all this, Clara kept her eyes averted, divesting herself of coat and scarf, bringing a paper bag of food to the kitchen table, putting the kettle on as May followed.

"I know we have you to thank. You are the one who had the nerve to get him started. You were the one, Clara."

"It was God, not me," Clara said gruffly.

May looked at her sharply, realizing this was not typical Clara. "Aren't you happy about Oba? To have him come back to the fold this way?"

"Of course I am."

May watched Clara lay out sliced cheese, a tin of crackers, a ring of smoked bologna.

"You are? You don't seem like it."

Clara gave her a cool glance. "May, we know each other too well. Alright, sit down, dear friend. Let me get the coffee. I have a lot to tell you."

What? "Dear friend?" A phrase such as this coming from Clara? She sat down, lifted Fronie to her lap, and waited.

Most of the story was unfolded, bit by bit, though she left out their strange encounter in the barn and her reaction to it. But she did include the whole mistake of having Sally Troyer do her cleaning.

"I mean, girls nowadays are so uncaring. She could not have given one hoot about that leg of Oba's. Not ever. She looked like the thought of his missing leg was going to make her throw up. And Oba feels like an oddity anyway. I mean it, May, I wanted to smack her."

"But you invited her to introduce them?"

"Yes. Of course. I thought it would be a good thing. Get him interested in a girl, give him a plan for the future."

"And he wasn't interested."

"No."

May was quiet for a moment, then said it was very good to see Oba wanting to give his life to God without the benefit of a girlfriend, which made it seem doubly sincere.

"I agree, May. But now where do I start?"

"You mean . . . ?"

"Who do I introduce him to now? Clearly, it will have to be someone special, a bit plain, left out of the popular crowd. I mean, Oba is very handsome, to my way of thinking. But it's that leg. And of course, he can be a complicated person."

When Oba and Andy arrived for lunch, they were cold and starving, clattering into the washhouse, talking all the while. May smiled, stirred the pot of chicken corn noodle soup, put bread in a pan to fry. Clara set the table, her face pinched and drawn, repeatedly straightening her covering, smoothing the brilliant blue pleats of her skirt. May noticed all this as the forenoon drew into noon hour, but kept her thoughts and opinions to herself.

Andy was delighted to see Clara and made quite a fuss about not having seen her in a coon's age. Clara told him lots of coons lived longer lives than these few weeks, which sent him into loud laughter, Oba smiling quietly.

"Hello, Clara," he said.

She had her back turned, but said something in reply. May could not be sure what it was. When she turned, he watched her, but she kept her eyes averted, downcast. She fiddled around with her water glass and then the knife by her plate.

The soup was served in deep bowls, a plate of saltines passed. Andy kept a lively conversation going, telling the women about Oba's deft accomplishments, able to fork manure with the best of them.

"I don't like it any better than I ever did, though. I helped Dat as a child. Pure misery then. Pure misery now."

But as Oba said it, he grinned at Andy, and Clara's heart flopped painfully. She couldn't be in his presence without coming too close to this frightening, unplanned, and helpless wasteland. She might easily lose all her self-confidence, her bold and orderly, well-managed way of life. She took sips of water, toyed with her soup, her throat choked with the threat of the returning lunacy. She was obviously losing her mind.

"So how's everything at the horse farm?" Oba asked Clara, looking directly at her, trying to draw her into the conversation. He'd noticed her strange withdrawal, a certain shyness, and wondered.

"Lucky had her foal."

"Good. Girl or boy?"

"Girl. What I was hoping for."

And then she blushed, a painful spread of color over her face, something none of them had ever seen. There was an awkward silence, till Andy remedied the situation by deftly changing the subject.

BY THE TIME the snowdrifts turned soggy, rivulets of dirty water ran everywhere, and the wind blew gently from the south, Clara's condition had worsened. She cried at the sight of the first dandelion poking its sturdy leaves through a crust of packed gravel and thought, *the poor, brave thing*. There was mud everywhere, mud and rivers of brown water carrying bits of straw and hay, and the robins and sparrows were chirping madly as they darted frantically through the air, searching for a good place to raise their young. The bluebirds returned, sitting on top of the bluebird house on the fence post, posting sentry for all marauders, feral cats, starlings, and aggressive house wrens.

Lucky's foal was taken to pasture, her mother's hooves pounding the wet turf, sending bits of slush flying. Clara leaned on the fence, her arms crossed on the top rail, and watched the long-legged creature flying effortlessly, as if invisible wings propelled the perfect hooves. She was poetry, a song in motion.

And she cried about that.

She drove her horse to town on a rainy day, her black bonnet and shoulders of her light black coat becoming quite wet. She thought of other women whose husbands hitched the horse to the buggy for them, and considered how nice that would be, then caught herself thinking these strange thoughts. Driving through the cold spring rain, she changed hands on the leather reins and shook the opposite one to restore circulation. This black horse named Ralph would never change. He wasn't happy unless he was running flat out, tugging on the reins as if he drew the buggy with his mouth. She loved the rhythm of his pounding hooves, the light whir of the buggy wheels, but with the water running along the reins into the buggy, he was hard to control.

An oncoming surrey hitched to a plodding fat horse moved past, the white-bearded driver waving a hand. There were two cars behind hers, so she drew off to the side of the road to allow them to pass.

The livestock auction was quiet today, but the combination hardware and grocery store had a line of buggies along the hitching rack and a row of colorful, gleaming cars parked along the front. People scurried through the rain, some of them wearing rubber boots and carrying umbrellas.

Clara loved the little village of Oakley, the houses crowded by the side of the road as if there were safety in numbers. Later in the year, colorful window boxes would appear on many of the houses, sporting red geraniums and brilliant cascades of petunias. The town folks liked to keep their village clean and picturesque, proud of their Swiss heritage and the rich, rolling farmlands spreading out around them.

She stopped at the end of the hitching rack, loosened the rein, and tied her horse securely. He was blowing hard, his sides heaving, which was perfectly normal, so she gave him a pat and walked into the store. On any given day, you were bound to run into folks you knew, and today was no different, various acquaintances stopping to say hello.

Clara was friendly enough, but never given to chatty, senseless conversation, so after brief hellos, she moved on, throwing grocery items into her cart.

She stood by the baking supply shelf, looking for pastry flour, when she heard the distinct giggling only a young girl was capable of.

"Oh, I know, Verna. Isn't he cute? But too old. They say he has a wooden leg. I don't know if I could deal with that."

"Really? I guarantee if that man would ask me, I'd be gone."

"Mom said he was English too long. He'll never make a good husband."

"That's mean. I hope he starts coming to the *singens*, cause if he does, I plan on flirting just a teeny bit."

More giggles as the girls moved off.

A hot rage crowded into Clara's chest, taking her breath away. She thought she might choke for one wild moment but was distracted by old Aaron Mast's wife, Drusilla, who accidentally pushed her cart into Clara's.

"Whoops! Ach my. I'm so clumsy."

"No, it's fine. These aisles are a bit narrow."

She barely remembered checking out or carrying paper bags to her buggy. She made her purchases at the feed store and got out of there as swiftly as possible, glancing sideways at all the men lounging around like bright-eyed lizards. She did not like men. Never had.

For a moment she felt her old courage well up. She held her head high and thought how she'd conquered many things in her life, and surely she would conquer this craziness about Oba, which was what it narrowed down to. She hoped he would go to the *singens* and find a pretty girl, because she was done. She had accomplished her goal of helping him make a life for himself and now her work was done. All she really had to do was eliminate these strange, melancholy feelings.

Yes, let him go. It was the only way she could ever return to her normal self. She looked forward to it, really. She did. The absence of craziness, the surge of power and strength to make decisions. She would simply go on living her life according to her terms, and no one else's.

OBA WAS BONE weary.

The stump of his leg throbbed painfully, the sheep's wool padding needed washing, and his good humor hovered on empty. It had rained all day and Andy had him breaking up concrete in the barn, a job he wanted done before the spring work began. He'd hung back, unsure of his ability, the balance to swing a sledgehammer, his muscles gone soft. But he found himself caught up in the work, enjoying Andy's lively banter and visiting with Joe Schrock when he came for the heifer he'd bought. Joe and the cattle truck driver were old men who lived in the area all their lives and often hung out at the livestock auctions, wells of local information. Oba found himself drawn into the conversation, a part of their circle.

How easy life was, how much better to be slowly emerging from the dark tendrils of bitterness that had him in its grip for too long. He was learning how to live a new life as a believer, receiving instructions from the home ministers every two weeks, on a church Sunday. May fitted him with a new pair of black broadfall trousers with a vest to match and a pure white cotton shirt. She tugged at his vest, smoothed his shoulder, told him he was good looking.

The wheelchair and the crutches were taken back to the attic, a fact Oba found unbelievable. Was he actually free of them?

He'd written his doctor a letter of appreciation last week but hadn't heard back. Arpachshad Brown, the no-good boy lying on the riverbank fishing—who would have thought he would ever turn out this way? More than ever, Oba wanted to follow in his steps. To overcome obstacles, to push on with determination.

And there was the matter of Clara.

He felt strong and true, on course. He knew exactly what he wanted, knew the direction he was taking gave him a sense of peace and belonging. It was all rather simple, really. Once love entered your heart, the person you loved was transformed into a new person, a magnet of beauty, and no one else would hold a candle to her. He had loved once, but Sam had been different. There had always been questions, doubt.

With Clara, there were none.

No matter that she was older. No matter that her face was not considered a standard of beauty, that her personality was abrasive like sandpaper. She had given her life to his well-being, had smacked him in the backside when he needed it, and she'd made him laugh ever since.

Yes, she was a beauty to him, with that unusual skin and gorgeous rippling red hair. But more than anything, she was completely devoid of simpering falseness, the trait he most deplored in women. She was wholly Clara, take her or leave her, and this he loved the most. She inspired him to be his best self.

He had a plan. He smiled to himself, thinking of the old tradition of asking a girl to marry when the strawberries bloomed in May. A summer engagement and a wedding in the fall. But no one would know, not even Andy and May. An engagement was top secret, guarded fiercely.

He thrilled to the thought of arriving unexpectedly some soft spring evening. He wasn't sure when, but he'd know when the time came. He knew he had a chance of winning her hand, as quiet and strange as she had become when he was around. He laughed aloud, thinking of their beginning. He had despised her, and she looked on him with as much respect as she'd had for a barn cat. Oh, but she'd accomplished what she set out to do, an admirable trait. Sometimes, he barely knew how to handle happiness.

And his thoughts rambled on, a wisp of happiness here, a shade of past sorrow there, but always there was Clara, and the fact he could stand upright on the formerly hated prosthesis, which seemed to be more and more efficient as time went on. He thought of the strawberry plants growing from rich soil, spreading jagged leaves, pushing buds that would turn into white flowers with a yellow center, the perfect sign of new love.

He still found himself battling old traits, however, which wasn't much of a surprise, with the fullness of his past. Not many young men had the experiences under his belt he had, but then, not many had lost their parents at eleven years of age. He hadn't been a young adult, still a child, caught in a maelstrom of grief and wrenching sorrow. Still reeling, numbed by loss, rejected by relatives, thrown into the the human slavery that was Melvin Amstutz's cotton farm. He hadn't planned on being Amish, had never wanted to return. But he also saw that he didn't want to be alone in the world, a cripple with no future.

He mused about God's existence. Of course He was there, had always been. It was merely his own back that had been turned, his own choice to bury himself in self-pity and a thick, life-draining bitterness. All that was behind him, although he realized he was not without faults, would certainly never be. He imagined life with Clara and smiled. He kept on smiling as he lay back on his pillows, crossed his hands behind his head. For the hundredth time, he moved the stump of his leg to cross his ankles, a habitual move, but there was no foot there. It was a comfort knowing Clara had seen it all, gamely helped him adjust the remains of his leg into the wool, then the prosthesis. She'd adjusted the straps to his thigh, her hands quick and sure, her face filled with concentration, never once self-conscious or repulsed. A clear stream of love flowed through his veins and he pictured her freckled face, her prominent nose, the quick intelligence of her green eyes.

When he proposed, she would say no. She would. But he wouldn't give up. A deep rumble of laughter began in his chest, spread to his throat until a sound of strangled mirth emerged, a sound of freedom from the clanking chains of despair that had held him for so much of his life. Clara had turned the key to unlock his chains.

IF MAY NOTICED a change in Oba, she said nothing, only thanked God with a heartfelt gratitude, a hope burning for his future. This was life as she knew it, had only wanted the same for Oba, had prayed on in spite of seemingly impossible hurdles. Her faith had been exercised through her love for her brother.

ALTHOUGH ELI LOVED to visit Clara's farm, he never displayed a love of horses. Not even a mild interest. He would watch them in the pasture, laugh at the antics of the long-legged foals, but he always shook his head when Clara asked him to ride.

"They're too high," he said as he stood stubbornly refusing her.

The day was sunny, with a brisk wind, one of those teasing days in April when the sun's warmth is soft and gentle, but the north wind refuses to let go. Andy and May had brought Oba and the children for a Saturday afternoon of fishing at Clara's pond, Andy saying a mess of bluegills would be great, with the pond water still being cold, the white fish filets firm and delicious.

Oba regaled them all with tales of fishing for salmon in Alaskan waters, the size and strength of them, the hooking and netting, drying the immense filets for the dogs. Clara strode ahead, one ear turned to his words. Eli hopped and skipped at her side, darting off to catch dragonflies, falling flat on his face in the deep grass before emerging with an irritated expression.

At the pond, May spread a blanket on the grass and set the wicker basket on top to hold down one edge, then found a few stones for the other corners before settling comfortably, her legs tucked beneath her pleated skirt.

She drew little Fronie onto her lap, held her small body tightly, and kissed the side of her face where the soft tendrils of her blond hair were like spun gold. She watched as Oba helped Eli put a fat night crawler on his hook, Andy bending over Lizzie as she held onto the bamboo rod. She felt a wellspring of love for the two men in her life, knew and recognized the fact of her many blessings. God was kind, a benevolent father, far greater in His love and wisdom than she had ever thought possible. His grace was a wonderful thing, His forgiveness new every morning. Her sins had been banished as far as the East is from the West, the way the Bible promised.

She watched as Clara walked away from Oba and Andy, plunked herself down beside a fresh growth of yellow daffodils, her alarmingly pink dress like an outsized rose. Her face bore no trace of good will, her eyebrows drawn down with the vertical line of irritation between them, her face pale, as if she didn't feel as healthy as usual.

Her freckles were quite prominent with the white pallor of her skin, her lips thin and unfriendly. May looked away, beginning to put the puzzle pieces together in her mind. Was it possible? *Ach, Clara.* May smiled to herself.

CLARA SAT DOWN firmly, harder than was necessary. She was peeved at Oba and Andy, the way Oba kept following her around with Andy watching every move. If Oba thought he would teach her how to fish, he had a surprise coming. She knew everything there was to know about fishing, did not need a man to show her how to do it.

She'd spent days at the farm pond, catching an amazing amount of bluegills and sunfish. She knew how to filet them with a swift slice of the sharp knife, could still hear her father's voice in her ear, exclaiming over the fine pan of fish filets.

Out of one corner of her eye, she watched Oba get to his feet, an awkward tangle of arms and one leg, repeated shoving and balancing till he stood upright. Her heart sank when he slowly made his way over to her.

"I know how to fish," she said to the bulrushes on the opposite side.

"That's not why I'm here."

"What else?" She felt him beside her, tall and imposing, but kept her eyes on the opposite bank.

"Oh, just wanted to be with you, see what you have to say. Did you notice the improvement with my walking?"

"No."

"Didn't you watch me walk?"

"Why would I?"

Oba looked out across the pond, watching the water rippling in the stiff breeze, a line of wavelets like ruched fabric, the sun scattering sparkles along the top.

"Clara, why would you not? You were instrumental in my recovery, and now you act like you can't stand me, can't have me around. What have I done?"

But his words were without conviction. He actually enjoyed her lack of composure, the awkward stab at driving him off, felt as if he knew what was bothering her. Or hoped he did.

After a long moment, she said, "You haven't done anything."

"Then why do you avoid me?"

She blinked, shrugged one shoulder.

He lowered himself to the grass, one leg sliding stiffly in front of him. "You look very nice in that pink dress. It reminds of the hibiscus flowers in Arkansas. Not that Arkansas holds many good memories. But I do remember them."

"Huh. You know I'm not pretty."

"You are to me."

She stared hard at the opposite bank, her eyes squinted to hide her feelings. He noticed her slender neck, the way her red hair escaped the confines of her covering at the nape. He had to stop himself from reaching out to touch the soft tendrils.

Suddenly, she shifted her gaze to his deep brown eyes, the eyes having started her unsettling flight into a new and strange territory. What she saw there was no different than being hurled into the unknown that first time. If anything, it was intensified. She tried to look away from the warm light in his eyes, but found she was held there, as helpless as the day she was born. Slowly, he reached out and placed a hand on her freckled face, a light stroke across her cheek with the back of his hand.

"You are beautiful, Clara."

Her face contorted in a sort of agony. "But I'm not. I never was. I never will be. I'm old and ugly. Please don't toy with me."

"I'm not toying." Oba smiled.

She was confused now, torn between allowing his words to sink in and taking flight in order to keep her wits about her. Common sense should always be the road taken.

"I would like if you would allow me to pay you a visit," he said, staring into her eyes with the same warm intensity. "Not to practice walking this time."

CHAPTER 10

THE STRAWBERRY PLANTS GREW TO A DEEP GREEN COLOR AND pushed their buds in response to the warmth of the spring sun, developing lovely white flowers with a yellow button center. Oba helped May spread straw between the rows, his tanned face open, a smile lurking behind his eyes.

Yes, the blooms were there, perfectly formed, a sign from his heritage. He wondered how many nervous young men had asked their girlfriends to be their wives in times past. He wasn't exactly worried about her response, not after that day at the pond, but he did not expect an easy answer. The one thing that did make him nervous was the big question of whether he should kiss her. He had no idea if she'd ever had a boyfriend before. He certainly did not want to shock her, or be repulsive in any way, but wasn't that how it was done? Certainly, in this age, the practice of "bundling," or cuddling beneath warm quilts in the winter when the house was cold, was an accepted practice among the Amish. This was, after all, a modern age, a time of newer, sleeker automobiles, electric wiring and appliances, telephones ringing, washing machines whirring. So if the practice of bundling went on, it was tolerated, but never discussed, each couple left to their own conscience, their own secrets never divulged.

He dressed carefully in a soft, white, short-sleeved shirt, a clean pair of black Sunday trousers, a narrow-brimmed straw hat. He took one look in the mirror above the small sink in the washhouse and let himself out the door when the driver arrived on time. He still did not trust himself to harness and hitch up a horse by himself, with the awkward motion of getting into the buggy, at a disadvantage from the time he put the harness on the horse's back.

He felt nothing but a bright elation as he chatted with old Tom who drove far too slowly and talked far too much, rolling down the window on his side at regular intervals to send a stream of brown tobacco juice down the side of his dusty blue coupe.

He took Clara by surprise, bent over in the garden, her bare feet covered in dust and streaks of mud where the water from the galvanized watering can had spilled onto her legs. (Clara wore her dresses shorter than most women.)

"Oh."

She straightened, a hand going to her frowzy hair, then to the dirt on her skirt. She bent to pick up her hoe, having dropped it at sight of him.

"Hello, Clara. I hope it's okay . . . a good time to visit?"

"Well, I guess so. I mean, I wouldn't know why not. It's just that I'm all messy from working in the garden."

"You want me to help finish?"

She shook her head, a question in her eyes.

"Go ahead. Wash up and change your dress. I'll wait on the porch.

"But . . ."

"I asked you if it's alright if I visit, and you didn't say no."

"But . . ."

"Is it alright?"

"Well, yes . . . I suppose you're already here so I can't really say no."

She found herself trembling, her breath coming in ragged gasps, had a clear sense of letting go, falling headlong. She decided to buy time by taking a bath. She felt ashamed of her freckled body, felt even more ashamed of using her best talcum powder. Should she wear shoes and stockings? Should she wear green, blue, or red? She decided on her latest acquisition, a dress of powder blue. (She'd bought it with Oba in mind.) Oh, shameful horrible thought.

She decided to leave her feet bare, not wanting to give the impression of dressing up for him. What in the world did he want? Hadn't he caused enough turmoil already? His hand on her cheek. Really? She looked up "beautiful" in her heavy, red Webster's dictionary, searching for some hidden meaning pertaining to her. He could not have meant she was beautiful, not in the way Sally Troyer was beautiful. Or Amanda Mast. There had to be some mystery to his words.

Softly, she opened the screen door and let herself out into the aching, mellowing evening when the golden rays of the setting sun turned everything into a brilliant replica of itself.

He patted the seat beside him, smiling.

"You look beautiful in that dress, Clara."

She sank into the swing beside him, feeling overwhelmed by his nearness. She shrank to the side and gripped the small links of the chain that held the wing. She said nothing.

He took a deep breath.

"Your porch is the most welcoming thing, Clara. It's deep and inviting, as if you feel at home on it. I love the wide pillars that support the roof."

"Thank you. It's a Sears and Roebuck house. It came in pieces and was assembled like a crib, or . . . or . . . oh, I don't know."

"A crib?"

"Well, you know, you . . . uh . . . assemble cribs."

"Did you ever do that?"

"Do what?"

"Assemble a crib?

"Of course not. I just . . . you know, saw it in the Sears catalog."

Her face was flaming, her mouth as dry as a drought in August. This was a terrible thing, talking about cribs, as if . . . oh, she couldn't think about it.

He was chuckling, a soft sound of merriment that set her on edge. He tactfully changed the subject, for which she would be eternally grateful.

"So tell me why you live alone, why you own a farm filled with all these horses."

She took a deep breath, then took the plunge. She told him honestly and forthrightly that she was never asked out on a date and quit "running around" at an early age, decided she'd had enough of listening to simpering—that's exactly what said, *simpering*—girlfriends talking about their dates, the young man in question always someone she would gladly have taken. Her father left her the farm, and she threw herself into the love of her life, horses. She finished with, "It was the only smart thing to do. Especially after the man tried to . . . you know, have his way with me."

Oba looked at her, astonished.

"I hated men after that."

Oba reached out and took her hand. He gently ran his thumb across the top of her narrow hand. Then raised it to his lips. She felt the soft dryness, felt the electricity pulse through her veins, but was helpless in the wake of the onslaught of emotion.

"I hope you don't feel that way about me."

She was quiet, so still he heard the whir of a sparrow's wings as it quietly took flight. Suddenly, without warning, she tore her hand out of his, sat up and forward on the swing, turned her upper body toward him, and said, low, "Oba."

He was speechless, could only stare at her.

"I mean it. I simply can't go on this way. Do you actually feel anything toward me? I mean, why are you doing this? I can't go on. Do you honestly feel attracted to me?" She was almost crying, yet she had to know.

And Oba realized she was a mature woman, not a young girl he would have to put on a display of flowery speeches for. Oba nodded, then pushed her back slightly before taking her hand. "I'm afraid you'll run, depending on what I say."

"No. I'll stay. But tell me nothing but the truth."

And he did. He told her how she had won his heart by her generous spirit, her honesty, and in time, her beauty had grown on him, like a desert flower on a cactus plant blending into its surroundings.

"I think, Clara, that love and beauty go hand in hand. I'm sure you've heard the phrase, beauty is in the eye of the beholder. Your beauty is not perceived by everyone, but to me, you are like a rare flower others might overlook at first glance."

"But I'm so homely," she wailed, clearly distraught. "Life was so much easier before ... before." She waved a hand, fluttered it helplessly.

He knew there was no other way to relate his true feelings, so he drew her tenderly to him until she rested in his arms. He was very gentle and very patient. The swing creaked softly. A smattering of sound came from the Rose of Sharon bush as a pair of cardinals chased each other among the branches. A horse snorted by the fence, then stomped its hooves to rid the skin of pesky horseflies.

Finally, she surrendered, lay her head on his shoulder. Her arm came up and around his waist. She caught the scent of soap, fresh air, and newly sprouted grass.

The solidness of him! The solid strength of his waist, his back. She had never known the touch of a man in tenderness. It seemed unfair, undeserved, this blessed liberty of laying her head on this wide chest, to feel the beating of his heart. And when she imagined she would die of sheer bliss, she felt the touch of his fingertips on her chin, a gentle prodding motion. She tilted her head slightly to look into his eyes, splendidly alight with what she could only describe as love and caring.

Slowly, so slowly, he bent his head, while she thought if she never breathed again, but died here in his arms, her whole life leading to this magical moment would have been worth the pain. And when he placed his perfect lips on hers, she felt the beginning of womanly wisdom, the fullness of life, touched by a pure love for the very first time. It was beautiful, astounding, surreal. She did not draw away from him, but allowed herself to be swept away into a new and wonderful love for a man. When he raised his head, he put both hands on the sides of her face, whispered hoarsely, clearly shaken.

"I love you, Clara. It's the truth. And more than anything on earth, I want you to be my wife."

To his horror, she burst into harsh, lonely cries of denial. Her head swung back and forth as moans of sadness tore through her throat.

"No, no, Oba."

"But . . . Clara. I love you."

"No, you don't. You don't. I just helped you with your leg and all that, and now you pity me. All you're doing is paying me back because you think you should."

"Please, Clara, no. It's not like that at all."

"Yes, it is. You just don't know it yet. I can't marry you. I'm a homely thing, covered in freckles. I'm as thin as a stick. I don't even have . . ." She waved a hand helplessly across the front of her dress. "You're perfect, Oba. You're the most handsome man I have ever seen. You have no idea what it feels like to be me. Imagine for one minute. I am not endowed with natural beauty. You won't want me. Oh, perhaps you feel this way now. You're a man, you have needs in your loneliness. That's all this is."

She got up off the swing, walked the length of the porch and back again. She told him brokenly she could not go and she couldn't stay. He smiled at her, a long, slow smile that made her sit down beside him, made her want to stay in his arms forever.

But she could not give in to him, she just couldn't.

For a long moment, there was silence between them, a silence stuffed full of unspoken words, until they tumbled from Oba in the form of a reminder of his own handicap. He became sullen then, a dark mood settling over his features. Turning to her, he asked it was alright if he showed her something, although he did not want to frighten her.

She nodded, her eyes on his.

Slowly, he got up off the swing, began to open the buttons of his shirt.

"Oba," Clara said hesitantly.

"No. You said you would look."

He shrugged the white shirt off his shoulders. At first, in the waning light of evening, she did not see. He turned slightly, and a hand went to her mouth.

"Oba, no!" she croaked, broken completely.

She saw the width of his shoulders, the narrow waist, the perfect back of a man, hideously crisscrossed by aged welts, red and purple, some of them white, mottled by lines and wrinkles, puffs of poorly healed flesh. It was a sordid ruination of his back, without imagining the pain and devastation to his soul.

With a strangled cry, she got to her feet, put both hands to his waist, and with tears running down her face, her eyes closed in anguish, she placed her wet face to the most terrible scars, and kissed them.

"Oba, oh, Oba," she murmured. "It's so terrible."

His shoulders heaved as broken cries burst out of him, terrible strangled choking sounds of a pain so deep and endless, there were no words to describe them.

He stepped away, kept his face hidden as he pulled his shirt on, then turned to her. She would always remember his half-buttoned, lopsided shirt, his arms spread wide, his palms up, his hands outstretched in the twilight.

"It's me. Oba. All of me."

She shook her head, her eyes agonized as she met this.

"Who?" she whispered.

"You know. May told you."

"Yes. But I had no idea the severity of it."

She took his arm, wiped her eyes with the back of her hand, and said, "Come, Oba. Let's light a lamp and go inside. I'm cold."

He wiped his own eyes, then gave a rueful laugh. "There you go, bossing me around again."

She tried to laugh, but the sound from her mouth was a small, sad cry. He was smiling when she placed a hand on each forearm to look into his eyes, and he put his hungry arms around her and drew her close. This time, he kissed her with abandon, and they drew apart, shaken, unwilling to admit just quite yet the perfect plan God was slowly unfolding.

They talked most of the night, and he asked her to marry him the second time. She told him if he only pitied her, she supposed that was something, after all, wasn't it? He assured her it was so much more than pity, but he was willing to wait for her answer.

When he decided to stay, she told him no respectable driver would come pick him up in the morning without gleefully telling anyone who had access to his blue coupe that he had picked up Oba Miller at Clara Yoder's house, in the morning.

Clara did not sleep at all, but lay wide-eyed, staring at the ceiling, questioning God and herself and Oba. Sometimes, she wished she had never met him, other times she knew she had to be with him for the remainder of her days.

"Oh, God, answer me. Come on, just show me."

She begged and bargained and prayed, made coffee at six o'clock, and watched Oba asleep on the couch in the living room, his arm flung to the floor, his face slightly pressed into the pillow. Would he love her in the alarming light of a sunlit morning? Her freckles, her long, beaked nose, like a homely fledgling bird. Would he love her when she got hopping mad, which was bound to happen sometime? Did a terribly scarred back and half of a leg equal one skinny freckled wife?

He awoke when she dropped a coffee mug, lifted himself off the couch, came to the kitchen with tousled hair and slightly swollen, sleepy eyes. He had never been more attractive. She seemed almost terrified, stayed as far away as possible when she poured their steaming cups of coffee.

"Good morning, Clara."

"I never say good morning. Just so you know."

He burst out laughing. "Does that mean you'll say yes, so I can prepare myself for the lack of being wished a good morning?"

"No."

"Come sit down, Clara."

She obeyed.

"I can hardly wait for our future. I am looking forward to living with someone who always speaks her mind, is the most honest person I know, who gets mad as a hornet, who is perfectly lovely, slim, red-haired, and freckled all over."

Slowly she exhaled, her eyes suddenly weary. "It's such a bunch of bologna," she said dryly.

He laughed uproariously this time. "See, I love that so much. I never know what will come out of your mouth. You will entertain me, delight me, just by listening to you."

"We got a bit emotional last night."

"We did. And I hope to get emotional with you quite often."

"Just be quiet about it now, okay?"

She got briskly to her feet, asked if he liked scrambled eggs or fried. Bacon or canned sausage.

She drove him home with Ralph, spoke a few words to May, and took off in a cloud of dust. She returned to the farm and cleaned three stalls before falling into bed, completely exhausted. She slept the night away and rose the next morning, rummaged in a drawer until she found her pen and paper, sat down at the kitchen table, and held her pen above the lined paper for a long moment.

Dear Oba,
Why don't you ask someone else to be your wife? I'm not good wife material.

That made her sound like a piece of fabric from Spector's, so she tore off the sheet of paper and began again.

Dear Oba,
I think a younger girl like Sally Troyer would be a much better match.

16   *Linda Byler*

She thought how much that sounded as if she was putting up a matching pair of horses, so she ripped that page off, crumpled it and threw it in the woodstove.

Dear Oba,
You could marry Amanda Mast. She's very pretty. You could have a whole row of children.

That was not appropriate either, so she tore that page off, let it flutter to the linoleum. Suddenly, she threw the pen and tablet across the kitchen where they hit the opposite wall and slid to the floor.

She decided anew that marriage was not for her, then spent a miserable week watching the driveway for Tom's old blue coupe. It rained nearly every day. Low clouds scudded across the horizon like churning, dirty wash water, the horses kicked up mud and brown water on the white board fence, and a skunk crawled under the stone foundation of the house and wouldn't come out. She left nuts and raisins, cold oatmeal, and bits of cookie at a place he might have been able to squeeze through and then chased the neighbor's dog out the drive with a broom when he ate everything, leaving the skunk underneath to spray the toxic scent that wafted through the floorboards as thick as if the skunk stood on the kitchen table.

All day Sunday she sat in the stench, now a bit milder after opening all the doors and windows, froze in the brisk spring breeze after the rain, and finally started a roaring fire in the kitchen range. She glared out the window and regretted the day she met May Miller. Like a wilting flower, a pansy. She had no backbone, or she would have let that spoiled Oba fend for himself out in the world. She made a list of reasons why Oba should not marry her, then a list of why he should, which only served to befuddle her even further.

She wished someone would come to visit, but when Elias Amstustz drove in, the surrey bulging with unkempt, snotty-nosed children, she ran upstairs and hid in the closet. She heard the door banging, the "Helloo! *Bisht do* (Are you here), Clara?" and gave no answer. When they piled back into the surrey and made their way out the drive, she felt like a traitor, a spy, or a liar, maybe all three.

And she watched the driveway.

By Wednesday of the following week, she came to the hard-won conclusion that she was meant to stay an old maid. Cut and dried.

She was deeply ashamed of her emotion. (She had kissed his back.) Had she really done that? The searing shame was like drowning in thick molasses.

She would gather her wits about her, then, and go on with her life. She thought of Oba and Sally, Oba and Amanda, doing what they had done on the porch swing, and a sort of rabid anger sliced through her.

She contemplated packing her things and moving to Wisconsin, where an Amish settlement was being pioneered by a few hardy Ohioans.

When Tom's blue coupe drove in and Oba got out on a gloomy Thursday evening, she slowly lay down her spoon, took a deep breath, and met him at the door. She flung herself into his waiting arms, sniffed and blubbered, and said yes.

"Yes, yes, yes. I will marry you, Oba."

And she did, that November, when the weather turned cold enough to keep the roast chicken and tapioca pudding, the mashed potatoes and gravy, the many pies and cakes. Andy's farm was dotted with Ohio folks dressed in their wedding finery, the family from Indiana sporting all the latest styles, wavy hair and smaller coverings, the men with neatly trimmed beards.

Everyone said they made a handsome pair, Clara having the glow of a bride in love. When they stood by the earnest old minister and he pronounced the sacred vows, more than one young girl felt confused.

Really. Clara Yoder of all people.

The day was like a rose in full bloom, they all agreed. Something was special. The singing in the afternoon rose with great volume, ascending to the heavens. It seemed as if the angels smiled down on the white farmhouse that day.

All May and Oba's remaining family, the aunts and uncles who had rejected them, were in attendance, and every last one apologized for any heartache they might have caused. None of them would ever know the extent both had suffered, but was it necessary? God would judge in the end. May and Oba had faced the brave journey of forgiveness, had found the road to be much harder than anything in their life, but possible. With the help of their faith in God, they had overcome severe and crippling bitterness and could now reap the benefits of their labors.

On their first evening in the cozy little house, Oba could tell he had been right in looking forward to life with Clara. She was heady with praise, admiration puffing her up like spring toadstools. She chortled to herself about her perfectly beautiful sister's jaw-dropping assessment of Oba, the desperate need to hide the fact they could not see how she could ever land a husband like him.

She told him all of it, unabashedly, honest, gleeful.

"They say we all have our day in the sun," she laughed. "Mine was so bright it was blinding today."

And Oba laughed, the sound of freedom from bitterness and unforgiveness. He could honestly say he loved the guests as one, harbored no ill will, which freed his heart to love Clara, his red-haired bride with the audacious spirit to match.

THE BRIGHT NOVEMBER moon created patterns of bare branches across the roof and the brown lawn on the horse farm. The cold, frosty air made the wooden siding creak after the warmth of the sunny day. The banked fire in the kitchen range popped and crackled. A lone coyote yipped in the woods by the pond, and a dog began to bark a warning to the few sheep and cows still in the pasture as the cold descended.

And since Oba could not easily kneel, they sat side by side on their marriage bed, her hand in his and bowed their heads in silent prayer, the old tradition handed down from the forefathers. Clara was not one given to long prayers, and Oba was only a fledgling in the faith, but their prayers were sincere, their hearts full of love, and God looked down with benevolence, with grace and acceptance, at two people battered by the storms of life, their sturdy raft now resting together on the shores of holy matrimony.

CHAPTER 11

IT WASN'T PERFECT, THIS THING CALLED MARRIAGE.

Clara decided this early on, but it was a bonus in life, an added blessing by which she was truly astounded. She often wondered if she was the only Amish wife who could have spent all her days looking at her husband. Simply observing his beloved face, the determination in his brown eyes as he attempted more and more of the work around the farm. It was a joy to wash his clothes and cook his meals, and never once had he been unkind.

There was a fullness to life, having a husband, and she rarely wanted to go back to her single state. Only occasionally, like when she wanted a quiet moment with the daily paper and Oba seemed to deem it necessary to talk incessantly, telling her all sorts of things about life in general. All the solitude he had ever found himself to be in had exploded into a myriad of thoughts that had to be delivered to her ears alone. At first, she had been thrilled, all these observations of life and she the sole recipient of his views. Sometimes, though, she wished he'd simply be quiet when she was reading.

And he never wanted to go visiting. She had to threaten and pout and carry on before he'd accompany her on a social call, then clam up and sit there like a rock until she finally consented to go home. Oh, it made her hopping mad. When she told him this, he shrugged, said he didn't like people. They made him nervous. He only liked her. Which made her smile, of course, but still.

And Oba was as delighted as he had always imagined himself to be. Clara was outspoken, funny, smart. She was entertaining, a bright, vivacious part of his life, and his love for her never wavered but grew as the years went by.

They were not blessed with children for quite a length of time, which Clara assured him was up to God, so what was he fussing about. Andy and May were so happy when a son was born to them, a son for Andy, named Andrew Weaver, Jr. A little junior.

Clara sat with May as the children crowded around her, beads of perspiration on her upper lip, her face the color of curdled milk, the large baby yelling his head off, and Clara thought all that could just pass her by and she'd be happy. Motherhood was a *schmottz* (pain).

But when she did finally conceive, she felt proud, with Oba beside himself with anticipation. She was as cranky as a wet hen, threw up every morning for four months, couldn't stand the smell of horses and their manure, neglected her chores, her garden, the dishes, and the laundry. She yelled at Oba when he tried to help with anything, then threw herself on the couch and wept great tears of frustration and self-pity. When a well-meaning friend told her she might have a hard time at her age, she snapped at her and walked away, then fumed to Oba, who nodded his head and agreed with his wife. There was nothing else to do these days except agree to whatever she said, knowing it would not go well if he didn't.

He told Andy he had no idea women could get so cranky, and Andy looked at him with a blank face, having never experienced such a thing with May.

When Clara was delivered of a squalling little redhead named Esther, a girl with all of her attributes, Oba was sure God was on his side, had blessed him beyond measure. They came home from the hospital with plenty of bottles, instructions about feeding canned milk mixed with boiled water and a bit of brown sugar, and that was that. No breastfeeding for Clara. The little thing didn't want anything to do with it, so Clara washed her hands of the whole deal, sterilized her bottles, and fed her with much less hassle.

Esther yelled and screamed, balled her angry little fists and resented the bottle, her mother, Oba's clumsy attempts at calming her, and anyone who tried to hold her. The whole process of having a baby caught Clara like a trap, and she spiraled into a deep, dark place of feeling useless, incapable, and bone-weary.

And when Esther was three months old, Clara was shocked into numb silence when she realized she would have another baby. She was so horrified, she didn't tell Oba for a length of time. When she finally did, he was thrilled, said he could hardly wait, he really couldn't.

So Clara found herself thrust headlong into a situation she could never have imagined. A newborn son named Emanuel, as bald as a baseball with eyes that appeared to be perpetually surprised. Oba cried at the sight of his son, but Clara stayed dry-eyed, thinking he looked a bit odd and wondering if something was wrong with him.

May kept Esther for three days, days in which her footsteps were directed by the outraged yells from one angry little one-year-old. She could never quite understand all this unhappiness from one adorable redheaded girlie, but told Andy she supposed every innocent new-born was brought into the world with a nature God had given then, impure like Adam and Eve. She said this very soberly to her husband, after finally getting her to sleep, and Andy looked at his delicate wife with so much love. It was only natural that she should find some loving reason to set little Esther free from blame, when he'd wondered what a good paddling would accomplish. He had no idea how Clara would manage with two babies only a year apart, so perhaps he'd need to extend his advice. He grinned, imagining the response.

To say Clara had her hands full was an understatement. For all her attitude—handling any situation with aplomb, working with horses, facing anything life handed her—these two babies almost did her in. Confined to the small house in the dead of winter, with Oba spending most of his time in the barn to get away from the chaos, Clara finally admitted to herself the thought she'd pushed away too long.

She should have stayed single.

But when Oba came in from the barn, the babies were both asleep (miracles did happen on occasion), the fire in the range crackled and popped, accompanying the swish of driven snow across the windows, and he looked at her with his sleepy brown eyes, she knew the devil only tempted her with those regrets. Of course she wanted Oba, wanted to be married. She loved him with her whole heart.

Slowly, a semblance of order was restored. Esther learned to walk, which seemed to put her in another frame of mind entirely. She wobbled from couch to chair and back again, immensely pleased at her accomplishment, while Oba and Clara egged her on, both comparing this to the times she had helped with the prosthesis, which was now like a part of his body. They looked at one another with the warm light of remembering.

"Did you love me back then?" Oba asked, a light of teasing in his eyes.

"No. You were bullheaded, stubborn."

"Just because you made me so mad, as pushy as you were."

"Nothing else would have worked."

Oba grinned. "I loved you back then, more than you could have known."

She shook her head, laughed ruefully. "You lie. You don't remember it now, but you couldn't stand the sight of me then."

"Maybe I didn't know I loved you, but I did. And I do still. You fill up my days with crazy situations that bring sparkles of enjoyment. Even when you're mad."

"Really? So that's all there ever was?"

"You want me to start on the rest of it?"

They were interrupted by the snuffling sound of a newborn waking, and Oba got to his feet. Clara heated the bottle, handed him a cloth diaper, and watched as he settled himself in the hickory rocker with Emanuel in the crook of his arm, the bottle held expertly. And she knew why she'd married him. He continued to surprise her, as he gained confidence with childcare, the responsibilities at the barn, the way he matured as the years went by. Esther loved her "Dat" in spite of her ill temper, climbing onto his lap at his slightest bidding, which was a huge help in her daily struggles.

Her days inched along, the weary winter a blur of sleepless nights, half-awake days, children crying, washing diapers and despairing over coughs, diaper rashes, bumped heads, and noses needing wiping. She held Emanuel over one shoulder, her hand thumping a rhythm to coax the elusive burp, with Esther clinging to her leg, the gray clouds scudding across the leaden sky, and wondered.

Who in the world came up with the idea about motherhood being so great? How was one supposed to keep cheerful thoughts in one's head when your whole life was like a bucket of horse feed turned upside down, shaken and scattered with birds coming to pick up the remains? There was no order to her days. Dishes piled up in the sink, laundry stayed heaped in the clothes hamper. The diaper pail was full and smelled to high heaven. She had two choices. Live like this, or do her dishes and laundry with unattended children crying in their cribs, guiltily stuffing articles of clothing through the wringer as fast as she could.

She had always been proud of keeping everything organized and under control—a clean barn, brushed and glowing horses, and an immaculate house she was never ashamed of.

And now.

The final straw came the day Oba yelled at her when he could not find a clean pair of denim trousers. She sat holding Emanuel when, at that very moment, a sour jet of half-digested milk shot across her shoulder and landed with a splat on the floor behind her.

She felt her face turn red, felt the hot retort rise in her throat and was powerless to stop it. She told him if he needed a clean pair of trousers, he could dig one out of the hamper or go do his chores in his underwear.

"Take your pick," she finished, bending to wipe the milk off the floor while holding Emanuel as best she could.

The truth of the matter was, she was sick and tired of gray days and wet laundry hanging on racks by the stove. It was like living in a giant, steaming closet. She could not abide the thought of looking at one more rack of limp socks and baby clothes. If the sun didn't shine all week, well then, he could do without trousers.

Oba was well versed in the ways of his wife, so he dutifully picked the cleanest pair available, went to the barn, and considered her lack of management since the children were born. He thought of the look on her face, the magenta red color of her skin when she was riled, and burst out laughing. Over and over, chuckles bubbled to the surface, and he was a happy man. This was one of the reasons he had married her, and one that never failed to delight him. She was so real, so human, wearing her ill temper and her good humor and every emotion in between like a brilliant cloak that could never be hidden.

He did his best to perform all of his fatherly duties, but she wouldn't let him close to the wringer washer, or the sink. She refused a *maud*, saying who wanted an incompetent idiot ruining her clothes and breaking her dishes. So he knew to hold the baby and keep his opinions to himself.

AFTER A FEW years went by, the babies grew into sunny little toddlers who ran across new-mown grass and squatted by the flower bed to stick their noses into daisies, giggling together as they glanced at their mother. Esther's red hair was like a brilliant flag, the little black covering on her head sliding away, hanging by its strings. The sun had already created a deepening of the freckles, a mirror of Clara's own scattering of them. Emanuel was neither blond nor red, but a color in between, with his father's huge brown eyes and dimples to match. He was round and firm, a strong little boy who could keep up with his sister's frenetic pace.

The sun shone, the breeze was soft and mellow, and Clara understood the poetry of motherhood. The bald, red-faced baby she'd been surprised by, the baby who terrified her a little bit, really had turned into the sweetest, most lovely little human. Esther, with her odd ways and angry howls of protest, was a constant source of amusement, and Clara loved her quick wit and ceaseless energy. Her temper tantrums bordered on hysterical, but as each year went by, they became less and less, until she became a quite presentable young lady.

But only if she felt like it.

They were raised with the rules of any normal Amish family, learned to love the barn and horses, the wide open fields and the scent of new-mown hay. They knew their father did not have two good legs the way other fathers did, and their mother was not always sweet or friendly, especially when she worked with the horses.

If they climbed the board fence, there were consequences, and if they ever dared to slip beneath it, well, they could only guess what would happen then. So they spent hours seated on small wooden benches, peering between the boards as their mother trained horses.

One hot, dusty afternoon, Emanuel accidentally got to his feet rather quickly, stumbled, and fell against the fence, spooking a rangy brown colt that didn't have an ounce of brains in his head. Clara was frustrated, overheated, thirsty, and tired, so when the horse tore the rope out of her grasp, knocked her over, and took off across the corral, she picked herself up, lifted her skirt to examine the brush burn on her knee, where the skin had made contact with the sharp gravel, then took out her frustrations on poor, unsuspecting Emanuel by giving a stern scolding.

She sat him severely on the bench and told Esther to watch out for her brother. Esther squinted up at her mother and told her to calm down, Emanuel hadn't meant to scare the horse.

Shocked, Clara said, "If I decide he needs to be scolded, then you need to respect that."

Esther looked straight ahead without changing her expression, before saying soft and low, "Your face is awful red."

She told Oba that evening, and he howled with genuine glee. "She's the one who will train you good and proper," he chortled.

"It's not funny."

"It is. She is your exact image, just everything."

"Is that a bad thing?"

"Of course not. You know why I married you. I love your spirit. Your endless quirkiness."

"Is that a word?"

And he laughed again.

It seemed as if the laughter welled up easily these days, like a spring that bubbled constantly, a sound quite familiar to his own ears. He reveled, wallowed in happiness. His past was like a dark line of clouds on a faraway horizon, a line of clouds holding no power. His marriage to Clara, the love of God, his faith, his children, all the blessings along the way, brought brilliant sunshine holding the clouds at bay. The deep-seated anxiety could be overcome, the isolation from normal society a thing of the past.

He didn't enjoy crowds, did not attend horse sales or go to neighboring districts to church, something Clara realized she would have to accept. So she went by herself, a regular figure, standing with her black coat and bonnet, watching every horse being sold, her experienced eye finding a good trotter, bidding for no more than he was worth. She was respected by the men in the ring and those standing or sitting around it, watching as she appraised each animal. When one of her own was being sold, everyone knew there would be a flurry of bidding, followed by a sale quite a few dollars more than others. She was Clara Yoder—well, Oba Miller's Clara now—horse dealer, an equine specialist, certainly.

Oba spent a great deal of time in the tack room, which they turned into a harness shop a few years later. He used the finest leather and sewed it on the immense cast-iron machine. In time, mastering the art of harness and bridle making became Oba's best accomplishment yet. He enjoyed the work, especially in the winter months, and found there was a good market for his fine leather products.

ELI WAS THE children's favorite cousin. Tall and strong, the color of dark honey with a cascade of springy black hair, he was the one they imitated, the one they talked about as they played.

He loved Oba's children as he loved his uncle and they spent hours together, playing in the cow stable, the creek, the woods, and the pasture. They knew where the bantam hen laid her eggs, where the barn cats had a nest of kittens, and which cow to stay away from. So on a hot summer day, when they asked May and Clara if they could go to the fields to watch the men at the threshing rig, they both said no. Eli was helping the men, and Lizzie was too young to be held responsible for the two little ones.

Esther frowned, stamped her narrow foot in frustration. "Come on, Mama," she said forcefully.

May exchanged a look with Clara. They both hid their smiles and shook their heads. No, it wasn't safe with the wagons being drawn behind trotting horses, carrying straw to the barn. Lizzie and Fronie shrugged and gave in, but not Esther, who clung to the base of the windmill by the barn and looked intently at the cluster of men, wagons, horses, and the big clattering monster chewing up sheaves of wheat and spitting out grain and straw. The rolls of dust and the clackety-clackety sound was almost more than she could resist. Fronie held Emanuel while Lizzie went to get a table and chairs after deciding they'd play church. Esther swung around the windmill, her skirts flying in a swirl of color, watching the thrilling sight of the threshing rig. She looked at her cousins, calculated the distance to the barn and down to the rig, then slowly took her hands off the steel rigging of the windmill, turned, and ran. In a flash, she was gone, slipping through barbed wire as slick as an eel, propelling herself forward with wiry muscles in her thin legs.

She could smell the straw dust, she could hear the roar of the gas engine, which created a whirl of excitement in her small chest. It was thrilling—the stamping of horses' feet, the heat, and a roaring sound that made her want to hop up and down, clap her hands with hard smacks. She didn't see the danger, didn't hear the driver climb on the wagon, lift the reins, and chirp to his horses. She only knew she heard her name being screamed in a tone of voice she had never heard. Through the dust and the roaring clattering sound, Eli barreled past the fast-moving wagon and she felt herself being grabbed and lifted, whisked away seconds before the loaded wagon was in the spot she had been standing.

"Esther!"

Eli looked down at her face, her expression unchanged, the complete absence of fear.

"What?"

"Why are you down here? That wagon could easily have run you over."

"I don't think so. Put me down. I want to watch."

Eli did not put her down, but carried her all the way to the house where he deposited her with the dire warning that perhaps someone should be keeping an eye on her, that she had almost been run over.

May was aghast, her face turning white, but Clara was clearly angry, her small strong-willed daughter disobeying her yet again. May flinched as she delivered a sound smack, then another, accompanied by dire threats.

Esther turned, took a deep breath as she looked her mother in the eye. "That wasn't necessary, Mam."

Clara's face turned red with fury, but she seemed to contain it well. She said evenly, "It was. I hope you know how dangerous it is to go to the threshing rig. The reason I spanked you is so you know if you do something you aren't supposed to do, there will be consequences."

May got down to her level, put an arm around her shoulders. "You could have been run over by a team of horses, sweetie."

"But I wasn't."

Clara rolled her eyes.

Eli spoke kindly. "Esther, you would have been if I hadn't seen you. You really do have to stay with your cousins while we're threshing."

"I wasn't run over," she said calmly.

Fronie and Lizzie watched, wide-eyed, saying nothing. They would never dare speak to their mother in such a bold manner.

Eli looked down at Esther and asked her to promise she would stay here for the rest of the day.

"Here? Right here in this kitchen?" she asked. "No, I'm going to stand by the windmill so I can watch you."

Clara immediately said, "No, you're not."

Which, of course, sent Esther into denial, bucking her mother's words with undeterred determination.

WHEN THE MEN came clattering in for the huge dinner the women had prepared, Esther was still at the windmill like a bright flower attached to the base. Clara's love of color was carried over to her daughter's clothing, which had been the reason Eli spied her quickly. He left the group of men to go to her and tell her dinner was ready. And she was a bright flower trotting beside Eli, her face lifted as she chattered away.

Clara and May were flushed with the heat and the effort of cooking huge amounts of food between caring for children. Toddlers fought for toys or had to be taken to the little wooden potty, which could never be neglected, even if you were not at home. Children were trained before the age of two, or the mother was considered lazy or unconcerned.

May's mother-in-law, Kettie, had volunteered her services, which May could not refuse politely, but she had come down with a summer cold and kept to her house, which May guiltily admitted to Clara was just fine with her.

A long table was spread in the back yard, with benches along each side. The white tablecloth was dotted with flowered china plates and glass tumblers, plates of butter, and small glass bowls of raspberry jam. There were bowls of applesauce, divided plates of sweet gherkins, slices of dill pickles, and mounds of red beets.

While the men washed up at the pump, May and Clara dished up bowls of steaming mashed potatoes, platters of fried chicken, and bowls of yellow chicken gravy seasoned with dots of fresh parsley and ground pepper. There were new peas, buttered noodles, and savory stuffing, pies, cakes, golden canned peaches, and tapioca pudding.

May beamed as the men thanked her, having eaten their fill of her good cooking, her house a place the men on the threshing crew always looked forward to. Most of the women on the threshing ring were good cooks, but May was outstanding. Andy stood with the close-knit group of men, a toothpick dangling from his mouth, listened to the praise of his *gut frau* (good wife), and smiled a long slow grin. He nodded his head and said, "Ya, ya. The day I met May, I was blessed indeed."

Oba stood a bit apart and caught Clara's eye and winked. She winked back, then gave him a bright smile. They had both decided life only got better after having two babies in the span of only one year, that nothing lasted forever, and if they survived that, they were up for anything.

Over and over, Oba realized his good fortune, the blessings he lived every day. He loved being with friends and family, loved his children and Clara with fierce dedication. He laughed freely at her fiery temper, enjoyed listening to her tales of drama, real or imagined. Everyone said Oba and Clara were an unlikely match, but surely one made in heaven.

And there were no more babies for them, with Clara getting past the childbearing years, and Oba blessed with the two they did have. Each day he prayed these two precious little souls would never have to experience half of the sorrow and heartache he and May had gone through.

And though the days were packed with blessings, only May knew the challenges Eli faced, the days when adversity raised its ugly visage in the form of unacceptance. She calmly took all of it upon herself, knew it was the reaping of her own sowing, but never once did she regret having Eli in her life.

He was the link to her first great love, the remembered times with Clinton, when she was bruised and battered by the unfairness of life, the times she had lived in the dark tunnel in Arkansas. She loved Andy with a new and steady love, expanded her heart to include him, when, first, there had been Clinton, then Eli.

And always Eli was the star that guided her caring, her concern. Would he stay with the heritage that meant so much to her and Andy? Would he ever completely fit in? Only God knew the answer to that question.

PART TWO

Eli

CHAPTER 12

THE TWO-STORY BRICK SCHOOL WAS LOCATED IN THE CENTER of the small Ohio town named Mayfield. It was the center of education for the children of the surrounding area, Amish, Swiss Mennonite, and the English (what the non-Amish were called). The regular people who drove their cars and had electricity and televisions, the women who dressed in pretty dresses or slacks and blouses, cut their hair, and wore lipstick on their lips.

Everyone was neighborly, each left the other to his or her religion and way of life, and all sent their children to Mayfield School, with different rooms for different grades, and four English teachers. There was talk of the Amish having their own schools, some of them seriously having meetings with officials, but here in Wayne County, many of the children were happy to go to school with their neighbor children—it really didn't matter if they were Amish or not.

Eli rode the yellow bus with his sister Lizzie, his happy personality and winning smile helping him over the rough spots, when an occasional off-hand remark from some unkind child would remind him he was the only dark-skinned boy in all of Mayfield School. And for the most part, he went smoothly through all his grades until he entered seventh grade and Dan Nissley partnered up with John Graham and decided to make life rough for the "black boy."

Mrs. Crouse was the teacher that year, a wide-shouldered and powerfully built woman in her fifties, hair crimped and curled, her small brown eyes missing nothing. She favored the English children and tolerated the rest of them. A few of the Amish and Swiss Mennonite children were sent to school with cropped denim trousers and bare feet, a brown U of liquid manure dried between their toes, having come from the cow stable to school. A faint smell of cow manure and bedwetting emanated from the innocent souls, the bane of the poor woman's existence, the evils of her job.

There were just so many children in one family, so they could not all be cared for in the way the English children were. Parents had a dozen children easily, sometimes more—preventing this blessing from God was unthinkable. Blessed is the man whose quiver is full, his children around his table. A great blessing, indeed. It was just that fourteen children ranging in age from five months to eighteen years was a houseful, and one busy mother could not always be counted on to tend to the smallest details.

So the odor rising from the tousled hair of the Amish children was only an accompanying scent to their bare feet. Baths were only on Saturday night, in a galvanized tub beside the kitchen stove, a sheet hung on a wire for privacy. The kettle hummed on the cherry-cheeked stove, heating water for the next group of little ones, six or more using the same water.

On occasion, one of the children would begin a frantic scratching, especially behind their ears, and a cold chill of fear would go through Mrs. Crouse's stomach. Lice. Cooties. After a thorough search through the unsuspecting child's head, she'd find the lice inhabiting the long, thick hair. Out came the kerosene or naphtha gas, a stiff brush, and a fine-toothed comb, and grim mothers who raked them through without mercy, blaming those sloppy Troyers. They came up with lice far too often. Mrs. Crouse threatened to quit after the last outbreak, but Mr. Tomlin, the principal, begged her to stay, said he'd give her a raise if she did. He'd bring in a nurse to check the children's heads every once in a while, he said.

Now there was this deal with Eli Miller getting picked on.

Mrs. Crouse sat down heavily, splayed her size-ten shoes in front of her, crossed her arms on her stomach, and decided the next time she heard Dan Nissley speak to Eli like that, he'd be hiked to the principal's office.

Eli was a bit of a mystery, no doubt, but she didn't plan on sticking her nose into affairs she shouldn't. He was Amish, indeed, but not white. Not as black as some, but certainly not white, with all that kinky black hair. Cleaner than most, but then, there were only three children in that family. A mystery.

She retrieved her lunchbox, snapped the lid open to look for the second powdered sugar doughnut she'd saved for after school, and came up empty. She sucked her teeth in dismay, remembering she'd eaten both for lunch. Well, she'd hurry up and get out of here, there were still a few in the box at home. There were, unless Willis got into them. He could stand to lose a few pounds, too.

The door opened slowly, and she looked up. Thought, *Mmhmm.*
"Yes?"

Dan Nissley was a big seventh grader, stood a good six inches above his classmates, his face large, rounded, with a peppering of sandy hair cut very short. He was shifty-eyed, one she couldn't trust—she just tried to keep him out of too much trouble.

"My pencil box was stolen yesterday," he blurted out, shifting his weight from one foot to the other.

"Really? And you're just mentioning it now?"

"Well, yeah."

"Are you sure it was stolen and you haven't misplaced it?"

"No. I mean, yes, I'm sure it was stolen."

"And who would need a new pencil box?"

"Eli. Eli Miller."

Mrs. Course had taught school for thirty-two years, and this was one of those times when she saw straight through this boy. He hated Eli. In some ways, it was hardly his fault. He was one of those boys who were raised to believe they were born superior to the colored race and had every right to make their lives miserable. Those boys rained all kinds of slang names on their heads and never felt a moment's guilt.

"So Eli stole your pencil box, and you're here to report it."

"Yes, ma'am."

"I'll address the problem in the morning then." She could only think of one descriptive word as he let himself out. Slunk. He slunk through the door.

She got to her feet, went to Eli's desk, bent over, and rummaged through the books and papers. She found the metal box in question. Of course it would be there, planted by Dan himself. So it wouldn't be worth raising a big stink about it; she'd merely keep both boys in at recess and let the truth speak for itself.

Which was what she did, and ever since, Dan had made school miserable for Eli. He was tripped by Dan's oversized shoe, locked into the bathroom Dan and one of his friends throwing all their weight against the door, taunted and teased unmercifully. As these things go, a few of the Amish boys who wanted to be considered a part of the popular group joined in the fray, until Eli was cornered on the playground by four of these bullies.

Eli had been taught to accept the fact he was different, take responsibility for his own behavior, and try his best to get along with everyone. His quiet, soft-spoken mother was the one he'd go to when things got rough, and she would tell him about Jesus, how the Christian way was to love your enemies, do good to them who hate you. But that did not seem to be working, as the pranks and name calling escalated to the encounter on the playground.

AFTER HE'D BEEN beaten and his straw hat stomped on until it was no longer wearable, he washed his face at the pump, held his injured shoulder in what he hoped was the correct position, and kept all his tears inside while he sat at his desk with the hurt like a ball of lead in his stomach. This time, he did not tell his mother, until she saw the remains of his straw hat.

His parents were not happy and went to see Dan Nissley's parents, after which they spoke to the teacher. Both of them seemed concerned, both of them promised to deal with the problem, but Andy and May came away with an unsettled feeling they had never experienced before. Was there a real concern, or was that a half sneer on Tom Nissley's face? Had Mrs. Crouse actually said it was time the boy stood up for himself? She seemed to be implying that Eli was cowardly, that somehow the encounter was his own fault.

These incidents kept coming, with May teaching Christian love and non-resistance. This was all well and good, until the day came when he had passed his fifteenth birthday and school was over and done with. He had passed all his grades and was sent home to work on the farm with his father. May sighed with relief. His school years had been exhausting for both of them—she felt like it was only her constant efforts to address problems with the teachers and instruct Eli at home that kept his head above water. Weeks would pass without incident, but always they were on edge, waiting for the next encounter, until his sunny nature became cloudier and cloudier.

Would he have fared better by hitting back as Mrs. Crouse suggested? Very likely. But it went against May's religion, her culture, her entire understanding of Scripture. To turn the other cheek, to go the second mile, to give a man your cloak also. Love your enemies. Pray for them that despitefully use you. She had no doubt Eli could have successfully whooped them all. He was tall for his age, with a strong build, outrunning all his classmates.

How hard she prayed, coming before the Lord in anguish, asking him to protect her son, to stay by his side. The teachings of Christ were not easily accepted by the young, when their nature was so against His teaching. The responsibility of his well-being, the choices she had made, the fear of his future, all of it was rolled together in a mass that lay heavily on her heart.

How long could she be patient with her telling of the Scripture? Was it fair to him to live here with her Amish heritage intact? How could a young black boy ever hope to find peace and lasting happiness in the Amish church with the lack of people like him?

He loved his work on the farm, so when school was behind him, his sunny disposition seemed to rebound. Every morning he helped with the milking, swinging the heavy pails with ease. He harnessed the huge draft horses, slinging the great leather harnesses over their backs, lifting the tongues of the wagons with seemingly very little effort. He plowed for days on end, walking behind the plow with ease, his face lifted to watch the flight of the birds, knowing what would happen when he heard the cry of the goshawk. He knew where the den of foxes was hidden beneath a pile of rocks, knew all the inhabitants in the groundhog community. When Andy despaired of the dangerous holes they created and sat in the fencerow with the shotgun, Eli never accompanied him. He couldn't stand the thought of killing one of those comical creatures resembling a fat little man with unfortunate buck teeth. He knew where the redbellied woodpeckers raised their young, watched anxiously as a mother deer came out of the woods, a delicate fawn by her side.

Nature filled a void in his soul, his heart. He was often lonely, with no friends to really call his own. All the boys his age were repeatedly told to be nice to Eli, be his friend, don't let him feel left out, take him along. Most obeyed as best they could, but no one wanted to be alone with him, to be singled out as the buddy of "black Eli," *da schwottz Eli*.

The farm was his favorite place to be, away from prying eyes and uncomfortable situations, but as he grew, Andy told May they could not always shield him from the questions, from well-meaning folks who asked blunt, hurtful things.

"Adopted one, didja?"

"Where's he come from?"

"Slavery's over, Andy." A knee-slapping guffaw, a stream of brown liquid sent into a Maxwell House coffee can.

May agreed to her husband's words but flinched inwardly, thinking of the unknown. She would gladly have given her life, stepped out in black skin and taken all the hurled knives and sledgehammers of racial division.

As he grew into adolescence, the time of self-awareness, of gauging the world around him with a critical eye turned on himself, Andy and May saw less and less of his great beaming smile.

ANDY ASKED IF Eli would like to ride along to the bank, pick up a few supplies for May, maybe go to the feed store. He was sweeping the packed cement of the forebay, pushing the wide broom rhythmically, his bowl-shaped straw hat hiding his face. He stopped, leaned on the broom handle, his face darkening as his eyes shifted away.

"No."

"Why, Eli?"

"I'll stay home."

Andy stepped closer. "What is it?"

"Dat, I'm older now. Those remarks the men make sometimes really hurt."

"They're teasing. They're hard on everyone else. They mean well."

"No, they don't."

Andy hesitated. Eli's brown eyes flashed as he opened his mouth, closed it again. He picked up the broom and hung it between the two nails designed for that purpose, before turning to his father.

"How would you like to ride in the spring wagon with black skin?"

"Your skin is not black."

"It may as well be."

"God loves you just he way you are."

"Tell that to the people in town. Tell it to the schools and churches. They don't believe it."

"But you don't understand, Eli. The Amish people aren't like that. You have always been accepted, in all fairness."

"Not by everyone."

"Look, Eli. Please don't harbor resentment toward the few who have narrow minds. There is not one human being anywhere on this earth who has everyone's approval. We all try and get along as best we can."

With the softening light in his eyes, Andy could tell his words were considered. Eli put his hands in his pockets, shrugged his shoulders, and said okay, he'd ride along.

Andy grinned at Eli when he changed his shirt.

"Might be someone you notice, huh?"

"Dat, stop it."

And both were silent. Both knew the implications of his words. How was one to think of a future in an unusual situation like this? Would he stay alone? Would he ever fit in, or be considered one who could choose a girl and marry her if the law of the day would not grant them a license to marry?

For the first time in his life, Andy fully realized the choice his wife had made to rejoin the Amish—the right choice for herself, no doubt in his mind—but what about her son? He mulled this over in his mind until he came up with the conclusion of Eli leaving the Amish culture and becoming integrated *mit die ausry* (with the outsiders). He would have to do that if he wanted to marry a dark-skinned girl.

Ah, May. His sweet wife and her terrible, tangled past. How innocent and alone, the day their parents died, how cruelly rejected by relatives, sent to Arkansas to fall prey to the unbridled Melvin Amstutz, to escape her unbearable situation with a black man. And still her heart longed for the home of her family here in Ohio.

Well, he could not worry about things that would not happen now, might never occur at all. He was not one to be bothered by fear of the future, always able to let his days meander past like a quiet stream. But he loved Eli, wanted what was best for him. He had loved seeing him grow into a tall young man, and now—or soon—he would need friends, a circle of young men and women with whom he could plan a future. He hoped May was not keeping her own concerns from him, the way she seemed preoccupied at times.

They rode to town that day, bounced high up on the spring wagon seat in the glorious sunshine, the gladiolus blooming profusely in

Annie Mast's roadside garden, groundhogs scuttling along to dive into the entrance of their burrows. Robins and sparrows chirped on fence posts and Holstein cows lifted their heads to watch them go by, their lower jaws constantly moving even as they watched.

"Old Roman Amstutz needs some help on his place," Andy observed, pointing in the direction of a small white house, the lawn unkempt, a goat tethered to a stake beside it. "I'll have to talk to a couple of men, see if we can get some of us together."

"How old is he? Is he the one who sits up front sleeping all day?" Eli asked with a small grin.

"He's probably in his upper nineties. He's pretty close to a hundred years old. Still does his own dishes and laundry, they say. He only has one daughter left, and she isn't as healthy as her father."

"Wow. I'd hate being that old."

"Many of us never get to live here on earth that long."

"Yeah."

There was a long pause, the only sound the rattle of the steel wheels on gravel, the sound of clopping hooves and the jingling of snaps and buckles on the leather harness.

Then Eli spoke suddenly. "I'll probably be shot."

Andy turned quickly. "Why would you say such a thing?"

"I'm dark-skinned. White people don't like us living the same way they do."

"Where did you learn that?"

Eli shrugged. "I read."

"Not all white people."

"Most of them."

"You'll be safe among the Amish. Everyone likes you here in our community."

"They don't, Dat."

"Who doesn't?"

"You'd be surprised."

Andy shook his head. It was hard to comprehend this fact. The thought of anyone disliking Eli because of his skin color was beyond his understanding. Eli was the most likable person Andy knew of, one with amazing talents for a boy of fifteen, always happy, his sunny smile a bright spot on the farm, in Andy's life. But folks didn't know that. The color of a person's skin set one apart from the other, it was true, no matter how he, Andy, tried to deny it to Eli. There had been some changes since the days of slavery, sure, but there was a constant tension, a taut line of misunderstanding and mistrust that had never been God's plan. This was troubling to Andy, hearing Eli say it in those earnest tones, almost childlike in its simplicity. Sometimes he felt as if Eli were the adult, a young man with knowledge far beyond his years.

"I don't belong here, you know."

Andy stared straight ahead, went cold all over. He wanted to take hold of Eli's shoulders, shake some sense into him, deny it with his whole being, but how could he do it in the face of such a simple truth?

"You do belong to us, Eli."

"I want to find my family someday. I want to find my father's brothers and sisters, see where he lived and worked. I want to see the area in Arkansas where Mam and Uncle Oba lived."

"Maybe we can do that," Andy said, but his mouth was dry with fear, his heart heavy with the weight of Eli's truth.

As they neared the grocery store, Andy reined in the fast-trotting horse, turned to the hitching post, and hopped to the ground. A heavyset man with his straw hat pushed back on his head waved at Andy before going back to untying his horse.

"How's it going there, Andy?" he called, as he folded the neck rope and stuck it beneath the seat in the mud-splattered surrey.

"Good, good. We're busy, thankful for our health."

"Yup, yup. Hey, we got church at our place on Sunday. Why don't you bring the family? We need new faces sometimes. Bring some of your ministers. You do that."

He turned to Eli. "Hello there, young man."

Eli's smile was quick, a brilliant flash in his dark, handsome face. "Hello."

"You come along, you hear? We'd be glad to have you."

"See if Dat decides to go," Eli answered respectfully.

"Sure, sure. Hey, see you Sunday." With that, he heaved himself into the surrey, clucked to his horse, and was off with a spray of gravel.

Andy watched Eli's face, poked an elbow into his ribs. "Now looky there, Eli."

Eli nodded, grinned widely.

But in the grocery store collecting items for May, he was accosted by silence, long evaluating stares from a few heavyset women with black bonnets and tight-sleeved dresses, their mouths grim with disapproval, a fact completely unnoticed by the affable, well-meaning Andy.

At the feed store, Eli's most dreaded place, the taunts were ribald, thrown out without reserve. His breath came quickly, but he held his head high. He imagined this was how the gladiators felt, facing fierce adversity in an enclosed arena, crowds roaring in approval as the fighting commenced.

"Hey there, Andy!"

"Brought Rufus, didja?"

Rufus. The name was a slang word for every black man who worked the fields.

"Easy there, Bill," Andy said evenly.

An uncomfortable silence ensued, rife with unspoken questions, full of the distaste the common white race held for one like Eli, especially one wearing the plain garb of the Amish.

Andy walked up to the counter while Eli waited uncomfortably, his hands thrust into this trouser pockets, his eyes on the tops of his shoes.

Bill, however, would not be deterred. "So whatcha plan on doing with Rufus? Marry him off to some white girl and raise a buncha halfbreeds?" A sneer accompanied the glittering yellow eyes.

A few men shook their heads, grunts of disapproval followed.

"Shut up, Bill. For once in your life, shut your mouth."

Andy listened, his back turned as he paid for his purchases. Then in a half-dozen strides, he confronted Bill, shoved his face into the now startled one of the offender.

"I have never heard anything quite as hurtful as that comment. You need to take responsibility for your cruelty and apologize."

Another sneer, an uttered oath.

Andy forgot all his teachings, forgot non-resistance, forgot where he was or who was watching. In one swift move, he grabbed the shirt-front of the unsuspecting Bill, shoved his face as close as possible, and ground out the demand for an apology.

"Say it. Now."

He brought back one of his huge fists, leaving Bill with no reason to think it would not be brought squarely into his nose.

He managed a stammered "sorry," his eyes rolling in his head, a line of spittle forming along the corners of his mouth.

Eli nodded, turned away, deeply ashamed of the whole unfortunate scene. Andy wasn't finished, but stood, telling everyone in the feed store if he ever heard another remark like that, they could expect something worse than what he'd done to Bill.

And they believed him. The incident was talked about for weeks, some snorting and saying so much for the peaceful Amish. What a joke. Others said Andy Weaver had every right to put Bill in his place, the way he loved that boy—he couldn't stand aside and allow that kind of evil to go on unchecked.

Andy had a long talk with Eli that day, his words mixed into the soft breeze and the smell of the pine trees and wild roses clinging to the stone fence by the side of the road. And Eli felt cherished and protected, knew a fierce devotion to his stepfather, felt the wonder of a love from a pure heart, which shored up the growing foundation of his own Christian life.

CHAPTER 13

OF COURSE MAY TOOK UP THE INVITATION TO ATTEND church at a neighboring district, her eyes shining at the prospect. She opened her sewing machine and cut a new navy blue dress for herself and robin's egg blue ones for Lizzie and Fronie. She soaked Andy and Eli's white shirts in lye soap and homemade bluing until they were so white they seemed a bit blue. She polished shoes, ironed the freshly washed coverings, and brushed the black wool hats. She hummed as she worked, looking forward to the social gathering after lunch, perhaps receiving an invitation to a friend's house for the evening meal. She smiled, thinking how Andy had accepted the invitation for her sake, knowing how much she loved to socialize now that she was fully incorporated into the Amish church, her past a distant blur, a mere forgotten shadow for most folks around her. Except for the few with a grudge against all manner of diversity, anyone who did not fully conform to their own rigid idea of righteousness.

Her small feet worked the cast-iron pedal up and down, the needle flashing as it stabbed repeatedly in the fabric, sewing a straight line down the center of a seam. She had to add a half inch to the sides of her dress pattern, but she smiled about that, too. She loved to cook for her big husband—and cook she did, using up the rich cream from the dairy, her own butter and buttermilk. She made sponge cakes and angel food cakes with the leftover egg whites after making her own noodles with the golden yolks. Every mound of creamy mashed potatoes was drizzled with foaming browned butter, every noodle dish enhanced with it. She baked bread twice a week, made butter-horn rolls and sandwich rolls. Flaky pie crusts were filled with seasonal fruit or rich custard made with whole milk, sugar, and eggs, a dark topping of cinnamon sprinkled with a lavish hand.

When Gertie died so long ago, she had learned to cook by trial and error, alone in the dark kitchen with the damp humidity of the Mississippi Delta clinging to every bread and pie dough, her face gleaming with drops of perspiration in the airless room. And Melvin had smacked his lips and eaten without complaint.

Her smile vanished as her thoughts picked up the thread of her past, but she soon broke into song, a trick she had taught herself years ago. When the sad, looming shadows descended, she praised God through the words of old hymns, which always brought rest for her soul. "Then in my dreams I'd be, nearer my God to Thee, nearer my God to Thee, nearer to Thee." She hummed along to the rhythm in her head, in her heart, felt the black clouds drift away like wind-pushed fog, the peace and calm returned.

THEY DID CHORES hurriedly, ate the oatmeal and egg sandwiches quickly, then dressed in their Sunday finery. Eli's shirt was pressed to perfection, dazzlingly white, and his black vest and trousers fit his tall form well. He stood taller than most of the boys his age, with a face that grew steadily more handsome as he matured.

Andy watched as he combed his hair in the small mirror above the sink, his eyes twinkling back at Eli.

"What?" Eli asked.

"Nothing." But he kept smiling.

It was not considered proper to heap words of praise on children, for fear of exploding vanity, creating a *grosfeelich* (proud) person who was in danger of ruining his own soul with lofty attitudes. Much better to teach them what true humility was, a humble view of their own nature, knowing well the ways of the sins of man.

They all piled on the two-seated spring wagon, the brown Standardbred named Sam drawing them along with his head held high, his satiny coat gleaming from Andy's prolonged brushing. The harness was cleaned and oiled, the spring wagon washed with buckets of soapy water and the garden hose. To attend services at a neighboring district meant there had been a bit more attention to detail than usual. They were not a *sloppich* (sloppy) family, but one who knew the virtues of cleanliness and hard work.

The morning was scented with the sweet smell of honeysuckle vines growing rampant across board fences or along the small locust trees by the side of the road. May inhaled deeply, lifted her face to catch Andy's smile.

"Love that smell," she murmured, tucking Junior a bit more safely into her arms.

He responded with a wave of his chubby arms, a wriggle of his strong little body, wanting down from her lap to stand gripping the dashboard. But May told him *no* quite firmly, knowing it simply wasn't safe. One sideways lurch and he could easily tumble out of the spring wagon, an incident completely unthinkable.

The farm where services were held was nestled among sloping farmland, the corn with heavy stalks and wide deep green leaves like a rippling sea of promise. The alfalfa had been cut once, like a good haircut, but was growing back in small, brilliantly colored green leaves. A prosperous farm always gave them reason to lift their hearts in gratitude to the Giver of all goodness.

Black surreys and two-seated spring wagons were moving in the long, winding drive, joining the ranks of the parked ones spread out along the large white barn and outbuildings. People clad in plain garb walked along the sidewalk or milled about close to the forebay of the barn where the men stood, greeting one another with hearty handshakes and friendly smiles. A beautiful morning, a time to congregate with loved ones, fill the soul with spiritual food for the coming week.

It was only when Eli was helping Andy unhitch the horse from the spring wagon that Andy saw the growing anxiety. Eli's nostrils were slightly extended, his mouth parted as his breathing sped up, his eyes wide with concern.

Ach my, Andy thought. *Does the poor boy suffer more than we know?* He felt the weight of responsibility.

But there was nothing to do. Eli could not always be protected by his father the way he had been at the feed store. Here, among his people, Eli was on his own in the morning before church services. He was alone, in his dark skin, standing tall, a magnet for curious looks or mean and uncouth remarks.

May's trusting heart, her inherent belief in the goodness of others, smoothed the way to be among a group of Amish folks like herself, believing everyone would always be kind, in spite of having gone through many experiences herself that contradicted this belief. But Eli was older now, a handsome young man with a ready smile, kindness toward everyone. Surely those traits would win over the hardest of hearts.

As it was, the displays of friendliness and generosity did win over the curious onlookers, many of them having heard of the *scwottsa boo* (black boy). But here he was, standing in front of them, his skin like dark honey, his hair tightly curled and as black as midnight. Polite glances were directed his way, a few curious ones longer than a glance, but no one could summon the courage to speak to him.

Eli stood alone, a half smile on his face. He tried to listen and feel a part of the scattered conversation. The group of boys and young men grew as more came to join them, all waiting together to be called upon to enter the house in a timely fashion. He felt poked and prodded. He felt as if an invasion of stares accosted him like a swarm of bees. His heart raced as his eyes blurred. He told himself to get over it, gather himself together. *Don't mind them,* he thought. *They probably don't know what to say either.*

He watched pigeons flapping their wings as they launched themselves off the peak of the barn roof. He thought how alike they all were, with only a variation of soft-hued feathers. He looked around, took notice of various shades of skin, all white. Blond hair, brown, or black, a redhead, but all to top off the normal white skin. *Birds of a feather*, he thought.

Who am I?

A raven. A crow. An imposter.

He felt his breath come in short puffs, felt the dryness of his lips. Why had he agreed to this?

Then, he was confronted by a tall form. A hand was thrust in his direction. Bewildered, Eli raised his eyes. He met dark eyes, as dark as his own, with a mild curiosity and the warmth of his smile.

"Hi! You must be Andy Weaver's Eli."

"I am."

The hand had a firm grip, taking him by surprise. His own hand felt weak, limp, and he was embarrassed by this.

"I've heard about you."

Eli raised his eyebrows, nodded, then lowered his eyes, suddenly quite self-conscious. He could not imagine the hearsay would have been good. He did not know how to respond to this, so he said nothing.

"I'm John. John Troyer. Are you sixteen yet?"

Eli shook his head.

"I just turned sixteen," John said, "so I run around."

Eli nodded, caught the twinkle of amusement in John's eye.

"Running around" was the English translation of *rumschpringa*, which seemingly included a broad spectrum of activities. There was always the Sunday evening German hymn singing, the gathering of youth at the same farm at which church services had been held. Long tables with benches on each side were set up in large rooms, the girls leading the way to be seated and begin the songs of praise. It was a good way for a young man to choose a girl he felt drawn to, as he covertly watched from behind the cover of a German hymnbook.

But that was only the tip of the many and widespread activities that abounded among the youth of the plain people. The "singing" was, of course, endorsed and approved of by every parent, a tradition that came from the early 1800s. But as in all of human nature, there were those with sharp consciences, careful, willing to obey, who never gave their parents reason to believe they would do anything offensive or immoral. Then there were those who never went into the house to help with the singing, but sneaked around outside, lifting warm bottles of beer hidden beneath buggy seats, lowering their heads to light cigarettes with stolen kitchen matches, vices they cared about much more than the singing.

These more liberal characters enjoyed the company of the "fast" girls, the ones whose hair was a bit more loose and wavy, the ones whose coverings were pushed back to show more of their hair and ears, the hems of their dresses quite a bit shorter than the obedient ones.

Some of them were allowed to have a Victrola in their bedrooms, the strains of Hank Williams heard softly from below. Sometimes a parent's eyes would shine with the remembered beat and he'd go to the bottom of the stairs and say, "Play 'Maple on the Hill,' Emmy." In these households the boys were allowed upstairs in the girls' rooms on Saturday night, where they played card games or sneaked away to a forbidden picture show in town, taking the girls who traded their plain clothing for sweaters and brightly designed poodle skirts, with bobby socks and brown-and-white saddle shoes, their hair caught up in a high ponytail.

It all came under the one word. *Rumschpringa.*

The couples who shyly dated within the rules of the parents became couples who entered marriage already well-versed in the ways of giving up one's own will, who loved God and their partner. The often raised a large brood of children with fairness, love, and discipline, became the bedrock of the community, the husbands ordained to the ministry, the children usually obedient as they built the church, generation after generation down through the years.

The more liberal, disobedient ones often suffered more of the setbacks, the way self-willed people will do. Eventually, they settled into the roles required of them, but would always dress their children in slightly fancier clothes, their consciences having been lulled into complacency at a young age. They all lived together with various levels of conservative views, the most important thing being learning to live in peace and harmony. It wasn't easy for any of them to pull out the beams in their own eyes, as the scripture says, before trying to help others pull out the splinters in theirs.

Then there was the matter of forgiveness, of dealing with ordinary troubles that crop up out of nowhere, sometimes needing wise intervention from the ministers or the bishop. But the driving force that kept them together was the love for God and fellow pilgrims, a contentment to adhere to rules and live in peace.

"So, where do you live?" John asked.

"Over closer to Oakley."

"Okay, yeah. We probably don't live too far apart, then."

Eli cleared his throat, unsure what he should say to that.

"I mean, you'll be looking for someone to accompany you to the singing on Sunday evening after you turn sixteen, won't you? I mean, two is always better than one, right?"

Eli nodded, met John's eyes, saw the friendliness and compassion before he allowed a slow grin to spread across his face, his white teeth and delighted eyes the start of a friendship.

Eli walked into the house behind John, sat beside him on the hard bench, and kept his gaze lowered to avoid the stares of the congregation. Many of them kept their eyes averted, out of duty, respectfully pretending there was nothing out of the ordinary. On some faces there were compressed lips, hidden disapproval; on others, the bright, open looks of love and acceptance.

He couldn't remember when exactly he spied her, or even if it was that day in church. He just knew he had to continue to catch a glimpse of her occasionally, like a necessary drink of water to keep him alive. At fifteen, he knew next to nothing about girls or dating or marriage; he just knew she looked like an angel, or at least the prettiest girl he had ever seen.

She sat quietly, her head lowered, her eyes to the hymnbook. She was as dark-haired as he was, with startling green eyes and skin tanned to a golden color, dressed in a quiet shade of gray. When she looked up, his eyes met hers unexpectedly. Both looked away quickly, but desperately wanted another glance, another stab at reality.

After the hymns were sung, the short sermon that followed seemed to float in and out of Eli's hearing and understanding. He struggled to comprehend what the minister was saying, felt a sense of shame. By the time the lengthy second sermon was over, he felt a deep misery, a catapult into an outer galaxy where he had no control over his destination.

He remembered to pray, a fervent request that God would direct his footsteps. He had no idea what had occurred, if anything, and so went about his days as usual. But he knew she had entered his life, and nothing would be the same.

Eli talked to May about this, in a joking kind of way, Andy joining into the teasing conversation with his good humor. But it was later that evening when May cried on Andy's shoulder, and he held her close to comfort her.

A union of two people of different races was simply not done. The United States government deemed it illegal, a blatant disrespect to the order of God, and therefore prohibited. So May knew the chances of Eli staying within the fold of the Amish was hardly possible, and this she would have to face bravely.

"But Andy," she sighed.

"What, my dear heart?"

"How can he enter the main society after having been raised in this ... this plain community? He'll always be caught between the two."

Long into the night, they spoke of Eli's future, but neither one came to a peaceful conclusion. They decided to cast all their cares on God alone, pray for strength to face whatever He chose to put them through.

HE REACHED HIS sixteenth birthday. May baked his favorite chocolate cake, spread the vanilla icing all around it, swirled expertly until it resembled a cake in the Betty Crocker cookbook. She made his favorite supper of chicken and mashed potatoes with filling and gravy, served a huge slice of the cake on his plate while they all sang "Happy Birthday." The three children clapped their hands and sang boisterously, without reserve. Eli joined in the festive mood, thanking his parents for the open courting buggy and the horse that would now belong to him.

John Troyer remained his true friend, the way he had promised. There was never any mention of his race, his past, nothing, but a simple acceptance of Eli himself. So on the first Sunday evening Eli attended the singing, he watched in fascination as John drove in with a girl beside him on the roofless courting buggy.

He blinked, drew the back of his hand across his eyes to clear his vision, but he knew it was her. The girl in church at the neighboring community. Eli was dressed in his Sunday best, a pale blue shirt with black trousers and vest, his hat pulled low to an attractive angle. When he climbed up onto the single seat, she met his gaze, smiled a genuine smile of welcome, before saying in a low voice, "Hello, Eli."

"Hello."

"This is Mattie, my sister."

"Your sister? I had no idea. I remember seeing you in church a while ago."

"I remember you too."

"I'm not easy to miss," he said with a small laugh.

She smiled but said nothing.

The seating arrangement on a courting buggy was a bit primitive at best, with only enough space for two seated side by side. When a third person was present, there were two options. One was for the two who were seated to slide their knees to one side, allowing the third passenger, usually the driver, to perch on the small space allotted him, or simply to sit on one knee of each one, which seemed to work best. Eli sat beside Mattie, and John perched on top of both, looked back, and grinned mischievously.

"I'm not quite two hundred pounds," he said.

The horse trotted willingly, the hooves pounding the macadam, the sweet breath of summer air creating a longing in Eli, a feeling of sadness he could not name. With this girl beside him, why would he feel that now? And yet, he knew.

He had John as his helper, his armor against the open taunts from a few of the less polite, the ones who viewed him with contempt.

Harry Mast was older, well past his twenty-first year, a bit of a bully, a heavy smoker and liberal troublemaker. He had never joined the church, dated only the most liberal girls, and was the only one who never hid his bottle of beer from the girls. Of course, he was a leader to those who were like-minded, but to the ones with better morals, he was someone to avoid.

Before the singing began, the group of boys waited to go inside. Eli felt nervous, shy, unwilling to admit even to himself that he felt out of place, a tremendous thistle in a field of verdant wildflowers. He heard a loud snort, smelled the spray of cigarette smoke blown in his face.

"Aren't you a bit out of your territory, there, huh?"

Before Eli could answer, John spoke loud and clear. "Leave him alone, Harry."

"What are you, his personal bodyguard?"

"That's what I am, yes."

Harry came even closer to Eli, shoved his white pimply face closer. "Mammy's boy. Why don't you go to Loos-i-anna where you belong?"

"I'm from Arkansas. Or my mother is. I was born here."

"You may as well go back and join the rest of the darkies. Pick that cotton, why don't you?"

"Maybe I will. I haven't decided what I want to do yet. My father is a farmer."

"Your real father ain't nothin'. Black, that's all he is."

"My father is dead."

"Good."

"Cut it out, Harry. Give him a break now." This from John, who was getting jumpier by the minute.

Eli lifted a hand, said it was okay, he was used to being heckled.

"I'm not serious, you know," Harry said, trying to make a joke out of his botched attempt at angering Eli.

"You likely are, but there's nothing I can do about it," Eli said.

This remark brought Harry up short. His eyes opened wide in surprise. "You used to it or what?"

"Yeah."

"Huh. So how do you swallow that?"

"I don't always."

It seemed as if the first evening at the hymn singing was the mark of Eli's character, the way many of the young men spoke to him afterward. Some of them were a bit ill at ease, others were filled with admiration, and the start of real acceptance followed. He was known as Andy's Eli, friendly, full of good humor and a sense of fun, the beginning of his years with the *rumschpringa* off to a good start.

He cherished every word with Mattie, every ride home with the large John perched on one knee. When the autumn rains brought a chill to the air, the canvas tarp was brought up over the three of them, a woolen blanket underneath. And Eli felt he could have spent the rest of his life happily huddled there together.

ONE SUNDAY EVENING when the rain was scissoring in from the east, driven by the first cold blast of early winter, they raised the outsized black buggy umbrella, the only protection against winter's harsh conditions. Eli was in charge of the unwieldy thing, hanging on to the carved wooden handle to tilt it in the right direction. With the trotting horse, the wind's power was tripled, so Eli needed to be alert to the slightest tugging of the umbrella, knowing how easily it could turn inside out, leaving the huddled occupants of the buggy exposed to the elements.

Mattie's face was lowered, her black bonnet hiding much of it. In horror, Eli noticed the water dripping steadily off the umbrella and onto her shoulder, surely soaking through to her clothing. His first concern was keeping her dry, so he forgot the tilt of the umbrella for only an instant, resulting in a *phwoop* of sound, a snap of metal parts, and the umbrella blew inside out, leaving them exposed to the hard, cold, slanting rain hitting their faces like small knives.

John yelled, Mattie shrieked, and Eli was mortified. How could he have allowed this to happen? He berated himself repeatedly, apologizing above the sound of driving, splashing rain, the clopping of hooves, and the grinding of steel-clad wheels on macadam.

"Nothing to do about it now, Eli. We'll get to your place soon."

Eli nodded and hung onto the ruined umbrella, then cast a sideways glance at Mattie, who had her head almost to her lap to ward off the worst of the deluge.

"Are you alright?" he shouted.

She responded with a quick nod, a bright smile with her face streaming water.

"Wet!" she shouted back and laughed out loud, the sound of tinkling bells and cymbals.

Eli could have fainted with relief and gratitude.

He insisted they come in and warm themselves, saying he'd get them some dry outerwear and another umbrella. He made cocoa with his mother's chocolate mixture, served it in thick mugs, and watched Mattie's expression as the warmth returned to her cheeks. John teased Eli about his umbrella skills. But it was in a good way.

May heard them in the kitchen, wrapped her warm housecoat around herself, and went to see if she could be of assistance.

"Sorry to wake you, Mam," Eli said.

Mattie's mouth literally hung open in surprise. This small blonde-haired woman was his mother? How could it be? How was anything like this possible? He towered over her, tall and dark, well, yes, almost black, with features very unlike his mother.

The kitchen was warm, the teakettle hummed quietly on the back of the stove, the hot cocoa warmed her soul. She spied the beauty of the red geraniums in coffee cans on the windowsill, caught the scent of flowery talcum powder, felt a sense of belonging as Eli exchanged a look with his mother.

The only thing that didn't seem to fit with the whole scene of warmth and love was the dark color of Eli's skin.

CHAPTER 14

E LI'S DAYS WERE FULL. EACH DAY WAS ANOTHER LESSON IN the way of the farm and he acquired skills quickly, steadily growing in the ways that counted as a good farm hand. Andy was always appreciative, swift to praise, slow to correct, which was a great boon to Eli's confidence. His days were filled with hard physical labor, and there was never a duty he didn't tackle willingly. He loved the heat of the sun, the odor of new-mown hay, the sound of clanking chains on harnesses, the great round hooves kicking up dust as they drew the farm equipment through the fields. He knew where the dangerous groundhog holes could present a threat if a horse's hooves went through, knew where the poisonous plants needed to be hoed away from fencerows. He had a quick mind, willing to see and absorb the necessary wisdom a good farmer would need to become successful.

In his sixteenth year, he appeared much older both in physical attributes and quiet knowledge. He was never tempted to run with the wild youth, thinking of the hurt and disbelief on his quiet mother's face, the disappointment on his kind father's. He endured unkind remarks with stoic courage, only occasionally getting rankled by Harry's persistent obnoxious comments.

He milked five cows every morning and evening, to Andy and May's four. He knew when every cow was due to freshen, watched at any time of day or night to confirm a successful birthing of a newborn calf. He cleaned the gutters in the cow stable, alongside Andy, and never tried to dodge the unsavory job. But his heart was not with the cows. He found the twice daily milking too repetitious, the exact demand on his time a duty he did not want to have his whole life. He had an avid interest in the massive-shouldered, loudmouthed farrier who came to the farm every few months, his great, rough voice bouncing off the rafters. He watched him set up his tools, build a hot, hot fire, shaping the horseshoes to precision. Here was a worthy talent. If he could be an apprentice . . .

As he performed his duties around the farm, he dreamed of becoming a mighty farrier, shoeing horses with ease, talking around the nails in his mouth, his shirt stained with dirt and the sweat of horses and his own body. But he never told Andy.

On a sizzling hot day, when the humidity made the nights long and uncomfortable, the farrier's green Dodge pickup rattled up to the barn. He unfolded his considerable length and width from behind the steering wheel and shouted for Andy without bothering to approach the house or place a knock on the door.

Eli rounded a corner of the barn, grinned, and said, "Hi."

"Hey there. Where's the boss?"

"There's a frolic at Yoni Weaver's."

"Barn raising?"

"No, they're actually taking the whole roof off, rafters and all, replacing the rotted timbers. Dat said it might be a dangerous job, and he needed me to stay here with you."

"Okay, okay." The farrier paused, looked straight into Eli's dark eyes, and asked how it came to be that he was an Amish negro.

"My mother . . . uh . . . my father was black."

"Was?"

"That's right . . . He died before I was born. Then my mother married Dat . . . Andy."

"Hm. Surprises me the Amish took you on."

There was no answer to that statement, so Eli remained silent.

Then, "So how's this going to go? You're gonna have to leave at some point. These plain folks won't allow you to marry a white girl."

Eli shook his head. "I don't know."

"'Course you know. It ain't gonna happen."

Eli turned away, called over his shoulder, "You want Duke or Fred?"

"Gimme Fred. He's easier on the back this early in the morning."

Fred followed Eli easily, keeping his head lowered as he was tied to the ring at the watering trough. He had been shod so many times, he knew there was nothing to fear, so he allowed his foot to be lifted as the farrier removed the cast iron shoes and sliced away at his hooves. The farrier built the fire to red hot coals in a bowl-like device, then proceeded to heat the new shoes, pounding them to the exact dimension on his anvil. Sweat ran off his face, his shirt already wringing wet, but he sang a bawdy song and grinned at Eli, who hovered over him, alert to every move he made.

"You'll get your nose pounded on this anvil," he shouted.

"Sorry." Eli backed away, embarrassed.

"You're curious? You wanna learn?"

His eyes shining, Eli nodded, smiling eagerly.

"It's a good profession, boy. Hardest work, but you can make a buck. You're built for it." He eyed Eli before bringing the hammer down with a thunderous blow. "You're gonna need a truck to get around."

"Couldn't I open a shop, people bring the horses?"

"Dunno how that would go down. Maybe the Amish. They could drive."

"You think it could work?"

"All you can do is try. I got more than enough work. Be glad to teach you."

A thrill ran though his veins. Here was a chance to prove himself as one capable of learning on his own, apart from the farm. It could perhaps be a glimpse into the world outside the farm. He longed to hear views and opinions, understand what went on in the world.

But when he told Andy about his dream, he was shocked to see the shadow of disapproval, the hurt and ensuing irritation. Except for that one time at the feed store, Eli had never seen or heard Andy raise his voice, and he had never experienced a moment's anger directed at him. So when he saw the expression in his eyes, he stepped away, leaned against the watering trough in the forebay of the barn and crossed his arms.

Andy set the pitchfork against the wall, his eyes searching Eli's face for a sign, anything to prove he was joking. "Come on, Eli," he said, serious.

"What?" A tinge of rebellion.

"Why would you want to leave the farm? You know I can't do without you."

"But why can't I have a chance to do something on my own?" He caught himself before he told Andy he could do whatever he chose, that he was not his son.

The spark of anger in Andy's eyes ignited the disappointment in Eli. It was all so sudden, coming on like a cyclone in the middle of a calm summer day. Andy felt Eli slipping away, tightened his grip on the friendly control he'd always had, the sense of panic rising. This was an unusual thing, this unexpected asking for something he was unwilling to give.

May noticed immediately.

The lack of a warm twinkle in her husband's blue eyes was plenty cause for alarm, but coupled with Eli's hooded eyes and angered countenance, it was very distressing. Her eyes pleaded with Andy, but when no reassurance was forthcoming, she turned her back and dished up the hot beef stew with shaking hands. She turned to set the bowl on the table, ready to receive Andy's bright smile, but her own slid off her face, leaving a question in her troubled eyes. She poured water, brought the dish of pickled red beet eggs, and sat with Fronie and Lizzie beside her on the bench.

"Junior is asleep," she said, quietly, her eyes going to Andy in bewilderment.

Without further ado, Andy bowed his head, the rest following suit for the quiet prayer. May's heart beat a staccato rhythm in her chest as she placed her fears on the throne of mercy. Now, after all this time, was she to be handed the limpid sheaves of her wrongdoing? *Oh God, have mercy.*

May, being the natural peacemaker, made nervous small talk, her glance going anxiously from face to face, hoping for a change of expression in both. The steaming beef stew turned dry in her mouth when Andy said calmly, "Eli thinks he wants to be a farrier."

"Oh?"

It was all May could say, knowing the helplessness her husband was experiencing. She cast a quick look on Eli's direction before taking up her glass and taking a sip of water.

"So what do you say?" Andy's voice was demanding, as if he was already accusing May of taking Eli's side in the argument.

May hesitated. She knew she wanted only the best for Eli—what he wanted, she wanted—but she felt the same about Andy, her husband, her confidant. Caught in the middle, she shrugged both shoulders, lifted her hands with palms up, and shook her head.

"I don't know. You need Eli."

"Of course I need Eli. I can't possibly go on farming without him." Eli's dark eyes flashed. "You can hire someone."

"Are you going to pay him?

"No."

Was it a flicker of fear in Andy's blue eyes, or was it naked disbelief? Calm, obedient Eli. To have him turn against his own wishes was beyond comprehension.

Then Eli spoke. He was calmer, sounding older than his years, and there was just a hint of bitterness in his voice. "You know I don't always want to be here on the farm. I like what I do here, but I can't depend on being the heir to this place. I don't know if I'll be able to stay in the future. Let's be honest—no Amish family is going to allow their white daughter to be married to me."

Andy bowed his head. May gave a small, sad cry.

"Oh, Eli. Don't say that. You're only sixteen."

"Mam, I thought about this since I was in school. You can't deny it."

So here it was. The burden of her sowing the seeds of sin. No matter the circumstances of her life with Melvin and Gertie Amstutz, her escape and time spent with Clinton would always have its repercussions, like a thrown stone in a still pool, the ripples going on and on through the generations. As she sat in the safety of her own farmhouse kitchen, surrounded by all the love and security she would ever need, she knew a moment of reckoning, knew she was caught in the helpless tide of her past. *Eli, Eli. Please don't say this to me. I can't accept this as the absolute, written-in-stone truth.*

The kitchen was so quiet, the sound of the ticking clock seemed deafening, the drip of the water faucet the sound of torture. May bowed her head as unbidden tears rose to the surface.

"I'm sorry, Mam. But this has to be faced. I won't be able to stay when the time comes for me to be married. You know as well as I do, marriage between black people and whites isn't legal."

"But you're not ready yet!" May burst out, tears streaming down her face.

"I'm preparing myself for when the time comes."

"After all we've done for you!" Andy shouted.

Lizzie and Fronie winced, then hid their faces in their hands. May shook her head, told the girls they were excused, said she thought Junior might be awake.

"Andy, please don't raise your voice," May begged. "We need to discuss this like adults and becoming upset won't help anything."

Andy looked at his wife's tear-stained face and said, "I'm sorry."

May gathered courage from that sincere statement, felt it rise in her heart as she gripped the tabletop. "I think Eli is right, Andy. You know he is."

"But maybe not. Maybe someone would accept him, as . . . as he is."

"As I am? How am I?"

Andy's eyes fell before Eli's. "You know what I mean."

"Say it."

"No . . . You're not completely black," Andy said, stumbling over the word.

"And if I were, would that make me even worse? Accepted even less?"

"Probably."

"And you think that is right? You think the color of my skin is how God will judge me at the end of my life."

"Of course not."

"Then why do men judge me? Why am I unfit to be a husband to a white woman?"

"Look, Eli. It's the law. It's the *ordnung* of our Amish church. We are not condemning the black race, just keeping the church the way God intended. Pure."

"So if I join the church, it would be a black stain on a pure white church? A shame and disgrace."

Andy looked defeated, weary. "I don't know."

"You do know. You don't have the nerve to say it."

May saw the flicker of anger before Andy rose to his feet, knocking the chair backward. He put both hands on the table, his great shoulders a hulking, formidable strength.

"If you obey us, you will stay here on the farm and forget all this nonsense."

And with that, he left the room, closing the door solidly behind him. Eli and May sat in silence after that. May's heart felt shattered, the heaviness in her chest enough to keep her from breathing. And gladly she would have succumbed to the utter weariness, the will to live an impenetrable mountain she had no energy to scale. It had come to this, and she was completely unprepared for the wretchedness.

"Mam."

"Yes, Eli?"

"I'm sorry."

"I know you are."

"Can you understand?"

"Yes."

As she had left, so long ago it seemed, so her son would leave. She had left out of sheer despair, could no longer abide the maelstrom of evil she had been subjected to, and would now have to bear the burden of her son's decision. As the handmaiden Hagar had been cast out by the jealous Sarah to roam the wilderness without understanding, so would her precious Eli be cast out, being of another race. But God knew. He had saved Hagar, heard her cry from the desert, where she had given up her son to die because of his thirst. And God heard her, had saved them. Hope welled up as she contemplated the story in the Old Testament, the lesson of Abraham and Sarah's impatience, after God had promised them a son. After years of no childbearing, Sarah had given Hagar to her husband, saying she was barren, and only later understood the folly of her actions. And yet, God had a perfect plan, had known all along how things would turn out, had known the handmaiden's son would be the beginning of a large and powerful race. A tribe who would always be at odds with the children of Israel.

In that moment, May realized she must let Eli go. In her heart, she had to release him to seek his own destiny. He had been conceived in sin, no matter how she had suffered at the hands of Melvin Amstutz. And yet, grace had been sufficient. She lived every day in the glory of her beloved Savior's forgiveness, never doubted the love that infused her days. But this, this parting was all a part of the sacrifice she had to make.

"Eli?"

"Hmm."

"Is there someone?"

"Yes."

"I was afraid of that."

For a few moments they sat together in silence.

"Mam, I'm happy here on the farm. If I was white, I would never leave. My home and heart are right here with you and Dat. I don't blame him for being upset."

"*Achy my.* You'll always be the same caring young boy we love. Somewhere, somehow, God will bless you. Now, are you planning to stay for a while yet?"

"Until I'm eighteen."

"Must you go? Can't you try and ... ?"

"Be alone for the rest of my life? I've thought about it. I don't know ..."

A long silence lay thickly between them, unspoken words steadily filling the space. May looked at the congealed beef stew, the slices of bread drying out on the plate, the unwashed dishes and laundry on the line, and knew a moment of unutterable sadness, a depression so thick and heavy she thought she would never be able to contain so much.

LIFE WENT ON. There was an apology, a return to the normal way of life, albeit with the thread of sadness standing out like a scarlet cord. The shadows May had so successfully overcome bunched up on the horizon and threatened to overtake the sweetness of Christ's love and forgiveness. But gradually, as the days went by and Andy and Eli worked side by side, the bitterness lessened. Andy's heart softened toward his son, this boy he had loved since the moment he fell in love with May. He started to feel an acceptance of Eli becoming a farrier, but he didn't tell Eli that. He intended to give it some time, see if Eli changed his mind.

ELI RESUMED HIS duties on the farm, kept his eye on the farrier's skill, and did what was expected of him.

John Troyer remained his friend, as did his sister Mattie, although she noticed the drawing away, the air rife with an icy chill she hadn't recognized before. It was mysterious, the way Eli's brown eyes avoided hers, the way he rarely included her in conversations.

Then, John came down with a severe case of strep throat and asked Eli to take his own team and pick up Mattie on Sunday evening. Would he do that for her? The request was based largely on

Mattie's broad hints, but Eli didn't need to know. They smiled, John and Mattie, their eyes shining a bit too brightly.

So Eli oiled his harnesses, brushed the best sorrel horse with the high-stepping gait, washed the black courting buggy, and shook the lap robes before deciding they smelled bad. He asked his mother to wash them in the wringer washer. Her eyes questioned him, but she did it anyway.

When he dressed with care, spending extra time by the wash basin in the kitchen, turning his face from side to side as he patted his hair with the palm of his hand, a wild hope rose in May, an erratic butterfly of *what if*. What if a miracle occurred? What if a genuine love would blossom, and the United States government and the Amish *ordnung* relaxed their views, and Eli could ask this Mattie Troyer and live peacefully among them, his coppery skin completely overlooked?

It had to be Mattie. There was no question.

But the shadows returned as he drove away. His suffering would only be worse if love were to blossom and then get stomped out by the rules they lived under. It all felt too cruel.

IN THE GOLDEN light of evening, Mattie Troyer was a vision of pure beauty. Eli drew in a soft breath and could not keep his eyes away from her perfectly heart-shaped face, the smooth black hair tucked beneath the white covering, the gladness in her emerald green eyes. He found himself short of breath, as if he had run to the Troyer farm, then realized his voice came out hoarse, garbled, the words falling haphazardly.

"Good evening, Eli," she said warmly.

He held the light lap robe to one side as she sprang lightly into the buggy, then reached across her lap to tuck it into the side. He quite despaired at the intimacy, the closeness of these narrow courting buggies, her presence awakening every thought he had of her. She was all he could ever ask for, all he would ever want but knew he could never have.

"How was your week, Eli?"

"Good. Busy. The crops are productive this summer, with all the rain."

"Yes. We're kept busy harvesting from the garden." She gave a rueful laugh. "I don't care if I never see another string bean."

A deep sadness welled up in him. He could smile, nod his head, think of some banal, worthless answer, but it did nothing for the heaviness in his chest. Too late, he realized the mistake of having agreed to pick her up, to ride alone in the achingly beautiful evening, when every climbing wild rose proclaimed its love, the scent of hollyhocks and wild primrose speaking of two hearts destined to be torn apart.

"You're being quiet, Eli."

"Sorry. Just thinking, I guess."

"A penny for your thoughts."

"It'll cost a lot more than a penny."

"Try me."

He turned to look at her, saw the invitation, the sincerity . . . and what was that look from her eyes? Like a deep, quiet pool, suddenly sent into choppy, restless wavelets. He knew it was against his conscience, against all well-ordered teaching, but he looked deep into those agitated eyes and asked, "How much do you want to go to the hymn singing?"

She answered with her steady gaze that spoke volumes of feeling, then slowly shook her head. "Not much."

He shook his head, as if acknowledging he was going against everything he knew was good and right. "We need to talk. Could we go to the park in Oakley, perhaps tie the horse and go for a walk?"

"It's alright with me." But her voice sounded husky, too quiet, as if every word was an effort.

"You sure?"

"I'm sure."

The road to Oakley was interminable, endless, the silence hanging above and around them, taking away the air they breathed. Mattie plucked nervously at the clean lap robe, kept her eyes downcast, the safety zone they both recognized.

There were dim electric lights surrounding the large grassy area complete with a baseball diamond, swings and slides, a pavilion with picnic tables, a perimeter of fir and oak trees. After tending to the horse, they walked slowly along the bike path surrounding the area, twilight turning everything into an object of perfect beauty. The absence of sunlight hid the weeds, the bare spots in the mown grass.

Still he could not find the proper words to discuss what was in his heart. The walk was completed in silence, both of them breathing too fast, as if they had run the entire way. When Eli sat down on the grass, he lowered his head as she sat beside him.

"You must think I have lost my mind."

"No, not at all. I . . ."

"I know. You're waiting till I work up the nerve to talk, but I'm not sure I can."

"Do you want me to try?"

"I don't know. There's just so much to say, and so little that can be said."

Suddenly, he took her hand, placed it on his knee, then placed his own beside it. For a long moment, neither one spoke. She felt the soft fabric of his dress trousers, the warmth of his hand beside hers. She turned her face to his, a question in her deep green eyes.

"Do you see, Mattie? There is our problem."

She nodded, coughed a little. She could not speak.

"My hand is black, yours is white." Slowly, he placed his hand over hers, then gathered it into his own.

She said quickly. "Not very black. Mine is tanned. Not very white."

He turned her hand over, revealing the white underside, then his own, which was decidedly lighter than the top, but still much darker than hers.

"Do you think there is something to be done about the difference in the color of our skin?"

"I don't know."

A thin sliver of the moon rose in the afterglow of the setting sun, like the thin sliver of hope that was banished by her words.

CHAPTER 15

Eli told her of the circumstances of his birth, the desperation driving his mother to Clinton, the black man from Arkansas who had befriended her. He told her of his father's sad death, his preceding spiral into alcohol, the hard times his mother had experienced before returning to her roots.

Night had fallen, the only available light from the dim yellow pole lights surrounding the area, the appearance of myriad stars, and the remaining sliver of the moon. Fireflies blinked across the grassy field, turning the ordinary into a magical landscape.

"But . . ." Mattie faltered.

"What? Go on."

"If the Amish community accepted your mother with her . . . um . . . baby, why can't they accept you now?"

"They do. I can never get married, is all."

"So what is your solution?"

"There are two. Stay Amish, remain single all my life. Go out into the world and find a nice girl with skin the color of mine. I'm black, Mattie."

"But only half."

"That doesn't matter. I'm not the right color to marry a white girl."

Mattie sighed, a sound as light as a moth settling on a flower. "I could go with you."

The announcement was unexpected, a thought Eli had never considered. To bring such heartache to an ordinary conservative family would be the epitome of selfishness. Blatant unkindness.

"I would never ask you to do that."

"I know you wouldn't. You're much too thoughtful. You're the kindest person I know."

"You don't know me very well."

"But I do. I have spent many Sunday evenings with you."

"I suppose you have."

"So, if we were both white—or both black—would I have a chance with you?" Mattie asked unexpectedly.

She knew it was too bold, but felt him slipping away into the vast unknown. When Eli didn't answer, she looked at him, found him with a troubled expression, a hard line of strength in his jaw.

"What am I suppose to say to that? We both know it's impossible."

"Just say yes or no, then we'll get into the buggy and go home."

"Of course I would ask you to be my girl. I have never had a moment's admiration for anyone else. From the first time I saw you, you have had a special place in my thoughts."

"But not your heart."

"I have never allowed you to enter. I can't do that."

She nodded, understood what he meant, having found herself in the same position numerous times. "Well, Eli, we're not going to solve anything by sitting here with our wishes. Things will likely never change, so if we want to be honorable upright citizens and obedient members of the Amish church, then I guess we're pretty much doomed to accept our fate."

He nodded.

Then, "Do you believe in prayer? Do you believe God answers prayer if we ask in faith, Eli?"

"I do, yes."

"Then why don't we both ask God to guide us? To help us?"

"When we already know the answer, should we keep on asking in case He may have changed his mind?"

Mattie laughed, but it was a sad sound of pretended mirth.

"I have to tell you before we go. I'm leaving next week. My mind is made up after tonight. I can't live here, knowing we don't have a future together."

She caught her breath. "Do you have to go? Can't you stay, and we'll still be able to see each other? Talk to each other?"

"It will only become more painful. The temptation to do the wrong thing will only increase. You know we both need to find the courage to put our feelings behind us, and God can bless us in other ways we can't understand now."

Eli convinced himself as he spoke, shored up the foundation of self-denial, until she began to weep so softly and delicately it felt like a dagger in his heart.

"Don't cry, Mattie. I'm not worth it. I'll be gone, and you'll find someone new, someone you never imagined you could love." He got to his feet to keep from pulling her into his arms, to erase the tears trembling on her eyelids. "Come, Mattie. We'll go home now. Forget about this evening. I never should have picked you up in the first place."

He did not help her to her feet, and offered no assistance to reach the buggy, but strode ahead, a tall, broad-shouldered figure intent on choosing the way of righteousness, to trod the narrow path with his heavy cross laid squarely on his shoulders.

She called out before he reached the horse. "Eli!"

He stopped, turned partway.

With a broken cry, she reached him, stood very close, put both hands on his forearms.

"This can't be it. I can't believe this will be the last time I will ever see you. I don't want anyone else. I will never love again, I don't care what you say, or they say. Whoever they are. I want you, and only you. I love your dark skin and your kindness, your curly hair, and your . . . your . . ."

Her voice faded away as she fell against him. He felt her hands leave his arms, felt the absence of her presence, and almost, he did the right thing, shook her off and walked away. Her words numbed his resolve, and he shook, as helpless as a dying leaf in a stiff gale.

"Don't, Mattie. Don't."

But his empty arms were filled with her supple body, as she pressed against him. Her arms came like strong bands around his waist, and with a groan, he lowered his face to her upturned one, her eyes luminous in the half light of the pole lamps.

"Kiss me just this once," she whispered through her tears.

Both of them could not have been prepared for the beauty of the meeting of their hearts. Eli was shaken to the core, finding her mouth repeatedly giving him the assurance of her love, her devotion. She awakened the face of his staunch denial, which he surrendered gladly, and loved her with every atom of his being. The sweetest, most satisfying declaration of a forbidden love, but only for a short time before they realized this was an indulgence which brought on the pain of their parting.

And still they clung to each other.

"I can't let you go," he whispered hoarsely.

A muffled cry was his answer, before she renewed her grasp on his waist.

THE HOUR WAS very late when Mattie's worried mother heard the rasp of steel buggy wheels on gravel. She breathed a sigh of relief, rolled over, and punched her pillow before becoming sleepy and relaxed. Thank goodness Mattie had finally come home. It was way later than usual.

THE KNOWLEDGE OF Eli's leaving didn't reach Mattie's mother till Friday when she shopped at the market in Oakley, but coupled with the news of her daughter's absence from the hymn singing and the late arrival on Sunday evening, the mother of many teenagers put two and two together. She had a talk with Mattie about the circumstances surrounding the past Sunday evening and was met with a flaming outburst of denial and told to mind her own business.

She berated herself for not having nipped this in the bud way back when it bothered her to see Mattie going away with that black Eli, and now here she was with all these imagined scenes roiling around in her head.

She knew Mattie cried in her room, had found crumpled handkerchiefs under her pillow, had seen her red-rimmed eyes. But she figured if he truly had left them the way Sam Ada had said, well then, she'd get over him. She couldn't bear to hear the truth, anyway, thinking of the awful mother she might have been, after all, her daughter falling low enough to actually consider black Eli. Well, he wasn't really black, but certainly not white, either.

She was deeply relieved he had left.

THE WEAVERS FOUND a handwritten note, the bed neatly made, and the brown suitcase missing along with a few changes of clothes. May was beside herself, weeping softly when no one was around, begging Andy to go after him.

Andy was overwhelmed with the responsibility of having all the farm work dumped on his shoulders. Lizzie stepped up and took on the milking Eli used to do, but that did not help with the dozens of other chores surrounding him. He wavered between pity for May, outrage against Eli, self blame, and a kind of crippling humility. The day he so gladly accepted Eli as his own, he could not have foreseen this sad end to having him as a beloved son. And he had been beloved. He had.

He justified himself to May, reminded her of the good times, of which there were plenty, but somehow could never quite get past the barrier of how he responded to Eli's idea of apprenticeship as a farrier.

Andy sat in the living room, his elbows resting on his big knees, his head bent as he listened to the soft heartbroken sounds of weeping, May curled on the opposite side of the sofa, the girls and Junior sound asleep upstairs. He wanted to take her into his arms, freely, the way he had always done, but knew he might only be tolerated, not accepted.

"May," he choked out.

There was no response.

"Please. Don't blame me. He would eventually have left anyway. It was that Mattie Troyer. He couldn't be here because of her."

"Don't, Andy. Don't say that. He could have at least stayed nearby if . . ." She didn't finish.

And Andy could only hang his head. He knew he could not comfort his wife, the way she felt he had failed Eli. She believed he had not loved Eli enough. And perhaps he hadn't. But the cold, hard truth had nothing to do with love, and everything to do with social laws, what the world considered right or wrong. Rules. Would he allow Lizzie or Fronie to marry someone of another race? Hard questions with no easy answers.

The crumbling of the complete trust between Andy and May, the devotion they took for granted, was harder for Andy than anything else. And he could not help being slightly aggravated at Eli for having disrupted the almost perfect peacefulness of his life on the farm with May. And at times, he felt a kind of self-hatred for having been caught unprepared, using blunt force in the face of feeling helpless. Blunt force in the way he had handled Eli's simple desire to learn the farrier trade. He might as well have hit him with a club.

May simply wept, wasting away in her pool of sorrow and fear, the hovering shadows completely taking over, snatching away her abiding faith in the goodness of God. Inwardly, she railed against the Amish *ordnung*, the US government, every law and ritual ever invented, then fell into a deep repentance, sitting in a spiritual heap of ashes dressed in spiritual sackcloth.

She read and reread the letter Eli wrote, filled with his love and appreciation, never blaming anyone. He had to accept his fate, so he would be traveling back to Arkansas to find his family, make a home, a name for himself as an experienced farrier. He wished them well and would return for a visit as soon as he was able.

How suddenly this had all come upon them, May thought. How unfair to have it dumped on her shoulders without warning. But still, she supposed the warnings had been there all along, only covered completely by a refusal to see and understand God's law.

Or was it God's law? Who made these rules? Her mind never rested, but sought ways to get around this horrible sense of loss. Without realizing it herself, she had doubled her loss by shutting out her beloved Andy, placing blame, pitying herself, which is the most often used fault of human nature.

May was not perfect, in spite of being an inspiration to those around her, a rare light of being the keeper of a serene and loving home. Andy gave her space to overcome the debilitating heartache before trying to work on their own broken trust. It was only after they cried together, allowed forgiveness to do its healing duty, that their lives were restored to the times of peace and happiness. The sun shone again, although with an even more generous light than before. Although they always keenly felt the absence of Eli's kind, sturdy presence.

HE CAME HOME after two years and nine months, on a brisk March morning when May was upstairs painting Lizzie's room a muted shade of pink, a color that suited the growing young girl's fancy, a fact that delighted May, allowed her to revel in the joy of having daughters.

She was moving the stepladder to reach a far corner when she thought she heard a knock on the front door. She was only a bit annoyed, her goal to finish the room by suppertime in jeopardy, but she laid down her brush before flying hurriedly down the stairs, peering through a living room window to find a black Ford pickup truck in the driveway.

She knew no one who drove a black Ford, but didn't hesitate to throw the door open, expecting to find a salesman, the Fuller Brush man having been a nuisance in the neighborhood.

"Hello, Mam."

She felt faint with shock and threw up her hands at the sight of her
tall, grown-up English son. Oh, he was so English, his hair cut short
against his scalp, his plaid shirt denying all traces of his ever having
been Amish.

"Eli! Oh, Eli. It's you!"

The March wind caught the screen door and slammed it against
the outside wall, but neither one noticed or cared. What was a broken
hinge compared to the joy of seeing her precious Eli?

He took her into his strong arms, and she felt redeemed, blessed
beyond measure. She looked into his kind brown eyes and found the
same love and admiration he had always had for his mother.

She made him sit at the kitchen table, brought him homemade
root beer, a cup of coffee, sugar cookies, and Swiss cheese, crackers,
and homemade beef bologna. Lizzie came to the kitchen, shy, standing awkwardly, before he noticed her, small, petite, with traces of his
mother's perfect features.

"Lizzie! Look at you!"

She giggled, but would not come closer.

The past two years had been lessons in survival. Mostly, he had
been treated well, especially among those who were extended family.
Roy and Martha had both passed on, after their move to Louisiana.
May said she would always regret never having been able to apologize
for the sad heartache she had caused them.

Eli could barely express the feeling of arriving to the town in
Arkansas, the town his father had called home, the outpouring of
love and unrestrained acceptance as one of them. Repeatedly tears
sprang to his eyes as he related the effusive welcome, the verbal out-
pouring of gladness that he had returned. They hadn't even known he
was born. He laughed as he recounted the time spent with relatives,
the way they expressed themselves, the warm hugs and good-natured
teasing. They were poor, for the most part, living happily with what
the Lord provided, resting easy on neighborhood porches after a day
in the fields. He voiced his anger with lowered brows, the hideous
unfairness of sharecropping, white men treating their counterparts

like dogs. Some of his cousins, though, were furthering their education, becoming lawyers or dentists, even bankers.

May was rapt, listening to the deepened voice of her son, marveling at this maturity, his attitude of fairness, the humility with which he delivered his thoughts and opinions.

"I guess we were born a step lower than the whites, I don't know. If things ever even out, it'll be long after I'm dead and gone." He shook his head, as if this statement was hard for him to believe.

"Oh, perhaps sooner, Eli," May said hopefully. "There's this thing going on called the civil rights movement. I read about it. Andy and I discuss it. He seems to think, if change comes, it will be slowly."

Eli nodded. He looked around, sighed contentedly. His eyes returned again and again to May's face, as if frequently seeing her would etch it more permanently in his memory.

When Andy came in to warm his hands, he stopped when he spied Eli, then lifted his hands in disbelief. There was only gladness in his welcome, a certainty to his booming, "Eli! Out of nowhere! Here you are!"

A firm handshake, their faces almost level. Man to man.

May suppressed the lump rising in her throat. All these years together and here they were, these two men sharing her life. One as beloved as the other. A quick prayer of gratitude.

He was staying a week, he said. And then he asked about Mattie Troyer. "And John," he added quickly. May passed on the small bit of information she knew, saying she hadn't heard anything at all unusual. Yes, she believed Mattie was among the instruction class to join church in the neighboring district. And then, he asked the hard questions—was she dating? Had she married someone?

Both Andy and May shook their heads and kept their faces impassive. Eli wondered if there was there a chance he could talk to her. Did they think it would be allowed? May trembled, a chill chasing itself up her spine, thinking of the dangerous consequences. She knew all too well the sown seeds of longing, and the repercussions, the doubt and fear.

"Eli, I don't think I would encourage you to see Mattie. I know it sounds harsh to you, as if I didn't care about your feelings, but I really think it would be best for you to move on. Really and truly move on, in body as well as spirit. Your thoughts need to release her. I'm afraid nothing good will come of this. You will only hurt people, cause division, setting relatives against one another. I beg you to let her go."

"But *you* didn't. You didn't just forget about the man you loved." Eli's voice was cold, hard.

May paused, remembering her first love, his smooth, dark skin, their very first kiss. She pushed the memories back but her voice quivered as she replied. "No, I didn't. And though I would never trade you for the world, there have been . . . consequences."

THE MARCH WIND was relentless, the bare branches of the oak tree by his upstairs bedroom scraping continuously across the shingled roof, tapping on the painted siding. It howled and moaned its way along the eaves, set a loose shingle to whirring, an annoying sound that grated on his raw nerves.

He rolled from side to side, flopped on his back, and stared wide-eyed at the ceiling. His main purpose for his return was to see about Mattie's welfare, he admitted it. But now his mother had made an honest effort to sidetrack him. He wanted to see her. He had to. Every turn of the truck's wheels had been the closing distance between them. Almost three years, and he'd tried honestly. He'd learned the ways of the world, sat in juke joints of the South and been introduced to the wiles of women. Thick as flies, hovering about, but he'd only felt annoyance. Never once had the night in the park left his mind, the sweetness of her outburst, declaring a love that mirrored his own. If he lived to be a hundred, that incident would surpass any other relationship.

How long did a person wait and hope? He didn't know. Long into the night, arrows of regret and doubt stung painfully. He was accosted by weakness, had no strength to say no. He knew he should get in his truck and drive away, but the thought of returning to the sweltering Mississippi Delta was more than he could tolerate.

Especially without seeing her.

He dozed fitfully, overslept, and missed his mother's breakfast. She offered to fry more eggs, fry more bacon in the cast iron skillet, but he said a bowl of oatmeal would do. He felt grumpy, out of place, disoriented.

May looked at her son. He had always worn the expression he felt in his heart, and this morning, his face was a map of misery.

"Eli."

"Hmm?"

He pushed away his oatmeal, raised his eyes to her, and she was shocked to see the despair, the lack of his usual bright interest in those around him. She sat across from him, her eyes deep wells of empathy.

"I know this is hard. But believe me, you'll do well to forget her."

"I know." He hung his head, lowered his eyes, picked at a thread on the tablecloth. "Why was I born, Mam? Why?"

"We don't always know, but it's very clear to God." She spoke quickly, grabbing at anything that came to mind. She was suddenly faced with a wild, irrational fear, that of Eli's despair becoming more than he had realized it could be.

"I have to see her."

"No, Eli, please. Please try and give in to God's will. I beg you."

She stood waving as long as she could see the black truck going out the drive, watched until the dust had settled, listened till she could no longer hear the chug of the engine. When she turned to go back inside, her shoulders drooped and her back was as rounded as a much older woman's. The full responsibility of her son's life was almost more than she could carry. She had always known it would come to this, but how could she have prepared herself for the poignant reality of his forbidden love?

ELI DROVE BLINDLY, slowly. He had to pass her place at least once. Just in case she might be walking along the road, driving a team of horses in the field, anything. Seeing her face just once more would be enough.

He loved the winding roads, the long level stretches and sloping hills and wooded areas of Ohio. He loved the slow, easy rhythm of life, the easy life of being with a group of people who were content. Who drove their well-cared-for horses with a whip dangling from the holder that was mostly there for decoration. He smiled to himself, remembering the times when the men discussed old Eph Weaver's whip, like a sign of real authority, over a horse they all knew did exactly as he pleased.

It wasn't that his folks in Arkansas weren't good to him. They were. He was like a celebrity, the prodigal son, the link to beloved Roy and Martha. He felt a sense of belonging, the dark-skinned relatives scattered thickly among the whites. Salt and pepper.

Whatever that was supposed to mean.

Sometimes, he had a hard time understanding the world, the people who occupied the towns and cities scattered across Arkansas. Or Louisiana. He knew it was the deep South, the home of descendants of slavery, the ancestors brought over from beloved African shores in deplorable conditions on white men's ships. After the Civil War, between the North and the South, slavery was successfully abolished, but like a scarlet thread refusing to break, the memory of wrongdoing persisted, the knowledge of having been the subject of terrible acts of outrage, being sold like animals, obedient women bearing the children of cruel slaveholders.

He shook his head to clear it. Would his people never free themselves from past atrocities? Some did. But there was strife. There were always those who would push back, demand their rights. Segregation. He hated the word. Separating the salt from the pepper, when together, they were so good, seasoning food so perfectly.

Wasn't that what God intended? Wasn't grace the same for all of mankind?

His heart beat thickly in his chest.

There.

There, nestled among the fir trees, the verdant crops rising like a beacon to her father's well-managed farm, was her home. The white two-story farmhouse where she ate and slept and worked, helping her mother and older sister with all the household chores.

Mattie. Just let me glimpse your sweet, perfect face. He stopped the truck, let the engine idle as his eyes searched the farm for any sign of life. He could have driven in, said he wanted to speak to John, but he wasn't sure of a welcome, the way he had deserted the Amish way of life, gone to live *mitt de hōchy* (with the higher up). The English. Ezra Troyer might think he came to mislead his son, and who knew what Mattie had told her family, so he probably would not be received with gladness.

He watched, waited, completely torn.

Should he venture into that driveway?

In the end, he merely put the truck in gear and drove slowly away, his eyes constantly going back for just one glimpse.

There was none, and so he drove, his shoulders slumped in the same despairing way as his mother's, the lump in his throat pushed back, his eyes dry, in the way of a courageous young man.

CHAPTER 16

IT WAS LATE SUMMER.

Summer in Arkansas was no laughing matter, the humidity wringing perspiration from a body like a twisted cloth. He thought he'd get used to it, but almost four years after having left Ohio to make his home among cousins and aunts and uncles, he still felt amazed at the power of the Delta heat. It was oppressive, watching the pulsing orange circle of fierce heat rise from the horizon and mount across the sky, the orange turning into a pale yellow that did nothing to diminish the blazing power.

He had given up his career as a farrier. With the automobile being everyone's form of transportation, horses were scattered throughout the countryside. The small Amish settlement had become even smaller as the value of cotton plummeted, the heat and humidity driving many families north to a more temperate climate. The remaining handful of Amish were contemplating a move as well, or that was the message his Uncle Orphus had given him.

He lived with Orphus and Lavinia, an older retired couple in their sixties, Orphus a brother to Clinton Brown's father Roy. It was a pleasant blue-sided house with black shutters outside of town, a pine forest in back, the road meandering along the level fields like a flat ribbon, cars traveling past on their way to the bank or for groceries or whatever business they needed to take care of.

Orphus suggested a job at the shoe factory, having worked there himself for forty-two years. He had an impeccable record, a pleasing number of laurels for having his years of labor behind him, the knowledge of having been treated well his entire life. He gave all the credit to his employer, to the shoe company, to the wonderful folks he worked with.

It was on this note that Eli applied for a job, with the recommendation of his Uncle Orphus. The pay was decent, the skill of cutting leather easily acquired. He soon got used to the expansive building with high ceilings and huge windows, the clacking of heavy cast iron sewing machines, the oiled wooden floors giving a squeaking sound as the workers entered on the seven o'clock shift.

He was grateful to be warm in winter and out of the sun's penetrating rays in summer, loved the smell of expensive leather, cutting into it like a daring high dive, hoping the heavy scissors would not disappoint.

In the evening, there was Lavinia's cooking to anticipate, the comfort of relatives and the culture in which they lived. There had been things to learn, to sort out in his mind. He had only known the Amish way of life through his teen years, so there was much to adjust to. The disregard to the wearing of particular clothes, the freedom to drive cars and to make use of modern conveniences. At church, God's graces were sung with abandon at emotional, soul-stirring services. Love of God was as thick as creamy pudding, eaten by enormous spoonfuls, the bowl of His grace miraculously filled over and over. They sang, they raised their dark arms and shouted the glory of the resurrection, the coming of Jesus as if it was the happiest event known to mankind. He had been raised with the dark questions of "Are you ready? Have you repented and done all you could to assure your sinful nature will be taken care of? It might not be." He found himself caught in a tide that contained rip currents of different views and values. He watched the flowered hats and dark hands adorned by many silver rings, bangles, and bracelets, dark lips enhanced with crimson lipstick, while tears of joy flowed freely at the thought of their Savior having died for them and risen victorious.

His worship had been solemn, laced with the fear of wrongdoing. Hair had to be cut in the proper fashion, a bowl cut, never shorn close to the scalp like the worldly men, and if anyone dared buck that rule, ministers would be at such a person's door. There were rules for shirts, trousers, and shoes. An equality was expected of each member, so when clothes followed a fashionable trend, there was always the fear of being an offense to the brethren, and everyone knew well, "now walkest thou not charitably." That was what had kept him from driving into the Troyer farm—the offense of driving that black truck. In Arkansas, there was so much love. So much freedom of expression, hugs, backslapping, shoulder-thumping exuberance at the sight of an acquaintance. Among the Amish, this gladness at seeing a friend was the same, but a restrained handshake would do, a sincere light of welcome in the eyes.

"Stuffy," Lavinia said of Eli, with an affectionate tone.

"Straitlaced," Orphus chuckled.

"Well, he was raised that way, the boy was. Sober as a cat," Lavinia said, a deep, rumbling chuckle shaking her massive chest.

And he was. Had been. Appearance mattered. The length of a dress, the size of a covering, the way you spoke and laughed in church. Quiet, well-mannered, aware of others' disapproval. Everything was orderly, restrained, days going by in smooth, unruffled fashion. There was gossip, and things went wrong now and then—a bout of drunken youths misbehaving, or the ultimate slap in the face when a twenty-one-year-old spurned the ways of the forefathers, left home, and lived a worldly life. The youth would be excommunicated, the solemn words creating a quiet sobbing among brokenhearted women, struggling to accept the years of shunning, the lost sheep caught in the evil hands of the devil. After a time, when the youth dared a visit to see his parents, the tears, threats, and pleading would be almost more than a person was able to handle. The pain of seeing a child having left the fold was as thick and choking as noxious fumes.

Oh, Eli wasn't exactly raised this way. He wasn't. For him, the return to his parents was different. He knew he would be received with love and grace, that as much as his leaving hurt his family, they understood that he had little choice. And when he left the second time, he had gone with their blessing, sent out to save heartache among other families—Mattie Troyer's family, specifically. Leaving was the honorable thing to do. There was no looking back, he knew, except that he was like Lot's wife, the rebel who went against God's Word and looked back to see the burning of Sodom and Gomorrah, after which she had turned into a pillar of salt. His mind had been filled with the warnings of the Old Testament.

Obedience was highly sought after by the Amish, the kind of obedience printed in trusting little hearts as they grew among the rules and dress codes of everyone around them. The world would always have its high fashion and fast cars, but that was not for anyone to judge. Such things were without, away from the structured, plain life, and God would be the one who judged—it was not for the Amish to decide who was right and who was wrong. There were many good people among *die hochy*, many kind and friendly neighbors and drivers, people who were living in the way their parents had raised them.

In Arkansas there were plenty of pretty colored girls with dark eyes and curly hair, most dressed in tight dresses and jeans and shirts, who would have loved to be his girlfriend and never tried to hide it. They came to visit Orphus and Lavinia, sashayed up to the porch like the long-lost cousins they were not, blew kisses and batted eyelashes, crossed one leg over the other and bobbed their feet, red slippers dangling like temptation itself. He was invited to ball games and dances, to family dinners on Sunday and juke joints on Saturday night, the hornet's nest of drama and wronged hearts, of men decent enough who defiled themselves before the night was over.

Eli wove in and out, like a basket he was finishing with care. After the status of long-lost relative wore off, he was merely one of them, a serious young man with some strange ways, but he was loved and accepted for the most part.

Every Friday night, he played baseball at the park for the black people. A few whites would show up to watch the game, but they'd never play, even if they'd been invited. They had a separate park for whites they could go to if they wanted to play their own game.

And time went on.

What was time? Days melting into weeks, weeks into months, and months into years. The years slipped by, and he could not make himself go back to see his family, could not face the thought of driving past the Troyer farm again. He hoped she was married. The sharp longing for his mother eventually loosened into a dull ache. He read her letters, wrote a few himself, but never asked about Mattie. Sometimes, he dreaded opening his mother's letters, for fear of receiving the news of Mattie's marriage or dating or upcoming engagement, anything that would leave him floundering helplessly, trying to accept the fact there was no hope.

She embodied all his hope, his dreams. He wanted the kind of life in which he could truly feel at home in spirit. In his heart, he was Amish. He was one of them. He wanted to stand against the board fence at Oakley Auction, one knee bent, the heel of his shoe caught on the lower rail, his thumbs hooked in his suspenders.

Most of all—and this was hard to understand—he missed the slow cadence, the easy rhythm and swell of the German plainsong in church. He missed the smell of leather harnesses, the salty sweat of the horses, the jingling of snaps and buckles as the steady draft horses pulled the plow along the furrow, the earth dark and gleaming, earthworms slick and wet, squirming to find a new home after being dislodged by the plow.

Sometimes he would watch the farmers in Arkansas, but the chug of the tractor was not the same. He'd tried to make friends with a few Amish families in the area, but they weren't exactly welcoming of a colored guy with too many questions.

In time, the Amish all moved out of Arkansas, sold their farms one by one, moved to Wisconsin or Illinois or Indiana. This saddened Eli, as if a part of him moved with them. Another emotion that was hard to understand. If he was born to a colored father, why couldn't he be content with his people? Why did he always feel as if he didn't quite belong?

He drove past the farm his mother told him about, her uncle's farm, where she and Oba spent their childhood days. He did this when he missed her, when he tried to imagine her doing chores in the barn or sweeping the front porch. Melvin Amstutz had not been a nice man, according to Oba, but May never said much about him. She'd said, more than once, it was her own fault she ran off with Clinton Brown.

He drove slowly past the farm on a lazy Sunday afternoon, picturing Oba and his mother. Weren't there three boys his mother talked about? Leviticus was the youngest, the one she always worried would not find his way—she had carried guilt her entire life for having deserted him.

The farm seemed shrouded in mystery, a sense of deception and misdeeds. Perhaps it was only May's voice that brought this on, the way her voice would lose all sense of joy, the lilt in her speech flattened by her remembering.

He shook off his sense of foreboding, of needing to know the honest circumstances of his birth. The thing bothering him most was how his sweet, unselfish, almost angelic mother could have been so wild, so promiscuous, to have run off during the night with a colored man.

Why had she done it?

Did Andy, his stepfather, know the truth? Why had he married her?

He knew Gertie had died but wasn't sure what had happened to Melvin. He decided to search for the three boys, or at least the one whose name he remembered. Leviticus. Leviticus Amstutz. So he searched the phone book. Went to the courthouse for record of his birth. He drove around the area, asked questions, but no one seemed to know a Leviticus.

He reasoned about the lack of a telephone number. If he was Amish, there would be none, and it was likely he had moved away. He spent all his spare time now obsessing, mulling over the circumstances of his birth, finding Ammon—or was it Enos, Ezra, Ephraim? He was never sure. Orphus told him about both of the older boys having been in and out of prison, terrorizing the neighborhood with fast cars and petty thefts, yelling racial slurs and putting their own lives in danger.

Orphus and Lavinia could share quite a few stories about Mr. Melvin, as he was known among the sharecroppers, but since Orphus had never worked for him personally, it was all hearsay, gossip, and there was always plenty of that to go around. He'd met him a couple of times in town, and he didn't seem like such a bad guy.

The information Eli gleaned as the years slipped by was only enough to keep him wondering. He tried to let it go, knowing the chances of speaking to someone who knew what had actually happened were very slim. But he kept his eyes and ears open.

HE WAS IN the local hardware store, buying a new kitchen spigot for Lavinia. The day had not gone well, the mercury in the outdoor thermometer climbing dangerously high, Orphus in his chair with his feet propped up on the hassock, no shirt, and a pair of pajama pants.

When the water gushed uncontrollably, Lavinia yelled and threatened and carried on, with Orphus heaving himself from the chair and heading downstairs to turn the water off at the tank. Eli lifted his water-soaked plate of grits and fried eggs, set it on the counter, and offered to buy a new spigot.

Which was where he was, when he heard the whining voice of the proprietor of Ace Hardware call out.

"Levi! Levi Amstutz! Well I'll be!"

Eli froze. Slowly, his hand dropped away from the box he was examining. He lost all sense of reason and slipped quickly toward the voice before peeping around the end of the aisle.

He saw a medium-sized man, well built, with dark hair and eyes, his hair cut neatly, well dressed in a plaid shirt and navy blue work pants. He was smiling as he shook hands.

"You're back! You back to stay?"

"I don't know yet."

"Really?"

"Yeah. Depends."

"On what?"

"Well, my wife and children aren't real keen on this heat."

"Hot it is. But only in summer."

Eli watched as Levi Amstutz shook his head, gave a small laugh. "I told Caroline we'll install an air conditioner, if we can afford it."

"I can sell you one."

"I'm sure you can."

The proprietor rang up his purchase, Levi handed over the money, pocketed his change, and said he'd be back if he needed more. As he turned to go, Eli stepped forward.

"Sir."

Levi turned, a question on his pleasant face. "Yes?"

"Uh... Are you... Is your father's name Melvin? Melvin Amstutz?"

"Indeed it is. Was. He passed away."

Eli hesitated. Perhaps he did not want to hear who he was. He took the plunge. "I'm Eli Weaver."

A puzzled look. A shrug of his shoulders.

"Do you . . . did you ever know a May . . . um . . . Miller?"

Instantly, there was recognition. "Why, yes."

"Her name is Merriweather Miller. May. She's Amish."

"Yes. Of course. May is my first cousin. She . . . she and her brother Oba came to live with us when they were, I don't know, nine or ten? Eleven maybe."

"Yes."

Eli could barely contain his excitement. The proprietor had gone back to helping another customer, after his face had swiveled from one to the other, incredulous.

"May is my mother," Eli said quietly.

"No!" The sound of disbelief was followed by a hand to his mouth. "I mean. I'm sorry. It's quite a shock."

Eli nodded, ashamed of his dark skin. Why this was so, he couldn't tell, except it gave away his mother's sin.

Levi recovered quickly. "Look, I have to get home. We're renting till we decide. Come over this evening. We'll talk. We live on Route 6, about two miles on the left. White bungalow. Black shutters. My car is red. Parked in the driveway."

"Thank you."

It was all Eli could think to say. He bought the spigot, paid for it in a daze, counted the hours till it was time to go. He helped Orphus install the new spigot, listened to his groans of pain as he lay on his back below the sink, trying repeatedly to tighten the spigot to the water pipe, with Lavinia shrieking above his laments.

"Get out from under there. Get out, Orphus. You're worthless. Let Eli get it. He's a lot younger and skinnier. Get outta there."

As always, Eli grinned, thought how unlike his own quiet mother, but he loved Lavinia. He knew her words were crude, belittling poor Orphus the way she did, but they loved each other with undying devotion that bordered on worship. It was just her way.

He didn't tell them where he was going. He simply left in his truck, driving down the way he'd been instructed until he found a home that fit the description he'd been given.

They were in the back yard—Levi, his wife, and their two children.

"Come on back. We're here," Levi called out.

His wife rose from the green-and-white webbed lawn chair, plump and pretty in her lavender house dress, her brown hair curling around her petite face.

She put out a welcoming hand, and Eli clasped it in his. The children came to stand with their parents, their hands extended in a way that Eli found to be extremely polite.

"This is Caroline, my wife. And Patty and Bobby."

Eli greeted them with a polite, "How do you do? I'm glad to meet you."

They nodded, said they were pleased to meet him, then went back to their game of croquet.

"Come. Sit down. Levi tells me you are a son to his cousin, May Miller."

Gratefully, Eli took the proffered chair, his knees taking on a sudden weakness, his heart thumping too loudly in his chest. He swallowed nervously, then swallowed again, unsure of how to proceed. There was so much he wanted to know, and he did not want to offend this seemingly perfect family.

"So, where do we begin?" Levi offered, with a warm smile.

"You go first. Tell me what you know."

Was it only the merest flicker of doubt that crossed Levi's face, or was it his heightened awareness? He shoved his hands into his pockets, stretched his legs.

"Well," he began, then looked to his wife for assistance. She gave him a beatific smile, which seemed to bolster his courage.

"I was three or four when they came. I remember May as a sister. My mother was sick a lot. She didn't like living on the farm. She didn't like Arkansas, being so far away from her family. I remember my mother as being extremely unhappy, so May brought sunshine into our lives. She sang, played games with us. She was very nice to us. Well, to me. Ammon wasn't nice to her. My father was a hard worker, very intense. With a temper. Oba didn't like him at all. They fought. But May picked up more and more of the housework as time went on, with my mother unwell. They went to church with us. We were one big happy family on the outside." He paused. "Amish as Amish could be," he said softly.

"I was Amish too. My mother is Amish."

Levi gave him a piercing look. "Still?"

"I gather by what she told me, she left the Amish when she . . . I don't know. Did she run away with my father? What happened? My father's name is Clinton Brown."

Again, the piercing gaze was directed at him. Then Levi lowered his face, shook his head from side to side. "Unbelievable. I often wondered what happened to her. In fact, after she left, I didn't want to go on living. She was all I had. When Oba left, it wasn't as hard. He fought with my father, I told you. But May . . ."

"Why did she leave?" Eli asked.

It was the question he'd wanted an answer to for most of his life. He felt as if he had never known the truth.

For a long moment, Levi said nothing. He looked off across the yard, his eyes unseeing. Obviously, he suppressed a strong emotion, his face working to contain it. Or conceal it.

"Was she the type to . . . to . . . you know, have boyfriends? Was she sneaking out a lot?"

"No."

The one word sounded strangled, coming from a place deep within. Suddenly, Levi looked straight at Eli, asked if he was strong enough to hear what he had to say.

"Strong? I hope so," Eli answered.

"My father was not a normal man, in any sense of the word. He beat Oba, with a whip. I can still picture his white face, his eyes like burning coals. He beat us. My two brothers carry the brunt of his cruelty, carry his nature. They have not . . . well, I'm still hoping they can turn their lives around."

"But what about my mother? He didn't beat her, surely?" Eli almost choked on the question.

"No, he didn't."

Again, there was a heavy silence, thick with unspoken words, words stuffed into the air between them, stifling their freedom to be relaxed, to have an easy exchange.

"He visited her upstairs, in her room, at night."

A sledgehammer's blow would not have hurt more. The breath was literally knocked out of him. His mouth opened and closed.

"No," he whispered. "Not that."

"These things are not spoken of. She never said a single word. I was a bedwetter, a young, troubled boy who lived with fear and anxiety. So I lay there."

Eli could not comprehend the strength and bravery of his dear mother. He could not imagine the days, years of shame. How long had she stayed? He wrestled with a thousand questions, a thousand pangs of pain and pity for one as sweet, as perfect as his mother.

Mam, Mam, was all he could think. His heart cried out to her, as words failed him completely. The tears were thick and hot, coursing down his cheeks and dropping on the grass at his feet. His heavy shoulders heaved with the pain of knowing what his beloved mother had endured. He shook all over, his tall frame trembling like a terrified child.

"I'm sorry," Levi said. Caroline placed a hand on her husband's shoulder, kept it there.

"Don't be," Eli choked, lifting his leg to reach for his handkerchief. He blew his nose, wiped his eyes, then shook his head, words failing him. Finally, he took a deep, shaking breath, swiped at his face, blindly, and said, "She couldn't have done anything to deserve that. I mean, no one could, but especially not my Mam."

"No. Oh my, no. She was a quiet whisper of a girl. Obedient. I imagine she thought of herself as a servant. She tried to get Oba to adopt her attitude. Do you know what happened to Oba?"

That was when the smiles could begin. Lemonade was served and the heaviness seemed to lift. Eli talked easily, remembering his mother's words, then telling them in colorful detail about Oba's return, his learning to walk with a prosthesis, the friendship and marriage with the unlikely Clara.

And Levi voiced his wish to travel to Ohio, to meet them all. To see May, especially.

"And this Andy Weaver? He's good to her?" he asked.

"Couldn't be better. He's a great guy. We parted ways because I can't have a future in the Amish church. I . . ." He spread his hands, indicating his skin color.

Levi and Caroline nodded with a hint of sadness in their eyes.

CHAPTER 17

Leviticus Amstutz was a man of ambition. He had married Caroline at a young age, after meeting her when he applied for his driver's license. She was a clerk at the courthouse, as young and as purposeful as he was. He managed a course through the mail, acquired his GED, and from there, worked his way into the University of Arkansas and studied law, while Caroline kept working to support them both. When the babies came, they moved to central Pennsylvania, where he took night classes at Penn State University and worked at an electronics place during the day. Now they were back, with Leviticus continuing his studies, although he would be completing them the following year. He hoped to work in civil rights as well as mental health laws.

He gave Caroline most of the credit, having stuck by him through the worst of times, scrimped and saved, living in cramped apartments while he was gone at night. She knew the rewards could come later, when he hung his shingle on the front lawn of a substantial home in a nice neighborhood. She just wasn't sure if she wanted to live in Arkansas, the low-lying Mississippi Delta with its heat and humidity, the poverty of the sharecroppers and the constant unrest between the colored people and the whites.

Levi was her beloved husband, the love of her life, after having lost both parents in an automobile crash when she was thirteen and a half years old. Her only sibling, Carson, was a scientist, spending years in the Colombian rainforest, studying foreign diseases, so she was alone, save for the single aunt who had raised her.

Levi had shared most of his traumatic upbringing, but this was new, this fact he shared with the handsome Eli. This dark person with the saddest, softest eyes she had ever encountered. Raised in the Amish church, same as Levi, they seemed to have much in common, but where Levi wanted nothing to do with any of them, which Caroline understood very well, Eli longed to return to his childhood people, the community he loved. His mother, Caroline gathered, was a special person.

Night fell, but the porch lights went on, and still they stayed, talking. The children were bathed and put to bed, Caroline returning with a tray of homemade chocolate chip cookies and a carafe of coffee, the flyswatter tucked under one arm.

"Bugs!" she said, setting the tray on a low table.

"They come with the territory," Levi said, reaching out to touch her arm.

"The heat and the bugs and the smell of the muddy river," she countered.

Eli contemplated this, listening quietly as they bantered back and forth, weighing all the pros and cons, finishing with the affordability of air conditioning, which was used in commercial buildings, but the high cost of purchasing a large, weighty unit was indeed questionable.

"The time will come when every household will be able to enjoy a cool interior during the summer," Levi remarked.

"I can't imagine," Caroline answered. "If this was possible, we could live anywhere comfortably."

Eli nodded. "If you're not Amish. No electricity there."

Levi grinned. "Well, I remember. We washed our feet in the granite tub by the back door, scuttled off to bed, shucked our clothes, and tumbled into the unwashed sheets, smelling to high heaven."

They all burst out laughing.

"It was life, though, and it had its good times. I remember May pushing me on the swing, the way it felt when my toes almost touched the branches. I adored her. She was like an angel. She looked like one."

"Still does. Yeah, she spoke of you, worried what would become of all of her boys. But especially you. She called you Leviticus."

"It's an old name from the Bible."

"I'm named Eliezer, after her father."

"Wow. That's quite a name."

"Glad our names are shortened to ones folks can pronounce."

As the night wore on, the bond between them deepened. Caroline yawned, slapped mosquitoes and other buzzing insects of the night, before she told them goodnight and went into the house.

After that, Levi and Eli were given free rein to discuss the many things pertaining to their views of life. Eli told him about Mattie Troyer, the girl of his dreams, one who claimed his heart so fully he could not become even remotely interested in anyone else, no matter the wiles, the many attractions placed before him.

"That's a tough one," Levi said. "So much against you. The law does not allow an interracial union, not yet. Law or not, what would the Amish church allow?"

"Not that. Never."

There was a comfortable silence between them as the night breeze whispered through the tress. A screech owl set up its undulating cry, an eerie sound that set Eli's teeth on edge. He slapped at a whining mosquito in his ear and watched a pair of headlights coming down the road, casting an arc of light across the house before it was gone.

After a while, he asked, "What do you mean, 'not yet'?"

"Well, there's a lot going on in law. Segregation is a hot topic right now. Schools, churches, places of business won't always have the dividing line, which is coming closer every year. I doubt if interracial marriage is too far behind."

"But that doesn't help my situation at all."

"It would be a first step."

Eli nodded. "You know, there's this story in the Old Testament, where Jacob worked seven years for Laban's daughter Rachel. Seven years is a long, long time."

"After which, he was given Leah, not the one he bargained for, so back to work he went for another seven years," Levi finished. "I've heard that story from the time I was old enough to go to church. It's an old favorite."

"So think about it. The way I feel about this Mattie Troyer. I do believe I would gladly work for the fourteen years, if it meant I could have her."

"You really would?"

"I would."

"You could always ask her father," Levi laughed.

"I can't joke about it."

"No. I imagine you couldn't."

"I'll stay single for many years. I simply have no desire to be with someone else. I can't see myself being married to anyone."

"I'm blessed beyond measure with Caroline. She's my guiding star. She's everything I have always dreamed of and more. I don't deserve her one bit. The way I was brought up, I was ill-prepared for a relationship, but she has helped me to grow, to see the world in a softer light. It's hard when your upbringing is based on discipline without love, barely even being liked. You're mistrustful, if that's a word. And she is the most trusting, the most loving person I know of. She reminds me of May, of your mother."

"She does."

"So when are we going to Ohio?"

"I can go anytime. All I have to do is tell my boss, and he'll get a substitute. He's easy to work for."

CAROLINE WAS IN the back seat with the children with Levi at the wheel and Eli beside him, the summer breeze laden with the smell of diesel exhaust, hot tarmac, and the acrid smell of stale, sunbeaten gravel by the side of the road. The tires hummed and the engine buzzed along as the air rearranged sleeves, hair not bound by a pony-tail holder, or anything loose in the car.

The children sat quietly, looking at the books Caroline provided, occasionally giggling or pointing fingers at humorous depictions, their heads almost touching as they turned the pages. Levi tapped his fingers on the steering wheel, the length of time behind the wheel making him antsy, just enough to make Eli laugh out loud.

A road trip was an event they all looked forward to, but as one tedious mile clicked into another one, the sun shone fiercely on the roof of the car, and the water Thermoses lay empty on the floor, everyone became cranky, including the children. Caroline managed to entertain them with books and stories, but after Levi began tapping the steering wheel too much, they decided it was time for a rest.

The rest area was nestled by the side of a mountain, the trees thick and green, like a fringe surrounding the rustic building containing restrooms, vending machines, maps, and literature of the surrounding states. Cars were parked in colorful rows, the occupants spilled around picnic tables, small charcoal grills spewing a stream of black smoke as the charcoal heated. There was ice for the Thermos jugs, and cold sodas to go with the sandwiches Caroline had packed. There was a budget to be considered, so meals at a restaurant were limited to once or twice.

They walked, stretched, found an empty picnic spot, and marveled at the tall mountains, the sky that seemed an otherworldly color of blue. Caroline spread a checked tablecloth and arranged small paper plates and cups. The children stood shyly, watching as older children chased each other across the wide expanse of green lawn.

They were ready to sit down when a large man of color approached them and greeted Eli with the familiarity of old comrades, the delight at seeing a dark face among a scattering of whites.

"Hey, brother! How are you?"

Eli grinned and stuck out a hand. "I'm well, thank you. And how are you?"

"Good. I'm good. It's nice to see a brother on occasion. So where you headed?"

"We're on our way to Ohio to see my mother." He gestured toward Levi and Caroline. "These people are going as well. Levi hasn't seen my mother since he was a child. They grew up together."

Nodding, he laughed, introduced himself as Harold Wells and politely acknowledged the introductions before wandering away, his hands in his trouser pockets, whistling softly.

Eli was strangely subdued after that chance encounter. He answered the questions Levi and Caroline asked, but they could tell something had upset him. After their return to the car, everything packed back in the trunk, back on the highway, Eli began to talk.

"See?"

"What?" Levi asked, confused.

"I'm just . . . I'm black. My skin is too dark to ever be accepted into the Amish church. Like that back there? I stick out in a crowd of white people—I don't belong—and no matter what, I can never change that. I try and kid myself, tell myself some kindly bishop will forgive my black skin, but you know it's not going to happen. They accepted my mother because she's white. She's white."

Levi looked over at him, amazed to see the despair, the hopelessness.

"They accepted her because she was one of them. I was the fruit of her mistake. I'll always be an outcast, as far as the Amish are concerned. They don't want me marrying into their pure white society." He swallowed, grimaced, his eyes squinting as he pulled down the sun visor. "You know I'm speaking the truth."

"But you've never tried. You don't know this for sure. If you do want to marry into the Amish church, you won't know until you try. The laws will change in the coming years."

"Don't. Don't tell me lies just to make me feel better."

Levi shook his head. "Would you rather turn around and go back home?"

"No. I want to see my mother."

"That is the only person?"

"Of course not."

Eli remained subdued, his thoughts a million miles away. He feigned sleep, became sullen, his mood darkening as they entered the state of Ohio. Levi allowed him this, spoke to Caroline in the back seat, checked the road atlas from time to time.

It was late afternoon when they drove slowly into the Weaver homestead driveway. The warm afternoon sun was slipping toward the west, with rays slanted from a layer of gray and white clouds, puffed up like rolls of cotton. The white barn and house were a beacon of light, a welcoming destination of love and warmth, a place he could call home. His eyes lit up with the anticipation he felt, and Levi could see the truth of this man's life in the homestead before them.

They were amazed to see the family lined up on the porch, eagerly awaiting their arrival. Andy, tall and wide, with graying hair, the side of his beard tinged in drops of white, and May, as small and petite as Levi remembered her, but her waist thickened with age. Lizzie was a young woman now, with the mixed features of both parents. Junior, a husky boy, with the thick wavy hair of his father, standing tall and strong. Fronie was the only one not there, having married Robert Mast, Eli's childhood bully.

There had never been more children, and so May accepted those God had given them, poured out all her love and compassion, and was grateful to be in their lives.

May stepped out to see Levi. She knew he was the one driving the car, but tears clouded her vision and she could not see his features clearly.

"Leviticus." The name was spoken with so much tenderness.

As they clasped one another in a glad embrace, the tears spilled unchecked from both of them, fueled by the memories of their time in Arkansas. May stepped back, a shaky smile bringing the gladness she felt.

"You're all grown up. Oh my. And this is Caroline." Another warm welcome, then to the children, and finally, Eli.

Andy greeted them with his broad grin and squinting blue eyes. Lizzie was a bit more reserved, but showed good manners and a sincere welcome.

Levi was amazed by the kindness, the normalcy of this fine Amish family. His own memories of his life with the Amish did not include the love, the obvious respect and appreciation of each other.

And when they gathered around the extended kitchen table laden with fried chicken and meatloaf, mashed potatoes and gravy, a filling made with toasted bread crumbs and chicken broth with vegetables, Levi could understand the longing in Eli's heart. There were buttered noodles and warmed green beans and ham, apple sauce and tomato slices, dishes of deep green sweet pickles, creamy coleslaw and deviled eggs. That was all before the many desserts, which included a tall layer cake made with caramel frosting and chunks of walnuts, fresh peach pie and creamy tapioca pudding, squares of multicolored Jell-o with piles of whipped cream, chocolate pie, and raspberry squares.

This was an Ohio Amish company dinner—the kind of dinner on which the talented housewife spent hours plying her culinary skills, cooking and baking, mixing and chopping, anxiously lifting golden pies from a wood-fired stove, inserting toothpicks in a baking cake, lifting to see if there was even a trace of batter adhering to it. All the love was put into the array of dishes, the energy and time spent pleasing the ones who would grace her table.

Levi knew nothing of this. He could not remember ever having been seated around a company table, never tasted desserts from an Amish cook. He sat back after the second prayer, rubbed his stomach contentedly, then gave May a wry smile.

"Our life at home must have been different than anyone's, or else no one in Arkansas cooked like this."

"Oh, I believe they did." May said. "Your father was not a social kind of person, so we never visited."

"There was so much missing in our home."

"There was. But it's all water under the bridge. As they say, it doesn't enrich a Christian life to look back at past sorrows and ... well, life back then wasn't easy, as you know. And Oba."

"Why isn't Oba here?" Levi asked.

May glanced at Andy, and they shared a moment of laughter.

"You have to understand. Oba's wife ... well, she pretty much wears the pants in that family. He doesn't care, though. In fact, I think he gets a tremendous kick out of his wife."

Caroline's laugh tinkled across the table. "Really?"

Andy nodded. "Never saw anything like it."

"They get along great," May added. "But like tonight. Something didn't suit her, so she won't budge. They'll be here for breakfast tomorrow."

"You mean, we get breakfast? Surely not like this?"

"Oh, you wait," Andy laughed.

They explained the menu, which had Caroline holding her stomach and rolling her eyes. They sat together on the front porch, sharing memories, talking about the past and the present.

Eli learned that Fronie had been married in the church services on a Sunday in April—not in November, the usual month for weddings—which explained everything to Eli. He understood why he had not been invited. It had been a small celebration with only a simple supper—not the kind of thing you invited family from out of town for. Little Daniel was born a few months after the wedding service.

Nothing more was said. Shame of this magnitude was not discussed but merely endured until a length of time had elapsed, erasing the worst of the dishonor. Eli understood, nodded his head, and remained silent. Silence covered so many unnecessary emotions quite effectively.

HE COULDN'T SLEEP. All he could think of was the space between him and the girl who took up all the space in his heart. Finally, he woke Levi by tapping softly on the door of their room, got the keys to the car, then drove to the Troyer farm in the dead of night. He didn't exactly have a plan—he just knew he needed to be nearer to her. He parked in a hayfield, sat there for a while, and then decided to walk a bit. Everyone would be asleep. He just needed some time to think and pray, and he hardly realized he was being drawn like a magnet nearer to her house. Suddenly, a dog seemingly the size of a horse exploded out of the forebay of the barn and sank his teeth into the calf of his leg without warning. Eli yelled in horror and pain and wrestled with the infuriated dog until the front door burst open and Mattie's father voiced a rough command. The dog slunk away as a flashlight's harsh beam was directed into Eli's face, his eyes wide with pain and shock.

He was ordered off the property, told never to come back, and if he ever caught him around there at night, he'd call the cops.

"But, I'm Eli. Eli Weaver," he ground out between clenched teeth, both hands wrapped around his bleeding lower leg.

The beam of the flashlight returned, and stayed.

"Well, I'll be. It is you."

An awkward silence followed, with Eli writhing in pain, the amount of blood seeping through his pants leg an alarming fact in itself.

"Well, what are you doing here at this hour?"

"I'm just . . . I'm sorry, I didn't intend to disturb anyone. I wanted to say hello to Mattie, but not tonight . . . I mean . . ." he stumbled awkwardly over his words. "Hey, I'm really sorry, but I think I need some help right now. . . your dog took quite a chunk out of my leg."

Mattie's father looked at him suspiciously, but helped him inside. The leg was tended to, wrapped in gauze with strips of white adhesive tape, the mother hovering anxiously. He was told to come back at an hour when most folks go visiting and to never come sneaking around at night. If he had something to say to Mattie, well, he could come right out and say it.

"Huh," was all Eli said to himself as he drove away, his leg throbbing, his pride shattered, his love for Mattie an ache in his heart.

Of course, there was explaining to do in the morning, with Levi and Caroline terribly concerned, saying he needed a doctor and May nodding her head in agreement. Eli insisted he was fine and tried to divert the attention elsewhere.

It was a relief when Clara and Oba arrived and the general out-pouring of joy and warm welcoming took away the focus on Eli's leg and the ridiculous predicament he had got himself into the night before. Oba was indeed thrilled to see Eli, to see him growing in stature, maturing into a person far beyond his years. Clara, as garrulous as ever, caught him in a crushing embrace, saying he looked much better with his hair cut like that.

He smiled, laughed, exclaimed about Emanuel growing so big, teased Esther until she eyed him with a calculating eye and told him he was exactly the color of a snapping turtle. Oh, she was her mother, complete with the red hair and unvarnished opinions, unafraid to throw them out, completely oblivious to the feelings they created after landing.

Eli laughed, told her if he was a snapping turtle, he was going to snap at her, and made like he was coming after her. But she put out a hand and held it with the palm out, said, "Stop being so *kindish* (childish)."

Clara threw back her head and guffawed a loud, unladylike burst of enjoyment. Her red hair was speckled with gray, which gave her the appearance of a squirrel, but besides that, she was her lean, sinewy self, dressed in a shocking shade of green. Oba laughed with her, his eyes shining with the merriment he lived with, being married to this extraordinary woman.

The dog bite was discussed, but May called from the kitchen, putting an end to further conversation. It was mid-forenoon and everyone was hungry, so the dishes of eggs, sausages, their own home-cured ham, fried potatoes, stacks of pancakes with warmed syrup, coffee cake, creamy oatmeal, and fresh peaches were relished.

Levi voiced his appreciation over and over, saying this was far beyond the fatted calf. Caroline soon fell into a conversation with Clara about the rights of horse owners, avidly listening to her colorful account of one of her horses being injured by a vehicle who failed to give her enough space on the road.

The whole time they spent together was filled with warmth and companionship, a time of renewing bonds that had never truly been severed. May became very sad when Ammon and Enos were mentioned, saying it was so unnecessary, such a waste to spend their lives in rebellion against their violent father and his unstable ways.

"I worried so much, especially for Ammon. He displayed so many of his father's own traits. It just seems so hard to accept."

Levi was astounded that May would care at all, the way both of those boys had made her life even harder. They had mocked her, teased her mercilessly, refused to do her bidding, and still she loved them. He supposed her capacity to forgive was, indeed, limitless. Was the love of the Savior in Heaven like that?

IN THE AFTERNOON, he drove over to the Troyer farm, got out of the car at the yard gate, then walked up to the porch and knocked on the door. His embarrassment from the previous night was overshadowed by the real possibility of seeing Mattie. She met him, a picture of beauty just inside the screen door, a sense of unreality taking his breath away.

"Hello, Mattie."

"Hello."

"Uh . . . are your parents home?"

"No."

He couldn't hide his relief. Had she heard about last night's incident? "May I speak to you?"

"Yes."

"Um." He stepped back. "Out here?"

She pushed open the screen door, stepped outside, and led the way to the cool recesses of the porch, the wisteria climbing up over the wooden trellis, keeping the porch shaded. There was the traditional wooden porch swing hanging from a chain, the pots of geranium growing in scarlet profusion.

She turned to face him, and his strength seeped away as if a serious onslaught of lightheadedness attacked him. Her eyes were jewels of light, gladness mixed with pain, a sadness so deep it wrenched his heart.

"I shouldn't have come here."

She nodded, only a slight dip of her head. "No, you shouldn't have."

CHAPTER 18

WHAT WAS THERE TO SAY AFTER THAT?

A part of Eli wanted to leave, to walk away without coming back, ever. She had agreed that he should not have come, so what else was left? He sat down, his head bowed. She sat beside him, as far away as possible, shrinking against the side of the wooden porch swing.

Katydids chirped their erratic song from somewhere in the wisteria. The high whine of a cicada followed, shutting out any other sound from the inhabitants of the flower bed. The farm seemed strangely deserted, the interior of the house as quiet as the rest of the place. An automobile appeared, passed by, followed by another. Mattie's hands moved restlessly in her lap, pleating and unpleating the fabric of her skirt.

Eli cleared his throat, felt close to tears.

"My Dat told me what happened last night, with the dog. They went visiting, to my oldest sister. So we have till milking time."

"They agreed to allow us to talk?"

"Yes."

"So, tell me, is that an encouragement or the final answer?"

"Eli, you know we already have the final answer."

"Which is?"

"No. If we ask, it will be 'no.'"

"But we haven't asked."

"I'm ready to move on, Eli," she whispered.

"You are?"

"I have to. Year after year and there is no hope, no change. If we give ourselves up, we can love again. We can both find a true partner, be happy."

"I have tried, Mattie. In Arkansas, it would be easy indeed, to move on. To ask a girl, to allow the relationship to develop, to think of marrying. But somehow, I can't bring myself to do it."

She caught her lower lip in her teeth, blinked her eyes furiously, the sting of her tears threatening to upset her composure. "We should never have met. Never allowed ourselves to feel the slightest attraction."

"We can't undo what has already happened. There is a reason for our . . . for the feelings we have. We can call it whatever we want, but we both know it's there."

"I don't want to encourage you to think of me, if we both know we can never be together."

"We do not know that yet."

She turned to face him, her eyes wide with disbelief.

"I have a new friend who is going to school to be a lawyer. He used to be Amish. Levi Amstutz from Arkansas. My mother lived with their family for years. Anyway, to shorten the long story, she had a special place in his heart, and we're back in Ohio to pay her a visit. Levi was raised on a cotton farm, was connected to sharecroppers all his life. Black people surrounded him and his brothers—on the farm, in town, in fact, everywhere he went—and he developed a strong interest in civil rights, in the question of the inequality around him. He began asking questions, then went to school after he left the Amish. He's really very intelligent. And here's what he says."

She found herself on the edge of her seat, her breath coming in short gasps. "What? What does he say?"

"He says he thinks there will be a change in the law of this country in the not too distant future."

"You mean . . . ?"

"That a person of color will be able to marry a white person."

"But is it right in the sight of God?"

"Who can say, Mattie? I know what I have in my heart, and I know it won't go away any time soon, so I figure God put it there, and if he wants to take it away, He will, in time."

"That doesn't answer my question."

"Well, my mother told me that Moses one of God's foremost servants ... well, he had a wife from Ethiopia. And God didn't seem to have a problem with that."

Mattie seemed to be contemplating this. "Besides, you aren't all black, only half."

"And if I were as dark as coal, should it make a difference?" Eli's words were laced with contempt.

"But Eli! You know it does. I feel like you're just trying to justify something you know is sinful."

"Because we are taught that."

"The whole world is. Is the whole world wrong?"

"Uh-huh." Eli had to rein in his utter disdain of the law, of men deciding what was right and what was wrong, being the conscience for everyone born on the earth. A hot rebellion against perceived rules raced through his veins. "So you've already decided to fling the possibility of a relationship by the wayside because you believe it's wrong. You're going along with the higher-ups, the lawmakers and congressmen, the bishops and ministers, and whoever else is listed on God's police force."

He was spitting with the force of his words. Like a hatchet, the edge of his words cut into the tender conscience she nurtured well by the obedience to her parents and the church.

"Stop it, Eli. Stop. When I hear you speaking in that tone of voice, I don't even want to be with you anymore. I cannot willfully go along with something that's wrong."

"It's not wrong."

She turned to look at him. The beloved profile, the caramel-colored cheekbone melding into the perfect contours of his straight nose, the tight black curls, now cut close to his head, the long dark lashes surrounding the deep liquid brown of his eyes. The strength of his neck and shoulders, the goodness of him.

What set one human being apart from another? Why could she not be drawn to someone else the way she was to him? Sometimes she felt as if she would gladly give her life for his. And still she did not understand it. She had never felt this way before, and hardly knew what to do with it. To be with him and her brother John had been moments of bliss, moments of stolen glances and the quickening of her blood. After experiencing feelings like she had with him, was it possible to ever live fully afterward? Or would she always walk through life half alive, for all the rest of her days? Was it right to keep asking God for an answer, if it was written in black and white? Were they not tempting God, which was one of the worst sins? Her mind tumbled over unanswered questions, one disappearing only to be replaced with another.

He signed, an inaudible sound of hopelessness. "I don't know what we're going to do."

"We are going to stay apart, Eli. You will go back to Arkansas, and you will put me out of your mind. I will stay here and do my best to find someone, or say yes to the next person who asks me out. I will develop the same kind of feelings I have for you. And you will do that as well. We must leave each other, and stay that way."

"You can't be serious, Mattie. I can't accept it."

"You can, and you will. In time."

"If you're so sure that is our only choice, how can you ever be sure how you felt about me in the first place?"

Slowly, she nodded her head, as if coming to a conclusion. Her heavy lids came down over her eyes, as the thick black lashes brushed her cheeks.

"Oh, I know how I feel. I know very well."

She lifted her eyes to find his gaze directed at her. She found the inner light burning in the center of his dark pupils, and the rest of the world disappeared as she was swept away by the power of his great love.

She opened her mouth to say something, anything to resist him, but what she did say was "I love you, Eli."

With a sound of overwhelming wonder, Eli said, "Mattie!"

She lowered her eyes, then, but stayed turned toward him. Slowly, she leaned forward, till her forehead almost rested on his chin. He could feel the aura of her, catch the scent of soap and shampoo, the salty aroma of delicate perspiration on a warm day. Without warning, she lifted her head, her eyes telling him everything her heart contained. Her hands on his shoulders, his arms finding a haven as they closed around her. She brought her lips to his, as light as the settling of a moth on a flower, before she moved away. Again, she brought her lips to his, in wonder.

As long as he lived, he never forgot the feel of her lips on his that afternoon beneath the wisteria. It was a sensation that would be sufficient for the remainder of his days, even if she was taken away from him by the rules of the church coupled with the laws of the country.

"I love you," he said hoarsely, before claiming her lips with his own, years of yearning and heartache released in this one intimate moment.

The only sound was the creaking of chains connected to hooks from the ceiling as the porch swing moved beneath their weight. A lean barn cat came around a corner of the porch, watched the two people caught up in the love they had confessed moments before, then sat down and began grooming the fur on her chest, her pink tongue making long, efficient strokes. A younger cat, barely more than a kitten, leaped up the steps and rubbed her side against the larger cat, before pouncing on a white moth. The mother cat watched, her eyes turning to slits, before she lowered herself on the boards of the porch floor and stretched comfortably.

Finally, they broke apart, but the only sound was the near inaudible sound of the kitten swiping at the moth. There was a muffled cry from the girl on the swing, before her shoulders heaved with sobs, a dry, rasping sound of desperation. He reached for her again, his own heart heavy with the hopelessness of their circumstances.

"You shouldn't have come today," she whispered. "We cannot see each other ever again. It's wrong, Eli, you know this is wrong."

"As wrong as it was for my father and mother."

"But it was!" she burst out.

"So I'm a product of something wrong. A mistake. I should never have been born."

"Don't say that. Please don't."

She reached in the pocket of her skirt for a delicate, lace-trimmed handkerchief, swiped at her nose as if the effort was far too much. Her shoulders drooped with so much weariness, as if she had run for miles without finding whatever it was she had run for.

"Mattie, my love, listen. We need to come up with a plan. We can elope, be English the way I am now, live together in defiance of society. We can stay apart. Or we can go talk to the bishop of your church. Take your parents with us."

"I can't break my parents' hearts. They would go to their graves with the weight of my lost soul. No, I can't run away with you. You would not require it of me. And we can't talk to the bishop. My parents would not allow that, would never accompany us. It's just asking too much."

He was tempted to tell her if she did none of these things, she did not love him, but he knew that was selfish and very childish. He knew all too well the ties that bind, the strong cords of duty and obedience to parents, the fear of wrongdoing and hell as a consequence.

"Alright. We can reach an agreement, my darling girl. I could say that over and over, since you told me you love me. You are my darling, my sweet and unforgettable love. I will return to my people in Arkansas, but we will write to each other. Every week. We will stay in touch, if only by letter. And if God chooses to disintegrate this love we share, He'll let us know in the form of an attraction to another person. Right?"

"Perhaps. I think it's the best we can do," she answered.

Still they stayed, talking, drinking in the astonishing amount of true love in each other's eyes, the giving and taking of their hearts'

secrets. A love newly proclaimed is a tender thing, and both were
reluctant to relinquish their hold on it. There were hopes, promises,
longings, dreams of a future created here in Ohio, married to each
other, living in harmony with the Amish church.

"I'm not desperately unhappy," he told Mattie, as he reached for
her hand. He held her sturdy hand in his, his thumb running restlessly along a small callus on the palm of her hand.

"I can wait," Mattie answered. "I've waited all these years, and I
can wait again. If our love is wrong, God will make it clear in time."
She sighed, a soft sound of resignation.

HE DROVE AWAY that day with her address tucked securely in his
pocket, his eyes streaming with tears of longing and frustration.
Later, when they had packed up and said goodbye to his family, he
asked to drive to keep himself occupied. But he almost missed his
exit onto Route 496, then drove erratically, forgetting to switch his
turn signals on when he pulled into the left lane. Levi made him stop
and get away from the wheel, and then drove with his mouth in a grim
line. He had a precious wife and children and no one was going to
put their lives in jeopardy, no matter how heartbroken they appeared
to be.

Caroline was very concerned, her brows furrowed in concentration, her eyes going to the slumping figure on the passenger side of
the front seat. He shouldn't have gone, Lord knows, she thought, but
the reality of it was evident. How hard it must be, how terribly hard.
Perhaps he could still forget about her eventually and find peace and
happiness with one of his own. She knew Levi would take it seriously,
would do all he could, but was the uphill battle really worth it? Were
Eli and Mattie being merely self-centered, determined to have their
own way without weighing the consequences? She didn't know.

MAY HAD A hard time returning to her busy schedule, finding herself wandering around the house in prayer, murmuring her requests
in half whispers, half sobs. Her heart was soft and tender, and when

Eli had returned yesterday, she felt as if she must surely die with the overwhelming pity she felt for him. To see the suffering in his eyes was almost more than she could bear. Having held him in her arms as a newborn baby, to marvel at the perfect face, fingers and toes, to feel blessed with the image of Clinton God had given her, to watch him grow and flourish, only to be bitterly saddened by his forbidden love. Oh, she should have been more aware. Warned him of these things. But she had, hadn't she?

Guilt at his birth rode in on the wings of the horrible dragon of remorse, self-loathing, the sin she had committed the day she ran off with Clinton. Her only escape route. Should she have escaped? And so the fires from the dragon's mouth consumed her until Andy came in for his usual dinner to find his wife distraught, lying on her bed with her face to the wall, Lizzie showing signs of worry as she did the washing and sweeping without being told.

Andy was a special gift to her, of this she was sure. His hand on her shoulder, his arms around her, the words of comfort and assurance. This was not her fault, never, not once, he crooned. He was the healing balm, the oxygen she needed to live and breathe, and she clung to every word, held them greedily to her heart. He offered to go with her for a visit to the bishop—they could just go over one evening and bring up the subject of Eli's plight. See what he said.

This, for some reason, was a huge blessing, an encouragement from her beloved, the husband God had given her. She gazed into this tender eyes, the squinting blue eyes she fell in love with, nodded her head, and felt blessed among women.

THE HORSE PLODDED steadily, his well-fed haunches rising and falling with every clack of his hooves. The green-headed horse flies took nose dives at the poor animal, who shook his head and swished his tail in protest.

"Must be a thunderstorm in the making. These flies are bad today," Andy said, snapping the reins for the second time.

May offered no reply, her thoughts wavering between fear and trepidation or casting her cares upon the Lord, her Savior and friend. She watched the miles go by, evaluated the cornfields and second cutting of hay, the state of John Mast's yard and garden, thinking how she would not like to live so close to the road. She'd be ashamed of her garden about this time, the way the weeds were taking over in the late corn. She watched Sally's snow-white laundry dancing in the fickle summer breeze and thought she'd have summer wash to bring in.

"Summer wash" was a description of the stiff towels and sheets brought on by the fierce heat of the sun and hardly a breeze to move it on the line. Baked laundry was what it was. But it was fresh and clean, so a bit of stiffness never hurt anyone. She noticed the way she hung up the underpants, all bunched together, to make less obvious the fact they wore these unmentionable articles of clothing.

She smiled a little.

Children were walking along the shoulder of the road, their feet dusty, their small black coverings and straw hats smashed down on their heads. The little girls on the wagon looked as if they'd rolled around in dust, but their white teeth flashed as they waved.

Andy slowed the horse, turned left, and commented on Noah Lambright's alfalfa before nearing the hitching rack in front of the small black cement barn. Abner Gingerich was in his seventies, had farmed here all his life, until his youngest daughter and her husband Noah took over the farm. A neat single-story house had been built on the east end of the lawn, a cement walkway between the two houses, the small Dawdy house a visible altar to the loving care of the elderly.

They walked up to the small porch together, knocked lightly, and entered upon the lisping, "Come on in."

The interior was shaded, cool, the scent of honeysuckle vine permeating the kitchen. Two hickory rockers were placed side by side, both filled with the thin figures of two white-haired people, both getting to their feet as hurriedly as possible.

"Hello, hello. Do come in. What a lovely surprise!" Abner said, with the enthusiasm of the lonely faced with loving visitors.

There were handshakes, words of welcome, with the aging wife scuttling off to the kitchen for cold mint tea she'd just steeped that morning and put in the icebox.

The tea was delicious and refreshing and the conversation flowed freely as they discussed the weather, crops, the latest death, twins born to a family close to Salesville. May sat beside the bishop's wife, Annie, and received tips on how to make good mint tea and the best way to get rid of beetles on the cabbage in the garden. If she lived to be a hundred years old, she would want to be the image of Annie, so sweet and so loving, every wrinkle in her face speaking of a life well lived.

Eventually, Andy opened the subject of Eli. He thought he saw a shadow cross the bishop's face, but perhaps he was being oversensitive. He related how Eli had been back for a visit with, of all people, one of Melvin Amstutz's boys, Leviticus.

"Oh my. Really? He's not Amish?" the bishop inquired.

"No, he's putting himself through school. Wants to become a lawyer."

"Really?" Again, the kind word, no judgment, only the acceptance of Andy's words.

"He was raised with the colored people and has a heart for them. His main interest is civil rights."

The elderly bishop shook his head. "That's a touchy subject these days. I hear they're de-segregating the schools in the South. I just don't know. You know how it's always been common knowledge of the black race being the descendants of Ham, the curse they have through his misdemeanor. But you know, Andy, that was in the Old Testament, and isn't grace free? *Die gnade unsers Herren* (The grace of our Lord) is for everyone since the New Testament, or since Christ's coming. I know and have known some good colored people." He paused, shook his head. "I don't like to see a white man feeling superior. Higher up."

May nodded, grasped a bit of hope.

Andy plunged ahead. "Now, our Eli, as you know, is half black."

The bishop nodded.

"If he were to return to the Amish and wished to marry a white girl, what would be his chances?"

Clearly the bishop was shocked at this question. He took a moment before asking, "And the girl? What does she say?"

"She would be willing to marry Eli, from what he's told us."

"But he's already no longer a young man. Why would he wait?"

"I think he's hoping the law will change."

The old bishop's head wagged from side to side. "I would certainly not want to be responsible for a union between a dark person and a white one. The laws of our land would hardly call it right, and we have to be law-abiding citizens above all. I'm just afraid it would not be good."

"But you said grace is for every race," Andy argued.

The bishop chuckled. "Indeed, I did. But to think of actually taking Eli into the church at his mature age, to think of being the one responsible for bringing about such a union, I just don't know. I never thought I would see the day when something like this was presented."

"You took me in," May said softly.

"Ah, yes, we did. But not without controversy."

Annie placed a hand on May's arm. "We have no regret about our decision. You have proved your dedication over and over."

"Thank you."

Annie nodded, her eyes sparkling with tears of kindness. "Well, in this matter, same as many others, the best thing is to take a day at a time. We shall see. My wish would be that Eli could find a nice girl, a good Christian church, and live according to God's purpose. I just don't know how anything else would work."

"Yes, it's true, and you're right. But why did you take me in, knowing I would bring this baby into the church?"

"Do you want to know why? We all hoped the baby would have lighter skin as he grew." Annie clucked, adding it was so *shaut* (such a shame).

"So there is no chance of Eli being incorporated into the Amish church with a white girl for his wife?" Andy asked.

"I would say no. Not now. But if the laws were to change, and this young couple felt their love was from God, I don't want to say definitely never. First, the law would have to uphold it, after which many votes would have to be taken. Do you truly feel you would be alright with half-black grandchildren? The physical traits might only be more problematic as time goes on. We want to keep the church pure, of course."

May's shoulders sagged. She seemed to shrink into her chair, become smaller and smaller, as if the bishop's words chiseled away at her well being.

"I just wish . . ." she began.

"Yes, I know, May. You are not in a position I envy. But I haven't said a definite yes or no. It would have to be decided after the law would allow it."

"We understand," Andy said, with a gentle kindness that only he could fully invoke.

THEY DROVE AWAY with more peaceful hearts, still saddened by the reality of the world, but strengthened in their love for the leaders of the church. Simply sharing the heavy load had made it lighter. The foundation of their faith was Jesus Christ, and He promised to share the yoke of heavy burdens, but here was a loving being in flesh and blood, directed by the Holy Spirit, a comfort to the hearts of the afflicted.

There had been no direct answers, only the promise of being with them in their times of trouble, but it was sufficient.

May leaned her head against Andy's shoulder and his hand came down to pat her knee reassuringly.

"It will be alright, May. We need to place our trust entirely on Him, which I know you already do so well."

CHAPTER 19

ELI MOVED AS IF ONE IN A DREAM. HIS DAYS WERE ENDLESSLY boring, the job he had previously enjoyed turning into a vast pool of drudgery in which he swam. He wanted to be in Ohio with her. Nothing here in Arkansas proved to be worth his time and energy.

Lavinia moved about the house like a barge on the Mississippi, her wide backside flower-bedecked, with the ribbons of her apron buried in the rolls of her soft flesh. She threatened and cajoled as he lay stretched out on the sofa, idly watching something on the black-and-white TV in the corner.

She reached down and snapped it off.

"Why you lay there all day?" she huffed, sliding her apron from the left to the right and back again.

"I'm tired, Lavinia."

"No, you're not tired. You're lazy. Ever since you come back from Ohio, it's like you got a bag o' coal tied to your backside. Face to the ground, back bent like an ol' man. No more mopin' around in this house."

"What do you want me to do?" Eli asked, rolling to a sitting position.

"Orphus is out there diggin' around, tryin' to locate the problem with the water leak. Why don't you help?"

"I had no idea. Sorry."

"You don't look it."

Some days he disliked everyone, even good-natured Orphus, who was likely out back digging as slowly as possible or not digging at all, but hanging over the vertical boards between his yard and his neighbor's, talking about catfish or the price of cotton. Which was pretty much what he found.

He stopped to see where Orphus had been plying the digging iron before picking it up and giving it a few thumps into the hard clay. In less than two minutes, he was soaked with sweat, so he shucked his shirt and went back to work. He watched Orphus pretending he didn't see him, knew every slam of the digging iron was one less for him. Eventually, he did come over and took a turn, before handing it over again.

On Saturday, the postman was early, so when he received a letter postmarked "Wooster, Ohio," he dropped the digging tool, took the yard in a few leaps, and jumped up on the porch, missing the steps entirely. With shaking hands, he tore the end off the envelope, his wet fingers scrabbling to retrieve the two folded pages of lined white paper. His eyes burned into the words, devouring her handwriting like a starving dog.

She was well, the days were hot and sunny. Autumn was on its way, she could tell by the flocks of blackbirds going south. Every single word skimmed across the top of her true feelings, her letter a mimic of all they had shared. His disappointment made his heart plummet to his stomach, until he felt nauseated. This letter could have been written by his sisters Lizzie or Fronie.

What had happened? Did she regret her days thinking of him? Had she forgotten her time with him by the wisteria vine? She'd told him outright she loved him and had meant it. *Oh, dear God.* What was the meaning of this?

An anger shot through him like an arrow. He stuffed the letter back in the envelope, carried it to his room, and flung it on the dresser. He stalked out to the kitchen, where Lavinia was washing red beets under the spigot in the sink, her back turned. When he slammed the refrigerator door hard enough to rock it from side to side, she turned, put her fists on her hips, and glared at him.

She pointed her fingers and told him if he was gonna act like a baby, he might as well go back out to Ohio, and she meant every word. Hadn't she and Orphus taken him in from the goodness of their hearts?

"Say it. Who took you in? And who didn't charge you rent? And who cooked for you, huh? Who?"

Eli felt deeply ashamed, humbled to the point of contrition. He hadn't meant to be this way. He could not see himself living here for the rest of his life, after being with Mattie in Ohio. He had to make a choice based on common sense and the need to live in the will of God.

But this letter. This awful misinterpretation of the love between them. He didn't care if the blackbirds were flying south or if she had tried her parents' new cookbook. He wanted to know how she felt about him.

Your friend, Mattie, she'd finished.

Really?

It was maddening, and now he'd been dressed down, thoroughly rebuked by Lavinia, and every word out of her mouth was true. He had turned into a depressed, self-absorbed beast, shoving off reluctantly to work and back again, lying around the house with no offer to help, no incentive to attend any social functions.

He showered, combed his hair, put on a decent shirt and fresh dungarees, and sauntered out of the house, determined to put the letter behind him. Perhaps she had been asked by a handsome fellow, accepted, and didn't have the heart to tell him. Well, two could play this game, and he rocked on the balls of his feet as he walked, flashed his white teeth at passing girls, talked big, strutted around, and did not enjoy any of it.

He walked home beneath the insect-infested street lights, swatting at mosquitoes and wishing he'd never been born. He kicked a tin can into the side of a car and resisted the glare of the motorist before breaking into a slow run, then a sprint, and finally reaching the house.

Fans whirred in the living room where Lavinia sat with Orphus waving a fan at her glistening face, Orphus in his sleeveless T-shirt and boxer shorts.

"What you all hepped up about?" she asked, her eyes going from the TV to his face.

"Just running home."

"Too hot to run."

"Goodnight, Orphus. Lavinia."

"G'night."

He read and reread the letter, but it only increased his despair. After tearing it into a hundred pieces, he tossed it into the waste can, watching the pieces drift down like snowflakes. Then he sat down on the too-small chair by his tiny desk, got out the paper and ink pen he kept there, and began to write.

Dearest Mattie,
Why did you write a letter like that?

He stopped, chewed the tip of his pen, grimaced, trashed the paper, and reached for another one. He started and stopped at least half a dozen times before he gave up and went to bed, where he tossed from the headboard to the footboard. In the morning he went to work at the shoe factory and didn't speak decently to anyone all day.

Lavinia made his favorite peach pie with a few of the late peaches still hanging on from the tree in the back yard. She piled it with whipped cream, just the way he liked it, then sat across from him and dug at him like a relentless bulldozer.

She wanted to know. She needed him to tell her why he was in such an awful mood since he'd returned from his home in Ohio. So Eli told her.

"I figured. Figured had somethin' to do with a girl. You after white girls, boy?"

"I am."

"Oh boy. It ain't gonna happen. Not with those Mennonites."

"Amish."

"Now how you figure? You can't go chasin' rainbows, and you know it. What's the matter with you?"

Orphus grunted assent from his stance at the stove, pouring himself one of his thick black mugs of coffee.

"It's not what you think. I'm waiting, year after year, I'm waiting."

He held up a hand when Lavinia opened her mouth. She closed it again, her black eyes snapping.

"I'm waiting, okay? Levi Amstutz said the law might change sooner than we think. He's in school. To be a lawyer. Civil rights and abuse. He's smart as a whip."

"Smart as a whip, is he now? Well, honey, let me tell you. You'll be old and gray, sitting on a chair with your cane, an' you'll still be waitin' and waitin'. You're black and that ain't going away. If the day comes that a black man can marry a white girl, I'll eat my hat, every one o' my hats."

Orphus smiled, shook his head. "You better listen to her, boy. Afraid she's right."

"But you don't know!" Eli burst out. "Change is coming. You watch. Look what happened after that woman, what was her name? Parks? Rosa Parks. Refused to give up her seat on the bus, was arrested for it, and they boycotted the bus system. Before the year ended, the Supreme Court ruled." Eli's speech became impassioned.

Lavinia held up a hand. "Yeah, yeah. One small thing, that bus riding. Not saying Mrs. Parks wasn't one brave woman, but if you face reality, it's gonna be a lo-o-ng while before you can get married to your white girl."

"But Dr. King is still doing his work. He was jailed, arrested, but he keeps right on going. I'm telling you, things will change."

Orphus shook his head. "If you've been a sharecropper all your life, your descendants will likely never see much change. My parents were free but stayed on picking cotton. This Martin Luther King best watch his step a little. Not saying, not saying."

He held up a hand to silence Eli, who leaned forward, his mouth open in protest.

"It's good. It's good, the work he's doin', but people don't change much inside. Alright, so we get to ride anywhere we want on city buses, our kids go to school with the white kids. Does that stop the hatin' on each other? Change comes slow, an' sometimes only on the outside."

Lavinia nodded, finishing her peach pie before pushing her plate away. "An' what about those Amish? You know anyone so set in tradition they're still wearing those same old clothes ain't changing their mind about marriage anytime soon."

"Don't say that," Eli burst out, before lowering his face in his hands, his elbows on his knees.

Lavinia reached over and patted his shoulder, kept her hand there, her fingers moving to comfort him, saying *ah, ah.* "You know, honey, truth hurts. But love ain't just for one person. It ain't. The ones we think we can't live without are often the ones we need to step along on the road God wants us on."

"I don't want anyone else!" Eli burst out, his face passionate with the force of his feelings.

Lavinia persisted, "But you will. You're barking up the wrong tree."

"No, I'm not. She loves me, and I love her."

But the outburst was laced with doubt.

He knew they were right.

THE DAYS IN Arkansas crawled by, one miserable day blending into another as Eli wrestled with his birth, his upbringing, life at home on the farm. He wrestled with his love for Mattie, wrote impassioned letters without receiving a reply. And still he wrote.

He told her of the hope in his heart, of only a few more years, and how Leviticus thought laws might change. He told her of the time that was coming, a time when they could be together as husband and wife. It was absolutely possible.

He spent many an evening with Levi and his family, sitting on the webbed lawn chairs in the back yard, the fireflies as thick as the stars in the night sky. They talked about his mother, her life with Levi, and Eli missed her with a physical ache.

He traveled home in the fall of the following year, determined to talk to Mattie, somehow. He held his slight mother in his strong arms, shook hands with Andy.

The barn had received a good coat of paint, gleaming white in the late afternoon sun. Everywhere, there were signs of prosperity—a new surrey in the carriage shed, a white picket fence surrounding the yard, more cows, and an addition of four new Belgian workhorses.

Eli looked deep into this mother's eyes and saw only peace and happiness, her face lined now, but with the lines of a cheerful spirit. She had lived with Andy all these years, and it had been a time of peace, of genuine happiness and belonging.

Clara and Oba arrived the second evening, Clara in the driver's seat with the reins held taut, the horse's neck arched as his flying feet scattered gravel, the two children hanging out the back, their elbows hung across the opening, unconcerned at the speed of yet another half-broke horse.

Oba grinned, slapped Eli's back, said he was looking good. Clara, her red hair fading with streaks of gray, pumped his hand with far too much enthusiasm, told him he was the best-looking man she'd ever seen, and why in the world didn't he find himself a wife?

He shrugged, told her Orphus and Lavinia spoiled him, then sat down to his mother's Ohio cooking. He basked in the spirit of closeness, the sense of family surrounding him, and realized he was truly at home. He ate fried chicken and "mush," the western dialect for mashed potatoes. He poured rich, golden chicken gravy over the filling, took a heaping serving spoon of buttered noodles, and thought how a person would always love the food of his childhood.

Things became awkward when Oba teased him about going to see Mattie Troyer. Clara kicked him beneath the table, and he gave her a wounded look, one Eli caught, but thought nothing of. Clara was always bossing him around, and this was not unusual. She changed the subject to the fact Oba had received a new and much better prosthesis. He was able to do just about anything he wanted with less effort, and wasn't that great?

Oba looked at his wife, who was still his beloved. He had only improved with age, his blond hair and beard darkened somewhat but still carrying the perfect symmetry of the Miller beauty. Clara was, however, the delight of his life, the star that guided him out of a deep, cloying depression into an existence filled with humor and achieved goals.

Their daughter Esther was well endowed with the same fiery spirit, a generous thatch of coppery hair and flashing green eyes, while Emanuel sprouted a head of strawberry blond hair and a quiet, gentle spirit.

He went to see Mattie Troyer that same evening and was met at the door by her mother, who seemed to hesitate for only an instant before telling him she would get Mattie.

And then she was there.

Dressed in a powder blue dress, her white covering setting off the ebony of her hair, the deep tan on her beautiful face, the green eyes like a still forest pool, but darker than he remembered.

"Hello, Eli."

"How are you, Mattie?"

He reached for both of her hands, but she backed away, proffering one with a formality, a stiffness.

"I'm well, thank you."

They shook hands with the same sense of politeness one would reserve for the meeting of a stranger.

"Mattie, I . . ." Eli stumbled over the words, felt an alarm rise within him.

She shook her head, her mouth in a firm line. "No, Eli. I . . . I am dating a young man from Mount Hope. He and I are getting married in the fall."

He stepped back, went numb all over. He opened his mouth to speak, but there were no words to form the shock and denial he felt.

"But why?" he croaked, finally.

"I'm sorry, Eli. I really am. In all fairness, I did not answer your letters. I gave you no encouragement. I just . . ."

She shrugged, her gaze drifting to the fern in the pot on the bench by the door.

"You didn't bother to tell me it was over?"

"We never dated."

"You know why we never dated."

She nodded. "I'm sorry. But you know as well as I do what we were up against. The laws of the country are one thing, but the rules and traditions of the plain church, quite another. And I respect my heritage and the *ordnung* of my people. Love is a fickle thing and a person needs to stay on guard. We mix up our own will for God's will, and it is so enticing to want what we cannot have."

She watched Eli's face darken, his eyebrows draw down by the force of his anger.

"Our love is not fickle, nor was it our own will," he ground out.

"Wasn't it?"

"No, not for me, it wasn't. I have never felt for anyone what I felt for you, and I never will. I will never marry anyone, never."

"Don't say that, Eli. Don't."

After that, there was nothing left to say. And still he could not leave.

Finally, he blurted out, "Do you love him?"

"I do. He is a very nice young man, and one I respect with my whole heart."

"But do you love him in the way you loved me? You know we had something special, we waited for years. How can you throw all that away? How?"

"Eli, you must remember, we were young, attracted to each other, our love was not the kind that brings peace and joy over many years. The kind that grows and blossoms into the real thing, not the heart-thumping infatuation where you really think you can't live one moment without knowing we can be together."

"Oh, so you had some strange spiritual enlightenment and you've risen above a mere mortal like me?"

Her eyes were wells of sadness when she lifted them to his.

"Alright, Eli, you know I loved you, and you loved me. But we can never be together, and you know that. I am going to marry a fine young man, and you will do well to find a young woman worthy of you."

"No!"

"Goodbye, Eli. I wish you God's blessing." And with that, she turned and went into the house, closing the screen door softly behind her.

There was nothing left for him to do but turn and go down the steps and out to his truck. He was blinded by tears, numb with the disintegration of his hopes and dreams, bitterly disappointed.

What was he to do?

How was he expected to live his life, his whole being yearning for life on the farm, the slow easy rhythm of Amish life, where God was with you in the fields, spoke to you through the rich smell of over-turned sod and waving grasses? Without his Amish parents, without any guidance, how was he expected to find true and lasting happiness, when all his roads had always led to Mattie Troyer?

When he returned, Clara and Oba had risen from their chairs, ready to depart after an evening with their closest relatives, a time they all looked forward to each week.

Eli slammed the screen door and flopped on a chair, put his head in his hands, as Clara glanced at May and raised her eyebrows. Nothing was said till Esther yelled from the doorway, telling her parents it was time to leave, she was getting sleepy. Clara told her to sit down, or go lie on the couch, they wanted to talk to Eli.

"You can talk to him some other time," she called out, and Oba told her firmly that they couldn't. She slouched away from the door, stomped her feet the whole way to the couch, and threw herself on it with an exaggerated sigh.

The remainder of the evening was spent in conversation, caring, and sharing their innermost thoughts and feelings. Clara told him about her life before Oba, when she had persuaded herself love was not for her and she lived an independent life.

Oba grinned. "Do you remember how rude I was to Clara at first? I could hardly stand her. Surely you remember?"

"I do."

"Well, think about it, Eli. God is in control of our destiny. We can make all the choices we want, but in the end, God allows everything to happen for a purpose. We rest in His hands."

"But why did He allow me to meet Mattie?"

"To prepare the way for the one he has for you."

"No. No. I refuse to believe it. How can I ever trust God again, ever?"

"You give your life to Him. Whatever He does, you have faith it is for your own good."

"Yeah, right."

Clara made coffee, the same bitter, black brew she always made. She set the thick, white mugs on the table, brought the cream and sugar, and sat close to Oba. Eli saw her place a hand on his thigh and keep it there, a gesture of affection and caring that touched a place deep inside him. Oh, it was true. Oba could not bear the sight of her in the beginning, could not imagine he would ever change. The unlikeliest couple ever. But all he could think of was Mattie being married to someone else, someone she didn't love. She couldn't love him in the way she loved Eli.

May sat on the sidelines, quiet as always, listening wisely, her heart an open wound for Eli. She had brought him into the world, through her own illegal alliance with Clinton, and like a field of golden wheat sheaves, her reaping lay before her in the despondent slope of Eli's shoulders, the pain and confusion in his brown eyes.

She spoke to him alone the following morning. She told him of her greatest fear, to have him follow the easy road of depravity, to fall into the snares of the devil, through every pleasure the world had to offer. She told him to stay true to God, to be in His army, to fight for what was right and good and true.

The hardest thing in the world was to tell him he could probably never be Amish, if he wanted a wife and children. All that he loved about the Amish could be found among others—that goodness, obedience, love, faith, all of it, could be found in the world. The choice was his.

And when he drove away, she watched the small puffs of gray dust well up behind the wheels of his truck and gently waft away in the early morning fog. She prayed he could find a happy and God-fearing life.

Too long, she had harbored a false hope, conceived the beginning of something she knew could never be. She let him go in her heart, opened her hands, and allowed the breeze to take her beloved Eli, freeing him the way she had always known she must do.

CHAPTER 20

HE WENT BACK TO THE SHOE FACTORY, BACK TO ORPHUS AND Lavinia. He felt smothered between the four walls of the factory and the small, brightly painted walls of the house. Lavinia kept her words to herself, did the cooking and the washing and the cleaning, and thought sure as God's mercy this boy was going through the wringer.

But as time went on, Eli's heart began to heal. As the juniper berries turned red and the waxy holly leaves shone among the dead brown leaves and yellow grass of late autumn, his whistling could be heard as he pruned the crabapple tree in the back yard.

He went to church, his white shirt bringing out the coppery tones of his skin, his hair black against the collar. He raised his voice when they stood to sing, worshipped God with arms outstretched, ate sweet potato pie and fried green tomatoes, ham hocks and okra, learned to appreciate the steady rhythm of this new life.

He knew he had no choice anymore. Not a whisper of hope among his dreams. Mattie Troyer had been a fantasy, a wanting of his heart that had never been God's will for his life.

As he gave in to his life in Arkansas, he began to appreciate the fact that he lived among people of his own birth, lived on in the culture of his father. He had never known him, but his blood ran in his veins, his skin color was the color of his own. He was raised white, in another culture, but he could never truthfully be a part of them.

ON HIS WAY home from work, he noticed a sign pointing to the center of town.

FARMER'S MARKET 8 TO 5.

Lavinia had been yelling about the Japanese beetles getting into her zucchini when the plants were at their most tender. She was hungry for fried squash, and look at that, they'd gone and ruined every last stalk and vine.

And because the late afternoon was golden with the promise of summer, the honeysuckle vines fragrant and sweet, he decided to see if he could find a few zucchini squash for Lavinia. He made a few wrong turns but found the group of vendors along the left side of Finch Street, lining the small town square.

Some of them were packing up the day's leftovers, wooden crates containing head lettuces and spring onions. Empty crates told of the produce having been sold, the cigar boxes of money opened, bills being counted. He found a parking space and went to the first vendor, a grizzled white man with a huge belly and denim overalls stretched snugly across it.

"Any zucchini left?"

"Nope. Sold the last one about a hour ago."

He moved on.

She walked down the street as if she owned it, carrying a crate of cucumbers as if it weighed no more than a crate of feathers, set it on an empty spot, and began to remove them, stacking them in neat rows along the few zucchini squash. Her dark hair was pulled back in a no-nonsense ponytail and she wore a floppy men's T-shirt over a pair of loose jeans. She looked up, annoyed at being distracted, then continued picking out the best cucumbers.

"Excuse me?" he said.

"Yeah."

"Those zucchini for sale?"

"Why wouldn't they be? They're on the table."

"I'll take them."

"Fifty."

She never looked at him. He took the zucchini, she took his money, he said thank you, and she never bothered with an answer. He thought she could surely learn some customer skills, couldn't imagine selling anything with that personality disorder.

HER NAME WAS Alice.

She lived on a farm about nine and a half miles out of town, along the Cottonwood Creek where the dirt road ran along some of the most fertile soil in the Mississippi Delta.

Her father's parents had been sharecroppers, lived in houses barely fit to raise a family, relying on the scrawny wages of the white landlord. They spent their days planting, hoeing, and picking cotton, spending sweet, humid evenings lounging on the crooked front porch with family gathered around them. No matter if it was a whole passel of young cousins, a distant uncle, or a great aunt, everyone was welcome on Richard and Dinah Hopkins's front porch.

Ten children, and the middle one named Richard, Jr., the one with a shrewd eye and lofty ambitions, the one determined to better himself and become a landowner, beholden to no one. In time, with hard work and a head for numbers, he acquired the old Townsend place from the town's chief alcoholic when the house fell to wreck and ruin.

Richard and Louise scrimped and saved, worked side by side, until the place looked nothing like it had before. The barn and outbuildings were red, the house a respectable blue with black shutters and a deep verandah along two sides. Richard had always longed for a porch wide and deep enough to accommodate a whole slew of relatives, just the way they'd been brought up. Evening was a time of catching up with each other's lives.

Alice was the middle child, like her father before her. There was Ralph and Harold, her, then Tina and Bobby. She had her father's work ethic, loved the soil and the outdoors, planted, tilled, and harvested alongside him. She had no interest in men, thought of them as shiftless, lazy. Most of them, anyway.

She'd been dating Harvey, but he showed no interest in the farm, just spiffed himself up in ridiculous clothes and pranced down the street with her hanging on to his arm like a faithful dog on a leash. They'd go to the cinema, eat a hamburger and French fries, while he regaled her with stories of his many accomplishments and wasn't a bit interested in any of her own. Especially not the farm.

After Harvey, she met Ammon Amstutz, who hoodwinked her into believing he was a good person for exactly two weeks before trying to kiss her in places completely inappropriate. After that, she decided so much for men—black, white, or in between, there were hardly any good ones left.

Her mother badgered her, saying her age was slipping up on her, and when was she ever going to stop being so picky? She couldn't cook, had no idea how to bake a good loaf of bread or a decent cake. How would she ever become a good wife? But she laughed her good-natured laugh, patted her shoulder, and said she could put up with an old maid in the house; the way she helped her father was a pure blessing, too.

Alice noticed Eli.

She thought, *Now that is one handsome man, with that skin the color of maple syrup, the wide shoulders and big brown eyes.*

But as she was known to do, when she felt an attraction, she immediately repelled him, her pride always turning her voice into an icy version of her real self. She'd never met a man who was truly worth her time. This one sure looked good, but she wasn't about to risk it.

He came walking down the street the following week and bent over to look at the green tomatoes as if to purchase them. She gave him a sidelong glance, then went right ahead stacking crates of green beans, keeping her back turned.

My, but he was one good-looking man. She turned to look at him, caught the smile he gave to Norah Downs and thought, *Oh, won't she eat that one up though.* She checked the zucchini supply, wishing she had done something with her hair.

Oh, lord, here he comes.

"Hello. How are you?"

She kept her back turned.

"Miss?"

"Yeah?"

"Zucchini?"

She pointed with her chin. "Help yourself."

He did. She gave him a paper bag, wouldn't look at him.

"May I ask what your name is?"

"Alice." She busied herself, riffling through the green beans, arranging the tops of the radishes.

"Just Alice?"

"Alice Hopkins."

He noticed her eyes, the way her eyebrows rose like the silhouette of a raven when it drifted on summer skies. Her skin was like dew on a ripe apple.

She actually looked at him then. Only a swift glance before turning away.

"Do you live around here?"

"Why do you want to know?"

"Oh, just curious. I didn't tell you my name."

She shrugged.

"I'm Eli Weaver."

She nodded.

"Do you know Orphus and Lavinia Brown?"

"No."

"They're my aunt and uncle. I live with them."

She turned away, raised her eyebrows to a buxom white woman wearing a tiny straw hat bedecked with limp daisies, her hair colored an electric shade of red. He moved aside till she finished serving her, became uncomfortable when another customer followed, then another. He tucked the brown paper bag under his arm and walked away. There would always be next week.

She found herself regretting every customer after he left. She tried to shrug off the fact that he would not bother returning, given her lack of interest, but couldn't quite stop hoping he'd try again. So she wore a red shirt the following week, tucked it into a pair of slacks, and wore sandals instead of going barefoot .

He noticed immediately and became bolder, asking her if he could drive out to see the place where the fine produce was grown. She said she guessed so, but not till after supper, as busy as they were in produce season.

Lavinia took notice. She pressed his white short-sleeved shirt, even pressed his second-best pair of jeans. She told him he needed a haircut, then gave him a tube of gel for his hair on Friday when he came home from work. Lord knew the boy did just fine in the looks department, but she certainly could help along now that it seemed like he was perking up around the edges.

When he did go get his hair cut and washed his truck, cleaned the inside, and hung up one of those foolish pine trees that smelled like rotten potatoes, she decided something was in the air, but far be it from her to try to find out what.

He hummed a song while he showered, sang while he buttoned his shirt. Something felt right, although he told himself not to get his hopes up too much.

It was late spring, early summer, the time of roses climbing over picket fences, the scent of blooming wildflowers and newly mown hay, tilled earth with cornstalks about a foot high. Immense level fields of cotton stretched to the tree-lined horizon, as if the uneven line of treetops served as a protective border for the cotton fields.

He thought of his ancestors, bent over the cotton, the burlap bags slung over one shoulder, working, working, every single day from dawn to dusk, entering hovels, living on bare necessities, no wages, no hope of ever being free.

Here he was, dark-skinned, driving his own truck, employed at a shoe factory, saving his wages, living free as the white men around him. He still didn't have some of the privileges they enjoyed, but so much had improved. A wave of appreciation for his life washed over him, the work of the civil rights leaders, the ways of the Amish instilled in him. He thought he just might qualify as one of the most blessed people on earth.

He found the farm without any wrong turns, which he took as a good omen. Finding himself suddenly shy, he shut off the engine and stayed behind the wheel, searching the deep front porch for a sign of her. This was far more than he had expected, really. The house was significant, the deep porch surrounding it amazing. The fields were dotted with all kinds of healthy plants, planted in deep rows, surrounded by wire fences and thick growths of newly planted fir trees.

A red Farmall tractor was parked by the barn, two flatbed wagons in good repair behind it. There was an open shed with long tables and wooden vegetable crates packed to the ceiling. All this was taken in by a long, sweeping glance before the door of the house was pushed open, and a man wearing overalls and a red bill cap was followed by a tall, slim woman who could only be her mother, he thought. When they reached his truck, they told him to come on up to the porch and set, Alice was still upstairs, they'd had a tractor break down that afternoon.

The introductions were casual—Rich and his wife Louise. Presented with a glass of lemonade with ice cubes and a wooden rocking chair, Eli felt immediately comfortable.

"Only Bobby at home anymore. Rest of 'em flew the coop. And Bobby's off playing baseball in town."

Eli was told about the other grown children. Harold had moved to Georgia to be a surveyor, with his wife Margaret and two kids, and Ralph lived in town working as a cotton gin mechanic. Tina got married at seventeen and lived in Detroit, Michigan with the biggest loser of all time, a drunk and a womanizer, no one to be proud of. Tina, apparently, was the wild child of the family, the black sheep. But they loved her and knew she'd figure life out eventually. Some folks just had to learn the hard way.

This was all said with a sense of good humor, of acceptance. Eli thought in passing that a daughter choosing a life like that would be a horrible tragedy to an Amish family. How was it that these calm, matter-of-fact parents seemed to accept it as no big deal? Perhaps he had been sheltered more than he realized.

When Alice appeared, he was surprised at his own reaction. She was like a vision in a pale pink dress, the skirt flaring around her slender hips, her bare feet making no sound on the wooden floor boards.

"Hello," she said softly, her voice low.

"Good evening."

"You wanted to see the fields?"

"Sure. Yes please, I mean . . . I'd love to." He stumbled over his words.

Smiling, they both turned and went down the steps, missing entirely the raising of Louise's fist as she hung back her head and whispered, "Finally!"

Alice showed him the way the potato bugs were controlled, the cucumbers planted a distance apart, the vines capable of growing three or four yards. The sweet corn was already higher than the corn grown in the fields for the animals.

He found himself mesmerized by the thick burr in the pronunciation of her words, the lilt in her voice when she spoke of her love of growing things. He told her he grew up on a farm in Ohio, had always hoped to own a farm one day, but was pretty much stuck in the shoe factory now. He didn't mention the sizable amount growing in his savings account in the bank in town. He didn't want to brag, and he could tell she was not easily impressed anyway.

He asked if she'd enjoy riding into town for ice cream. She said yes. He opened the truck door for her, then closed it carefully after she was seated, before going around to his side and getting behind the wheel. As the truck moved off, Richard looked at Louise and both raised their eyebrows and grinned.

"This just might be the one," Louise chortled.

"Oh man!" Richard exulted.

They were ready to give over the farm. Ready to let Alice take over, the only one who ever showed the slightest interest in growing things. Bobby was well on the way to having a career in baseball, had already secured a scholarship at the University of Arkansas. The last thing on his mind was growing and selling garden produce. The two oldest boys hated the searing heat of summer, hated the work they'd had to endure as boys on the farm, so that left Alice if the Hopkins farm was meant to continue.

But Alice needed a husband. Indeed she did. Which, up to this point, had seemed pretty hopeless. Whatever was wrong with Harvey, they never did find out, but he'd seemed ambitious, interested. As the sun sank behind the jagged line of trees, they rose and went indoors to avoid the worst of the mosquitos.

THE TRUCK TIRES hummed on the macadam, the radio played a soft melodious chorus, the air coming through the open windows laden with the scent of Arkansas in early summer. They drove out to the ice cream shop on Route 155, where the river made a wide bend before joining the Mississippi. Eli went around to her side, opened the door, and helped her out with a hand on her elbow. She hardly knew what to say or do—no one had ever done that before.

The middle-aged white lady pushed back the small window and said, "Help you?"

"Yes. I'll have a dish of strawberry," Eli said.

"Same for me," Alice nodded.

They were seated at a wooden picnic table, the air thick with the scent of the slow-moving river, the scent of hidden logs and lazy fish swimming close by, of turtles sunning on the banks and bullfrogs hiding just below the surface. Mosquitoes whined and white moths circled crazily around the lights of the small ice cream building.

"This is really good," Eli offered, suddenly quite shy.

He had found her presence in the truck a bit intimidating. His hand on the gear shift had been far too close to the fabric of her skirt, the song on the radio too achingly lovely. It was more comfortable out here in the air, but still he was very aware of their nearness to each other.

"It is good."

They ate a few more mouthfuls of ice cream before Eli tried again.

"Were you born and raised on the farm?"

"Yes."

"The only place you ever lived?"

"Mm-hmm."

"Can you believe I was raised on an Amish farm in Ohio?"

She looked at him, puzzled. "What's that?"

"A type of religion, a culture."

"You mean, like Jewish or Catholic?"

"Sort of. It's Christian. I guess you go to church?"

"We do. I was baptized at sixteen."

He felt a huge wave of relief listening to her humble confession. He had to restrain himself from reaching for her hand, from putting an arm around her waist to tell her how glad he was.

"Although," she continued, "of late, I'm not going very regularly. Seems as if I don't have the heart for it or something."

"You're busy. Probably you feel tired is all."

She smiled genuinely for the first time. "That's good of you to say that. Anyway, explain about the Amish."

So he told her of his birth, his upbringing, his mother, and how he ended up in Arkansas. She listened quietly and scraped the last of her ice cream from the dish before getting up to place it in the trash can.

"So you weren't accepted? And you're only half black?" She shook her head.

"It took me a long time to face the facts."

"Yeah, well." She looked off across the street, her eyes following the vehicles that came and went. She slapped at a mosquito on her leg. "You think things will be different someday?" she asked.

"Hardly. The Amish are slow to change. Tradition is very meaningful to them. I always respected that. Valued it, really."

"That explains a lot about you."

"How?"

"You're different than most men."

"In a good way?"

"Yes."

Their eyes met and held in the dim, faraway light of the ice cream place. Words were not necessary the way they flowed unspoken between them. The attraction was more than physical beauty, more than both wanting a relationship that would be genuine. Both recognized an inherent goodness in the other, coupled with the caution stemming from failed romances.

On the way home, the night air held a hint of a chill, a too-cold breeze, so he suggested rolling the windows up to stay warm. She agreed, then began to laugh, a slow, rolling chuckle that turned into an all-out sound of sheer delight.

"What's so funny about rolling up the window?"

"Oh, now don't be offended, okay? But I hate the smell of that stupid little pine tree. It smells like wet diapers!"

Eli burst out laughing, a deep sound that came from his stomach. "Huh! You really mean that?" he asked, turning to look at her. "I hung that thing up for your benefit. You know, impressing the lady."

She was still smiling, wiped her eyes, and said, "Let me tell you, little pine trees that smell like wet diapers do not impress me at all. Sorry."

After that moment of honesty, the true lighthearted banter could begin. They turned up the radio, sang along with the words.

He walked her to the front door, did not hold her hand and certainly did not kiss her goodnight. He told her he'd enjoyed his time with her immensely, and she thanked him for the ice cream.

As he turned to go back down the steps, the rose-colored draperies fell back into place, as Richard and Louise scuttled, giggling like school children, back to bed, where they lay staring at the ceiling.

Finally, Louise spoke. "He never even kissed her goodnight."

"I know."

"You think this isn't the one, then?"

"Wait and see."

But there was no way around it, disappointment lay between them like a third person, making it hard for them to go back to sleep.

CHAPTER 21

"MY ZUCCHINI PLANTS ARE RESURRECTED FROM THE DEAD," Lavinia told Orphus at the supper table as she spooned a second helping of rice and beans onto her plate. She lifted the salt shaker and sprinkled a generous amount over it, then lifted her fork.

"You mean them beetles left 'em alone after all this time?" he answered, putting the final touches on spreading apple butter on every corner of his bread.

"They did. I'm going to have a bumper crop."

No more zucchini buying, Eli thought, but gave no hint of his thoughts. But never mind, he didn't need an excuse to see her now. He hadn't asked for her telephone number, but he felt certain she'd be happy to see him at the farmer's market. Somehow, he couldn't picture driving up to her house without a clear invitation. Too many memories of the Troyer farm, the choking sensation in his chest. The desperation. It had been real, hadn't it? He had been so sure, so convinced God would make a way, would see to it that he could have the love of his life. Had it all been his own will? His nature to long for something he could not have?

On a Friday in the late afternoon, it seemed as if he had nothing at all to fight against. The day was golden, the air like liquid sunshine flowing through him, flowing around him, down the street to the farmer's market where he found her waiting on a harried old gentleman who was near blind and almost deaf.

He stood by the green beans and watched her deal patiently with the elderly gentleman. She never acknowledged Eli but kept trying to tell the man there was a difference between zucchini and cucumbers. And no, the corn wouldn't be in till after the middle of July.

He thought perhaps she would turn to him with the roll of her eyes or say something about the inept old man, but she merely watched him shamble away, the smooth seat of his trousers and loose shoe sole speaking of his poverty.

She gave him the full benefit of her smile, her straight white teeth flashing from her dark face. Her hair was slicked back away from her face in a tight bun, making her eyes appear even larger, with thick black lashes. Had he ever thought white skin and green eyes beautiful? God had certainly created beauty in different ways and created the eye of the beholder as well.

"How's it going?" he asked.

"Good. I'm actually having a great day."

"Are you up for ice cream again tomorrow evening?" he asked.

"Only ice cream? Nothing else?" she asked, then smiled again.

"Oh. You want to go some place nice?"

"I do."

"Okay, Alice. You dress up, and we'll go."

She smiled, easily, freely. He smiled back, and they stood there like two people alone in the world, till a customer cleared her throat and said, "Excuse me?"

THE EVENING WAS memorable, awash in fireflies and her dark beauty. She was stunning in a white dress with a straight skirt. He knew he was falling for her too soon, too recklessly, but he didn't care.

She ordered the steak and baked potato, and he said he'd have the same, and they laughed together, her eyes like liquid gold. She asked if they were always going to do that, and he said of course they would.

They clinked their glasses in a toast to their happy times, come what may, and for an instant, Eli felt as if he could cry with happiness.

THEN, LIKE A dark omen of trouble, Tina came home, battered and bruised, smoking cigarettes, and harboring ill feelings toward them all, especially Alice. She brought her three untrained children, who ran around the house breaking things and talking back to anyone who tried to straighten them out. She cursed at Alice, called Eli "that high yellow pansy," and made fun of him to his face.

Alice became withdrawn, ashamed of the chaos the family was descending into. Eli could no longer pick up Alice at the house, but instead he met her at the end of the produce fields where they could walk across the field to his truck.

"You can't let her do this to you," Eli told her for the hundredth time.

She shrank back in a corner of the truck, her arms crossed defensively, the smile he cherished turned into a scowl, her eyebrows lowered in anger.

They drove down the road, neither one aware of where they were going, or what they would do. They never dressed up and went out for a good meal at a fine restaurant, could only sneak away on occasion.

"It's not me, Eli. It's my parents. They're afraid if they don't protect her, she'll . . . well, she's threatening to take her own life. She was treated worse than most animals. Dad is working on her to try and get her into a hospital for treatment. Mom can't do a thing with her. Those kids! Ugh. Oh, Eli, you have no idea."

She began to cry, softly at first. He slowed, pulled off the road, then reached for her, pulled her into his arms, and simply held her, stroked her back, and told her to cry it out. A great sense of pity overwhelmed him to think of his, yes, *his*, beautiful girl thrown into this bewildering situation with seemingly no solution.

She drew back and wiped her eyes with the tip of her shirt. Silently, he handed over his clean handkerchief.

"You okay?" he asked, as he tenderly gazed into her swollen eyes.

"I am. I'm always the strong one, the one who can handle everything. But I feel like I can't stand living in the same house with Tina and those kids. And I see no way out of it. Ever."

Marry me. Please marry me, was the only thought in his mind. He wished he could say it, wished he could do it, but knew it was far too soon, too sudden. There was the farm, all the work to consider, the household duties doubled with the children cavorting unchecked.

"I wish I could help," he said, meaning every word.

"You're too good, too kind. Sometimes I'm not sure you're real."

"I'm very real. You don't know me very well yet. I can be a very unpleasant person if I want to be."

She lifted her head, drew back to look into his deep brown eyes. He looked at her, the dark symmetry of her perfect face, and knew the time was right to let her know how deeply he felt about her. Slowly, he bent his head, found the softness of her mouth, and kissed her very gently, then drew her even closer into his arms.

She sighed, lifted dewy eyes to his, where they stayed for a long while, their hearts' secrets exchanged without words.

WHEN THE SUMMER was over, Tina finally agreed to be hospitalized, and Louise took over the care of the children. In a matter of weeks, order was restored, with the children responding to the discipline coupled with real attention and caring.

Ben and Tim were the biggest problems, with Judy coming in close behind. Raised in a squalid inner-city apartment with an abusive, drunken father, they had to be taught the basics of society, good manners; stealing and cheating were both met with consequences.

Week by week, Eli heard of their progress and saw the change in Alice as she reached one solution, then another. By the time the last of the produce was harvested, the air had a decided nip to it and she was restored to her normal, cheery self.

When Tina returned with an arsenal of medication, she was given a choice. To allow the family to parent the three children, or move into her own house, a small rental property close to a mile away. Eli was allowed to sit in at family discussions by this time, although he had a hard time feeling welcomed by the troubled Tina.

Ben yelled that he was going absolutely nowhere, and Tim pounded the table with a fist. Judy began to cry, sobbing loudly, her mouth opened as far as it could possibly go. Tina became distraught and argued all the reasons why their ultimatum was unfair until Richard put a stop to everything by announcing calmly that it would be best if they moved.

Eli did his best to help, scouring the secondhand shops for furniture, dishes, and towels to equip Tina's new place. He worked side by side with Alice, encouraging Tina when she showed interest in lining the cupboard shelves with paper, then piling the dishes into neat sections. Tina was frail and her face and arms were scattered with scars of past abuse, as was her mind, heart, and thoughts. Everything, just everything, was an insurmountable obstacle for her, and this Eli recognized quickly. If she was given one small duty and then given plenty of time to perform it, she made much more progress than if she was thrown into the day without clear directions given. Eli managed to guide her without being patronizing, and while still giving her space to do things her own way. When Alice saw the results of Eli's understanding, her heart was filled with so much love and gratitude, she could hardly wait till he came home from work and drove to her house to help along with the job of moving Tina into her own home.

And in this way, he was incorporated into the family, became a fixture, a huge asset where Tina and her children were concerned. Eventually, he won over the children with his good humor, their adoration bordering on worship when he took them to the river and taught them how to fish. Alice packed a picnic basket with all kinds of healthy food, and Tina sat on the blanket, her knees drawn up like a child, her arms wrapped around them, a small smile on her thin, dark face.

Eli was amazed at the likeness of his own life on the farm with his parents and siblings in Ohio. The work was always there, from early spring till late frost, except in a different way. He found himself thrilled with the tender new growth, the ongoing harvesting and replanting of green beans, lima beans, red beets, okra, the heavy, round heads of cabbage placed into wooden crates and lugged on the back of the flatbed wagon.

Alice worked side by side with her father, seemingly never tiring of the heat, the insects, and the dirt. Eli put in his days cutting leather at the shoe factory, watching the clock every afternoon until he could escape the confines of the four walls to drive out to the farm to Alice and her family.

Sometimes, it seemed as if Ohio was only a scattered dream. Had he ever been Amish at heart? He supposed he was, sheltered in the way young children were kept from much of the influences that form the world outside. He truly loved his mother, his stepfather, and siblings, knew he had been blessed beyond measure. But would he still be happy there, knowing his future would have to be spent alone? Or would God have provided a wife and children in time?

Only sometimes, these thoughts of life with the Amish took away the peace and happiness he was finding here in Arkansas. He was slowly learning to love the land, the heat, and the scent of mud and silt in the low-lying delta.

What was home?

Home was where your father and mother made a secure place within four walls, a place of rest and acceptance, a place where love wasn't questioned. The church they attended together was the spiritual home, where he found the beginning of his faith, but neither of them were meant to be. The circumstances of his birth were no fault of his own, and yet he had to make this sacrifice of leaving his mother, enter into the culture of a father he had never met.

There were the photographs.

Proudly, Lavinia had brought the album to him, sat beside him, and laid it across his lap, her eyes closed, her chin tilted with the importance of this moment. From the pages of the album emerged a handsome colored man, a complete stranger in whose lineage he was born. His blood ran in his veins, his African ancestry dwelt within his cells. He felt no connection. Numb to any emotion, he slowly scanned the pages. Clinton Brown. Clinton and Roy, his father. Black as any colored person could be. His eyes slid to the backs of his own hands. Light in comparison, with his white mother's Swiss ancestry mixed in. Clinton and his mother, Martha. Lavinia with a whole bunch of nieces and nephews. Arpachshad. The doctor. He certainly didn't resemble one back then. Clinton with a slim black girl, dressed in a fancy suit, a flower in the lapel of the coat.

He looked at Lavinia, growled a question about his father staying with the black girl. Lavinia drew back, smacked his arm.

"Now don't go questioning the works of the Lord Jesus," she said sharply. "You here for a good reason."

He made no reply, simply flipped the pages before closing the cover of the album, laying it aside, and getting to his feet. Lavinia looked up, questioned his dark mood.

"I don't know. Probably it would have been better if I hadn't been born."

Lavinia hissed and thumped a hand on the arm of the couch. "Now don't you start, young man. Don't you even start. Those are the words the devil put in your head. Pity, pity myself. You were conceived, born, and grew up with His blessing, young man, and don't you forget it. There isn't a hair on your head He doesn't know about, and His love follows you wherever you go. So stop it."

"How did my father die? How come no one can tell me why he isn't alive today?"

"Nobody knows."

And Eli had to be content with that unsatisfying answer. Content in the knowledge his mother had been in horrendous circumstances, left the farm in desperation with the only available form of escape, which was her secret friend, Clinton Brown. He could not allow himself to imagine a life without his sweet, blond-haired, brown-eyed mother, the love and nurturing she had given him.

In spite of all he had left, he knew Orphus and Lavinia had been the ones who awakened him to the futility of a life with Mattie Troyer. He knew his own soft-spoken mother had truly believed God would provide a way for him to have the desires of his heart, would have given her own life if it made it a possibility. In spite of her prayers, her earnest good wishes, it had all been a selfish desire, one God had not included in His plan.

His days of soul searching had been bitter, an unending cycle of letting go and starting over. His love for Mattie had been true, pure, one he had never doubted, and yet it had not been meant to be. How could all this come about so unexpectedly?

He hummed along with the radio, felt the late summer dust in the air, the time of ripe pumpkins and gourds, the rustle of brown cornstalks and late tomatoes rotting on the vine. He was visited by a sense of joy, an outpouring of excitement for the future, living in the land of his roots, with those of his culture. He knew as surely as the sky above there was real promise of a life well lived here in Arkansas, with God at the helm of his small vessel.

HE ATTENDED THE South Baptist Church with Alice's family one Sunday when the frost was thick on the pumpkin vines, the train could be heard in the river bottoms, the long, lonely wail of the whistle as clear as day.

He was in awe of the power and the glory of God's Word. He sang and swayed, clapped his hands, and worshipped God along with those surrounding him. And he found them beloved. He found a deep sense of belonging, one totally absent of the need to prove himself, to prove the merits of his dark skin. Here was acceptance, pure and unrestrained. He was gathered into the arms of love and rejoiced with those who honored God in their own way.

And he was one of them.

He found himself making comparisons with the well-ordered, proper way of being seated in the Amish church that was held in various houses across the settlement. The slow, easy rhythm of plainsong from the thick black *Ausbund*, the German hymns of the forefathers. The drone of one gentle preacher's voice or the fiery calling of another. The silent tears of one who was moved by the fervent message. How they believed in order, to be circumspect with praise and devotion, to pray in silence hidden away behind closed doors. And God was there. Yes, He was.

He was here, too, in this white church with the steeple reaching to the Heavens, the air thick with the scent of oak leaves and chrysanthemums piled along the altar, something strictly forbidden among the Amish—there could be no decorating of flowers in God's house.

And he smiled to himself after services when he saw two women dressed in pink roll their eyes and say, just loud enough for him to hear, "That Betsy outdid herself with those brown leaves. Ugliest thing I ever see," punctuated by self-righteous sniffs and lifting of chins. He thought of the time he overheard Annie tell Verna Mast that Emmie's pies were hardly edible, she didn't know why she wouldn't realize it once and change her shortening to lard. This at the dinner table in church. He smiled again, thinking of human beings scattered all over the world, Christians indeed, but prone to the ways of the flesh.

He reached over and squeezed Alice's hand. She raised her liquid brown eyes to his and raised her eyebrows. He repeated the gesture with his own.

ON CHRISTMAS DAY, when the fencerows were bursting with the glossy green leaves of the holly bushes, bright red berries dotting the greenery, the brown grasses of winter appearing restful, a time of dormancy promising the renewal of new growth, Eli and Alice walked hand in hand down the long country road.

There was a chill in the air, enough to increase their steps to a brisk pace, getting away from the uproarious crowd in the house seemingly bursting with extended family, food, music, and loud conversation. Alice was laughing, saying he would never want to be at another Christmas dinner with her family, the way the house was rocking on its foundation. He stopped, reached out to place both hands on her shoulders, gently turning her to face him. She looked up, her dark eyes questioning him.

"Alice." His voice was laced with seriousness. Her eyes fell before the light in his. "I want to spend every Christmas with you and your family as long as I live. This is where I belong." He hesitated, then reached up to place the palms of his hands on either side of her face. "I love you, Alice."

She kept her eyes lowered, her heart racing.

He lifted her chin, looked deep into her eyes as she looked into the light shining from the depth of his heart. Slowly, he bent to place his lips on hers, a declaration of his true devotion and love. She responded with a glad cry of welcome, her arms drawing him into an embrace of strength and oneness. As his lips claimed hers again, he felt the beginning of a deep emotion from the center of his being.

"I love you, too, Eli." She spoke softly, barely above a whisper, but the words were etched on his heart forever.

"How soon can we be married?" he asked.

"You haven't asked me yet."

They laughed together.

"Will you marry me, Alice? Please tell me you'll be my wife."

"I will. Oh yes, yes, yes!"

Her face was radiant with the joy of the moment, her eyes lit like stars with dark liquid gold. Eli began to hum, a soft sound from a remembered song, then held her hand and began a slow rhythm of dance.

She laid her head on his shoulder, closed her eyes, and was swept away by the realization of a dream she had never imagined would actually come true.

A mockingbird twittered from the top branch of a magnolia tree, its raucous cry turning from the imitation of a robin, to the soft, warbling of a wren. The bird cocked its head, the bright eyes observing the dance in the middle of a country road, then set up with the joyous mating call of the southern meadowlark before spreading its wings and flying across the telephone wire.

And still they danced.

THE ANNOUNCEMENT WAS met with the expected revelry. Mistletoe was dangled above their heads as raucous congratulations shook the walls of the overflowing house. Eli found himself enveloped in too many hugs to count, too many handclasps and shoulder thumpings to know which wish of well-being came from who. Alice never left his side, but stayed by him, wanting to be close, as he wanted to be with her.

Lavinia almost knocked them over with the force of her elaborate congratulations. She cried into her lace-edged handkerchief, tried to say the proper words, but ended up snuffling and hiccoughing into the bit of muslin, her mouth twisted and wobbling with the failed attempt at decorum.

Orphus called him "son," saying he'd be glad to give him a loan if he needed it for the down payment on a house.

"Listen to the man!" Lavinia shrieked. "He doesn't have two cents to rub together."

Orphus drew himself to his full height, his chest widened as he drew back his shoulders and announced the fact he had a nice nest egg, and he had no plans of letting her in on his little secret. She smacked an open palm against his considerable girth and said again, "Listen to him!"

Eli smiled and laughed freely, the realization of having arrived at some invisible destination like an undeserved liberty. He reveled in this new freedom, knowing this was exactly where he belonged till the end of his days on earth.

Alice brought a plate of food, snuggled beside him on the living room sofa, shared the crackers and crab pâté, the fruit salad and Christmas cake. They sang the old Christmas hymns around the piano, with Orphus pounding out a high crescendo, faces lifted in praise for the birth of the Savior.

Only for a moment, when he was alone in the stillness of his room, did he wonder how Christmas Day was celebrated at home on the farm, with Clara and Oba, the sisters and husbands, grandchildren underfoot. His slight blond-haired mother with her quiet smile, the way she managed to cook a wondrous meal, with Andy on the sidelines, his eyes twinkling with good humor.

He would probably never stop missing them, and yet he knew he was exactly where he belonged.

CHAPTER 22

S HE SAT DOWN HARD, REACHED OUT TO PLACE A HAND ON the edge of the table to steady herself. Her first thought was, *Oh no, no.*

But here was the white invitation, embossed with golden calla lilies, with the words staring at her like an unwanted truth.

Eli, oh Eli. This is not what I want from you.

She read and reread the cruel words, the words she had hoped never to see. Eli Weaver and Alice Hopkins. Whoever she was, she was not good enough for him. She found herself shaking with anger, with a fierce jealousy, coupled with a despair at her own failure.

He was so English, so far gone from his upbringing, his Amish roots, the culture where he truly belonged. Far away in Arkansas, he had strayed from all they had taught him, learned the ways of the world.

Oh, she had let him go, hadn't she? She had opened her heart and given him to God, to direct his life in the best way possible, but here, on this invitation to his wedding, was the absolute proof he would never return. The ache began somewhere in the region of her stomach, before reaching her heart and breaking it into a thousand pieces.

Andy found her at the kitchen table, her head in her hands, the invitation flung to the floor. He sat down, calmly bent to pick up the white envelope, read the contents, and gazed across the room. May made no attempt at conversation; the only sound came from the ticking of the clock on the living room wall.

Andy inhaled softly, said, "May."

"Andy, I can't talk about it."

"Why can't you talk about it?"

She turned reddened, tormented eyes to his. "Did you read it?"

"Yes. It's a wedding invitation."

"But . . . but I can't be glad for him. She's English. Look at her name."

Andy nodded. "May, I thought you told him it was alright to leave the Amish. You knew he had no chance here. It's not fair to require him to live among us without the chance of a wife, a family of his own."

When she began shaking her head back and forth, whimpering sounds of denial coming from her throat, he pressed his lips into a straight line and got up from his chair, put on his coat and hat and went to the barn. He felt his patience thinning, knew if he stayed, he would say hurtful things, words meant to ease the inevitable transition of her son, but words that would instead injure her more.

As he returned to his work, he found himself praying, praying for his wife and for Eli, the divide between them, but a necessary one bound to occur sometime in both of their lives. God knew he loved them both, but knew he would have to stay strong to help May accept Eli's choice.

As it so often happened, it was Clara who sat down at the kitchen table the day before the storm and did not smooth any of the edges, but told her up front in her blunt manner.

"You're being a baby, May, kicking your high chair because you can't have your own way. Stop it."

May wept into her coffee cup, wiped her nose, and told Clara she had no idea how badly this hurt. This was not what she wanted for Eli, after raising him Amish. She wanted him dressed in suspenders and broadfall trousers, a straw hat, and a bowl hair cut, driving a horse and buggy, one of God's people. She always imagined he'd come back to Ohio, get rid of that truck and be Amish.

"And live a celibate life? A monk? A priest? Dedicate his life to God alone? Would you require that of him, just to see him dressed in plain clothes? God's people? What are you talking about, May?"

May was shocked into silence. She had often been subject to Clara's outbursts, but never one like this. Every red-gray hair was static with indignation, her face closely resembling a red beet egg, her skinny arms waving madly.

"I'm afraid you're misled, May. God's people are everywhere, all over the world, in every culture, in ever color. All believers are God's people. Who in the world put that in your head?"

May's soft brown eyes filled with tears. "No one. Not really. I just, well, had a conversation the other day with Albert Barb. You know, Bert's wife, Barb. She asked about Eli." Her voice became softer and softer till she was whispering.

"May, you can't listen to her. She's one among hundreds who believes a person has to wear plain clothes to be in good standing with God. You can't be right with God based on merits alone. Not at all."

And Clara proceeded in kindness, carrying out the duty of angels sent by the prayers of her loving husband. She helped May to see the beauty of allowing Eli a life unhindered by his different skin color. Wrong as it might be, it was here, this racial divide, and by the look of it, it was not going away any time soon.

"Eli will be okay, May. You just need to see him—he's probably happier than you can imagine. We have our invitation, too, so we'll go together. You'll see."

Again, Clara was the strong one, the one who took May's hand and helped her across the tough times. Andy was there to bolster her courage, to gently allow her newfound knowledge to unfold. He held her in his strong arms, stroked her lovely blond hair, and told her he loved her and she was one of the best mothers on the planet.

SPRING CAME LATE that year, winter holding the state of Ohio in its icy claws till late March. Firewood ran empty, water pipes in barns froze. Snow banks rose six feet or more, until finally, the first week in April, May heard the soft sighing of the wind at night. Water ran from the eaves as snow melted from rooftops and the sun shone and drew new green shoots from the thawing soil. Crocuses showed their delicate faces in lavender, purple, and yellow hues, before a few bold daffodils nodded their yellow bonnets on the south side of the house.

May opened the sewing machine and sewed blue dresses for herself, Lizzie, and Fronie, then helped her daughters with the grandchildren's wedding clothes. They hired a bus from Wooster, piled into it on the nineteenth of April, and traveled the long distance from Ohio to Arkansas, an entourage of Ohio Amish dressed in snow white coverings and new straw hats.

DOWN SOUTH IN Arkansas, there was plenty of hustle and bustle going on, the simple white church buzzing with frenzied activity as Louise and Roberta Clemens took on the job of decorating the interior with fresh flowers. There were white and pink tulips, white roses bought from the largest florist in the neighboring town of Harrisville, silk ribbon and bows, white urns and vases. It was all a hodgepodge of color and greenery, with Roberta calmly in the middle, knowing exactly what she was doing, Louise dashing here and there without getting anything accomplished, until Roberta told her to go back home and help the people they'd hired to cook the food.

"I ain't doin' it, Roberta. We're paying them good money, so why would I?" Louise barked at her best friend.

"Well then, you go back and set in that there pew and bow your head and say a prayer, for you to keep from flying apart." She shook her fingers. "Git. Git. Go."

"You're serious?"

"I am perfectly, dead serious. Now git."

Roberta hummed as she worked, sorted through flowers, tacked and taped and called for Louise when she needed her, and by late afternoon, the interior of the church was scented with the fresh smell of spring flowers, the perfect setting for Eli to meet his bride at the altar.

THE MORNING OF Eli's wedding day dawned bright and clear, the sun emerging over the green budded trees with an orange light, turning white clouds lavender and navy blue, as beautiful a sunrise as anyone had ever seen. He was at home with Lavinia and Orphus, his last morning with his aunt and uncle before he'd be off on his honeymoon with his beloved Alice. No matter how hard she tried, Lavinia shed tears; Eli was too nervous to eat anything except a slice of toast before he thanked them for all they had done for him.

He stepped out of the house to a brand new day, drove his truck out to the farm, to Alice and her family, and to the arrival of his family from Ohio.

When the bus chugged up the drive, the row of maple trees with their new green leaves forming a canopy over the gravel, the freshly mowed lawn falling away on either side, Eli stood by the front door with Alice by his side, eager to welcome his family. He found himself feeling anxious, hoping for approval. He had not been aware of the uneasiness till the bus actually came to a stop and he saw Andy alight first.

His stepfather, still with the good-humored smile on his tanned face, the crow's feet at his eyes, the straw hat bent at an angle. Alice held his hand as they stepped forward, their wide smiles mirrored in Andy's face.

May stepped off next and found Eli's eyes immediately. A glad cry came from her lips, and she rushed into his arms, murmuring his name brokenly. Eli was the first to step away, to put a hand on Alice's back and introduce her to his mother.

May found her to be quite beautiful, with a warm light in her brown eyes, her skin glowing with a jewel tone, the dark hue bringing back the memories of Clinton. Eli was disappointed to see his mother extend a hand for a formal handshake, but was glad Alice seemed to accept it as normal. There was Oba, the glad reunion, followed by the gregarious Clara, who pounded his back so hard he winced.

Sisters, husbands, grandchildren, dizzying introductions, Alice doing her best to keep them all straight. They all met the remainder of the family, then went to change into wedding clothes, freshen up, stretch their legs before they needed to be at the church.

Eli walked alone with his mother, while Alice went to her bedroom with sisters and cousins, the time of preparation for a young bride.

May was quiet but did her best to appear courageous, a trait Eli picked up immediately. She was hurting, and he knew it, but she would never own up to the fact, so he made small talk, which was unbearable.

"You're well, Mam?"

"Oh yes, I'm still young."

"You are, really."

"I'm happy for you, Eli. She's a nice girl. I'm sure you'll be very happy together."

"Thank you."

"Is this where you'll live?"

"About a mile down the road. I'll show you on the way to church."

"Did you purchase the house?"

"Yes."

"That's good."

"Mam."

"Hm?"

"I know you're disappointed, I know how much this hurts to see me get married in an English wedding. But I can't be otherwise. Please say you understand, Mam. Try to accept Alice. I know you were always hoping I'd be one of you, and I am, in spirit. I go to church, I worship the same God, I believe in the plan of salvation just the way you taught me, Mam."

He also knew her pride would not allow her to show emotion, so he took from the rest of the conversation what he could get. He could look into her brown eyes and thank her truly for everything she had done for him, and she looked into his with all the love and caring of a mother who is giving her son to another woman, a new wife who would claim him as her husband, the two woven together as one, with her blessing.

"You are here, Eli. Here where I lived and worked. They were not all good, but the years of living on the farm allowed me to have you, and that was a blessing."

"Thank you, Mam."

They returned, and he joined the men, the hollow disappointment of his time with his mother fluttering in his chest. It was the only sadness, the only bittersweet part of his day. He felt as if his mother had only given a fraction of what she could have imparted, but knew he had to be content with his portion.

THE CHURCH WAS filled to capacity, the air heady with the scent of spring flowers, the dark faces adorned with every color and hue of flower-bedecked hats imaginable. Brilliant dresses of every pattern and color, swaths of tulle and lace, fancy belt buckles and shoes with encrusted jewels. Men in light-colored suits and dark ones. Children dressed like flowers, swinging their patent leather shoes, swiveling around to watch for newcomers.

Along the front, the pews to the left were reserved for the groom's family. The white bowl-shaped coverings and blue dresses were neat and clean, the plain cut of the men's suits in stark contrast to the jubilation of color around them. Their white faces were in stark relief to the many dark hued ones, but they were all as one, united in the joy of Eli and Alice.

There, May thought. *There is my reaping. My blood will flow in the veins of his children.*

The aging minister appeared, and May was swept away by the power of his great love, his manner of speaking a balm to her anxious heart. Mesmerized, May sat under his spell as he brought the love of her Savior in a new and powerful way.

When the music swelled, Eli appeared and stood to the minister's right, her handsome son, smiling, a light of happiness shining from his dark eyes. And when the music introduced Alice on the arm of her father, the congregation stood and turned to watch the procession, the Amish relatives a step behind, unaware of the traditions of an English wedding.

Alice's eyes were downcast beneath the white veil, the low-cut white gown revealing her rounded neck and shoulders. She was like a vision, walking slowly to the flower-bedecked altar, up the steps to Eli, where her father handed her over to him. Eli looked down at his beautiful bride with a look of such pure joy and happiness May began to weep softly, unabashedly.

What was this if it wasn't a blessing? Had she been too blinded by tradition to see this union for what it was?

Oh, but it's not what I want, dear God, not what I want. I want to see him in an Amish house with an Amish bride dressed in the plain navy blue dress with the white organdy cape and apron. I want to see him farm the rich soil of Ohio, with a straw hat and a pair of Belgian horses.

"Not my will, but Thine be done."

She heard the words as clearly as if they were played on the organ. She felt the presence of God, felt as if He stood beside her, giving her the insight to see He was here, among these people. He was here with Eli, with Alice, and His love included every believer who had ever walked the face of the earth and would continue to do just that until the end of time.

It's not what I want, no, no. But if it be Thy will, if you promise to keep them in the circle of Your love, I can accept this, today.

She sat, her head bowed, a small thin figure so infinitely set apart from those around her. She thanked God for the gift of His wisdom. He knew she needed Him at her darkest hour. Hadn't she suffered enough, riding into the state of Arkansas years after her fractured childhood, the memory of Melvin Amstutz still alive and well? Here was the fruit of her desperation, the wrong that had brought an end to an even greater wrong. *What else could I have done?*

She felt forgiven, yes, she felt cleansed of past wrongs, but here in Arkansas, old demons raised their ugly heads as memories blew in like a thin white curtain on a summer breeze. Why had God allowed this time here in Arkansas? What purpose could He possibly have had?

When Andy reached for her hand and held it, she looked up at him, found his twinkling blue eyes containing so much love, she felt bewildered, pulled back from the abyss of her past. She gave him the love she felt for him, squeezed his hand in appreciation, and realized she had put her hand to the plow and looked back, exactly what the Bible asked her to forego.

"I love you," he whispered in her ear.

At that moment, the minister pronounced them man and wife and Eli lifted the veil and bent his head perfectly to kiss his bride in full view of everyone.

May was shocked. And the congregation clapped. They clapped! Oh, mercy, this was awful. She felt her face burn, felt deeply embarrassed. She watched in horror as Andy clapped, grinning broadly. Clara was enthused, raising one arm, Oba laughing openly. Oh, shame on them. What were they teaching the grandchildren?

She sat apart, her face averted, her hands clutched in her lap, the slight frown on her face. And when the minister pronounced "Mr. and Mrs. Eli Weaver" to the crowd, there were cheers and yells of approval and more handclapping and whistling.

May had never seen Eli look as radiantly happy, his wife on his arm as they made their way to the door to receive the congratulations of friends and relatives.

AT THE RECEPTION, back on the wide lawn of the farm, Levi and his wife joined the family table. They were all hungry, ready to enjoy the array of food served in huge bowls, family style. There were pitchers of Southern iced tea poured over ice, with wedges of lemon, something May decided she would get the recipe for and serve at her next company meal. It was delicious. Clara tapped her glass and winked at May, who winked back, and both knew what the other was thinking. Fried chicken, ham, gravy, sweet potatoes, and scalloped potatoes. And that was only the beginning.

Eli sat with Alice, the huge flowered wedding cake between them, the flowering apricot tree behind them, the budding maples on each side, the perfect frame for a young bride and her handsome groom.

Oh, but didn't he look relaxed and happy.

May kept her watch, the way anxious mothers will keep tabs on sons, or daughters, stepping out into new territory. He looked genuinely pleased with himself, without a trace of the old inhibition. And in all fairness, if she could let go of her own idea of God's will, set aside the love of tradition, she could fling her arms in the air and open her mouth to sing lovely praises to the God they all worshipped.

She found Eli alone for a few minutes and quietly put her arms around him, laid her small blond head with the white covering on his chest, and told him over and over how much she loved him and how much she wished him the best of God's blessings. She found Alice, held her to her heart, and welcomed her to the family, and said she hoped they would come for a visit quite often and to stay as long as they liked.

And Eli knew she had given everything there was to give, all her love and acceptance, her complete gathering in of her colored son and the wife he had chosen, along with the life they would live together in Arkansas.

But as the bus rumbled down the highway, away from Arkansas and the son she left there, she knew, too, there was nothing she could to do change what had been. *The past is our history*, she thought, *forgiven or unforgiven, our reaping is what we have here on earth.*

We reap what we sow. And gladly we reap, even if the day is long and the sheaves are heavy. We toil and carry and do what we must, because this is what the Lord has chosen for us to do, so that we may be heirs to the kingdom. His blood cleanses our sin, white as snow, but as long as we are mortals on earth, there will be disappointment, trials, mistakes will be made, and so we go forth, reaping and sowing, sowing and reaping.

She laid her head against the window frame, feigned sleep, but a constant parade of memories marched through her mind. Her newborn Eli, at Clara's house. His first time to church, when she wanted to hide him beneath her shawl. His first steps. How precious the day Andy accepted him as his own, and he truly had, always. How long she had been in denial, refusing to see the futility of his pursuing an Amish girl. And here she was, leaving Arkansas with her hopes and dreams dashed to the ground. But they were her hopes and dreams, and not God's plan for Eli.

She would let him go. She would surrender her will to God, release him from the bonds that held him to her. Today, on this bus, in this hour, she would finally do the right thing in her heart and allow him the peace of mind, the freedom to live and love among people who had welcomed him in and made him at home.

THE END.

ABOUT THE AUTHOR

LINDA BYLER WAS RAISED IN AN AMISH FAMILY AND IS AN active member of the Amish church today. Growing up, Linda loved to read and write. In fact, she still does. Linda is well known within the Amish community as a columnist for a weekly Amish newspaper. She writes all her novels by hand in notebooks.

Linda is the author of seven series of novels, all set among the Amish communities of North America: Lizzie Searches for Love, Sadie's Montana, Lancaster Burning, Hester's Hunt for Home, the Dakota Series, The Long Road Home, and the Buggy Spoke Series for younger readers. Linda has also written several Christmas romances set among the Amish: *Mary's Christmas Goodbye, The Christmas Visitor, The Little Amish Matchmaker, Becky Meets Her Match, A Dog for Christmas, A Horse for Elsie,* and *The More the Merrier.* Linda has coauthored *Lizzie's Amish Cookbook: Favorite Recipes from Three Generations of Amish Cooks!, Amish Christmas Cookbook,* and *Amish Soups & Casseroles.*

READ THE WHOLE TRILOGY

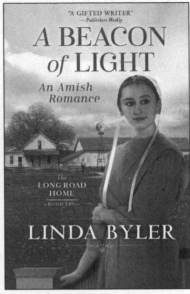

BOOK ONE

BOOK TWO

BOOK THREE

OTHER BOOKS BY
LINDA BYLER

LIZZIE SEARCHES FOR LOVE SERIES

BOOK ONE

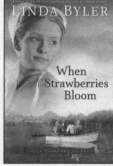

BOOK TWO

BOOK THREE

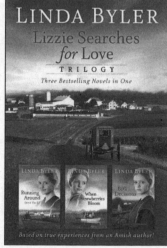

TRILOGY

COOKBOOK

SADIE'S MONTANA SERIES

BOOK ONE

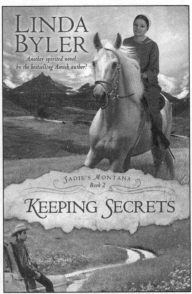

BOOK TWO

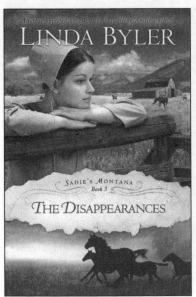

BOOK THREE

TRILOGY

LANCASTER BURNING SERIES

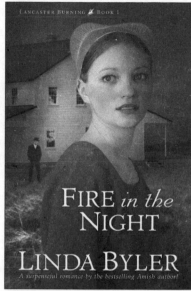

BOOK ONE

BOOK TWO

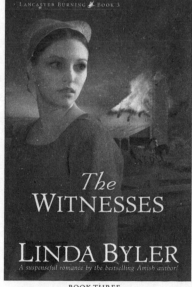

BOOK THREE

TRILOGY

HESTER'S HUNT FOR HOME SERIES

BOOK ONE

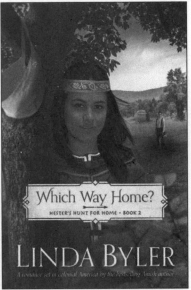

BOOK TWO

BOOK THREE

TRILOGY

THE DAKOTA SERIES

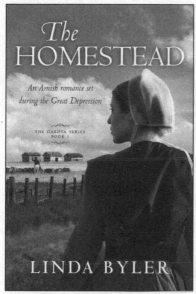

BOOK ONE

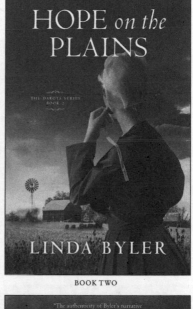

BOOK TWO

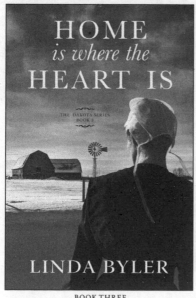

BOOK THREE

TRILOGY

CHRISTMAS NOVELLAS

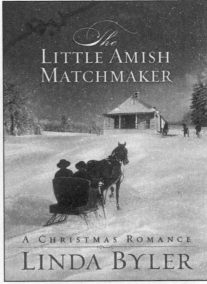

THE CHRISTMAS VISITOR

LITTLE AMISH MATCHMAKER

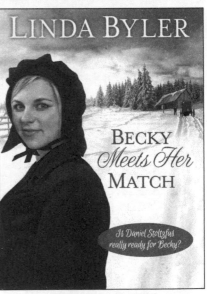

MARY'S CHRISTMAS GOODBYE

BECKY MEETS HER MATCH

A DOG FOR CHRISTMAS

A HORSE FOR ELSIE

THE MORE THE MERRIER

CHRISTMAS COLLECTIONS

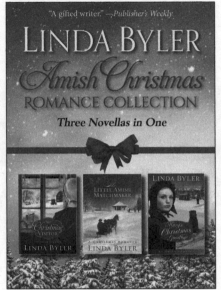

AMISH CHRISTMAS ROMANCE COLLECTION

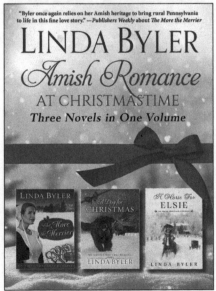

AMISH ROMANCE AT CHRISTMASTIME

NEW RELEASES

THE HEALING

A SECOND CHANCE

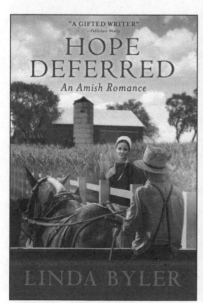

HOPE DEFERRED

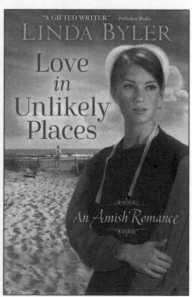

LOVE IN UNLIKELY PLACES

Buggy Spoke Series for Young Readers

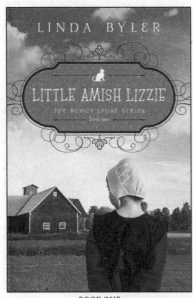

BOOK ONE

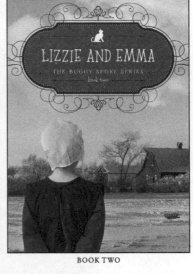

BOOK TWO

BOOK THREE